REFLEX

Dick Francis has written forty-one international bestsellers and is widely acclaimed as one of the world's finest thriller writers. His awards include the Crime Writers' Association's Cartier Diamond Dagger for his outstanding contribution to the crime genre, and an honorary Doctorate of Humane Letters from Tufts University of Boston. In 1996 Dick Francis was made a Mystery Writers of America Grand Master for a lifetime's achievement and in 2000 he received a CBE in the Queen's Birthday Honours list.

Dick Francis

ENQUIRY
&
REFLEX

PAN BOOKS

Enquiry first published in Great Britain 1969 by Michael Joseph
First published 1971 by Pan Books
Reflex first 1964 by Michael Joseph. First published 1976 by Pan Books

This omnibus edition published 2004 by Pan Books
an imprint of Pan Macmillan Ltd
Pan Macmillan, 20 New Wharf Road, London N1 9RR
Basingstoke and Oxford
Associated companies throughout the world
www.panmacmillan.com

ISBN 0 330 43256 7

1 3 5 7 9 8 6 4 2

A CIP catalogue record for this book is available from
the British Library.

Phototypeset by Intype London Ltd
Printed and bound in Great Britain by
Mackays of Chatham plc, Chatham, Kent

ENQUIRY

PART ONE

FEBRUARY

CHAPTER ONE

Yesterday I lost my licence.

To a professional steeplechase jockey, losing his licence and being warned off Newmarket Heath is like being chucked off the medical register, only more so.

Barred from race riding, barred from racecourses. Barred, moreover, from racing stables. Which poses me quite a problem, as I live in one.

No livelihood and maybe no home.

Last night was a right so-and-so, and I prefer to forget those grisly sleepless hours. Shock and bewilderment, the feeling that it couldn't have happened, it was all a mistake . . . this lasted until after midnight. And at least the disbelieving stage had had some built-in comfort. The full thudding realization which followed had none at all. My life was lying around like the untidy bits of a smashed teacup, and I was altogether out of glue and rivets.

This morning I got up and percolated some coffee and looked out of the window at the lads bustling around in the yard and mounting and cloppeting away up the road to the Downs, and I got my first real taste of being an outcast.

Fred didn't bellow up at my window as he usually did, 'Going to stay there all day, then?'

This time, I was.

None of the lads looked up . . . they more or less kept their eyes studiously right down. They were quiet, too. Dead quiet. I watched Bouncing Bernie heave his ten stone seven on to the gelding I'd been riding lately, and there was something apologetic about the way he lowered his fat bum into the saddle.

And he, too, kept his eyes down.

Tomorrow, I guessed, they'd be themselves again. Tomorrow they'd be curious and ask questions. I understood that they weren't despising me. They were sympathetic. Probably too sympathetic for their own comfort. And embarrassed: that too. And instinctively delicate about looking too soon at the face of total disaster.

When they'd gone I drank my coffee slowly and wondered what to do next. A nasty, very nasty, feeling of emptiness and loss.

The papers had been stuck as usual through my letterbox. I wondered what the boy had thought, knowing what he was delivering. I shrugged. Might as well read what they'd said, the Goddamned pressmen, God bless them.

The *Sporting Life*, short on news, had given us the headlines and the full treatment.

'Cranfield and Hughes Disqualified.'

There was a picture of Cranfield at the top of the page, and halfway down one of me, all smiles, taken the day I won the Hennessy Gold Cup. Some little sub-editor letting his irony loose, I thought sourly, and printing the most cheerful picture he could dig out of the files.

The close-printed inches north and south of my happy face were unrelieved gloom.

' "The Stewards said they were not satisfied with my explanation," Cranfield said. "They have withdrawn my licence. I have no further comment to make." '

Hughes, it was reported, had said almost exactly the same. Hughes, if I remembered correctly, had in fact said nothing whatsoever. Hughes had been too stunned to put one word collectedly after another, and if he had said anything at all it would have been unprintable.

I didn't read all of it. I'd read it all before, about the other people. For 'Cranfield and Hughes' one could substitute any other trainer and jockey who had been warned off. The newspaper reports on these occasions were always the same; totally uninformed. As a racing Enquiry was a private trial the ruling authorities were not obliged to open the proceedings to the public or the Press, and as they were not obliged to, they never did. In fact like many another inward-looking concern they seemed to be permanently engaged in trying to stop too many people from finding out what was really going on.

The *Daily Witness* was equally fog-bound, except that Daddy Leeman had suffered his usual rush of purple prose to the head. According to him:

'Kelly Hughes, until now a leading contender for this season's jump-jockeys' crown, and fifth on the list last year, was sentenced to an indefinite suspension of his licence. Hughes, thirty, left the hearing ten minutes after Cranfield. Looking pale and grim, he confirmed that he had lost his licence, and added "I have no further comment." '

They had remarkable ears, those pressmen.

I put down the paper with a sigh and went into the bedroom to exchange my dressing-gown for trousers and a jersey, and after that I made my bed, and after that I sat on it, staring into space. I had nothing else to do. I had nothing to do for as far ahead as the eye could see. Unfortunately I also had nothing to think about except the Enquiry.

Put baldly, I had lost my licence for losing a race. More precisely, I had ridden a red-hot favourite into second place in the Lemonfizz Crystal Cup at Oxford

6

in the last week of January, and the winner had been an unconsidered outsider. This would have been merely unfortunate, had it not been that both horses were trained by Dexter Cranfield.

The finishing order at the winning post had been greeted with roars of disgust from the stands, and I had been booed all the way to the unsaddling enclosure. Dexter Cranfield had looked worried more than delighted to have taken first and second places in one of the season's big sponsored steeplechases, and the Stewards of the meeting had called us both in to explain. They were not, they announced, satisfied with the explanations. They would refer the matter to the Disciplinary Committee of the Jockey Club.

The Disciplinary Committee, two weeks later, were equally sceptical that the freak result had been an accident. Deliberate fraud on the betting public, they said. Disgraceful, dishonest, disgusting, they said. Racing must keep its good name clean. Not the first time that either of you have been suspected. Severe penalties must be inflicted, as a deterrent to others.

Off, they said. Warned off. And good riddance.

It wouldn't have happened in America, I thought in depression. There, all runners from one stable, or one owner, for that matter, were covered by a bet on any of them. So if the stable's outsider won instead of its favourite, the backers still collected their money. High time the same system crossed the Atlantic. Correction, more than high time; long, long overdue.

The truth of the matter was that Squelch, my red-hot favourite, had been drying under me all the way up the straight, and it was in the miracle class that I'd finished as close as second, and not fifth or sixth. If he hadn't carried so many people's shirts, in fact, I wouldn't have exhausted him as I had. That it had been Cranfield's other runner Cherry Pie who had passed me ten yards from the finish was just the worst sort of luck.

Armed by innocence, and with reason to believe that even if the Oxford Stewards had been swayed by the crowd's hostile reception, the Disciplinary Committee were going to consider the matter in an atmosphere of cool common-sense, I had gone to the Enquiry without a twinge of apprehension.

The atmosphere was cool, all right. Glacial. Their own common-sense was taken for granted by the Stewards. They didn't appear to think that either Cranfield or I had any.

The first faint indication that the sky was about to fall came when they read out a list of nine previous races in which I had ridden a beaten favourite for Cranfield. In six of them, another of Cranfield's runners had won. Cranfield had also had other runners in the other three.

'That means,' said Lord Gowery, 'that this case

before us is by no means the first. It has happened again and again. These results seem to have been unnoticed in the past, but this time you have clearly overstepped the mark.'

I must have stood there looking stupid with my mouth falling open in astonishment, and the trouble was that they obviously thought I was astonished at how much they had dug up to prove my guilt.

'Some of those races were years ago,' I protested. 'Six or seven, some of them.'

'What difference does that make?' asked Lord Gowery. 'They happened.'

'That sort of thing happens to every trainer now and then,' Cranfield said hotly. 'You must know it does.'

Lord Gowery gave him an emotionless stare. It stirred some primeval reaction in my glands, and I could feel the ripple of goose pimples up my spine. He really believes, I thought wildly, he really believes us guilty. It was only then that I realized we had to make a fight of it; and it was already far too late.

I said to Cranfield, 'We should have had that lawyer,' and he gave me an almost frightened glance of agreement.

Shortly before the Lemonfizz the Jockey Club had finally thrown an old autocratic tradition out of the twentieth century and agreed that people in danger of losing their livelihood could be legally represented at their trials, if they wished. The concession was so new that there was no accepted custom to be guided by. One or two people had been acquitted with lawyers' help who would presumably have been acquitted anyway; and if an accused person engaged a lawyer to defend him, he had in all cases to pay the fees himself. The Jockey Club did not award costs to anyone they accused, whether or not they managed to prove themselves innocent.

At first Cranfield had agreed with me that we should find a lawyer, though both of us had been annoyed at having to shell out. Then Cranfield had by chance met at a party the newly elected Disciplinary Steward who was a friend of his, and had reported to me afterwards, 'There's no need for us to go to the expense of a lawyer. Monty Midgely told me in confidence that the Disciplinary Committee think the Oxford Stewards were off their heads reporting us, that he knows the Lemonfizz result was just one of those things, and not to worry, the Enquiry will only be a formality. Ten minutes or so, and it will be over.'

That assurance had been good enough for both of us. We hadn't even seen any cause for alarm when three or four days later Colonel Sir Montague Midgely had turned yellow with jaundice and taken to his bed, and it had been announced that one of the Committee, Lord Gowery, would deputize for him in any Enquiries which might be held in the next few weeks.

Monty Midgely's liver had a lot to answer for. Whatever he had intended, it now seemed all too appallingly clear that Gowery didn't agree.

The Enquiry was held in a large lavishly furnished room in the Portman Square headquarters of the Jockey Club. Four Stewards sat in comfortable armchairs along one side of a polished table with a pile of papers in front of each of them, and a shorthand writer was stationed at a smaller table a little to their right. When Cranfield and I went into the room the shorthand writer was fussing with a tape-recorder, unwinding a lead from the machine which stood on his own table and trailing it across the floor towards the Stewards. He set up a microphone on a stand in front of Lord Gowery, switched it on, blew into it a couple of times, went back to his machine, flicked a few switches, and announced that everything was in order.

Behind the Stewards, across a few yards of plushy dark red carpet, were several more armchairs. Their occupants included the three Stewards who had been unconvinced at Oxford, the Clerk of the Course, the Handicapper who had allotted the Lemonfizz weights, and a pair of Stipendiary Stewards, officials paid by the Jockey Club and acting at meetings as an odd mixture of messenger boys for the Stewards and the industry's private police. It was they who, if they thought there had been an infringement of the rules, brought it to the notice of the Stewards of the meeting concerned, and advised them to hold an Enquiry.

As in any other job, some Stipendiaries were reasonable men and some were not. The Stipe who had been acting at Oxford on Lemonfizz day was notoriously the most difficult of them all.

Cranfield and I were to sit facing the Stewards' table, but several feet from it. For us, too, there were the same luxurious armchairs. Very civilized. Not a hatchet in sight. We sat down, and Cranfield casually crossed his legs, looking confident and relaxed.

We were far from soul-mates, Cranfield and I. He had inherited a fortune from his father, an ex-soap manufacturer who had somehow failed to acquire a coveted peerage in spite of donating madly to every fashionable cause in sight, and the combination of wealth and disappointed social ambition had turned Cranfield *fils* into a roaring snob. To him, since he employed me, I was a servant; and he didn't know how to treat servants.

He was, however, a pretty good trainer. Better still, he had rich friends who could afford good horses. I had ridden for him semi-regularly for nearly eight years, and although at first I had resented his snobbish little ways, I had eventually grown up enough to find them amusing. We operated strictly as a business team, even after all that time. Not a flicker of friendship. He would have been outraged at the very idea, and I didn't like him enough to think it a pity.

He was twenty years older than me, a tallish, thin Anglo-Saxon type with thin fine mousy hair, greyish-blue eyes with short fair lashes, a well-developed straight nose, and aggressively perfect teeth. His bone structure was of the type acceptable to the social circle in which he tried to move, but the lines his outlook on life had etched in his skin were a warning to anyone looking for tolerance or generosity. Cranfield was mean-minded by habit and open handed only to those who could lug him upwards. In all his dealings with those he considered his inferiors he left behind a turbulent wake of dislike and resentment. He was charming to his friends, polite in public to his wife, and his three teenage children echoed his delusions of superiority with pitiful faithfulness.

Cranfield had remarked to me some days before the Enquiry that the Oxford Stewards were all good chaps and that two of them had personally apologized to him for having to send the case on to the Disciplinary Committee. I nodded without answering. Cranfield must have known as well as I did that all three of the Oxford Stewards had been elected for social reasons only; that one of them couldn't read a number board at five paces, that another had inherited his late uncle's string of racehorses but not his expert knowledge, and that the third had been heard to ask his trainer which his own horse was, during the course of a race. Not one of the three could read a race at anything approaching the standard of a racecourse commentator. Good chaps they might well be, but as judges, frightening.

'We will show the film of the race,' Lord Gowery said.

They showed it, projecting from the back of the room on to a screen on the wall behind Cranfield and me. We turned our armchairs round to watch it. The Stipendiary Steward from Oxford, a fat pompous bully, stood by the screen, pointing out Squelch with a long baton.

'This is the horse in question,' he said, as the horses lined up for the start. I reflected mildly that if the Stewards knew their job they would have seen the film several times already, and would know which was Squelch without needing to have him pointed out.

The Stipe more or less indicated Squelch all the way round. It was an unremarkable race, run to a well-tried pattern: hold back at the start, letting someone else make the pace; ease forwards to fourth place and settle there for two miles or more; move smoothly to the front coming towards the second last fence, and press on home regardless. If the horse liked that sort of race, and if he were good enough, he would win.

Squelch hated to be ridden any other way. Squelch was, on his day, good enough. It just hadn't been his day.

The film showed Squelch taking the lead coming into the second last fence. He rolled a bit on landing, a sure sign of tiredness. I'd had to pick him up and urge him into the last, and it was obvious on the film. Away from the last, towards the winning post, he'd floundered about beneath me, and if I hadn't been ruthless he'd have slowed to a trot. Cherry Pie, at the finish, came up surprisingly fast and passed him as if he'd been standing still.

The film flicked off abruptly and someone put the lights on again. I thought that the film was conclusive and that that would be the end of it.

'You didn't use your whip,' Lord Gowery said accusingly.

'No, sir,' I agreed. 'Squelch shies away from the whip. He has to be ridden with the hands.'

'You were making no effort to ride him out.'

'Indeed I was, sir. He was dead tired, you can see on the film.'

'All I can see on the film is that you were making absolutely no effort to win. You were sitting there with your arms still, making no effort whatsoever.'

I stared at him. 'Squelch isn't an easy horse to ride, sir. He'll always do his best but only if he isn't upset. He has to be ridden quietly. He stops if he's hit. He'll only respond to being squeezed, and to small flicks on the reins, and to his jockey's voice.'

'That's quite right,' said Cranfield piously. 'I always give Hughes orders not to treat the horse roughly.'

As if he hadn't heard a word, Lord Gowery said, 'Hughes didn't pick up his whip.'

He looked enquiringly at the two Stewards flanking him, as if to collect their opinions. The one on his left, a youngish man who had ridden as an amateur, nodded non-committally. The other one was asleep.

I suspected Gowery kicked him under the table. He woke up with a jerk, said, 'Eh? Yes, definitely,' and eyed me suspiciously.

It's a farce, I thought incredulously. The whole thing's a bloody farce.

Gowery nodded, satisfied. 'Hughes never picked up his whip.'

The fat bullying Stipe was oozing smugness. 'I am sure you will find this next film relevant, sir.'

'Quite,' agreed Gowery. 'Show it now.'

'Which film is this?' Cranfield enquired.

Gowery said, 'This film shows Squelch winning at Reading on January 3rd.'

Cranfield reflected. 'I was not at Reading on that day.'

'No,' agreed Gowery. 'We understand you went to the Worcester meeting instead.' He made it sound suspicious instead of perfectly normal. Cranfield had run a hot young hurdler at Worcester and had wanted to see how he shaped. Squelch, the established star, needed no supervision.

The lights went out again. The Stipe used his baton to point out Kelly Hughes riding a race in Squelch's distinctive colours of black and white chevrons and a black cap. Not at all the same sort of race as the Lemonfizz Crystal Cup. I'd gone to the front early to give myself a clear view of the fences, pulled back to about third place for a breather at midway, and forced to the front again only after the last fence, swinging my whip energetically down the horse's shoulder and urging him vigorously with my arms.

The film stopped, the lights went on, and there was a heavy accusing silence. Cranfield turned towards me, frowning.

'You will agree,' said Gowery ironically, 'that you used your whip, Hughes.'

'Yes, sir,' I said. 'Which race did you say that was?'

'The last race at Reading,' he said irritably. 'Don't pretend you don't know.'

'I agree that the film you've just shown was the last race at Reading, sir. But Squelch didn't run in the last race at Reading. The horse in that film was Wanderlust. He belongs to Mr Kessel, like Squelch does, so the colours are the same, and both horses are by the same sire, which accounts for them looking similar, but the horse you've just shown is Wanderlust. Who does, as you saw, respond well if you wave a whip at him.'

17

There was dead silence. It was Cranfield who broke it, clearing his throat.

'Hughes is quite right. That is Wanderlust.'

He hadn't realized it, I thought in amusement, until I'd pointed it out. It's all too easy for people to believe what they're told.

There was a certain amount of hurried whispering going on. I didn't help them. They could sort it out for themselves.

Eventually Lord Gowery said, 'Has anyone got a form book?' and an official near the door went out to fetch one. Gowery opened it and took a long look at the Reading results.

'It seems,' he said heavily, 'that we have the wrong film. Squelch ran in the sixth race at Reading, which is of course usually the last. However, it now appears that on that day there were seven races, the Novice Chase having been divided and run in two halves, at the beginning and end of the day. Wanderlust won the *seventh* race. A perfectly understandable mix-up, I am afraid.'

I didn't think I would help my cause by saying that I thought it a disgraceful mix-up, if not criminal.

'Could we now, sir,' I asked politely, 'see the right film? The one that Squelch won.'

Lord Gowery cleared his throat. 'I don't, er, think we have it here. However,' he recovered fast, 'we don't need it. It is immaterial. We are not considering the Reading result, but that at Oxford.'

I gasped. I was truly astounded. 'But sir, if you watch Squelch's race, you will see that I rode him at Reading exactly as I did at Oxford, without using the whip.'

'That is beside the point, Hughes, because Squelch may not have needed the whip at Reading, but at Oxford he did.'

'Sir, it *is* the point,' I protested. 'I rode Squelch at Oxford in exactly the same manner as when he won at Reading, only at Oxford he tired.'

Lord Gowery absolutely ignored this. Instead he looked left and right to his Stewards alongside and remarked, 'We must waste no more time. We have three or four witnesses to call before lunch.'

The sleepy eldest Steward nodded and looked at his watch. The younger one nodded and avoided meeting my eyes. I knew him quite well from his amateur jockey days, and had often ridden against him. We had all been pleased when he had been made a Steward, because he knew at first hand the sort of odd circumstances which cropped up in racing to make a fool of the brightest, and we had thought that he would always put forward or explain our point of view. From his downcast semi-apologetic face I now gathered that we had hoped too much. He had not so far contributed one single word to the proceedings, and he looked, though it seemed extraordinary, intimidated.

As plain Andrew Tring he had been lighthearted, amusing, and almost reckless over fences. His recently inherited baronetcy and his even more recently acquired Stewardship seemed on the present showing to have hammered him into the ground.

Of Lord Plimborne, the elderly sleepyhead, I knew very little except his name. He seemed to be in his seventies and there was a faint tremble about many of his movements as if old age were shaking at his foundations and would soon have him down. He had not, I thought, clearly heard or understood more than a quarter of what had been said.

An Enquiry was usually conducted by three Stewards, but on this day there were four. The fourth, who sat on the left of Andrew Tring, was not, as far as I knew, even on the Disciplinary Committee, let alone a Disciplinary Steward. But he had in front of him a pile of notes as large if not larger than the others, and he was following every word with sharp hot eyes. Exactly where his involvement lay I couldn't work out, but there was no doubt that Wykeham, second Baron Ferth, cared about the outcome.

He alone of the four seemed really disturbed that they should have shown the wrong film, and he said quietly but forcefully enough for it to carry across to Cranfield and me, 'I did advise against showing the Reading race, if you remember.'

Gowery gave him an icelance of a look which would have slaughtered thinner-skinned men, but against Ferth's inner furnace it melted impotently.

'You agreed to say nothing,' Gowery said in the same piercing undertone. 'I would be obliged if you would keep to that.'

Cranfield had stirred beside me in astonishment, and now, thinking about it on the following day, the venomous little exchange seemed even more incredible. What, I now wondered, had Ferth been doing there, where he didn't really belong and was clearly not appreciated.

The telephone bell broke up my thoughts. I went into the sitting-room to answer it and found it was a jockey colleague ringing up to commiserate. He himself, he reminded me, had had his licence suspended for a while three or four years back, and he knew how I must be feeling.

'It's good of you, Jim, to take the trouble.'

'No trouble, mate. Stick together, and all that. How did it go?'

'Lousy,' I said. 'They didn't listen to a word either Cranfield or I said. They'd made up their minds we were guilty before we ever went there.'

Jim Enders laughed. 'I'm not surprised. You know what happened to me?'

'No. What?'

'Well, when they gave me my licence back, they'd called the Enquiry for the Tuesday, see, and then for some reason they had to postpone it until the Thursday afternoon. So along I went on Thursday afternoon and they hummed and hahed and warned me as to my future conduct and kept me in suspense for a bit before they said I could have my licence back. Well, I thought I might as well collect a Racing Calendar and take it home with me, to keep abreast of the times and all that, so, anyway, I collected my Racing Calendar which is published at twelve o'clock on Thursdays, twelve o'clock mind you, and I opened it, and what is the first thing I see but the notice saying my licence has been restored. So how about *that*? They'd published the result of that meeting two hours before it had even begun.'

'I don't believe it,' I said.

'Quite true,' he said. 'Mind you, that time they were giving my licence back, not taking it away. But even so, it shows they'd made up their minds. I've always wondered why they bothered to hold that second Enquiry at all. Waste of everyone's time, mate.'

'It's incredible,' I said. But I did believe him: which before my own Enquiry I would not have done.

'When are they giving you your licence back?' Jim asked.

'They didn't say.'

'Didn't they tell you when you could apply?'

'No.'

Jim shoved one very rude word down the wires. 'And that's another thing, mate, you want to pick your moment right when you *do* apply.'

'How do you mean?'

'When I applied for mine, on the dot of when they told me I could, they said the only Steward who had authority to give it back had gone on a cruise to Madeira and I would have to wait until he turned up again.'

CHAPTER TWO

When the horses came back from second exercise at midday my cousin Tony stomped up the stairs and trod muck and straw into my carpet. It was his stable, not Cranfield's, that I lived in. He had thirty boxes, thirty-two horses, one house, one wife, four children, and an overdraft. Ten more boxes were being built, the fifth child was four months off, and the overdraft was turning puce. I lived alone in the flat over the yard and rode everything which came along.

All very normal. And, in the three years since we had moved in, increasingly successful. My suspension meant that Tony and the owners were going to have to find another jockey.

He flopped down gloomily in a green velvet armchair.

'You all right?'

'Yes,' I said.

'Give me a drink, for God's sake.'

I poured half a cupful of J and B into a chunky tumbler.

'Ice?'

'As it is.'

I handed him the glass and he made inroads. Restoration began to take place.

Our mothers had been Welsh girls, sisters. Mine had married a local boy, so that I had come out wholly Celt, shortish, dark, compact. My aunt had hightailed off with a six-foot-four languid blond giant from Wyoming who had endowed Tony with most of his physique and double his brain. Out of USAAF uniform, Tony's father had reverted to ranch-hand, not ranch owner, as he had led his in-laws to believe, and he'd considered it more important for his only child to get to ride well than to acquire any of that there fancy book learning.

Tony therefore played truant for years with enthusiasm, and had never regretted it. I met him for the first time when he was twenty-five, when his Pa's heart had packed up and he had escorted his sincerely weeping Mum back to Wales. In the seven years since then he had acquired with some speed an English wife, a semi-English accent, an unimpassioned knowledge of English racing, a job as assistant trainer, and a stable of his own. And also, somewhere along the way, an unquenchable English thirst. For Scotch.

He said, looking down at the diminished drink, 'What are you going to do?'

'I don't know, exactly.'

'Will you go back home?'

'Not to live,' I said. 'I've come too far.'

He raised his head a little and looked round the room, smiling. Plain white walls, thick brown carpet, velvet chairs in two or three greens, antique furniture, pink and orange striped curtains, heavy and rich. 'I'll say you have,' he agreed. 'A big long way from Coedlant Farm, boyo.'

'No farther than your prairie.'

He shook his head. 'I still have grass roots. You've pulled yours up.'

Penetrating fellow, Tony. An extraordinary mixture of raw intelligence and straws in the hair. He was right; I'd shaken the straws out of mine. We got on very well.

'I want to talk to someone who has been to a recent Enquiry,' I said, abruptly.

'You want to just put it behind you and forget it,' he advised. 'No percentage in comparing hysterectomies.'

I laughed, which was truly something in the circumstances. 'Not on a pain for pain basis,' I explained. 'It's just that I want to know if what happened yesterday was . . . well, unusual. The procedure, that is. The form of the thing. Quite apart from the fact that most of the evidence was rigged.'

'Is that what you were mumbling about on the way home? Those few words you uttered in a wilderness of silence?'

'Those,' I said, 'were mostly "they didn't believe a word we said".'

'So who rigged what?'

'That's the question.'

He held out his empty glass and I poured some more into it.

'Are you serious?'

'Yes. Starting from point A, which is that I rode Squelch to win, we arrive at point B, which is that the Stewards are convinced I didn't. Along the way were three or four little birdies all twittering their heads off and lying in their bloody teeth.'

'I detect,' he said, 'that something is stirring in yesterday's ruins.'

'What ruins?'

'You.'

'Oh.'

'You should drink more,' he said. 'Make an effort. Start now.'

'I'll think about it.'

'Do that.' He wallowed to his feet. 'Time for lunch. Time to go back to the little nestlings with their mouths wide open for worms.'

'Is it worms, today?'

'God knows. Poppy said to come, if you want.'

I shook my head.

'You must eat,' he protested.

'Yes.'

He looked at me consideringly. 'I guess,' he said, 'that you'll manage.' He put down his empty glass. 'We're here, you know, if you want anything. Company. Food. Dancing girls. Trifles like that.'

I nodded my thanks, and he clomped away down the stairs. He hadn't mentioned his horses, their races, or the other jockeys he would have to engage. He hadn't said that my staying in the flat would be an embarrassment to him.

I didn't know what to do about that. The flat was my home. My only home. Designed, converted, furnished by me. I liked it, and didn't want to leave.

I wandered into the bedroom.

A double bed, but pillows for one.

On the dressing chest, in a silver frame, a photograph of Rosalind. We had been married for two years when she went to spend a routine weekend with her parents. I'd been busy riding five races at Market Rasen on the Saturday, and a policeman had come into the weighing-room at the end of the afternoon and told me unemotionally that my father-in-law had set off with his wife and mine to visit friends and had misjudged his overtaking distance in heavy rain and had driven head on into a lorry and killed all three of them instantly.

It was four years since it had happened. Quite often I could no longer remember her voice. Other times she seemed to be in the next room. I had loved her passionately, but she no longer hurt. Four years was a long time.

I wished she had been there, with her tempestuous nature and fierce loyalty, so that I could have told her about the Enquiry, and shared the wretchedness, and been comforted.

That Enquiry . . .

Gowery's first witness had been the jockey who had finished third in the Lemonfizz, two or three lengths behind Squelch. About twenty, round faced and immature, Master Charlie West was a boy with a lot of natural talent but too little self-discipline. He had a great opinion of himself, and was in danger of throwing away his future through an apparent belief that rules only applied to everyone else.

The grandeur of Portman Square and the trappings of the Enquiry seemed to have subdued him. He came into the room nervously and stood where he was told, at one end of the Stewards' table: on their left, and to our right. He looked down at the table and raised his eyes only once or twice during his whole testimony. He didn't look across to Cranfield and me at all.

Gowery asked him if he remembered the race.

'Yes, sir.' It was a low mumble, barely audible.

'Speak up,' said Gowery irritably.

The shorthand writer came across from his table and moved the microphone so that it was nearer Charlie West. Charlie West cleared his throat.

29

'What happened during the race?'

'Well, sir . . . Shall I start from the beginning, sir?'

'There's no need for unnecessary detail, West,' Gowery said impatiently. 'Just tell us what happened on the far side of the course on the second circuit.'

'I see, sir. Well . . . Kelly, that is, I mean, Hughes, sir . . . Hughes . . . Well . . . Like . . .'

'West, come to the point.' Gowery's voice would have left a lazer standing. A heavy flush showed in patches on Charlie West's neck. He swallowed.

'Round the far side, sir, where the stands go out of sight, like, for a few seconds, well, there, sir . . . Hughes gives this hefty pull back on the reins, sir . . .'

'And what did he say, West?'

'He said, sir, "OK. Brakes on, chaps." Sir.'

Gowery said meaningfully, though everyone had heard the first time and a pin would have crashed on the Wilton, 'Repeat that, please, West.'

'Hughes, sir, said, "OK. Brakes on, chaps." '

'And what did you take him to mean by that, West?'

'Well sir, that he wasn't trying, like. He always says that when he's pulling one back and not trying.'

'*Always?*'

'Well, something like that, sir.'

There was a considerable silence.

Gowery said formally, 'Mr Cranfield . . . Hughes . . . You may ask this witness questions, if you wish.'

I got slowly to my feet.

'Are you seriously saying,' I asked bitterly, 'that at any time during the Lemonfizz Cup I pulled Squelch back and said "OK. Brakes on, chaps"?'

He nodded. He had begun to sweat.

'Please answer aloud,' I said.

'Yes. You said it.'

'I did not.'

'I heard you.'

'You couldn't have done.'

'I heard you.'

I was silent. I simply had no idea what to say next. It was too like a playground exchange: you did, I didn't, you did, I didn't . . .

I sat down. All the Stewards and all the officials ranked behind them were looking at me. I could see that all, to a man, believed West.

'Hughes, are you in the habit of using this phrase?' Gowery's voice was dry acid.

'No, sir.'

'Have you *ever* used it?'

'Not in the Lemonfizz Cup, sir.'

'I said, Hughes, have you *ever* used it?'

To lie or not to lie . . . 'Yes, sir, I have used it, once or twice. But not on Squelch in the Lemonfizz Cup.'

'It is sufficient that you said it at all, Hughes. We will draw our own conclusions as to *when* you said it.'

He shuffled one paper to the bottom of his pack and picked up another. Consulting it with the unseeing token glance of those who know their subject by heart, he continued, 'And now, West, tell us what Hughes did after he had said these words.'

'Sir, he pulled his horse back, sir.'

'How do you know this?' The question was a formality. He asked with the tone of one already aware of the answer.

'I was just beside Hughes, sir, when he said that about brakes. Then he sort of hunched his shoulders, sir, and give a pull, sir, and, well, then he was behind me, having dropped out, like.'

Cranfield said angrily. 'But he finished in front of you.'

'Yes, sir.' Charlie West flicked his eyes upwards to Lord Gowery, and spoke only to him. 'My old horse couldn't act on the going, sir, and Hughes came past me again going into the second last, like.'

'And how did Squelch jump that fence?'

'Easy, sir. Met it just right. Stood back proper, sir.'

'Hughes maintains that Squelch was extremely tired at that point.'

Charlie West left a small pause. Finally he said, 'I don't know about that, sir, I thought as how Squelch would win, myself, sir. I still think as how he ought to have won, sir, being the horse he is, sir.'

Gowery glanced left and right, to make sure that his colleagues had taken the point. 'From your position during the last stages of the race, West, could you see whether or not Hughes was making every effort to win?'

'Well, he didn't look like it, sir, which was surprising, like.'

'Surprising?'

'Yes, sir. See, Hughes is such an artist at it, sir.'

'An artist at what?'

'Well, at riding what looks from the stands one hell of a finish, sir, while all the time he's smothering it like mad.'

'Hughes is in the habit of not riding to win?'

Charlie West worked it out. 'Yes, sir.'

'Thank you, West,' Lord Gowery said with insincere politeness. 'You may go and sit over there at the back of the room.'

Charlie West made a rabbit's scurry towards the row of chairs reserved for those who had finished giving evidence. Cranfield turned fiercely to me and said, 'Why didn't you deny it more vehemently, for God's sake? Why the hell didn't you insist he was making the whole thing up?'

'Do you think they'd believe me?'

He looked uneasily at the accusing ranks opposite, and found his answer in their inplacable stares. All the same, he stood up and did his best.

'Lord Gowery, the film of the Lemonfizz Cup does not bear out West's accusation. At no point does Hughes pull back his horse.'

I lifted my hand too late to stop him. Gowery's and Lord Ferth's intent faces both registered satisfaction. They knew as well as I did that what West had said was borne out on the film. Sensing that Squelch was going to run out of steam, I'd given him a short breather a mile from home, and this normal everyday little act was now wide open to misinterpretation.

Cranfield looked down at me, surprised by my reaction.

'I gave him a breather,' I said apologetically. 'It shows.'

He sat down heavily, frowning in worry.

Gowery was saying to an official, 'Show in Mr Newtonnards,' as if Cranfield hadn't spoken. There was a pause before Mr Newtonnards, whoever he was, materialized. Lord Gowery was looking slightly over his left shoulder, towards the door, giving me the benefit of his patrician profile. I realized with almost a sense of shock that I knew nothing about him as a person, and that he most probably knew nothing about me. He had been, to me, a figure of authority with a capital A. I hadn't questioned his right to rule over me. I had assumed naïvely that he would do so with integrity, wisdom, and justice.

So much for illusions. He was leading his witnesses in a way that would make the Old Bailey reel. He heard truth in Charlie West's lies and lies in my truth.

He was prosecutor as well as judge, and was only admitting evidence if it fitted his case.

He was dispersing the accepting awe I had held him in like candyfloss in a thunderstorm, and I could feel an unforgiving cynicism growing in its stead. Also I was ashamed of my former state of trust. With the sort of education I'd had, I ought to have known better.

Mr Newtonnards emerged from the waiting-room and made his way to the witnesses' end of the Stewards' table, sporting a red rosebud in his lapel and carrying a large blue ledger. Unlike Charlie West he was confident, not nervous. Seeing that everyone else was seated he looked around for a chair for himself, and not finding one, asked.

After a fractional pause Gowery nodded, and the official-of-all-work near the door pushed one forwards. Mr Newtonnards deposited into it his well-cared-for pearl-grey-suited bulk.

'Who is he?' I said to Cranfield. Cranfield shook his head and didn't answer, but he knew, because his air of worry had if anything deepened.

Andrew Tring flipped through his pile of papers, found what he was looking for, and drew it out. Lord Plimborne had his eyes shut again. I was beginning to expect that: and in any case I could see that it didn't matter, since the power lay somewhere between Gowery and Ferth, and Andy Tring and Plimborne were so much window-dressing.

Lord Gowery too picked up a paper, and again I had the impression that he knew its contents by heart.

'Mr Newtonnards?'

'Yes, my lord.' He had a faint cockney accent overlaid by years of cigars and champagne. Mid-fifties, I guessed; no fool, knew the world, and had friends in show business. Not too far out: Mr Newtonnards, it transpired, was a bookmaker.

Gowery said, 'Mr Newtonnards, will you be so good as to tell about a certain bet you struck on the afternoon of the Lemonfizz Cup?'

'Yes, my lord. I was standing on my pitch in Tattersall's when this customer come up and asked me for five tenners on Cherry Pie.' He stopped there, as if that was all he thought necessary.

Gowery did some prompting. 'Please describe this man, and also tell us what you did about his request.'

'Describe him? Let's see, then. He was nothing special. A biggish man in a fawn coat, wearing a brown trilby and carrying race glasses over his shoulder. Middle-aged, I suppose. Perhaps he had a moustache. Can't remember, really.'

The description fitted half the men on the racecourse.

'He asked me what price I'd give him about Cherry Pie,' Newtonnards went on. 'I didn't have any price chalked on my board, seeing Cherry Pie was such an outsider. I offered him tens, but he said it wasn't

36

enough, and he looked like moving off down the line. Well...' Newtonnards waved an expressive pudgy hand '... business wasn't too brisk, so I offered him a hundred to six. Couldn't say fairer than that now, could I, seeing as there were only eight runners in the race? Worst decision I made in a long time.' Gloom mixed with stoicism settled on his well-covered features.

'So when Cherry Pie won, you paid out?'

'That's right. He put down fifty smackers I paid him nine hundred.'

'Nine hundred pounds?'

'That's right, my lord,' Newtonnards confirmed easily, 'nine hundred pounds.'

'And we may see the record of this bet?'

'Certainly.' He opened the big blue ledger at a marked page. 'On the left, my lord, just over halfway down. Marked with a red cross. Nine hundred and fifty, ticket number nine seven two.'

The ledger was passed along the Stewards' table. Plimborne woke up for the occasion and all four of them peered at the page. The ledger returned to Newtonnards, who shut it and let it lie in front of him.

'Wasn't that a very large bet on an outsider?' Gowery asked.

'Yes it was, my lord. But then, there are a lot of mugs about. Except, of course, that once in a while they go and win.'

'So you had no qualms about risking such a large amount?'

'Not really, my lord. Not with Squelch in the race. And anyway, I laid a bit of it off. A quarter of it, in fact, at thirty-three. So my actual losses were in the region of four hundred and eighty-seven pounds ten. Then I took three hundred and two-ten on Squelch and the others, which left a net loss on the race of one eight five.'

Cranfield and I received a glare in which every unit of the one eight five rankled.

Gowery said, 'We are not enquiring into how much you lost, Mr Newtonnards, but into the identity of the client who won nine hundred pounds on Cherry Pie.'

I shivered. If West could lie, so could others.

'As I said in my statement, my lord, I don't know his name. When he came up to me I thought I knew him from somewhere, but you see a lot of folks in my game, so I didn't think much of it. You know. So it wasn't until after I paid him off. After the last race, in fact. Not until I was driving home. Then it came to me, and I went spare, I can tell you.'

'Please explain more clearly,' Gowery said patiently. The patience of a cat at a mousehole. Anticipation making the waiting sweet.

'It wasn't him, so much, as who I saw him talking to. Standing by the parade ring rails before the first race. Don't know why I should remember it, but I do.'

'And who did you see this client talking to?'

'Him.' He jerked his head in our direction. 'Mr Cranfield.'

Cranfield was immediately on his feet.

'Are you suggesting that I advised this client of yours to back Cherry Pie?' His voice shook with indignation.

'No, Mr Cranfield,' said Gowery like the North Wind, 'the suggestion is that the client was acting on your behalf and that it was you yourself that backed Cherry Pie.'

'That's an absolute lie.'

His hot denial fell on a lot of cold ears.

'Where is this mysterious man?' he demanded. 'This unidentified, unidentifiable nobody? How can you possibly trump up such a story and present it as serious evidence? It is ridiculous. Utterly, utterly ridiculous.'

'The bet was struck,' Gowery said plonkingly, pointing to the ledger.

'And I saw you talking to the client,' confirmed Newtonnards.

Cranfield's fury left him gasping for words, and in the end he too sat down again, finding like me nothing to say that could dent the preconceptions ranged against us.

'Mr Newtonnards,' I said, 'would you know this client again?'

He hesitated only a fraction. 'Yes, I would.'

'Have you seen him at the races since Lemonfizz day?'

'No. I haven't.'

'If you see him again, will you point him out to Lord Gowery?'

'If Lord Gowery's at the races.' Several of the back ranks of officials smiled at this, but Newtonnards, to give him his due, did not.

I couldn't think of anything else to ask him, and I knew I had made no headway at all. It was infuriating. By our own choice we had thrust ourselves back into the bad old days when people accused at racing trials were not allowed a legal defendant. If they didn't know how to defend themselves: if they didn't know what sort of questions to ask or in what form to ask them, that was just too bad. Just their hard luck. But this wasn't hard luck. This was our own stupid fault. A lawyer would have been able to rip Newtonnards' testimony to bits, but neither Cranfield nor I knew how.

Cranfield tried. He was back on his feet.

'Far from backing Cherry Pie, I backed Squelch. You can check up with my own bookmaker.'

Gowery simply didn't reply. Cranfield repeated it.

Gowery said, 'Yes, yes. No doubt you did. It is quite beside the point.'

Cranfield sat down again with his mouth hanging open. I knew exactly how he felt. Not so much banging the head against a brick wall as being actively attacked by a cliff.

They waved Newtonnards away and he ambled easily off to take his place beside Charlie West. What he had said stayed behind him, stuck fast in the officials' minds. Not one of them had asked for corroboration. Not one had suggested that there might have been a loophole in identity. The belief was written plain on their faces: if someone had backed Cherry Pie to win nine hundred pounds, it must have been Cranfield.

Gowery hadn't finished. With a calm satisfaction he picked up another paper and said, 'Mr Cranfield, I have here an affidavit from a Mrs Joan Jones, who handled the five-pound selling window on the Totalizator in the paddock on Lemonfizz Cup day, that she sold ten win-only tickets for horse number eight to a man in a fawn raincoat, middle-aged, wearing a trilby. I also have here a similar testimony from a Mr Leonard Roberts, who was paying out at the five-pound window in the same building, on the same occasion. Both of these Tote employees remember the client well, as these were almost the only five-pound tickets sold on Cherry Pie, and certainly the only large block. The Tote paid out to this man more than eleven hundred pounds in cash. Mr Roberts advised him not to carry so much on his person, but the man declined to take his advice.'

There was another accusing silence. Cranfield looked totally nonplussed and came up with nothing to say.

This time, I tried for him. 'Sir, did this man back any other horses in the race, on the Tote? Did he back all, or two or three or four, and just hit the jackpot by accident?'

'There was no accident about this, Hughes.'

'But did he, in fact, back any other horses?'

Dead silence.

'Surely you asked?' I said reasonably.

Whether anyone had asked or not, Gowery didn't know. All he knew was what was on the affidavit. He gave me a stony stare, and said, 'No one puts fifty pounds on an outsider without good grounds for believing it will win.'

'But sir . . .'

'However,' he said, 'we will find out.' He wrote a note on the bottom of one of the affidavits. 'It seems to me extremely unlikely. But we will have the question asked.'

There was no suggestion that he would wait for the answer before giving his judgement. And in fact he did not.

CHAPTER THREE

I wandered aimlessly round the flat, lost and restless. Reheated the coffee. Drank it. Tried to write to my parents, and gave it up after half a page. Tried to make some sort of decision about my future, and couldn't.

Felt too battered. Too pulped. Too crushed.

Yet I had done nothing.

Nothing.

Late afternoon. The lads were bustling round the yard setting the horses fair for the night, and whistling and calling to each other as usual. I kept away from the windows and eventually went back to the bedroom and lay down on the bed. The day began to fade. The dusk closed in.

After Newtonnards they had called Tommy Timpson, who had ridden Cherry Pie.

Tommy Timpson 'did his two' for Cranfield and rode such of the stable's second strings as Cranfield cared to give him. Cranfield rang the changes on three jockeys: me, Chris Smith (at present taking his time over a fractured skull) and Tommy. Tommy got the crumbs and deserved better. Like many trainers, Cranfield couldn't spot talent when it was under his nose, and it wasn't until several small local trainers had asked for his services that Cranfield woke up to the fact that he had a useful emerging rider in his own yard.

Raw, nineteen years old, a stutterer, Tommy was at his worst at the Enquiry. He looked as scared as a two-year-old colt at his first starting gate, and although he couldn't help being jittery it was worse than useless for Cranfield and me.

Lord Gowery made no attempt to put him at ease but simply asked questions and let him get on with the answers as best he could.

'What orders did Mr Cranfield give you before the race? How did he tell you to ride Cherry Pie? Did he instruct you to ride to win?'

Tommy stuttered and stumbled and said Mr Cranfield had told him to keep just behind Squelch all the way round and try to pass him after the last fence.

Cranfield said indignantly, 'That's what he *did*. Not what I told him to do.'

Gowery listened, turned his head to Tommy, and said again, 'Will you tell us what instructions Mr Cranfield gave you *before* the race? Please think carefully.'

Tommy swallowed, gave Cranfield an agonized glance, and tried again. 'M...M...M...Mr Cranfield s...s...said to take my p...p...pace from S...

S . . . Squelch and s . . . s . . . stay with him as long as I c . . . c . . . could.'

'And did he tell you to win?'

'He s . . . s . . . said of course g . . . go . . . go on and w . . . w . . . win if you c . . . c . . . can, sir.'

These were impeccable instructions. Only the most suspicious or biased mind could have read any villainy into them. If these Stewards' minds were not suspicious and biased, snow would fall in the Sahara.

'Did you hear Mr Cranfield giving Hughes instructions as to how he should ride Squelch?'

'N . . . No, sir. M . . . Mr Cranfield did . . . didn't g . . . give Hughes any orders at all, sir.'

'Why not?'

Tommy ducked it and said he didn't know. Cranfield remarked furiously that Hughes had ridden the horse twenty times and knew what was needed.

'Or you had discussed it with him privately, beforehand?'

Cranfield had no explosive answer to that because of course we *had* discussed it beforehand. In general terms. In an assessment of the opposition. As a matter of general strategy.

'I discussed the race with him, yes. But I gave him no specific orders.'

'So according to you,' Lord Gowery said, 'you intended both of your jockeys to try to win?'

'Yes. I did. My horses are always doing their best.'

Gowery shook his head. 'Your statement is not borne out by the facts.'

'Are you calling me a liar?' Cranfield demanded.

Gowery didn't answer. But yes, he was.

They shooed a willing Tommy Timpson away and Cranfield went on simmering at boiling point beside me. For myself, I was growing cold, and no amount of central heating could stop it. I thought we must now have heard everything, but I was wrong. They had saved the worst until last, building up the pyramid of damning statements until they could put the final cap on it and stand back and admire their four-square structure, their solid, unanswerable edifice of guilt.

The worst, at first, had looked so harmless. A quiet slender man in his early thirties, endowed with an utterly forgettable face. After twenty-four hours I couldn't recall his features or remember his voice, and yet I couldn't think about him without shaking with sick impotent fury.

His name was David Oakley. His business, enquiry agent. His address, Birmingham.

He stood without fidgeting at the end of the Stewards' table holding a spiral-bound notebook which he consulted continually, and from beginning to end not a shade of emotion affected his face or his behaviour or even his eyes.

'Acting upon instructions, I paid a visit to the flat of Kelly Hughes, jockey, of Corrie House training stables,

46

Corrie, Berkshire, two days after the Lemonfizz Crystal Cup.'

I sat up with a jerk and opened my mouth to deny it, but before I could say a word he went smoothly on.

'Mr Hughes was not there, but the door was open, so I went in to wait for him. While I was there I made certain observations.' He paused.

Cranfield said to me, 'What is all this about?'

'I don't know. I've never seen him before.'

Gowery steamrollered on. 'You found certain objects.'

'Yes, my lord.'

Gowery sorted out three large envelopes, and passed one each to Tring and Plimborne. Ferth was before them. He had removed the contents from a similar envelope as soon as Oakley had appeared, and was now, I saw, watching me with what I took to be contempt.

The envelopes each held a photograph.

Oakley said, 'The photograph is of objects I found on a chest of drawers in Hughes' bedroom.'

Andy Tring looked, looked again, and raised a horrified face, meeting my eyes accidentally and for the first and only time. He glanced away hurriedly, embarrassed and disgusted.

'I want to see that photograph,' I said hoarsely.

'Certainly.' Lord Gowery turned his copy round and

pushed it across the table. I got up, walked the three dividing steps, and looked down at it.

For several seconds I couldn't take it in, and when I did, I was breathless with disbelief. The photograph had been taken from above the dressing chest, and was sparkling clear. There was the edge of the silver frame and half of Rosalind's face, and from under the frame, as if it had been used as a paperweight, protruded a sheet of paper dated the day after the Lemon-fizz Cup. There were three words written on it, and two initials.

As agreed. Thanks. D.C.

Slanted across the bottom of the paper, and spread out like a pack of cards, were a large number of ten-pound notes.

I looked up, and met Lord Gowery's eyes, and almost flinched away from the utter certainty I read there.

'It's a fake,' I said. My voice sounded odd. 'It's a complete fake.'

'What is it?' Cranfield said from behind me, and in his voice too everyone could hear the awareness of disaster.

I picked up the photograph and took it across to him, and I couldn't feel my feet on the carpet. When he had grasped what it meant he stood up slowly and in a low biting voice said formally, 'My lords, if you believe this, you will believe anything.'

It had not the slightest effect.

Gowery said merely, 'That is your handwriting, I believe.'

Cranfield shook his head. 'I didn't write it.'

'Please be so good as to write those exact words on this sheet of paper.' Gowery pushed a plain piece of paper across the table, and after a second Cranfield went across and wrote on it. Everyone knew that the two samples would look the same, and they did. Gowery passed the sheet of paper significantly to the other Stewards, and they all compared and nodded.

'It's a fake,' I said again. 'I never had a letter like that.'

Gowery ignored me. To Oakley he said, 'Please tell us where you found the money.'

Oakley unnecessarily consulted his notebook. 'The money was folded inside this note, fastened with a rubber band, and both were tucked behind the photo of Hughes's girlfriend, which you see in the picture.'

'It's not true,' I said. I might as well not have bothered. No one listened.

'You counted the money, I believe?'

'Yes, my lord. There was five hundred pounds.'

'There was no money,' I protested. Useless. 'And anyway,' I added desperately, 'why would I take five hundred for losing the race when I would get about as much as that for winning?'

I thought for a moment that I might have scored a hit. Might have made them pause. A pipe dream. There was an answer to that, too.

'We understand from Mr Kessel, Squelch's owner,' Gowery said flatly, 'that he pays you ten per cent of the winning stake money through official channels by cheque. This means that all presents received by you from Mr Kessel are taxed; and we understand that as you pay a high rate of tax your ten per cent from Mr Kessel would have in effect amounted to half, or less than half, of five hundred pounds.'

They seemed to have enquired into my affairs down to the last penny. Dug around in all directions. Certainly I had never tried to hide anything, but this behind-my-back tin-opening made me feel naked. Also, revolted. Also, finally, hopeless. And it wasn't until then that I realized I had been subconsciously clinging to a fairytale faith that it would all finally come all right, that because I was telling the truth I was bound to be believed in the end.

I stared across at Lord Gowery, and he looked briefly back. His face was expressionless, his manner entirely calm. He had reached his conclusions and nothing could overthrow them.

Lord Ferth, beside him, was less bolted down, but a great deal of his earlier heat seemed to have evaporated. The power he had generated no longer troubled Gowery at all, and all I could interpret from his expression was some kind of resigned acceptance.

There was little left to be said. Lord Gowery briefly summed up the evidence against us. The list of former races. The non-use of the whip. The testimony of Charlie West. The bets struck on Cherry Pie. The riding orders given in private. The photographic proof of a pay off from Cranfield to Hughes. .

'There can be no doubt that this was a most flagrant fraud on the racing public ... No alternative but to suspend your licences ... And you, Dexter Cranfield, and you, Kelly Hughes, will be warned off Newmarket Heath until further notice.'

Cranfield, pale and shaking, said, 'I protest that this has not been a fair hearing. Neither Hughes nor I are guilty. The sentence is outrageous.'

No response from Lord Gowery. Lord Ferth, however, spoke for the second time in the proceedings.

'Hughes?'

'I rode Squelch to win,' I said. 'The witnesses were lying.'

Gowery shook his head impatiently. 'The Enquiry is closed. You may go.'

Cranfield and I both hesitated, still unable to accept that that was all. But the official near the door opened it, and all the ranks opposite began to talk quietly to each other and ignore us, and in the end we walked out. Stiff legged. Feeling as if my head were a floating football and my body a chunk of ice. Unreal.

There were several people in the waiting-room outside, but I didn't see them clearly. Cranfield, tight lipped, strode away from me, straight across the room and out of the far door, shaking off a hand or two laid on his sleeve. Dazed, I started to follow him, but was less purposeful, and was effectively stopped by a large man who planted himself in my way.

I looked at him vaguely. Mr Kessel. The owner of Squelch.

'Well?' he said challengingly.

'They didn't believe us. We've both been warned off.'

He hissed a sharp breath out between his teeth. 'After what I've been hearing, I'm not surprised. And I'll tell you this, Hughes, even if you get your licence back, you won't be riding for me again.'

I looked at him blankly and didn't answer. It seemed a small thing after what had already happened. He had been talking to the witnesses, in the waiting-room. They would convince anyone, it seemed. Some owners were unpredictable anyway, even in normal times. One day they had all the faith in the world in their jockey, and the next day, none at all. Faith with slender foundations. Mr Kessel had forgotten all the races I had won for him because of the one I had lost.

I turned blindly away from his hostility and found a

more welcome hand on my arm. Tony, who had driven up with me instead of seeing his horses work.

'Come on,' he said. 'Let's get out of here.'

I nodded and went down with him in the lift, out into the hall, and towards the front door. Outside there we could see a bunch of newspaper reporters waylaying Cranfield with their notebooks at the ready, and I stopped dead at the sight.

'Let's wait till they've gone,' I said.

'They won't go. Not before they've chewed you up too.'

We waited, hesitating, and a voice called behind me, 'Hughes.'

I didn't turn round. I felt I owed no one the slightest politeness. The footsteps came up behind me and he finally came to a halt in front.

Lord Ferth. Looking tired.

'Hughes. Tell me. Why in God's name did you do it?'

I looked at him stonily.

'I didn't.'

He shook his head. 'All the evidence ...'

'You tell me,' I said, rudely, 'why decent men like Stewards so easily believe a lot of lies.'

I turned away from him, too. Twitched my head at Tony and made for the front door. To hell with the Press. To hell with the Stewards and Mr Kessel. And to hell with everything to do with racing. The upsurge of fury took me out of the building and fifty yards along the pavement in Portman Square and only evaporated into grinding misery when we had climbed into the taxi Tony whistled for.

Tony thumped up the stairs to the darkened flat. I heard him calling.

'Are you there, Kelly?'

I unrolled myself from the bed, stood up, stretched, went out into the sitting-room and switched on the lights. He was standing in the far doorway, blinking, his hands full of tray.

'Poppy insisted,' he explained.

He put the tray down on the table and lifted off the covering cloth. She'd sent hot chicken pie, a tomato, and about half a pound of Brie.

'She says you haven't eaten for two days.'

'I suppose not.'

'Get on with it, then.' He made an instinctive line for the whisky bottle and poured generously into two tumblers.

'And here. For once, drink this.'

I took the glass and a mouthful and felt the fire trickle down inside my chest. The first taste was always the best. Tony tossed his off and ordered himself a refill.

I ate the pie, the tomato, and the cheese. Hunger, I

hadn't consciously felt rolled contentedly over and slept.

'Can you stay a bit?' I asked.

'Natch.'

'I'd like to tell you about the Enquiry.'

'Shoot,' he said with satisfaction. 'I've been waiting.'

I told him all that had happened, almost word for word. Every detail had been cut razor sharp into my memory in the way that only happens in disasters.

Tony's astonishment was plain. 'You were framed!'

'That's right.'

'But surely no one can get away with that?'

'Someone seems to be doing all right.'

'But was there *nothing* you could say to prove . . .'

'I couldn't think of anything yesterday, which is all that matters. It's always easy to think of all the smart clever things one *could* have said, afterwards, when it's too late.'

'What would you have said, then?'

'I suppose for a start I should have asked who had given that so-called enquiry agent instructions to search my flat. Acting on instructions, he said. Well, *whose* instructions? I didn't think of asking, yesterday. Now I can see that it could be the whole answer.'

'You assumed the Stewards had instructed him?'

'I suppose so. I didn't really think. Most of the time I was so shattered that I couldn't think clearly at all.'

'Maybe it *was* the Stewards.'

'Well, no. I suppose it's barely possible they might have sent an investigator, though when you look at it in cold blood it wouldn't really seem likely, but it's a tear drop to the Atlantic that they wouldn't have supplied him with five hundred quid and a forged note and told him to photograph them somewhere distinctive in my flat. But that's what he did. Who instructed him?'

'Even if you'd asked, he wouldn't have said.'

'I guess not. But at least it might have made the Stewards think a bit too.'

Tony shook his head. 'He would still have said he found the money behind Rosalind's picture. His word against yours. Nothing different.'

He looked gloomily into his glass. I looked gloomily into mine.

'That bloody little Charlie West,' I said. 'Someone got at him, too.'

'I presume you didn't in fact say "Brakes on, chaps"?'

'I did say it, you see. Not in the Lemonfizz, of course, but a couple of weeks before, in that frightful novice 'chase at Oxford, the day they abandoned the last two races because it was snowing. I was hitting every fence on that deadly bad jumper that old Almond hadn't bothered to school properly, and half the other runners were just as green, and a whole bunch of us had got left about twenty lengths behind the four who were any use, and sleet was falling, and I didn't relish ending

56

up with a broken bone at nought degrees centigrade, so as we were handily out of sight of the stands at that point I shouted, "OK. Brakes on, chaps," and a whole lot of us eased up thankfully and finished the race a good deal slower than we could have done. It didn't affect the result, of course. But there you are. I did say it. What's more, Charlie West heard me. He just shifted it from one race to another.'

'The bastard.'

'I agree.'

'Maybe no one got at him. Maybe he just thought he'd get a few more rides if you were out of the way.'

I considered it and shook my head. 'I wouldn't have thought he was *that* much of a bastard.'

'You never know.' Tony finished his drink and absent-mindedly replaced it. 'What about the bookmaker?'

'Newtonnards? I don't know. Same thing, I suppose. Someone has it in for Cranfield too. Both of us, it was. The Stewards couldn't possibly have warned off one of us without the other. We were knitted together so neatly.'

'It makes me livid,' Tony said violently. 'It's wicked.'

I nodded. 'There was something else, too, about that Enquiry. Some undercurrent, running strong. At least, it was strong at the beginning. Something between Lord Gowery and Lord Ferth. And then Andy Tring, he was sitting there looking like a wilted lettuce.' I shook my head in puzzlement. 'It was like a couple of heavy animals lurking in the undergrowth, shaping up to fight each other. You couldn't see them, but there was a sort of quiver in the air. At least, that's how it seemed at one point . . .'

'Stewards are men,' Tony said with bubble-bursting matter-of-factness. 'Show me any organization which doesn't have some sort of power struggle going on under its gentlemanly surface. All you caught was a whiff of the old brimstone. State of nature. Nothing to do with whether you and Cranfield were guilty or not.'

He half convinced me. He polished off the rest of the whisky and told me not to forget to get some more.

Money. That was another thing. As from yesterday I had no income. The welfare state didn't pay unemployment benefits to the self-employed, as all jockeys remembered every snow-bound winter.

'I'm going to find out,' I said abruptly.

'Find out what?'

'Who framed us.'

'Up the Marines,' Tony said unsteadily. 'Over the top, boys. Up and at 'em.' He picked up the empty bottle and looked at it regretfully. 'Time for bed, I guess. If you need any help with the campaign, count on my Welsh blood to the last clot.'

He made an unswerving line to the door, turned, and gave me a grimace of friendship worth having.

'Don't fall down the stairs,' I said.

PART TWO

MARCH

CHAPTER FOUR

Roberta Cranfield looked magnificent in my sitting-room. I came back from buying whisky in the village and found her gracefully draped all over my restored Chippendale. The green velvet supported a lot of leg and a deep purple size-ten wool dress, and her thick long hair the colour of dead beech leaves clashed dramatically with the curtains. Under the hair she had white skin, incredible eyebrows, amber eyes, photogenic cheekbones and a petulant mouth.

She was nineteen, and I didn't like her.

'Good morning,' I said.

'Your door was open.'

'It's a habit I'll have to break.'

I peeled the tissue wrapping off the bottle and put it with the two chunky glasses on the small silver tray I had once won in a race sponsored by some sweet manufacturers. Troy weight, twenty-four ounces: but ruined by the inscription, K. HUGHES, WINNING JOCKEY, STARCHOCS SILVER STEEPLECHASE. Starchocs indeed. And

I never ate chocolates. Couldn't afford to, from the weight point of view.

She flapped her hand from a relaxed wrist, indicating the room.

'This is all pretty lush.'

I wondered what she had come for. I said, 'Would you like some coffee?'

'Coffee and cannabis.'

'You'll have to go somewhere else.'

'You're very prickly.'

'As a cactus,' I agreed.

She gave me a half-minute unblinking stare with her liquid eyes. Then she said, 'I only said cannabis to jolt you.'

'I'm not jolted.'

'No. I can see that. Waste of effort.'

'Coffee, then?'

'Yes.'

I went into the kitchen and fixed up the percolator. The kitchen was white and brown and copper and yellow. The colours pleased me. Colours gave me the sort of mental food I imagined others got from music. I disliked too much music, loathed the type of stuff you couldn't escape in restaurants and airliners, didn't own a record-player, and much preferred silence.

She followed me in from the sitting-room and looked around her with mild surprise.

'Do all jockeys live like this?'

'Naturally.'

'I don't believe it.'

She peered into the pine-fronted cupboard I'd taken the coffee from.

'Do you cook for yourself?'

'Mostly.'

'*Recherché* things like *shashlik*?' An undercurrent of mockery.

'Steaks.'

I poured the bubbling coffee into two mugs and offered her cream and sugar. She took the cream, generously, but not the sugar, and perched on a yellow-topped stool. Her copper hair fitted the kitchen, too.

'You seem to be taking it all right,' she said.

'What?'

'Being warned off.'

I didn't answer.

'A cactus,' she said, 'isn't in the same class.'

She drank the coffee slowly, in separate mouthfuls, watching me thoughtfully over the mug's rim. I watched her back. Nearly my height, utterly self-possessed, as cool as the stratosphere. I had seen her grow from a demanding child into a selfish fourteen-year-old, and from there into a difficult-to-please debutante and from there to a glossy imitation model girl heavily tinged with boredom. Over the eight years I had ridden for her father we had met briefly and spoken seldom, usually in parade rings and outside the weighing-room, and on the occasions when she did speak to me she seemed to be aiming just over the top of my head.

'You're making it difficult,' she said.

'For you to say why you came?'

She nodded. 'I thought I knew you. Now it seems I don't.'

'What did you expect?'

'Well . . . Father said you came from a farm cottage with pigs running in and out of the door.'

'Father exaggerates.'

She lifted her chin to ward off the familiarity, a gesture I'd seen a hundred times in her and her brothers. A gesture copied from her parents.

'Hens,' I said, 'not pigs.'

She gave me an up-stage stare. I smiled at her faintly and refused to be reduced to the ranks. I watched the wheels tick over while she worked out how to approach a cactus, and gradually the chin came down.

'Actual hens?'

Not bad at all. I could feel my own smile grow genuine.

'Now and then.'

'You don't look like . . . I mean . . .'

'I know exactly what you mean,' I agreed. 'And it's high time you got rid of those chains.'

'Chains? What are you talking about?'

'The fetters in your mind. The iron bars in your soul.'

64

'My mind is all right.'

'You must be joking. It's chock-a-block with ideas half a century out of date.'

'I didn't come here to . . .' she began explosively, and then stopped.

'You didn't come here to be insulted,' I said ironically.

'Well, as you put it in that well-worn hackneyed phrase, no, I didn't. But I wasn't going to say that.'

'What did you come for?'

She hesitated. 'I wanted you to help me.'

'To do what?'

'To . . . to *cope* with Father.'

I was surprised, first that Father needed coping with, and second that she needed help to do it.

'What sort of help?'

'He's . . . he's so *shattered*.' Unexpectedly there were tears standing in her eyes. They embarrassed and angered her, and she blinked furiously so that I shouldn't see. I admired the tears but not her reason for trying to hide them.

'Here are you,' she said in a rush, 'walking about as cool as you please and buying whisky and making coffee as if no screaming avalanche had poured out on you and smothered your life and made every thought an absolute bloody hell, and maybe you don't understand how anyone in that state needs help, and come to that I don't understand why *you* don't need help, but anyway, Father *does*.'

'Not from me,' I said mildly. 'He doesn't think enough of me to give it any value.'

She opened her mouth angrily and shut it again and took two deep controlling breaths. 'And it looks as though he's right.'

'Ouch,' I said ruefully. 'What sort of help, then?'

'I want you to come and talk to him.'

My talking to Cranfield seemed likely to be as therapeutic as applying itching powder to a baby. However, she hadn't left me much room for kidding myself that fruitlessness was a good reason for not trying.

'When?'

'Now . . . Unless you have anything else to do.'

'No,' I said carefully. 'I haven't.'

She made a face and an odd little gesture with her hands. 'Will you come now, then . . . please?'

She herself seemed surprised about the real supplication in that 'please'. I imagined that she had come expecting to instruct, not to ask.

'All right.'

'Great.' She was suddenly very cool, very employer's daughter again. She put her coffee mug on the draining board and started towards the door. 'You had better follow me, in your car. It's no good me taking you, you'll need your own car to come back in.'

'That is so,' I agreed.

She looked at me suspiciously, but decided not to pursue it. 'My coat is in your bedroom.'

'I'll fetch it for you.'

'Thank you.'

I walked across the sitting-room and into the bedroom. Her coat was lying on my bed in a heap. Black and white fur, in stripes going round. I picked it up and turned, and found she had followed me.

'Thank you so much.' She presented her back to me and put her arms in the coat-putting-on position. On went the coat. She swivelled slowly, buttoning up the front with shiny black saucers. 'This flat really is fantastic. Who is your decorator?'

'Chap called Kelly Hughes.'

She raised her eyebrows. 'I know the professional touch when I see it.'

'Thank you.'

She raised the chin. 'Oh well, if you won't say . . .'

'I would say. I did say. I did the flat myself. I've been whitewashing pigsties since I was six.'

She wasn't quite sure whether to be amused or offended, and evaded it by changing the subject.

'That picture . . . that's your wife, isn't it?'

I nodded.

'I remember her,' she said. 'She was always so sweet to me. She seemed to know what I was feeling. I was really awfully sorry when she was killed.'

I looked at her in surprise. The people Rosalind had

67

been sweetest to had invariably been unhappy. She had had a knack of sensing it, and of giving succour without being asked. I would not have thought of Roberta Cranfield as being unhappy, though I supposed from twelve to fifteen, when she had known Rosalind, she could have had her troubles.

'She wasn't bad, as wives go,' I said flippantly, and Miss Cranfield disapproved of that, too.

We left the flat and this time I locked the door, though such horses as I'd had had already bolted. Roberta had parked her Sunbeam Alpine behind the stables and across the doors of the garage where I kept my Lotus. She backed and turned her car with aggressive poise, and I left a leisurely interval before I followed her through the gates, to avoid a competition all the eighteen miles to her home.

Cranfield lived in an early Victorian house in a hamlet four miles out of Lambourn. A country gentleman's residence, estate agents would have called it: built before the Industrial Revolution had invaded Berkshire and equally impervious to the social revolution a hundred years later. Elegant, charming, timeless, it was a house I liked very much. Pity about the occupants.

I drove up the back drive as usual and parked alongside the stable yard. A horsebox was standing there with its ramp down, and one of the lads was leading a

horse into it. Archie, the head lad, who had been helping, came across as soon as I climbed out of the car.

'This is a God-awful bloody business,' he said. 'It's
wicked, that's what it is. Downright bloody wicked.'

'The horses are going?'

'Some owners have sent boxes already. All of them
will be gone by the day after tomorrow.' His weather-
beaten face was a mixture of fury, frustration, and
anxiety. 'All the lads have got the sack. Even me. And
the missus and I have just taken a mortgage on one
of the new houses up the road. Chalet bungalow, just
what she'd always set her heart on. Worked for years,
she has, saving for it. Now she won't stop crying. We
moved in only a month ago, see? How do you think
we're going to keep up the payments? Took every
pound we had, what with the deposit and the solicitors,
and curtains and all. Nice little place, too, she's got it
looking real nice. And it isn't as if the Guvnor really
fiddled the blasted race. That Cherry Pie, anyone could
see with half an eye he was going to be good some day.
I mean, if the Guvnor had done it, like, somehow all
this wouldn't be so bad. I mean, if he deserved it, well
serve him right, and I'd try and get a bit of compen-
sation from him because we're going to have a right
job selling the house again. I'll tell you, because there's
still two of them empty, they weren't so easy to sell in
the first place, being so far out of Lambourn ... I'll tell
you straight, I wish to God we'd never moved out of

the Guvnor's cottage, dark and damp though it may be . . . George,' he suddenly shouted at a lad swearing and tugging at a reluctant animal, 'don't take it out on the horse, it isn't *his* fault . . .' He bustled across the yard and took the horse himself, immediately quietening it and leading it without trouble into the horsebox.

He was an excellent head lad, better than most, and a lot of Cranfield's success was his doing. If he sold his house and got settled in another job, Cranfield wouldn't get him back. The training licence might not be lost for ever, but the stable's main prop would be.

I watched another lad lead a horse round to the waiting box. He too looked worried. His wife, I knew, was on the point of producing their first child.

Some of the lads wouldn't care, of course. There were plenty of jobs going in racing stables, and one lot of digs was much the same as another. But they too would not come back. Nor would most of the horses, nor many of the owners. The stable wasn't being suspended for a few months. It was being smashed.

Sick and seething with other people's fury as well as my own, I walked down the short stretch of drive to the house. Roberta's Alpine was parked outside the front door and she was standing beside it looking cross.

'So there you are. I thought you'd ratted.'

'I parked down by the yard.'

'I can't bear to go down there. Nor can Father. In

fact, he won't move out of his dressing-room. You'll have to come upstairs to see him.'

She led the way through the front door and across thirty square yards of Persian rug. When we had reached the foot of the stairs the door of the library was flung open and Mrs Cranfield came through it. Mrs Cranfield always flung doors open, rather as if she suspected something reprehensible was going on behind them and she was intent on catching the sinners in the act. She was a plain woman who wore no make-up and dressed in droopy woollies. To me she had never talked about anything except horses, and I didn't know whether she could. Her father was an Irish baron, which may have accounted for the marriage.

'My father-in-law, Lord Coolihan . . .' Cranfield was wont to say: and he was wont to say it far too often. I wondered whether, after Gowery, he was the tiniest bit discontented with the aristocracy.

'Ah, there you are, Hughes,' Mrs Cranfield said. 'Roberta told me she was going to fetch you. Though what good you can do I cannot understand. After all, it was you who got us into the mess.'

'I what?'

'If you'd ridden a better race on Squelch, none of this would have happened.'

I bit back six answers and said nothing. If you were hurt enough you lashed out at the nearest object. Mrs Cranfield continued to lash.

'Dexter was thoroughly shocked to hear that you had been in the habit of deliberately losing races.'

'So was I,' I said dryly.

Roberta moved impatiently. 'Mother, do stop it. Come along, Hughes. This way.'

I didn't move. She went up three steps, paused, and looked back. 'Come on, what are you waiting for?'

I shrugged. Whatever I was waiting for, I wouldn't get it in that house. I followed her up the stairs, along a wide passage, and into her father's dressing-room.

There was too much heavy mahogany furniture of a later period than the house, a faded plum-coloured carpet, faded plum plush curtains, and a bed with an Indian cover.

On one side of the bed sat Dexter Cranfield, his back bent into a bow and his shoulders hunched round his ears. His hands rolled loosely on his knees, fingers curling, and he was staring immovably at the floor.

'He sits like that for hours,' Roberta said on a breath beside me. And, looking at him, I understood why she had needed help.

'Father,' she said, going over and touching his shoulder. 'Kelly Hughes is here.'

Cranfield said, 'Tell him to go and shoot himself.'

She saw the twitch in my face, and from her expression thought that I minded, that I believed Cranfield too thought me the cause of all his troubles. On the whole I decided not to crystallize her fears by saying I thought Cranfield had said shoot because shoot was in his mind.

'Hop it,' I said, and jerked my head towards the door.

The chin went up like a reflex. Then she looked at the husk of her father, and back to me, whom she'd been to some trouble to bring, and most of the starch dissolved.

'All right. I'll be down in the library. Don't go without . . . telling me.'

I shook my head, and she went collectedly out of the room, shutting the door behind her.

I walked to the window and looked at the view. Small fields trickling down into the valley. Trees all bent one way by the wind off the Downs. A row of pylons, a cluster of council-house roofs. Not a horse in sight. The dressing-room was on the opposite side of the house to the stables.

'Have you a gun?' I asked.

No answer from the bed. I went over and sat down beside him. 'Where is it?'

His eyes slid a fraction in my direction and then back. He had been looking past me. I got up and went to the table beside his bed, but there was nothing lethal on it, and nothing in the drawer.

I found it behind the high mahogany bedhead. A finely wrought Purdey more suitable for pheasants. Both barrels were loaded. I unloaded them.

'Very messy,' I remarked. 'Very inconsiderate. And anyway, you didn't mean to do it.'

I wasn't at all sure about that, but there was no harm in trying to convince him.

'What are you doing here?' he said indifferently.

'Telling you to snap out of it. There's work to be done.'

'Don't speak to me like that.'

'How, then?'

His head came up a little, just like Roberta's. If I made him angry, he'd be halfway back to his normal self. And I could go home.

'It's useless sitting up here sulking. It won't achieve anything at all.'

'*Sulking?*' He was annoyed, but not enough.

'Someone took our toys away. Very unfair. But nothing to be gained by grizzling in corners.'

'*Toys* ... You're talking nonsense.'

'Toys, licences, what's the difference. The things we prized most. Someone's snatched them away. Tricked us out of them. And nobody except us can get them back. Nobody else will bother.'

'We can apply,' he said without conviction.

'Oh, we can apply. In six months' time, I suppose. But there's no guarantee we'd get them. The only sensible thing to do is to start fighting back right now and find out who fixed us. Who, and why. And after that I'll wring his bloody neck.'

74

He was still staring at the floor, still hunched. He couldn't even look me in the face yet, let alone the world. If he hadn't been such a climbing snob, I thought uncharitably, his present troubles wouldn't have produced such a complete cave-in. He was on the verge of literally not being able to bear the public disgrace of being warned off.

Well, I wasn't so sure I much cared for it myself. It was all very well knowing that one was not guilty, and even having one's closest friends believe it, but one could hardly walk around everywhere wearing a notice proclaiming 'I am innocent. I never done it. It were all a stinking frame-up.'

'It's not so bad for you,' he said.

'That's perfectly true.' I paused. 'I came in through the yard.'

He made a low sound of protest.

'Archie seems to be seeing to everything himself. And he's worried about his house.'

Cranfield made a waving movement of his hand as much as to ask how did I think he could be bothered with Archie's problems on top of his own.

'It wouldn't hurt you to pay Archie's mortgage for a bit.'

'*What?*' That finally reached him. His head came up at least six inches.

'It's only a few pounds a week. Peanuts to you. Life

or death to him. And if you lose him you'll never get so many winners again.'

'You ... you ...' He spluttered. But he still didn't look up.

'A trainer is as good as his lads.'

'That's stupid.'

'You've got good lads just now. You've chucked out the duds, the rough and lazy ones. It takes time to weed out and build up a good team, but you can't get a high ratio of winners without one. You might get your licence back but you won't get these lads back and it'll take years for the stable to recover. If it ever does. And I hear you have already given them all the sack.'

'What else was there to do?'

'You could try keeping them on for a month.'

His head came up a little more. 'You haven't the slightest idea what that would cost me. The wages come to more than four hundred pounds a week.'

'There must still be quite a lot to come in in training fees. Owners seldom pay in advance. You won't have to dig very deep into your own pocket. Not for a month, anyway, and it might not take as long as that.'

'What might not?'

'Getting our licences back.'

'Don't be so bloody ridiculous.'

'I mean it. What is it worth to you? Four weeks' wages for your lads? Would you pay that much if there was a chance you'd be back in racing in a month? The owners would send their horses back, if it was as quick as that. Particularly if you tell them you confidently expect to be back in business almost immediately.'

'They wouldn't believe it.'

'They'd be uncertain. That should be enough.'

'There isn't a chance of getting back.'

'Oh yes there damn well is,' I said forcefully. 'But only if you're willing to take it. Tell the lads you're keeping them on for a bit. Especially Archie. Go down to the yard and tell them now.'

'*Now*.'

'Of course,' I said impatiently. 'Probably half of them have already read the Situations Vacant columns and written to other trainers.'

'There isn't any point.' He seemed sunk in fresh gloom. 'It's all hopeless. And it couldn't have happened, it simply could *not* have happened at a worse time. Edwin Byler was going to send me his horses. It was all fixed up. Now of course he's telephoned to say it's all off, his horses are staying where they are, at Jack Roxford's.'

To train Edwin Byler's horses was to be presented with a pot of gold. He was a North country businessman who had made a million or two out of mail order, and had used a little of it to fulfil a long held ambition to own the best string of steeplechasers in Britain. Four of his present horses had in turn cost more than anyone had paid before. When he wanted, he bid. He only

wanted the best, and he had bought enough of them
to put him for the two previous seasons at the top of
the Winning Owners' list. To have been going to train
Edwin Byler's horses, and now not to be going to, was
a refined cruelty to pile on top of everything else.

To have been going to *ride* Edwin Byler's horses . . .
as I would no doubt have done . . . that too was a thrust
where it hurt.

'There's all the more point, then,' I said. 'What more
do you want in the way of incentive? You're throwing
away without a struggle not only what you've got but
what you might have . . . Why in the Hell don't you get
off your bed and behave like a gentleman and show
some spirit?'

'Hughes!' He was outraged. But he still sat. He still
wouldn't look at me.

I paused, considering him. Then, slowly, I said, 'All
right, then. I'll tell you why you won't. You won't
because . . . to some degree . . . you are in fact guilty.
You made sure Squelch wouldn't win. And you backed
Cherry Pie.'

That got him. Not just his head up, but up, trembling,
on to his feet.

CHAPTER FIVE

'How dare you?'

'Frankly, just now I'd dare practically anything.'

'You said we were framed.'

'So we were.'

Some of his alarm subsided. I stoked it up again.

'You handed us away on a plate.'

He swallowed, his eyes flicking from side to side, looking everywhere except at me.

'I don't know what you mean.'

'Don't be so weak,' I said impatiently. 'I rode Squelch, remember? Was he his usual self? He was not.'

'If you're suggesting,' he began explosively, 'that I doped . . .'

'Oh, of course not. Anyway, they tested him, didn't they? Negative result. Naturally. No trainer needs to dope a horse he doesn't want to win. It's like swatting a fly with a bull-dozer. There are much more subtle methods. Undetectable. Even innocent. Maybe you

79

should be kinder to yourself and admit that you quite innocently stopped Squelch. Maybe you even did it subconsciously, wanting Cherry Pie to win.'

'Bull,' he said.

'The mind plays tricks,' I said. 'People often believe they are doing something for one good reason, while they are subconsciously doing it for another.'

'Twaddle.'

'The trouble comes sometimes when the real reason rears its ugly head and slaps you in the kisser.'

'Shut up.' His teeth and jaw were clenched tight.

I drew a deep breath. I'd been guessing, partly. And I'd guessed right.

I said, 'You gave Squelch too much work too soon before the race. He lost the Lemonfizz on the gallops at home.'

He looked at me at last. His eyes were dark, as if the pupils had expanded to take up all the iris. There was a desperate sort of hopelessness in his expression.

'It wouldn't have been so bad,' I said, 'if you had admitted it to yourself. Because then you would never have risked not engaging a lawyer to defend us.'

'I didn't mean to over-train Squelch,' he said wretchedly. 'I didn't realize it until afterwards. I did back him, just as I said at the Enquiry.'

I nodded. 'I imagined you must have done. But you backed Cherry Pie as well.'

He explained quite simply, without any of his usual

superiority. 'Trainers are often caught out, as you know, when one of their horses suddenly develops his true form. Well, I thought Cherry Pie might just be one of those. So I backed him, on the off chance.'

Some off chance. Fifty pounds with Newtonnards and fifty pounds on the Tote. Gross profit, two thousand.

'How much did you have on Squelch?'

'Two hundred and fifty.'

'Whew,' I said. 'Was that your usual sort of bet?'

'He was odds on . . . I suppose a hundred is my most usual bet.'

I had come to the key question, and I wasn't sure I wanted to ask it, let alone have to judge whether the answer was true. However . . .

'Why,' I said matter-of-factly, 'didn't you back Cherry Pie with your own usual bookmaker?'

He answered without effort, 'Because I didn't want Kessel knowing I'd backed Cherry Pie, if he won instead of Squelch. Kessel's a funny man, he takes everything personally, he'd as like as not have whisked Squelch away . . .' He trailed off, remembering afresh that Squelch was indeed being whisked.

'Why should Kessel have known?'

'Eh? Oh, because he bets with my bookmaker too, and the pair of them are as thick as thieves.'

Fair enough.

'Well, who was the middle-aged man who put the bets on for you?'

'Just a friend. There's no need to involve him. I want to keep him out of it.'

'Could Newtonnards have seen you talking to him by the parade ring before the first race?'

'Yes,' he said with depression. 'I did talk to him. I gave him the money to bet with.'

And he still hadn't seen any danger signals. Had taken Monty Midgley's assurance at its face value. Hadn't revealed the danger to me. I could have throttled him.

'What did you do with the winnings?'

'They're in the safe downstairs.'

'And you haven't been able to admit to anyone that you've got them.'

'No.'

I thought back. 'You lied about it at the Enquiry.'

'What else was there to do?'

By then, what indeed. Telling the truth hadn't done much for me.

'Let's see, then.' I moved over to the window again, sorting things out. 'Cherry Pie won on his merits. You backed him because he looked like coming into form rather suddenly. Squelch had had four hard races in two months, and a possibly over-zealous training gallop. These are the straight facts.'

'Yes . . . I suppose so.'

'No trainer should lose his licence because he didn't tell the world he might just possibly have a flier. I never see why the people who put in all the work shouldn't have the first dip into the well.'

Owners, too, were entitled. Cherry Pie's owner, however, had died three weeks before the Lemonfizz, and Cherry Pie had run for the executors. Someone was going to have a fine time deciding his precise value at the moment of his owner's death.

'It means, anyway, that you do have a fighting fund,' I pointed out.

'There's no point in fighting.'

'You,' I said exasperatedly, 'are so soft that you'd make a marshmallow look like granite.'

His mouth slowly opened. Before that morning I had never given him anything but politeness. He was looking at me as if he'd really noticed me, and it occurred to me that if we did indeed get our licences back he would remember that I'd seen him in pieces, and maybe find me uncomfortable to have around. He paid me a retainer, but only on an annual contract. Easy enough to chuck me out, and retain someone else. Expediently, and not too pleased with myself for it, I took the worst crags out of my tone.

'I presume,' I said, 'that you do want your licence back?'

'There isn't a chance.'

'If you'll keep the lads for a month, I'll get it back for you.'

Defeatism still showed in every sagging muscle, and he didn't answer.

I shrugged. 'Well, I'm going to try. And if I give you your licence back on a plate it will be just too bad if Archie and the lads have gone.' I walked towards the door and put my hand on the knob. 'I'll let you know how I get on.'

Twisted the knob. Opened the door.

'Wait,' he said.

I turned round. A vestige of starch had returned, mostly in the shape of the reappearance of the mean lines round his mouth. Not so good.

'I don't believe you can do it. But as you're so cocksure, I'll make a bargain with you. I'll pay the lads for two weeks. If you want me to keep them on for another two weeks after that, you can pay them yourself.'

Charming. He'd made two thousand pounds out of Cherry Pie and had over-trained Squelch and was the direct cause of my being warned off. I stamped on a violent inner tremble of anger and gave him a cold answer.

'Very well. I agree to that. But you must make a bargain with me too. A bargain that you'll keep your mouth tight shut about your guilt feelings. I don't want to be sabotaged by you hairshirting it all over the place and confessing your theoretical sins at awkward moments.'

'I am unlikely to do that,' he said stiffly.

I wasn't so sure. 'I want your word on it,' I said.

He drew himself up, offended. It at least had the effect of straightening his backbone.

'You have it.'

'Fine.' I held the door open for him. 'Let's go down to the yard, then.'

He still hesitated, but finally made up his mind to it, and went before me through the door and down the stairs.

Roberta and her mother were standing in the hall, looking as if they were waiting for news at a pithead after a disaster. They watched the reappearance of the head of the family with a mixture of relief and apprehension, and Mrs Cranfield said tentatively, 'Dexter? . . .'

He answered irritably, as if he saw no cause for anxiety in his having shut himself away with a shotgun for thirty-six hours, 'We're going down to the yard.'

'Great,' said Roberta practically smothering any tendency to emotion from her mother, 'I'll come too.'

Archie hurried to meet us and launched into a detailed account of which horses had gone and which were about to go next. Cranfield hardly listened and certainly didn't take it in. He waited for a gap in the flow, and when he'd waited long enough, impatiently interrupted.

'Yes, yes, Archie, I'm sure you have everything in hand. That is not what I've come down for, however. I want you to tell the lads at once that their notice to leave is withdrawn for one month.'

Archie looked at me, not entirely understanding.

'The sack,' I said, 'is postponed. Pending attempts to get wrongs righted.'

'Mine too?'

'Absolutely,' I agreed. 'Especially, in fact.'

'Hughes thinks there is a chance we can prove ourselves innocent and recover our licences,' Cranfield said formally, his own disbelief showing like two heads. 'In order to help me keep the stable together while he makes enquiries, Hughes has agreed to contribute one half towards your wages for one month.' I looked at him sharply. That was not at all what I had agreed. He showed no sign of acknowledging his reinterpretation (to put it charitably) of the offer I had accepted, and went authoritatively on. 'Therefore, as your present week's notice still has five days to run, none of you will be required to leave here for five weeks. In fact,' he added grudgingly, 'I would be obliged if you would all stay.'

Archie said to me, 'You really mean it?' and I watched the hope suddenly spring up in his face and thought that maybe it wasn't only my own chance of a future that was worth eight hundred quid.

'That's right,' I agreed. 'As long as you don't all spend the month busily fixing up to go somewhere else at the end of it.'

'What do you take us for?' Archie protested.

'Cynics,' I said, and Archie actually laughed.

I left Cranfield and Archie talking together with most of the desperation evaporating from both of them, and walked away to my aerodynamic burnt-orange car. I didn't hear Roberta following me until she spoke in my ear as I opened the door.

'Can you really do it?' she said.

'Do what?'

'Get your licences back.'

'It's going to cost me too much not to. So I guess I'll have to or . . .'

'Or what?'

I smiled. 'Or die in the attempt.'

It took me an hour to cross into Gloucestershire and almost half as long to sort out the geography of the village of Downfield, which mostly seemed to consist of cul-de-sacs.

The cottage I eventually found after six misdirections from local inhabitants was old but not beautiful,

well painted but in dreary colours, and a good deal
more trustworthy than its owner.

When Mrs Charlie West saw who it was, she tried
to shut the front door in my face. I put out a hand that
was used to dealing with strong horses and pulled her
by the wrist, so that if she slammed the door she would
be squashing her own arm.

She screeched loudly. An inner door at the back of
the hall opened all of six inches, and Charlie's round
face appeared through the crack. A distinct lack of
confidence was discernible in that area.

'He's hurting me,' Mrs West shouted.

'I want to talk to you,' I said to Charlie over her
shoulder.

Charlie West was less than willing. Abandoning his
teenage wife, long straight hair, Dusty Springfield eye-
lashes, beige lipstick and all, he retreated a pace and
quite firmly shut his door. Mrs West put up a loud
and energetic defence to my attempt to establish
further contact with Master Charlie, and I went through
the hall fending off her toes and fists.

Charlie had wedged a chair under the door handle.

I shouted through the wood. 'Much as you deserve
it, I haven't come here to beat you up. Come out and
talk.'

No response of any sort. I rattled the door. Repeated
my request. No results. With Mrs West still stabbing
around like an agitated hornet I went out of the front

door and round the outside to try to talk to him through the window. The window was open, and the sitting-room inside was empty.

I turned round in time to see Charlie's distant back-view disappearing across a field and into the next parish. Mrs West saw him too, and gave a nasty smile.

'So there,' she said triumphantly.

'Yes,' I said. 'I'm sure you must be very proud of him.'

The smile wobbled. I walked back down their garden path, climbed into the car, and drove away.

Round one slightly farcically to the opposition.

Two miles away from the village I stopped the car in a farm gateway and thought it over. Charlie West had been a great deal more scared of me than I would have supposed, even allowing for the fact that I was a couple of sizes bigger and a fair amount stronger. Maybe Charlie was as much afraid of my fury as of my fists. He almost seemed to have been expecting that I would attempt some sort of retaliation, and certainly after what he had done, he had a right to. All the same, he still represented my quickest and easiest route to who, if not to why.

After a while I started up again and drove on into the nearest town. Remembered I hadn't eaten all day, put away some rather good cold beef at three-thirty in a home-made café geared more to cake and scones, dozed in the car, waited until dark, and finally drove back again to Charlie's village.

There were lights on in several rooms of his cottage. The Wests were at home. I turned the car and re-tracked about a hundred yards, stopping half on and half off a grassy verge. Climbed out. Stood up.

Plan of attack: vague. I had had some idea of ringing the front-door bell, disappearing and waiting for either Charlie or his dolly wife to take one incautious step outside to investigate. Instead, unexpected allies materialized in the shape of one small boy and one large dog.

The boy had a torch, and was talking to his dog, who paused to dirty up the roadside five yards ahead.

'What the hell d'you think you were at, you bloody great nit, scoffing our Mum's stewing steak? Gor blimey mate, don't you ever learn nothing? Tomorrow's dinner gone down your useless big gullet and our Dad will give us both a belting this time I shouldn't wonder, not just you, you senseless rotten idiot. Time you knew the bloody difference between me Mum's stewing steak and dog meat, it is straight, though come to think of it there isn't all that difference, 'specially as maybe your eyes don't look at things the same. Do they? I damn well wish you could talk, mate.'

I clicked shut the door of the car and startled him,

and he swung round with the torch searching wildly. The beam caught me and steadied on my face.

The boy said, 'You come near me and I'll set my dog on you.' The dog, however, was still squatting and showed no enthusiasm.

'I'll stay right here, then,' I said amicably, leaning back against the car. 'I only want to know who lives in that cottage over there, where the lights are.'

'How do I know? We only come to live here the day before yesterday.'

'Great ... I mean, that must be great for you, moving.'

'Yeah. Sure. You stay there, then. I'm going now.' He beckoned to the dog. The dog was still busy.

'How would it be if you could offer your Mum the price of the stewing steak? Maybe she wouldn't tell your Dad, then, and neither you nor the dog would get a belting.'

'Our Mum says we mustn't talk to strange men.'

'Hmm. Well, never mind then. Off you go.'

'I'll go when I'm ready,' he said belligerently. A natural born rebel. About nine years old, I guessed.

'What would I have to do for it?' he said, after a pause.

'Nothing much. Just ring the front-door bell of that cottage and tell whoever answers that you can't stop your dog eating the crocuses they've got growing all along the front there. Then when they come out to see, just nip off home as fast as your dog can stagger.'

It appealed to him. 'Steak probably cost a good bit,' he said.

'Probably.' I dug into my pocket and came up with a small fistful of pennies and silver. 'This should leave a bit over.'

'He doesn't really have to eat the crocuses, does he?'

'No.'

'OK, then.' Once his mind was made up he was jaunty and efficient. He shovelled my small change into his pocket, marched up to Charlie's front door, and told Mrs West, who cautiously answered it, that she was losing her crocuses. She scolded him all the way down the path, and while she was bending down to search for the damage, my accomplice quietly vanished. Before Mrs West exactly realized she had been misled I had stepped briskly through her front door and shut her out of her own house.

When I opened the sitting-room door Charlie said, without lifting his eyes from a racing paper, 'It wasn't him again, then.'

'Yes,' I said, 'it was.'

Charlie's immature face crumpled into a revolting state of fear and Mrs West leaned on the door bell. I shut the sitting-room door behind me to cut out some of the din.

'What are you so afraid of?' I said loudly.

'Well . . . you . . .'

'And so you damn well ought to be,' I agreed. I took a step towards him and he shrank back into his armchair. He was brave enough on a horse, which made this abject cringing all the more unexpected, and all the more unpleasant. I took another step. He fought his way into the upholstery.

Mrs West gave the door bell a rest.

'Why did you do it?' I said.

He shook his head dumbly, and pulled his feet up on to the chair seat in the classic womb position. Wishful regression to the first and only place where the world couldn't reach him.

'Charlie, I came here for some answers, and you're going to give them to me.'

Mrs West's furious face appeared at the window and she started rapping hard enough to break the glass. With one eye on her husband to prevent him making another bolt for it, I stepped over and undid the latch.

'Get out of here,' she shouted. 'Go on, get out.'

'You get in. Through here, I'm not opening the door.'

'I'll fetch the police.'

'Do what you like. I only want to talk to your worm of a husband. Get in or stay out, but shut up.'

She did anything but. Once she was in the room it took another twenty minutes of fruitless slanging before I could ask Charlie a single question without her loud voice obliterating any chance of an answer.

Charlie himself tired of it first and told her to stop, but at least her belligerence had given him a breathing space. He put his feet down on the floor again and said it was no use asking those questions, he didn't know the answers.

'You must do. Unless you told those lies about me out of sheer personal spite.'

'No.'

'Then why?'

'I'm not telling you.'

'Then I'll tell you something, you little louse. I'm going to find out who put you up to it. I'm going to stir everything up until I find out, and then I'm going to raise such a stink about being framed that sulphur will smell like sweet peas by comparison, and you, Master Charlie West, *you* will find yourself without a licence, not me, and even if you get it back you'll never live down the contempt everyone will feel for you.'

'Don't you talk to my Charlie like that!'

'Your Charlie is a vicious little liar who would sell you too for fifty pounds.'

'It wasn't fifty,' she snapped triumphantly. 'It was five hundred.'

Charlie yelled at her and I came as near to hitting him as the distance between my clenched teeth. Five hundred pounds. He'd lied my licence away for a hand-out that would have insulted a tout.

'That does it,' I said. 'And now you tell me who paid you.'

The girl wife started to look as frightened as Charlie, and it didn't occur to me then that my anger had flooded through that little room like a tidal wave.

Charlie stuttered, 'I d . . . d . . . don't know.'

I took a pace towards him and he scrambled out of his chair and took refuge behind it.

'K . . . k . . . keep away from me. I don't know. I don't know.'

'That isn't good enough.'

'He really doesn't know,' the girl wailed. 'He really doesn't.'

'He does,' I repeated furiously.

The girl began to cry. Charlie seemed to be on the verge of copying her.

'I never saw . . . never saw the bloke. He telephoned.'

'And how did he pay you?'

'In two . . . in two packages. In one-pound notes. A hundred of them came the day before the Enquiry, and I was to get . . .' His voice trailed away.

'You were to get the other four hundred if I was warned off?'

He nodded, a fractional jerk. His head was tucked into his shoulders, as if to avoid a blow.

'And have you?'

'What?'

'Have you had it yet? The other four hundred?'

His eyes widened, and he spoke in jerks. 'No . . . but . . . of course . . . it . . . will . . . come.'

'Of course it won't,' I said brutally. 'You stupid treacherous little ninny.' My voice sounded thick, and each word came out separately and loaded with fury.

Both of the Wests were trembling, and the girl's eye make-up was beginning to run down her cheeks.

'What did he sound like, this man on the telephone?'

'Just . . . just a man,' Charlie said.

'And did it occur to you to ask *why* he wanted me warned off?'

'I said . . . you hadn't done anything to harm me . . . and he said . . . you never know . . . supposing one day he does . . .'

Charlie shrank still farther under my astounded glare.

'Anyway . . . five hundred quid . . . I don't earn as much as you, you know.' For the first time there was a tinge of spite in his voice, and I knew that in truth jealousy had been a factor, that he hadn't in fact done it entirely for the money. He'd got his kicks, too.

'You're only twenty,' I said. 'What exactly do you expect?'

But Charlie expected everything, always, to be run entirely for the best interests of Charlie West.

I said, 'And you'll be wise to spend that money carefully, because, believe me, it's going to be the most expensive hundred quid you've ever earned.'

'Kelly...' He was halfway to entreaty. Jealous, greedy, dishonest, and afraid. I felt not the remotest flicker of compassion for him, only a widening anger that the motives behind his lies were so small.

'And when you lose your licence for this, and I'll see that you do, you'll have plenty of time to understand that it *serves you right*.'

The raw revenge in my voice made a desert of their little home. They both stood there dumbly with wide miserable eyes, too broken up to raise another word. The girl's beige mouth hung slackly open, mascara halfway to her chin, long hair straggling in wisps across her face and round her shoulders. She looked sixteen. A child. So did Charlie. The worst vandals are always childish.

I turned away from them and walked out of their cottage, and my anger changed into immense depression on the drive home.

CHAPTER SIX

At two o'clock in the morning the rage I'd unleashed on the Wests looked worse and worse.

To start with, it had achieved nothing helpful. I'd known before I went there that Charlie must have had a reason for lying about me at the Enquiry. I now knew the reason to be five hundred pounds. Marvellous. A useless scrap of information out of a blizzard of emotion.

Lash out when you're hurt . . . I'd done that, all right. Poured out on them the roaring bitterness I'd smothered under a civilized front ever since Monday.

Nor had I given Charlie any reason to do me any good in future. Very much the reverse. He wasn't going to be contrite and eager to make amends. When he'd recovered himself he'd be sullen and vindictive.

I'd been taught the pattern over and over. Country A plays an isolated shabby trick. Country B is outraged and exacts revenge. Country A is forced to express apologies and meekly back down, but thoroughly resents it. Country A now holds a permanent grudge, and harms Country B whenever possible. One of the classic variations in the history of politics and aggression. Also applicable to individuals.

To have known about the pitfalls and jumped in regardless was a mite galling. It just showed how easily good sense lost out to anger. It also showed me that I wasn't going to get results that way. A crash course in detection would have been handy. Failing that, I'd have to start taking stock of things coolly, instead of charging straight off again towards the easiest looking target, and making another mess of it.

Cool stock-taking . . .

Charlie West hadn't wanted to see me because he had a guilty conscience. It followed that everyone else who had a guilty conscience wouldn't want to see me. Even if they didn't actually spring off across the fields, they would all do their best to avoid my reaching them. I was going to have to become adept – and fast – at entering their lives when their backs were turned.

If Charlie West didn't know who had paid him, and I believed that he didn't, it followed that perhaps no one else who had lied knew who had persuaded them to. Perhaps it had all been done on the telephone. Long-distance leverage. Impersonal and undiscoverable.

Perhaps I had set myself an impossible task and I

should give up the whole idea and emigrate to Australia.

Except that they had racing in Australia, and I wouldn't be able to go. The banishment covered the world. Warned off. Warned off.

Oh God.

All right, so maybe I did let the self-pity catch up with me for a while. But I was privately alone in my bed in the dark, and I'd jeered myself out of it by morning.

Looking about as ragged as I felt, I got up at six and pointed the Lotus's smooth nose towards London, NW7, Mill Hill.

Since I could see no one at the races I had to catch them at home, and in the case of George Newtonnards, bookmaker, home proved to be a sprawling pink-washed ranch-type bungalow in a prosperous suburban road. At eight-thirty a.m. I hoped to find him at breakfast, but in fact he was opening his garage door when I arrived. I parked squarely across the entrance to his drive, which was hardly likely to make me popular, and he came striding down towards me to tell me to move.

I climbed out of the car. When he saw who it was, he stopped dead. I walked up the drive to meet him, shivering a little in the raw east wind and regretting I wasn't snug inside a fur-collared jacket like his.

'What are you doing here?' he said sharply.

'I would be very grateful if you would just tell me one or two things . . .'

'I haven't time.' He was easy, self-assured, dealing with a small-sized nuisance. 'And nothing I can say will help you. Move your car, please.'

'Certainly . . . Could you tell me how it was that you came to be asked to give evidence against Mr Cranfield?'

'How it was? . . .' He looked slightly surprised. 'I received an official letter, requiring me to attend.'

'Well, why? I mean, how did the Stewards know about Mr Cranfield's bet on Cherry Pie? Did you write and tell them?'

He gave me a cool stare. 'I hear,' he said, 'that you are maintaining you were framed.'

'News travels.'

A faint smile. 'News always travels – towards me. An accurate information service is the basis of good bookmaking.'

'How did the Stewards know about Mr Cranfield's bet?'

'Mm. Well, yes, that I don't know.'

'Who, besides you, knew that you believed that Cranfield had backed Cherry Pie?'

'He did back him.'

'Well, who besides you knew that he had?'

'I haven't time for this.'

'I'll be happy to move my car . . . in a minute or two.'

His annoyed glare gradually softened round the edges into a half-amused acceptance. A very smooth civilized man, George Newtonnards.

'Very well. I told a few of the lads . . . other bookmakers, that is. I was angry about it, see? Letting myself be taken to the cleaners like that. Me, at my age, I should know better. So maybe one of them passed on the word to the Stewards, knowing the Enquiry was coming up. But no, I didn't do it myself.'

'Could you guess which one might have done? I mean, do you know of anyone who has a grudge against Cranfield?'

'Can't think of one.' He shrugged. 'No more than against any other trainer who tries it on.'

'Tries it on?' I echoed, surprised. 'But he doesn't.'

'Oh yeah?'

'I ride them,' I protested. 'I should know.'

'Yes,' he said sarcastically. 'You should. Don't come the naïve bit with me, chum. Your friend Chris Smith, him with the cracked skull, he's a proper artist at strangulation, wouldn't you say? Same as you are. A fine pair, the two of you.'

'You believe I pulled Squelch, then?'

'Stands to reason.'

'All the same, I didn't.'

'Tell it to the Marines.' A thought struck him. 'I

don't know any bookmakers who have a grudge against Cranfield, but I sure know one who has a grudge against *you*. A whopping great life-sized grudge. One time, he was almost coming after you with a chopper. You got in his way proper, mate, you did indeed.'

'How? And who?'

'You and Chris Smith, you were riding two for Cranfield . . . about six months ago. It was . . . right at the beginning of the season anyway . . . in a novice 'chase at Fontwell. Remember? There was a big holiday crowd in from the South Coast because it was a bit chilly that day for lying on the beach . . . anyway, there was a big crowd all primed with holiday money . . . and there were you and Chris Smith on these two horses, and the public fancying both of them, and Pelican Jobberson asked you which was off, and you said you hadn't an earthly on yours, so he rakes in the cash on you and doesn't bother to balance his book, and then you go and ride a hell of a finish and win by a neck, when you could have lost instead without the slightest trouble. Pelican went spare and swore he'd be even with you when he got the chance.'

'I believed what I told him,' I said. 'It was that horse's first attempt over fences. No one could have predicted he'd have been good enough to win.'

'Then why did you?'

'The owner wanted to, if possible.'

'Did he bet on it?'

103

'The owner? No. It was a woman. She never bets much. She just likes to see her horses win.'

'Pelican swore you'd backed it yourself, and put him off so that you could get a better price.'

'You bookmakers are too suspicious for your own good.'

'Hard experience proves us right.'

'Well, he's wrong this time,' I insisted. 'This bird friend of yours. If he asked me ... and I don't remember him asking ... then I told him the truth. And anyway, any bookmaker who asks jockeys questions like that is asking for trouble. Jockeys are the worst tipsters in the world.'

'Some aren't,' he said flatly. 'Some are good at it.'

I skipped that. 'Is he still angry after all these months? And if so, would he be angry enough not just to tell the Stewards that Cranfield backed Cherry Pie, but to bribe other people to invent lies about us?'

His eyes narrowed while he thought about it. He pursed his mouth, undecided. 'You'd better ask him yourself.'

'Thanks.' Hardly an easy question.

'Move your car now?' he suggested.

'Yes.' I walked two steps towards it, then stopped and turned back. 'Mr Newtonnards, if you see the man who put the money on for Mr Cranfield, will you find out who he is ... and let me know?'

'Why don't you ask Cranfield?'

'He said he didn't want to involve him.'

'But you do?'

'I suppose I'm grasping at anything,' I said. 'But yes, I think I do.'

'Why don't you just quieten down and take it?' he said reasonably. 'All this thrashing about . . . you got copped. So, you got copped. Fair enough. Sit it out, then. You'll get your licence back, eventually.'

'Thank you for your advice,' I said politely, and went and moved my car out of his gateway.

It was Thursday. I should have been going to Warwick to ride in four races. Instead, I drove aimlessly back round the North Circular Road wondering whether or not to pay a call on David Oakley, enquiry agent and imaginative photographer. If Charlie West didn't know who had framed me, it seemed possible that Oakley might be the only one who did. But even if he did, he was highly unlikely to tell me. There seemed no point in confronting him, and yet nothing could be gained if I made no attempt.

In the end I stopped at a telephone box and found his number via enquiries.

A girl answered. 'Mr Oakley isn't in yet.'

'Can I make an appointment?'

She asked me what about.

'A divorce.'

She said Mr Oakley could see me at 11.30, and asked me my name.

'Charles Crisp.'

'Very well, Mr Crisp. Mr Oakley will be expecting you.'

I doubted it. On the other hand, he, like Charlie West, might in general be expecting some form of protest.

From the North Circular Road I drove ninety miles up the M1 motorway to Birmingham and found Oakley's office above a bicycle and radio shop half a mile from the town centre.

His street door, shabby black, bore a neat small nameplate stating, simply, 'Oakley'. There were two keyholes, Yale and Chubb, and a discreetly situated peephole. I tried the handle of this apparent fortress, and the door opened easily under my touch. Inside, there was a narrow passage with pale blue walls leading to an uncarpeted staircase stretching upwards.

I walked up, my feet sounding loud on the boards. At the top there was a small landing with another shabby black door, again similarly fortified. On this door, another neat notice said, 'Please ring'. There was a bell push: I gave it three seconds' work.

The door was opened by a tall strong-looking girl dressed in a dark coloured leather trouser-suit. Under the jacket she wore a black sweater, and under the trouser legs, black leather boots. Black eyes returned my scrutiny, black hair held back by a tortoiseshell band fell straight to her shoulders before curving inwards. She seemed at first sight to be about twenty-four, but there were already wrinkle lines round her eyes, and the deadness in their expression indicated too much familiarity with dirty washing.

'I have an appointment,' I said. 'Crisp.'

'Come in.' She opened the door wider and left it for me to close.

I followed her into the room, a small square office furnished with a desk, typewriter, telephone, and four tall filing cabinets. On the far side of the room there was another door. Not black; modern flat hardboard, painted grey. More keyholes. I eyed them thoughtfully.

The girl opened the door, said through it, 'It's Mr Crisp,' and stood back for me to pass her.

'Thank you,' I said. Took three steps forwards, and shut myself in with David Oakley.

His office was not a great deal larger than the ante-room, and no thrift had been spared with the furniture. There was dim brown linoleum, a bentwood coat stand, a small cheap armchair facing a grey metal desk, and over the grimy window, in place of curtains, a tough-looking fixed frame covered with chicken wire. Outside the window there were the heavy bars and supports of a fire escape. The Birmingham sun, doing its best against odds, struggled through and fell in wrinkled honeycomb shadows on the surface of an ancient safe.

In the wall on my right, another door, firmly closed. With yet more keyholes.

Behind the desk in a swivel chair sat the proprietor of all this glory, the totally unmemorable Mr Oakley. Youngish. Slender. Mouse-coloured hair. And this time, sunglasses.

'Sit down, Mr Crisp,' he said. Accentless voice, entirely emotionless, as before. 'Divorce, I believe? Give me the details of your requirements, and we can arrive at a fee.' He looked at his watch. 'I can give you just ten minutes, I'm afraid. Shall we get on?'

He hadn't recognized me. I thought I might as well take advantage of it.

'I understand you would be prepared to fake some evidence for me . . . photographs?'

He began to nod, and then grew exceptionally still. The unrevealing dark glasses were motionless. The pale straight mouth didn't twitch. The hand lying on the desk remained loose and relaxed.

Finally he said, without any change of inflection, 'Get out.'

'How much do you charge for faking evidence?'

'Get out.'

I smiled. 'I'd like to know how much I was worth.'

'Dust,' he said. His foot moved under the desk.

'I'll pay you in gold dust, if you'll tell me who gave you the job.'

He considered it. Then he said, 'No.'

The door to the outer office opened quietly behind me.

Oakley said calmly, 'This is not a Mr Crisp, Didi. This is a Mr Kelly Hughes. Mr Hughes will be leaving.'

'Mr Hughes is not ready,' I said.

'I think Mr Hughes will find he is,' she said.

I looked at her over my shoulder. She was carrying a large black-looking pistol with a very large black-looking silencer. The whole works were pointing steadily my way.

'How dramatic,' I said. 'Can you readily dispose of bodies in the centre of Birmingham?'

'Yes,' Oakley said.

'For a fee, of course, usually,' Didi added.

I struggled not to believe them, and lost. All the same . . .

'Should you decide after all to sell the information I need, you know where to find me.' I relaxed against the back of the chair.

'I may have a liking for gold dust,' he said calmly. 'But I am not a fool.'

'Opinions differ,' I remarked lightly.

There was no reaction. 'It is not in my interest that you should prove you were . . . shall we say . . . set up.'

'I understand that. Eventually, however, you will wish that you hadn't helped to do it.'

He said smoothly. 'A number of other people have

said much the same, though few, I must confess, as quietly as you.'

It occurred to me suddenly that he must be quite used to the sort of enraged onslaught I'd thrown at the Wests, and that perhaps that was why his office . . . Didi caught my wandering glance and cynically nodded.

'That's right. Too many people tried to smash the place up. So we keep the damage to a minimum.'

'How wise.'

'I'm afraid I really do have another appointment now,' Oakley said. 'So if you'll excuse me? . . .'

I stood up. There was nothing to stay for.

'It surprises me,' I remarked, 'that you're not in jail.'

'I am clever,' he said matter-of-factly. 'My clients are satisfied, and people like you, . . . impotent.'

'Someone will kill you, one day.'

'Will you?'

I shook my head. 'Not worth it.'

'Exactly,' he said calmly. 'The jobs I accept are never what the victims would actually kill me for. I really am not a fool.'

'No,' I said.

I walked across to the door and Didi made room for me to pass. She put the pistol down on her desk in the outer office and switched off a red bulb which glowed brightly in a small switchboard.

'Emergency signal?' I enquired. 'Under his desk.'

'You could say so.'

'Is that gun loaded?'

Her eyebrows rose. 'Naturally.'

'I see.' I opened the outer door. She walked over to close it behind me as I went towards the stairs.

'Nice to have met you, Mr Hughes,' she said unemotionally. 'Don't come back.'

I walked along to my car in some depression. From none of the three damaging witnesses at the Enquiry had I got any change at all, and what David Oakley had said about me being impotent looked all too true.

There seemed to be no way of proving that he had simply brought with him the money he had photographed in my flat. No one at Corrie had seen him come or go: Tony had asked all the lads, and none of them had seen him. And Oakley would have found it easy enough to be unobserved. He had only had to arrive early, while everyone was out riding on the Downs at morning exercise. From seven-thirty to eight-thirty the stable yard would be deserted. Letting himself in through my unlocked door, setting up his props, loosing off a flash or two, and quietly retreating . . . The whole process would have taken him no more than ten minutes.

It was possible he had kept a record of his shady transactions. Possible, not probable. He might need to keep some hold over his clients, to prevent their later denouncing him in fits of resurgent civil conscience. If he did keep such records, it might account for the multiplicity of locks. Or maybe the locks were simply to discourage people from breaking in to search for records, as they were certainly discouraging me.

Would Oakley, I wondered, have done what Charlie West had done, and produced his lying testimony for a voice on the telephone? On the whole, I decided not. Oakley had brains where Charlie had vanity, and Oakley would not involve himself without his clients up tight too. Oakley had to know who had done the engineering.

But stealing that information . . . or beating it out of him . . . or tricking him into giving it . . . as well as buying it from him . . . every course looked as hopeless as the next. I could only ride horses. I couldn't pick locks, fights, or pockets. Certainly not Oakley's.

Oakley and Didi. They were old at the game. They'd invented the rules. Oakley and Didi were senior league.

How did anyone get in touch with Oakley, if they needed his brand of service?

He could scarcely advertise.

Someone had to know about him.

I thought it over for a while, sitting in my car in the car park wondering what to do next. There was only one person I knew who could put his finger on the pulse of Birmingham if he wanted to, and the likelihood was that in my present circumstances he wouldn't want to.

However . . .

I started the car, threaded a way through the one-way streets, and found a slot in the crowded park behind the Great Stag Hotel. Inside, the ritual of Business Lunch was warming up, the atmosphere thickening nicely with the smell of alcohol, the resonance of fruity voices, the haze of cigars. The Great Stag Hotel attracted almost exclusively a certain grade of wary, prosperous, level-headed businessmen needing a soft background for hard options, and it attracted them because the landlord, Teddy Dewar, was that sort of man himself.

I found him in the bar, talking to two others almost indistinguishable from him in their dark grey suits, white shirts, neat maroon ties, seventeen-inch necks, and thirty-eight-inch waists.

A faint glaze came over his professionally noncommittal expression when he caught sight of me over their shoulders. A warned-off jockey didn't rate too high with him. Lowered the tone of the place, no doubt.

I edged through to the bar on one side of him and ordered whisky.

'I'd be grateful for a word with you,' I said.

He turned his head a fraction in my direction, and

without looking at me directly answered. 'Very well. In a few minutes.'

No warmth in the words. No ducking of the unwelcome situation, either. He went on talking to the two men about the dicky state of oil shares, and eventually smoothly disengaged himself and turned to me.

'Well, Kelly . . .' His eyes were cool and distant, waiting to see what I wanted before showing any real feeling.

'Will you lunch with me?' I made it casual.

His surprise was controlled. 'I thought . . .'

'I may be banned,' I said, 'but I still eat.'

He studied my face. 'You mind.'

'What do you expect . . .? I'm sorry it shows.'

He said neutrally, 'There's a muscle in your jaw . . . Very well: if you don't mind going in straightaway.'

We sat against the wall at an inconspicuous table and chose beef cut from a roast on a trolley. While he ate his eyes checked the running of the dining-room, missing nothing. I waited until he was satisfied that all was well and then came briefly to the point.

'Do you know anything about a man called David Oakley? He's an enquiry agent. Operates from an office about half a mile from here.'

'David Oakley? I can't say I've ever heard of him.'

'He manufactured some evidence which swung things against me at the Stewards' Enquiry on Monday.'

'Manufactured?' There was delicate doubt in his voice.

'Oh yes,' I sighed. 'I suppose it sounds corny, but I really was not guilty as charged. But someone made sure it looked like it.' I told him about the photograph of money in my bedroom.

'And you never had this money?'

'I did not. And the note supposed to be from Cranfield was a forgery. But how could we prove it?'

He thought it over.

'You can't.'

'Exactly,' I agreed.

'This David Oakley who took the photograph ... I suppose you got no joy from him.'

'No joy is right.'

'I don't understand precisely why you've come to me.' He finished his beef and laid his knife and fork tidily together. Waiters appeared like genii to clear the table and bring coffee. He waited still noncommittally while I paid the bill.

'I expect it is too much to ask,' I said finally. 'After all, I've only stayed here three or four times, I have no claim on you personally for friendship or help ... and yet, there's no one else I know who could even begin to do what you could ... if you will.'

'What?' he said succinctly.

'I want to know how people are steered towards David Oakley, if they want some evidence faked. He

115

as good as told me he is quite accustomed to do it. Well . . . how does he get his clients? Who recommends him? I thought that among all the people you know, you might think of someone who could perhaps pretend he wanted a job done . . . or pretend he had a friend who wanted a job done . . . and throw out feelers, and see if anyone finally recommended Oakley. And if so, who.'

He considered it. 'Because if you found one contact you might work back from there to another . . . and eventually perhaps to a name which meant something to you? . . .'

'I suppose it sounds feeble,' I said resignedly.

'It's a very outside chance,' he agreed. There was a long pause. Then he added, 'All the same, I do know of someone who might agree to try.' He smiled briefly, for the first time.

'That's . . .' I swallowed. 'That's marvellous.'

'Can't promise results.'

CHAPTER SEVEN

Tony came clomping up my stairs on Friday morning after first exercise and poured half an inch of Scotch into the coffee I gave him. He drank the scalding mixture and shuddered as the liquor bit.

'God,' he said. 'It's cold on the Downs.'

'Rather you than me,' I said.

'Liar,' he said amicably. 'It must feel odd to you, not riding.'

'Yes.'

He sprawled in the green armchair. 'Poppy's got the morning ickies again. I'll be glad when this lousy pregnancy is over. She's been ill half the time.'

'Poor Poppy.'

'Yeah ... Anyway, what it means is that we ain't going to that dance tonight. She says she can't face it.'

'Dance? ...'

'The Jockey's Fund dance. You know. You've got the tickets on your mantel over there.'

'Oh ... yes. I'd forgotten about it. We were going together.'

'That's right. But now, as I was saying, you'll have to go without us.'

'I'm not going at all.'

'I thought you might not.' He sighed and drank deeply. 'Where did you get to yesterday?'

'I called on people who didn't want to see me.'

'Any results?'

'Not many.' I told him briefly about Newtonnards and David Oakley, and about the hour I'd spent with Andrew Tring.

It was because the road home from Birmingham led near his village that I'd thought of Andrew Tring, and my first instinct anyway was to shy away from even the thought of him. Certainly visiting one of the Stewards who had helped to warn him off was not regulation behaviour for a disbarred jockey. If I hadn't been fairly strongly annoyed with him I would have driven straight on.

He was disgusted with me for calling. He opened the door of his prosperous sprawling old manor house himself and had no chance of saying he was out.

'Kelly! What are you doing here?'

'Asking you for some explanation.'

'I've nothing to say to you.'

'You have indeed.'

He frowned. Natural good manners were only just

118

preventing him from retreating and shutting the door in my face. 'Come in then. Just for a few minutes.'

'Thank you,' I said without irony, and followed him into a nearby small room lined with books and containing a vast desk, three deep armchairs and a colour television set.

'Now,' he said, shutting the door and not offering the armchairs, 'why have you come?'

He was four years older than me, and about the same size. Still as trim as when he rode races, still outwardly the same man. Only the casual, long-established changing-room friendliness seemed to have withered somewhere along the upward path from amateurship to Authority.

'Andy,' I said, 'do you really and honestly believe that Squelch race was rigged?'

'You were warned off,' he said coldly.

'That's far from being the same thing as guilty.'

'I don't agree.'

'Then you're stupid,' I said bluntly. 'As well as scared out of your tiny wits.'

'That's enough, Kelly. I don't have to listen to this.' He opened the door again and waited for me to leave. I didn't. Short of throwing me out bodily he was going to have to put up with me a little longer. He gave me a furious stare and shut the door again.

I said more reasonably, 'I'm sorry. Really, I'm sorry. It's just that you rode against me for at least five years ... I'd have thought you wouldn't so easily believe I'd deliberately lose a race. I've never yet lost a race I could win.'

He was silent. He knew that I didn't throw races. Anyone who rode regularly knew who would and who wouldn't, and in spite of what Charlie West had said at the Enquiry, I was not an artist at stopping one because I hadn't given it the practice.

'There was that money,' he said at last. He sounded disillusioned and discouraged.

'I never had it. Oakley took it with him into my flat and photographed it there. All that so-called evidence, the whole bloody Enquiry in fact, was as genuine as a lead sixpence.'

He gave me a long doubtful look. Then he said, 'There's nothing I can do about it.'

'What are you afraid of?'

'Stop saying I'm afraid,' he said irritably. 'I'm not afraid. I just can't do anything about it, even if what you say is true.'

'It is true ... and maybe you don't think you are afraid, but that's definitely the impression you give. Or maybe ... are you simply overawed? The new boy among the old powerful prefects. Is that it? Afraid of putting a foot wrong with them?'

'Kelly!' he protested; but it was the protest of a touched nerve.

I said unkindly, 'You're a gutless disappointment,'

and took a step towards his door. He didn't move to open it for me. Instead he put up a hand to stop me, looking as angry as he had every right to.

'That's not fair. Just because I can't help you . . .'

'You could have done. At the Enquiry.'

'You don't understand.'

'I do indeed. You found it easier to believe me guilty than to tell Gowery you had any doubts.'

'It wasn't as easy as you think.'

'Thanks,' I said ironically.

'I don't mean . . .' He shook his head impatiently. 'I mean, it wasn't all as simple as you make out. When Gowery asked me to sit with him at the Enquiry I believed it was only going to be a formality, that both you and Cranfield had run the Lemonfizz genuinely and were surprised yourselves by the result. Colonel Midgley told me it was ridiculous having to hold the Enquiry at all, really. I never expected to be caught up in having to warn you off.'

'Did you say,' I said, 'that Lord Gowery asked you to sit with him?'

'Of course. That's the normal procedure. The Stewards sitting at an Enquiry aren't picked out of a hat . . .'

'There isn't any sort of rota?'

'No. The Disciplinary Steward asks two colleagues to officiate with him . . . and that's what put me on the spot, if you must know, because I didn't want to say no to Lord Gowery . . .' He stopped.

'Go on,' I urged without heat. 'Why not?'

'Well because ...' He hesitated, then said slowly, 'I suppose in a way I owe it to you ... I'm sorry Kelly, desperately sorry, I do know you don't usually rig races ... I'm in an odd position with Gowery and it's vitally important I keep in with him.'

I stifled my indignation. Andrew Tring's eyes were looking inward and from his expression he didn't very much like what he could see.

'He owns the freehold of the land just north of Manchester where our main pottery is.' Andrew Tring's family fortunes were based not on fine porcelain but on smashable teacups for institutions. His products were dropped by washers-up in schools and hospitals from Waterloo to Hong Kong, and the pieces in the world's dustbins were his perennial licence to print money.

He said, 'There's been some redevelopment round there and that land is suddenly worth about a quarter of a million. And our lease runs out in three years ... We have been negotiating a new one, but the old one was for ninety-nine years and no one is keen to renew for that long ... The ground rent is in any case going to be raised considerably, but if Gowery changes his mind and wants to sell that land for development, there's nothing we can do about it. We only own the buildings ... We'd lose the entire factory if he didn't renew the lease ... And we can only make cups and saucers so cheaply because our overheads are small ...

If we have to build or rent a new factory our prices will be less competitive and our world trade figures will slump. Gowery himself has the final say as to whether our lease will be renewed or not, and on what terms . . . so you see, Kelly, it's not that I'm afraid of him . . . there's so much more at stake . . . and he's always a man to hold it against you if you argue with him.'

He stopped and looked at me gloomily. I looked gloomily back. The facts of life stared us stonily in the face.

'So that's that,' I agreed. 'You are quite right. You can't help me. You couldn't, right from the start. I'm glad you explained . . .' I smiled at him twistedly, facing another dead end, the last of a profitless day.

'I'm sorry, Kelly . . .'

'Sure,' I said.

Tony finished his fortified breakfast and said, 'So there wasn't anything sinister in Andy Tring's lily-livered bit on Monday.'

'It depends what you call sinister. But no, I suppose not.'

'What's left, then?'

'Damn all,' I said in depression.

'You can't give up,' he protested.

'Oh no. But I've learned one thing in learning nothing, and that is that I'm getting nowhere because

I'm me. First thing Monday morning I'm going to hire me my own David Oakley.'

'Attaboy,' he said. He stood up. 'Time for second lot, I hear.' Down in the yard the lads were bringing out the horses, their hooves scrunching hollowly on the packed gravel.

'How are they doing?' I asked.

'Oh . . . so so. I sure hate having to put up other jocks. Given me a bellyful of the whole game, this business has.'

When he'd gone down to ride I cleaned up my already clean flat and made some more coffee. The day stretched emptily ahead. So did the next day and the one after that, and every day for an indefinite age.

Ten minutes of this prospect was enough. I searched around and found another straw to cling to: telephoned to a man I knew slightly at the BBC. A cool secretary said he was out, and to try again at eleven.

I tried again at eleven. Still out. I tried at twelve. He was in then, but sounded as if he wished he weren't.

'Not Kelly Hughes, the . . .' His voice trailed off while he failed to find a tactful way of putting it.

'That's right.'

'Well . . . er . . . I don't think . . .'

'I don't want anything much,' I assured him resignedly. 'I just want to know the name of the outfit who make the films of races. The camera patrol people.'

'Oh.' He sounded relieved. 'That's the Racecourse

Technical Services. Run by the Levy Board. They've a virtual monopoly, though there's one other small firm operating sometimes under licence. Then there are the television companies, of course. Did you want any particular race? Oh ... the Lemonfizz Crystal Cup, I suppose.'

'No,' I said. 'The meeting at Reading two weeks earlier.'

'Reading ... Reading ... Let's see, then. Which lot would that be?' He hummed a few out-of-tune bars while he thought it over. 'I should think ... yes, definitely the small firm, the Cannot Lie people. Cannot Lie, Ltd. Offices at Woking, Surrey. Do you want their number?'

'Yes, please.'

He read it to me.

'Thank you very much,' I said.

'Any time ... er ... well ... I mean ...'

'I know what you mean,' I agreed. 'But thanks anyway.'

I put down the receiver with a grimace. It was still no fun being everyone's idea of a villain.

The BBC man's reaction made me decide that the telephone might get me nil results from the Cannot Lie brigade. Maybe they couldn't lie, but they would certainly evade. And anyway, I had the whole day to waste.

The Cannot Lie office was a rung or two up the

luxury ladder from David Oakley's, which wasn't saying a great deal. A large rather bare room on the second floor of an Edwardian house in a side street. A rickety lift large enough for one slim man or two starving children. A well-worn desk with a well-worn blonde painting her toenails on top of it.

'Yes?' she said, when I walked in.

She had lilac panties on, with lace. She made no move to prevent me seeing a lot of them.

'No one in?' I asked.

'Only us chickens,' she agreed. She had a South London accent and the smart back-chatting intelligence that often goes with it. 'Which do you want, the old man or our Alfie?'

'You'll do nicely,' I said.

'Ta.' She took it as her due, with a practised come-on-so-far-but-no-further smile. One foot was finished. She stretched out her leg and wiggled it up and down to help with the drying.

'Going to a dance tonight,' she explained. 'In me peep-toes.'

I didn't think anyone would concentrate on the toes. Apart from the legs she had a sharp pointed little bosom under a white cotton sweater and a bright pink patent leather belt clasping a bikini-sized waist. Her body looked about twenty years old. Her face looked as if she'd spent the last six of them hopping.

'Paint the other one,' I suggested.

'You're not in a hurrry?'

'I'm enjoying the scenery.'

She gave a knowing giggle and started on the other foot. The view was even more hair-raising than before. She watched me watching, and enjoyed it.

'What's your name?' I asked.

'Carol. What's yours?'

'Kelly.'

'From the Isle of Man?'

'No. The land of our fathers.'

She gave me a bright glance. 'You catch on quick, don't you?'

I wished I did. I said regretfully, 'How long do you keep ordinary routine race films?'

'Huh? For ever, I suppose.' She changed mental gear effortlessly, carrying straight on with her uninhibited painting. 'We haven't destroyed any so far, that's to say. Course, we've only been in the racing business eighteen months. No telling what they'll do when the big storeroom's full. We're up to the eyebrows in all the others with films of motor races, golf matches, three-day events, any old things like that.'

'Where's the big storeroom?'

'Through there.' She waved the small pink enamelling brush in the general direction of a scratched once-cream door. 'Want to see?'

'If you don't mind.'

'Go right ahead.'

She had finished the second foot. The show was over. With a sigh I removed my gaze and walked over to the door in question. There was only a round hole where most doors have a handle. I pushed against the wood and the door swung inwards into another large high room, furnished this time with rows of free standing bookshelves, like a public library. The shelves, however, were of bare functional wood, and there was no covering on the planked floor.

Well over half the shelves were empty. On the others were rows of short wide box files, their backs labelled with neat typed strips explaining what was to be found within. Each box proved to contain all the films from one day's racing, and they were all efficiently arranged in chronological order. I pulled out the box for the day I rode Squelch and Wanderlust at Reading, and looked inside. There were six round cans of sixteen-millimetre film, numbered one to six, and space enough for another one, number seven.

I took the box out to Carol. She was still sitting on top of the desk, dangling the drying toes and reading through a woman's magazine.

'What have you found then?'

'Do you lend these films to anyone who wants them?'

'Hire, not lend. Sure.'

'Who to?'

'Anyone who asks. Usually it's the owners of the

horses. Often they want prints made to keep, so we make them.'

'Do the Stewards often want them?'

'Stewards? Well, see, if there's any doubt about a race the Stewards see the film on the racecourse. That van the old man and our Alfie's got develops it on the spot as soon as it's collected from the cameras.'

'But sometimes they send for them afterwards?'

'Sometimes, yeah. When they want to compare the running of some horse or other.' Her legs suddenly stopped swinging. She put down the magazine and gave me a straight stare.

'Kelly . . . Kelly Hughes?'

I didn't answer.

'Hey, you're not a bit like I thought.' She put her blonde head on one side, assessing me. 'None of those sports writers ever said anything about you being smashing looking and dead sexy.'

I laughed. I had a crooked nose and a scar down one cheek from where a horse's hoof had cut my face open, and among jockeys I was an also-ran as a bird-attracter.

'It's your eyes,' she said. 'Dark and sort of smiley and sad and a bit withdrawn. Give me the happy shivers, your eyes do.'

'You read all that in a magazine,' I said.

'I never!' but she laughed.

'Who asked for the film that's missing from the box?' I said. 'And what exactly did they ask for?'

She sighed exaggeratedly and edged herself off the desk into a pair of bright pink sandals.

'Which film is that?' She looked at the box and its reference number, and did a Marilyn Monroe sway over to a filing cabinet against the wall. 'Here we are. One official letter from the Stewards' secretary saying please send film of last race at Reading . . .'

I took the letter from her and read it myself. The words were quite clear: 'the last race at Reading'. Not the sixth race. The last race. And there had been seven races. It hadn't been Carol or the Cannot Lie Co who had made the mistake.

'So you sent it?'

'Of course. Off to the authorities, as per instructions.' She put the letter back in the files. 'Did you in, did it?'

'Not that film, no.'

'Alfie and the old man say you must have made a packet out of the Lemonfizz, to lose your licence over it.'

'Do you think so too?'

'Stands to reason. Everyone thinks so.'

'Man in the street?'

'Him too.'

'Not a cent.'

'You're a nit, then,' she said frankly. 'Whatever did you do it for?'

'I didn't.'

'Oh yeah?' She gave me a knowing wink. 'I suppose you have to say that, don't you?'

'Well,' I said, handing her the Reading box to put back in the storeroom. 'Thanks anyway.' I gave her half a smile and went away across the expanse of mottled linoleum to the door out.

I drove home slowly, trying to think. Not a very profitable exercise. Brains seemed to have deteriorated into a mushy blankness.

There were several letters for me in the mailbox on my front door, including one from my parents. I unfolded it walking up the stairs, feeling as usual a million miles away from them on every level.

My mother had written the first half in her round regular handwriting on one side of a large piece of lined paper. As usual there wasn't a full stop to be seen. She punctuated entirely with commas.

Dear Kelly,

Thanks for your note, we got it yesterday, we don't like reading about you in the papers, I know you said you hadn't done it, son, but no smoke without fire is what Mrs Jones the post office says, and it is not nice for us what people are saying about you round here, all the airs and graces they say you are and pride goes before a fall and all that, well the pullets have started laying at last, we are painting your old room for Auntie Myfanwy who is coming to live here her arthritis is too bad for those stairs she has, well Kelly, I wish I could say we want you to come home but your Da is that angry and now Auntie Myfanwy needs the room anyway, well son, we never wanted you to go for a jockey, there was that nice job at the Townhall in Tenby you could have had, I don't like to say it but you have disgraced us, son, there's horrid it is going into the village now, everyone whispering, your loving Mother.

I took a deep breath and turned the page over to receive the blast from my father. His writing was much like my mother's as they had learned from the same teacher, but he had pressed so hard with his ballpoint that he had almost dug through the paper.

Kelly,

You're a damned disgrace boy. It's soft saying you didn't do it. They wouldn't of warned you off if you didn't do it. Not lords and such. They know what's right. You're lucky you're not here I would give you a proper belting. After all that scrimping your Ma did to let you go off to the University. And people said you would get too ladidah to speak to us, they were right. Still, this is worse, being a cheat. Don't you come back here, your Ma's that upset, what with that cat Mrs Jones saying things. It would be best to say don't send us any more money into the bank. I asked the manager but he said only you can cancel a banker's order so you'd better do it. Your Ma says it's as bad as you being in prison, the disgrace and all.

He hadn't signed it. He wouldn't know how to, we had so little affection for each other. He had despised me from childhood for my liking school, and had mocked me unmercifully all the way to college. He showed his jolly side only to my two older brothers, who had had what he considered a healthy contempt for education: one of them had gone into the Merchant Navy and the other lived next door and worked alongside my father for the farmer who owned the cottages.

When in the end I had turned my back on all the years of learning and taken to racing my family had again all disapproved of me, though I guessed they would have been pleased enough if I'd chosen it all along. I'd wasted the country's money, my father said; I wouldn't have been given all those grants if they'd known that as soon as I was out I'd go racing. That was probably true. It was also true that since I'd been racing I'd paid enough in taxes to send several other farm boys through college on grants.

I put my parents' letter under Rosalind's photograph. Even she had been unable to reach their approval, because they thought I should have married a nice girl from my own sort of background, not the student daughter of a colonel.

They had rigid minds. It was doubtful now if they would ever be pleased with me, whatever I did. And if I got my licence back, as like as not they would think I had somehow cheated again.

You couldn't take aspirins for that sort of pain. It stayed there, sticking in knives. Trying to escape it I went into the kitchen, to see if there was anything to eat. A tin of sardines, one egg, the dried-up remains of some Port Salut.

Wrinkling my nose at that lot I transferred to the sitting-room and looked at the television programmes.

Nothing I wanted to see.

I slouched in the green velvet armchair and watched the evening slowly fade the colours into subtle greys. A certain amount of peace edged its way past the dragging gloom of the last four days. I wondered almost academically whether I would get my licence back before or after I stopped wincing at the way people looked at me, or spoke to me, or wrote about me. Probably the easiest course would be to stay out of sight, hiding myself away.

Like I was hiding away at that minute, by not going to the Jockeys' Fund dance.

The tickets were on the mantel. Tickets for Tony and Poppy, and for me and the partner I hadn't got

134

around to inviting. Tickets which were not going to be used, which I had paid twelve fund-raising guineas for.

I sat in the dark for half an hour thinking about the people who would be at the Jockeys' Fund dance.

Then I put on my black tie and went to it.

CHAPTER EIGHT

I went prepared to be stared at.

I was stared at.

Also pointed out and commented on. Discreetly, however, for the most part. And only two people decisively turned their backs.

The Jockeys' Fund dance glittered as usual with titles, diamonds, champagne, and talent. Later it might curl round the edges into spilled drinks, glassy eyes, raddled make-up, and slurring voices, but the gloss wouldn't entirely disappear. It never did. The Jockeys' Fund dance was one of the great social events of the steeplechasing year.

I handed over my ticket and walked along the wide passage to where the lights were low, the music hot, and the air thick with smoke and scent. The opulent ballroom of the Royal Country Hotel, along the road from Ascot racecourse.

Around the dancing area there were numbers of large circular tables with chairs for ten or twelve round each, most of them occupied already. According to the chart in the hall, at table number thirty-two I would find the places reserved for Tony and me, if in fact they were still reserved. I gave up looking for table thirty-two less than halfway down the room because whenever I moved a new battery of curious eyes swivelled my way. A lot of people raised a hello but none of them could hide their slightly shocked surprise. It was every bit as bad as I'd feared.

A voice behind me said incredulously, 'Hughes!'

I knew the voice. I turned round with an equal sense of the unexpected. Roberta Cranfield. Wearing a honey-coloured silk dress with the top smothered in pearls and gold thread and her copper hair drawn high with a trickle of ringlets down the back of her neck.

'You look beautiful,' I said.

Her mouth opened. 'Hughes!'

'Is your father here?'

'No,' she said disgustedly. 'He wouldn't face it. Nor would Mother. I came with a party of neighbours but I can't say I was enjoying it much until you turned up.'

'Why not?'

'You must be joking. Just look around. At a rough guess fifty people are rubber-necking at you. Doesn't it make you cringe inside? Anyway, I've had quite enough of it myself this evening, and I didn't even *see* the damned race, let alone get myself warned off.' She stopped. 'Come and dance with me. If we're hoisting the flag we may as well do it thoroughly.'

'On one condition,' I said.

'What's that?'

'You stop calling me Hughes.'

'What?'

'Cranfield, I'm tired of being called Hughes.'

'Oh!' It had obviously never occurred to her. 'Then . . . Kelly . . . how about dancing?'

'Enchanted, Roberta.'

She gave me an uncertain look. 'I still feel I don't know you.'

'You never bothered.'

'Nor have you.'

That jolted me. It was true. I'd disliked the idea of her. And I didn't really know her at all.

'How do you do?' I said politely. 'Come and dance.'

We shuffled around in one of those affairs which look like formalized jungle rituals, swaying in rhythm but never touching. Her face was quite calm, remotely smiling. From her composure one would have guessed her to be entirely at ease, not the target of turned heads, assessing glances, half-hidden whispers.

'I don't know how you do it,' she said.

'Do what?'

'Look so . . . so matter of fact.'

'I was thinking exactly the same about you.'

She smiled, eyes crinkling and teeth gleaming, and incredibly in the circumstances she looked happy.

We stuck it for a good ten minutes. Then she said we would go back to her table, and made straight off to it without waiting for me to agree. I didn't think her party would be pleased to have me join them, and half of them weren't.

'Sit down and have a drink, my dear fellow,' drawled her host, reaching for a champagne bottle with a languid hand. 'And tell me all about the bring-back-Cranfield campaign. Roberta tells me you are working on a spot of reinstatement.'

'I haven't managed it yet,' I said deprecatingly.

'My dear chap . . .' He gave me an inspecting stare down his nose. He'd been in the Guards, I thought. So many ex-Guards' officers looked at the world down the sides of their noses: it came of wearing those blinding hats. He was blond, in his forties, not unfriendly. Roberta called him Bobbie.

The woman the other side of him leaned over and drooped a heavy pink satin bosom perilously near her brimming glass.

'Do tell me,' she said, giving me a thorough gaze from heavily made-up eyes, 'what made you come?'

'Natural cussedness,' I said pleasantly.

'Oh.' She looked taken aback. 'How extraordinary.'

'Joined to the fact that there was no reason why I shouldn't.'

'And are you enjoying it?' Bobbie said. 'I mean to say, my dear chap, you are somewhat in the position of a rather messily struck-off doctor turning up four days later at the British Medical Association's grandest function.'

I smiled.'Quite a parallel.'

'Don't needle him Bobbie,' Roberta protested.

Bobbie removed his stare from me and gave it to her instead. 'My dear Roberta, this cookie needs no little girls rushing to his defence. He's as tough as old oak.'

A disapproving elderly man on the far side of the pink bosom said under his breath. 'Thick skinned, you mean.'

Bobbie heard, and shook his head. 'Vertebral,' he said. 'Different altogether.' He stood up. 'Roberta, my dear girl, would you care to dance?'

I stood up with him.

'No need to go, my dear chap. Stay. Finish your drink.'

'You are most kind,' I said truthfully. 'But I really came tonight to have a word with one or two people . . . If you'll excuse me, I'll try to find them.'

He gave me an odd formal little inclination of the head, halfway to a bow. 'Come back later, if you'd care to.'

'Thank you,' I said. 'Very much.'

He took Roberta away to dance and I went up the

stairs to the balcony which encircled the room. There were tables all round up there too, but in places one could get a good clear view of most people below. I spent some length of time identifying them from the tops of their heads.

There must have been about six hundred there, of whom I knew personally about a quarter. Owners, trainers, jockeys, Stewards, pressmen, two or three of the bigger bookmakers, starters, judges, Clerks of Courses, and all the others, all with their wives and friends and chattering guests.

Kessel was there, hosting a party of twelve almost exactly beneath where I stood. I wondered if his anger had cooled since Monday, and decided if possible not to put it to the test. He had reputedly sent Squelch off to Pat Nikita, a trainer who was a bitter rival of Cranfield's, which had been rubbing it in a bit. The report looked likely to be true, as Pat Nikita was among the party below me.

Cranfield and Nikita regularly claimed each other's horses in selling races and were apt to bid each other up spitefully at auctions. It was a public joke. So in choosing Nikita as his trainer, Kessel was unmistakably announcing worldwide that he believed Cranfield and I had stopped his horse. Hardly likely to help convince that we hadn't.

At one of the most prominent tables, near the dancing space, sat Lord Ferth, talking earnestly to a large

lady in pale blue ostrich feathers. All the other chairs
round the table were askew and unoccupied, but while
I watched the music changed to a Latin rhythm, and
most of the party drifted back. I knew one or two of
them slightly, but not well. The man I was chiefly looking for was not among them.

Two tables away from Lord Ferth sat Edwin Byler,
gravely beckoning to the waiter to fill his guests' glasses,
too proud of his home-made wealth to lift the bottle
himself. His cuddly little wife on the far side of the
table was loaded with half the stock of Hatton Garden
and was rather touchingly revelling in it.

Not to be going to ride Edwin Byler's string of super
horses ... The wry thrust of regret went deeper than I
liked.

There was a rustle behind me and the smell of Roberta's fresh flower scent. I turned towards her.

'Kelly? ...'

She really looked extraordinarily beautiful.

'Kelly ... Bobbie suggested that you should take me
in to supper.'

'That's generous of him.'

'He seems to approve of you. He said ...' She
stopped abruptly. 'Well, never mind what he said.'

We went down the stairs and through an archway to
the supper room. The light there was of a heartier
wattage. It didn't do any damage to Roberta.

Along one wall stretched a buffet table laden with

aspic-shining cold meats and oozing cream gateaux. Roberta said she had dined at Bobbie's before coming on to the dance and wasn't hungry, but we both collected some salmon and sat down at one of the twenty or so small tables clustered into half of the room.

Six feet away sat three fellow jockeys resting their elbows among a debris of empty plates and coffee cups.

'Kelly!' One of them exclaimed in a broad northern voice. 'My God. Kelly. Come over here, you old so and so. Bring the talent with you.'

The talent's chin began its familiar upward tilt.

'Concentrate on the character, not the accent,' I said.

She gave me a raw look of surprise, but when I stood up and picked up her plate, she came with me. They made room for us, admired Roberta's appearance, and didn't refer to anyone being warned off. Their girls, they explained, were powdering their noses, and when the noses reappeared, immaculate, they all smiled goodbye and went back to the ballroom.

'They were kind.' She sounded surprised.

'They would be.'

She fiddled with her fork, not looking at me. 'You said the other day that my mind was in chains. Was that what you meant... that I'm inclined to judge people by their voices... and that it's wrong?'

'Eton's bred its rogues,' I said. 'Yes.'

'Cactus. You're all prickles.'

'Original sin exists.' I said mildly. 'So does original

virtue. They both crop up regardless. No respecters of birth.'

'Where did you go to school?'

'In Wales.'

'You haven't a Welsh accent. You haven't any accent at all. And that's odd really, considering you are only . . .' Her voice trailed away and she looked aghast at her self-betrayal. 'Oh dear . . . I'm sorry.'

'It's not surprising,' I pointed out. 'Considering your father. And anyway, in my own way I'm just as bad. I smothered my Welsh accent quite deliberately. I used to practise in secret, while I was still at school, copying the BBC news announcers. I wanted to be a Civil Servant, and I was ambitious, and I knew I wouldn't get far if I sounded like the son of a Welsh farm labourer. So in time this became my natural way of talking. And my parents despise me for it.'

'Parents!' she said despairingly. 'Why can we never escape them? Whatever we are, it is because of *them*. I want to be *me*.' She looked astonished at herself. 'I've never felt like this before. I don't understand . . .'

'Well I do.' I said, smiling. 'Only it happens to most people around fifteen or sixteen. Rebellion, it's called.'

'You're mocking me.' But the chin stayed down.

'No.'

We finished the salmon and drank coffee. A large loudly chattering party collected food from the buffet and pushed the two tables next to us together so that they could all sit at one. They were well away on a tide of alcohol and bonhomie, loosened and expansive. I watched them idly. I knew four of them, two trainers, one wife, one owner.

One of the trainers caught sight of me and literally dropped his knife.

'That's Kelly Hughes,' he said disbelievingly. The whole party turned round and stared. Roberta drew a breath in distress. I sat without moving.

'What are you doing here?'

'Drinking coffee,' I said politely.

His eyes narrowed. Trevor Norse was not amused. I sighed inwardly. It was never good to antagonize trainers, it simply meant one less possible source of income: but I'd ridden for Trevor Norse several times already, and knew that it was practically impossible to please him anyway.

A heavy man, six feet plus, labouring under the misapprehension that size could substitute for ability. He was much better with owners than with horses, tireless at cultivating the one and lazy with the other.

His brainless wife said brightly, 'I hear you're paying Dexter's lads' wages, because you're sure you'll get your licence back in a day or two.'

'What's all that?' Norse said sharply. 'Where did you hear all that nonsense?'

'Everyone's talking about it, darling,' she said protestingly.

145

'Who's everyone?'

She giggled weakly. 'I heard it in the ladies, if you must know. But it's quite true, I'm sure it is. Dexter's lads told Daphne's lads in the local pub, and Daphne told Miriam, and Miriam was telling us in the ladies . . .'

'Is it true?' Norse demanded.

'Well, more or less,' I agreed.

'Good Lord.'

'Miriam said Kelly Hughes says he and Dexter were framed, and that he's finding out who did it.' Mrs Norse giggled at me. 'My *dear*, isn't it all such fun.'

'Great,' I said dryly. I stood up, and Roberta also.

'Do you know Roberta Cranfield?' I said formally, and they all exclaimed over her, and she scattered on them a bright artificial smile, and we went back and tried another dance.

It wasn't altogether a great idea because we were stopped halfway round by Daddy Leeman of the *Daily Witness* who raked me over with avid eyes and yelled above the music was it true I was claiming I'd been framed. He had a piercing voice. All the nearby couples turned and stared. Some of them raised sceptical eyebrows at each other.

'I really can't stand a great deal more of this,' Roberta said in my ear. 'How can you? Why don't you go home now?'

'I'm sorry,' I said contritely. 'You've been splendid. I'll take you back to Bobbie.'

'But you? . . .'

'I haven't done what I came for. I'll stay a bit longer.'

She compressed her mouth and started to dance again. 'All right. So will I.'

We danced without smiling.

'Do you want a tombola ticket?' I asked.

'No.' She was astonished.

'You might as well. I want to go down that end of the room.'

'Whatever for?'

'Looking for someone. Haven't been down that end at all.'

'Oh. All right, then.'

She stepped off the polished wood on to the thick dark carpet, and threaded her way to the clear aisle which led down to the gaily decorated tombola stall at the far end of the ballroom.

I looked for the man I wanted, but I didn't see him. I met too many other eyes, most of which hastily looked away.

'I hate them,' Roberta said fiercely. 'I hate people.'

I bought her four tickets. Three of them were blanks. The fourth had a number which fitted a bottle of vodka.

'I don't like it much,' she said, holding it dubiously.

'Nor do I.'

'I'll give it to the first person who's nice to you.'

'You might have to drink it yourself.'

We went slowly back down the aisle, not talking.

147

A thin woman sprang up from her chair as we approached her table and in spite of the embarrassed holding-back clutches of her party managed to force her way out into our path. We couldn't pass her without pushing. We stopped.

'You're Roberta Cranfield, aren't you?' she said. She had a strong-boned face, no lipstick, angry eyes, and stiffly regimented greying hair. She looked as if she'd had far too much to drink.

'Excuse us,' I said gently, trying to go past.

'Oh no you don't,' she said. 'Not until I've had my say.'

'Grace!' wailed a man across the table. I looked at him more closely. Edwin Byler's trainer, Jack Roxford. 'Grace dear, leave it. Sit down, dear,' he said.

Grace dear had no such intentions. Grace dear's feelings were far too strong.

'Your father's got exactly what he deserves, my lass, and I can tell you I'm glad about it. Glad.' She thrust her face towards Roberta's, glaring like a mad woman. Roberta looked down her nose at her, which I would have found as infuriating as Grace did.

'I'd dance on his grave,' she said furiously. 'That I would.'

'Why?' I said flatly.

She didn't look at me. She said to Roberta, 'He's a bloody snob, your father. A bloody snob. And he's got what he deserved. So there. You tell him that.'

'Excuse me,' Roberta said coldly, and tried to go forwards.

'Oh no you don't.' Grace clutched at her arm. Roberta shook her hand off angrily. 'Your bloody snob of a father was trying to get Edwin Byler's horses away from us. Did you know that? Did you know that? All those grand ways of his. Thought Edwin would do better in a bigger stable, did he? Oh, I heard what he said. Trying to persuade Edwin he needed a grand top-drawer trainer now, not poor little folk like us, who've won just rows of races for him. Well, I could have laughed my head off when I heard he'd been had up. I'll tell you. Serves him right, I said. What a laugh.'

'Grace,' said Jack Roxford despairingly. 'I'm sorry, Miss Cranfield. She isn't really like this.'

He looked acutely embarrassed. I thought that probably Grace Roxford was all too often like this. He had the haunted expression of the for-ever apologizing husband.

'Cheer up then, Mrs Roxford,' I said loudly. 'You've got what you want. You're laughing. So why the fury?'

'Eh?' She twisted her head round at me, staggering a fraction. 'As for you, Kelly Hughes, you just asked for what you got, and don't give me any of that crap we've been hearing this evening that you were framed, because you know bloody well you weren't. People like you and Cranfield, you think you can get away with murder, people like you. But there's justice somewhere

149

in this world sometimes and you won't forget that in a hurry, will you now, Mr Clever Dick.'

One of the women of the party stood up and tried to persuade her to quieten down, as every ear for six tables around was stretched in her direction. She was oblivious to them. I wasn't.

Roberta said under her breath, 'Oh God.'

'So you go home and tell your bloody snob of a father,' Grace said to her, 'that it's a great big laugh him being found out. That's what it is, a great big laugh.'

The acutely embarrassed woman friend pulled her arm, and Grace swung angrily round from us to her. We took the brief opportunity and edged away round her back, and as we retreated we could hear her shouting after us, her words indistinct above the music except for 'laugh' and 'bloody snob'.

'She's *awful*,' Roberta said.

'Not much help to poor old Jack,' I agreed.

'I do hate scenes. They're so messy.'

'Do you think all strong emotions are messy?'

'That's not the same thing,' she said. 'You can have strong emotions without making scenes. Scenes are disgusting.'

I sighed. 'That one was.'

'Yes.'

She was walking, I noticed, with her neck stretched very tall, the classic signal to anyone watching that she was not responsible or bowed down or amused at being involved in noise and nastiness. Rosalind, I reflected nostalgically, would probably have sympathetically agreed with dear disturbed Grace, led her off to some quiet mollifying corner, and reappeared with her eating out of her hand. Rosalind had been tempestuous herself and understood uncontrollable feelings.

Unfortunately at the end of the aisle we almost literally bumped into Kessel, who came in for the murderous glance from Roberta which had been earned by dear Grace. Kessel naturally misinterpreted her expression and spat first.

'You can tell your father that I had been thinking for some time of sending my horses to Pat Nikita, and that this business has made me regret that I didn't do it a long time ago. Pat has always wanted to train for me. I stayed with your father out of a mistaken sense of loyalty, and just look how he repaid me.'

'Father has won a great many races for you,' Roberta said coldly. 'And if Squelch had been good enough to win the Lemonfizz Cup, he would have done.'

Kessel's mouth sneered. It didn't suit him.

'As for you, Hughes, it's a disgrace you being here tonight and I cannot think why you were allowed in. And don't think you can fool me by spreading rumours that you are innocent and on the point of proving it. That's all piffle, and you know it, and if you have any

151

ideas you can reinstate yourself with me that way, you are very much mistaken.'

He turned his back on us and bristled off, pausing triumphantly to pat Nikita on the shoulder, and looking back to make sure we had noticed. Very small of him.

'There goes Squelch,' I said resignedly.

'He'll soon be apologizing and sending him back,' she said, with certainty.

'Not a hope. Kessel's not the humble-pie kind. And Pat Nikita will never let go of that horse. Not to see him go back to your father. He'd break him down first.'

'Why are people so jealous of each other!' she exclaimed.

'Born in them,' I said. 'And almost universal.'

'You have a very poor opinion of human nature.' She disapproved.

'An objective opinion. There's as much good as bad.'

'You can't be objective about being warned off,' she protested.

'Er . . . no,' I conceded. 'How about a drink?'

She looked instinctively towards Bobbie's table, and I shook my head. 'In the bar.'

'Oh . . . still looking for someone?'

'That's right. We haven't tried the bar yet.'

'Is there going to be another scene?'

'I shouldn't think so.'

'All right, then.'

We made our way slowly through the crowd. By

then the fact that we were there must have been known to almost everyone in the place. Certainly the heads no longer turned in open surprise, but the eyes did, sliding into corners, giving us a surreptitious once-over, probing and hurtful. Roberta held herself almost defiantly straight.

The bar was heavily populated, with cigar smoke lying in a haze over the well-groomed heads and the noise level doing justice to a discotheque. Almost at once through a narrow gap in the cluster I saw him standing against the far wall, talking vehemently. He turned his head suddenly and looked straight at me, meeting my eyes briefly before the groups between us shifted and closed the line of sight. In those two seconds, however, I had seen his mouth tighten and his whole face compress into annoyance; and he had known I was at the dance, because there was no surprise.

'You've seen him,' Roberta said.

'Yes.'

'Well . . . who is it?'

'Lord Gowery.'

She gasped. 'Oh no, Kelly.'

'I want to talk to him.'

'It can't do any good.'

'You never know.'

'Annoying Lord Gowery is the last, positively the

last way of getting your licence back. Surely you can see that?'

'Yes ... he's not going to be kind, I don't think. So would you mind very much if I took you back to Bobbie first?'

She looked troubled. 'You won't say anything silly? It's Father's licence as well, remember.'

'I'll bear it in mind,' I said flippantly. She gave me a sharp suspicious glance, but turned easily enough to go back to Bobbie.

Almost immediately outside the bar we were stopped by Jack Roxford, who was hurrying towards us through the throng.

'Kelly,' he said, half panting with the exertion. 'I just wanted to catch you ... to say how sorry I am that Grace went off the deep end like that. She's not herself, poor girl ... Miss Cranfield, I do apologize.'

Roberta unbent a little. 'That's all right, Mr Roxford.'

'I wouldn't like you to believe that what Grace said ... all those things about your father ... is what I think too.' He looked from her to me, and back again, the hesitant worry furrowing his forehead. A slight, unaggressive man of about forty-five; bald crown, nervous eyes, permanently worried expression. He was a reasonably good trainer but not enough of a man of the world to have achieved much personal stature. To me, though I had never ridden for him, he had always been friendly, but his restless anxiety-state made him tiring to be with.

'Kelly,' he said, 'if it's really true that you were both framed, I do sincerely hope that you get your licences back. I mean, I know there's a risk that Edwin will take his horses to your father, Miss Cranfield, but he did tell me this evening that he won't do so now, even if he could . . . But please believe me, I hold no dreadful grudge against either of you, like poor Grace . . . I do hope you'll forgive her.'

'Of course, Mr Roxford,' said Roberta, entirely placated. 'Please don't give it another thought. And oh!' she added impulsively, 'I think you've earned this!' and into his astonished hands she thrust the bottle of vodka.

CHAPTER NINE

When I went back towards the bar I found Lord Gowery had come out of it. He was standing shoulder to shoulder with Lord Ferth, both of them watching me walk towards them with faces like thunder.

I stopped four feet away, and waited.

'Hughes,' said Lord Gowery for openers, 'you shouldn't be here.'

'My lord,' I said politely. 'This isn't Newmarket Heath.'

It went down badly. They were both affronted. They closed their ranks.

'Insolence will get you nowhere,' Lord Ferth said, and Lord Gowery added, 'You'll never get your licence back, if you behave like this.'

I said without heat, 'Does justice depend on good manners?'

They looked as if they couldn't believe their ears. From their point of view I was cutting my own throat, though I had always myself doubted that excessive meekness got licences restored any quicker than they would have been without it. Meekness in the accused brought out leniency in some judges, but severity in others. To achieve a minimum sentence, the guilty should always bone up on the character of their judge, a sound maxim which I hadn't had the sense to see applied even more to the innocent.

'I would have thought some sense of shame would have kept you away,' Lord Ferth said.

'It took a bit of an effort to come,' I agreed.

His eyes narrowed and opened again quickly.

Gowery said, 'As to spreading these rumours ... I say categorically that you are not only not on the point of being given your licence back, but that your suspension will be all the longer in consequence of your present behaviour.'

I gave him a level stare and Lord Ferth opened his mouth and shut it again.

'It is no rumour that Mr Cranfield and I are not guilty,' I said at length. 'It is no rumour that two at least of the witnesses were lying. These are facts.'

'Nonsense,' Gowery said vehemently.

'What you believe, sir,' I said, 'doesn't alter the truth.'

'You are doing yourself no good, Hughes.' Under his heavy authoritative exterior he was exceedingly angry. All I needed was a bore hole and I'd get a gusher.

I said, 'Would you be good enough to tell me who suggested to you or the other Stewards that you should seek out and question Mr Newtonnards?'

There was the tiniest shift in his eyes. Enough for me to be certain.

'Certainly not.'

'Then will you tell me upon whose instructions the enquiry agent David Oakley visited my flat?'

'I will not.' His voice was loud, and for the first time, alarmed.

Ferth looked in growing doubt from one of us to the other.

'What is all this about?' he said.

'Mr Cranfield and I were indeed wrongly warned off,' I said. 'Someone sent David Oakley to my flat to fake that photograph. And I believe Lord Gowery knows who it was.'

'I most certainly do not,' he said furiously. 'Do you want to be sued for slander?'

'I have not slandered you, sir.'

'You said . . .'

'I said you knew who sent David Oakley. I did not say that you knew the photograph was a fake.'

'And it wasn't,' he insisted fiercely.

'Well,' I said. 'It was.'

There was a loaded, glaring silence. Then Lord Gowery said heavily, 'I'm not going to listen to this,' and turned on his heel and dived back into the bar.

Lord Ferth, looking troubled, took a step after him.

I said, 'My lord, may I talk to you?' And he stopped and turned back to me and said, 'Yes, I think you'd better.'

He gestured towards the supper room next door and we went through the archway into the brighter light. Nearly everyone had eaten and gone. The buffet table bore shambled remains and all but two of the small tables were unoccupied. He sat down at one of these and pointed to the chair opposite. I took it, facing him.

'Now,' he said. 'Explain.'

I spoke in a flat calm voice, because emotion was going to repel him where reason might get through. 'My lord, if you could look at the Enquiry from my point of view for a minute, it is quite simple. I know that I never had any five hundred pounds or any note from Mr Cranfield, therefore I am obviously aware that David Oakley was lying. It's unbelievable that the Stewards should have sent him, since the evidence he produced was faked. So someone else did. I thought Lord Gowery might know who. So I asked him.'

'He said he didn't know.'

'I don't altogether believe him.'

'Hughes, that's preposterous.'

'Are you intending to say, sir, that men in power positions are infallibly truthful?'

He looked at me without expression in a lengthening

silence. Finally he said, as Roberta had done, 'Where did you go to school?'

In the usual course of things I kept dead quiet about the type of education I'd had because it was not likely to endear me to either owners or trainers. Still, there was a time for everything, so I told him.

'Coedlant Primary, Tenby Grammar, and LSE.'

'LSE . . . you don't mean . . . the London School of Economics?' He looked astonished.

'Yes.'

'My God . . .'

I watched while he thought it over. 'What did you read there?'

'Politics, philosophy, and economics.'

'Then what on earth made you become a jockey?'

'It was almost an accident,' I said. 'I didn't plan it. When I'd finished my final exams I was mentally tired, so I thought I'd take a sort of paid holiday working on the land . . . I knew how to do that, my father's a farm-hand. I worked at harvesting for a farmer in Devon and every morning I used to ride his 'chasers out at exercise, because I'd ridden most of my life, you see. He had a permit, and he was dead keen. And then his brother, who raced them for him, broke his shoulder at one of the early Devon meetings, and he put me up instead, and almost at once I started winning . . . and then it took hold of me . . . so I didn't get around to being a Civil Servant, as I'd always vaguely intended, and ... well ... I've never regretted it.'

'Not even now?' he said with irony.

I shook my head. 'Not even now.'

'Hughes ...' His face crinkled dubiously. 'I don't know what to think. At first I was sure you were not the type to have stopped Squelch deliberately ... and then there was all that damning evidence. Charlie West saying you had definitely pulled back ...'

I looked down at the table. I didn't after all want an eye for an eye, when it came to the point.

'Charlie was mistaken,' I said. 'He got two races muddled up. I did pull back in another race at about that time ... riding a novice 'chaser with no chance, well back in the field. I wanted to give it a good schooling race. That was what Charlie remembered.'

He said doubtfully, 'It didn't sound like it.'

'No,' I agreed. 'I've had it out with Charlie since. He might be prepared to admit now that he was talking about the wrong race. If you will ask the Oxford Stewards, you'll find that Charlie said nothing to them directly after the Lemonfizz, when they made their first enquiries, about me not trying. He only said it later, at the Enquiry in Portman Square.' Because in between some beguiling seducer had offered him five hundred pounds for the service.

'I see.' He frowned. 'And what was it that you asked Lord Gowery about Newtonnards?'

'Newtonnards didn't volunteer the information to the Stewards about Mr Cranfield backing Cherry Pie, but he did tell several bookmaker colleagues. Someone told the Stewards. I wanted to know who.'

'Are you suggesting that it was the same person who sent Oakley to your flat?'

'It might be. But not necessarily.' I hesitated, looking at him doubtfully.

'What is it?' he said.

'Sir, I don't want to offend you, but would you mind telling me why you sat in at the Enquiry? Why there were four of you instead of three, when Lord Gowery, if you'll forgive me saying so, was obviously not too pleased at the arrangement.'

His lips tightened. 'You're being uncommonly tactful all of a sudden.'

'Yes, sir.'

He looked at me steadily. A tall thin man with high cheekbones, strong black hair, hot fiery eyes. A man whose force of character reached out and hit you, so that you'd never forget meeting him. The best ally in the whole 'chasing set up, if I could only reach him.

'I cannot give you my reasons for attending,' he said with some reproof.

'Then you had some . . . reservations . . . about how the Enquiry would be conducted?'

'I didn't say that,' he protested. But he had meant it.

'Lord Gowery chose Andrew Tring to sit with him

at the hearing, and Andrew Tring wants a very big concession from him just now. And he chose Lord Plimborne as the third Steward, and Lord Plimborne continually fell asleep.'

'Do you realize what you're saying?' He was truly shocked.

'I want to know how Lord Gowery acquired all that evidence against us. I want to know why the Stewards' Secretaries sent for the wrong film. I want to know why Lord Gowery was so biased, so deaf to our denials, so determined to warn us off.'

'That's slanderous . . .'

'I want you to ask him,' I finished flatly.

He simply stared.

I said, 'He might tell you. He might just possibly tell you. But he'd never in a million years tell *me*.'

'Hughes . . . You surely don't expect . . .'

'That wasn't a straight trial, and he knows it. I'm just asking you to tackle him with it, to see if he will explain.'

'You are talking about a much respected man,' he said coldly.

'Yes, sir. He's a baron, a rich man, a Steward of long standing. I know all that.'

'And you *still* maintain? . . .'

'Yes.'

His hot eyes brooded. 'He'll have you in court for this.'

'Only if I'm wrong.'

'I can't possibly do it,' he said, with decision.

'And please, if you have one, use a tape-recorder.'

'I told you . . .'

'Yes, sir, I know you did.'

He got up from the table, paused as if about to say something, changed his mind, and as I stood up also, turned abruptly and walked sharply away. When he had gone I found that my hands were trembling, and I followed him slowly out of the supper room feeling a battered wreck.

I had either resurrected our licences or driven the nails into them, and only time would tell which.

Bobbie said, 'Have a drink, my dear fellow. You look as though you've been clobbered by a steamroller.'

I took a mouthful of champagne and thanked him, and watched Roberta swing her body to a compelling rhythm with someone else. The ringlets bounced against her neck. I wondered without disparagement how long it had taken her to pin them on.

'Not the best of evenings for you, old pal,' Bobbie observed.

'You never know.'

He raised his eyebrows, drawling down his nose, 'Mission accomplished?'

'A fuse lit, rather.'

He lifted his glass. 'To a successful detonation.'

'You are most kind,' I said formally.

The music changed gear and Roberta's partner brought her back to the table.

I stood up. 'I came to say goodbye,' I said. 'I'll be going now.'

'Oh not yet,' she exclaimed. 'The worst is over. No one's staring any more. Have some fun.'

'Dance with the dear girl,' Bobbie said, and Roberta put out a long arm and pulled mine, and so I went and danced with her.

'Lord Gowery didn't eat you then?'

'He's scrunching the bones at this minute.'

'Kelly! If you've done any damage . . .'

'No omelettes without smashing eggs, love.'

The chin went up. I grinned. She brought it down again. Getting quite human, Miss Cranfield.

After a while the hot rhythm changed to a slow smooch, and couples around us went into clinches. Bodies to bodies, heads to heads, eyes shut, swaying in the dimming light. Roberta eyed them coolly and prickled when I put my arms up to gather her in. She danced very straight, with four inches of air between us. Not human enough.

We ambled around in that frigid fashion through three separate wodges of glutinous music. She didn't come any closer, and I did nothing to persuade her, but equally she seemed to be in no hurry to break it up. Composed, cool, off-puttingly gracious, she looked as flawless in the small hours as she had when I'd arrived.

'I'm glad you were here,' I said.

She moved her head in surprise. 'It hasn't been exactly the best Jockeys' Fund dance of my life . . . but I'm glad I came.'

'Next year this will be all over, and everyone will have forgotten.'

'I'll dance with you again next year,' she said.

'It's a pact.'

She smiled, and just for a second a stray beam of light shimmered on some expression in her eyes which I didn't understand.

She was aware of it. She turned her head away, and then detached herself altogether, and gestured that she wanted to go back to the table. I delivered her to Bobbie, and she sat down immediately and began powdering a non-shiny nose.

'Goodnight,' I said to Bobbie. 'And thank you.'

'My dear fellow. Any time.'

'Goodnight, Roberta.'

She looked up. Nothing in the eyes. Her voice was collected. 'Goodnight, Kelly.'

I lowered myself into the low-slung burnt-orange car in the park and drove away thinking about her. Roberta

Cranfield. Not my idea of a cuddly bed mate. Too cold, too controlled, too proud. And it didn't go with that copper hair, all that rigidity. Or maybe she was only rigid to me because I was a farm labourer's son. Only that, and only a jockey . . . and her father had taught her that jockeys were the lower classes dear and don't get your fingers dirty . . .

Kelly, I said to myself, you've a fair-sized chip on your shoulder, old son. Maybe she does think like that, but why should it bother you? And even if she does, she spent most of the evening with you . . . although she was really quite careful not to touch you too much. Well . . . maybe that was because so many people were watching . . . and maybe it was simply that she didn't like the thought of it.

I was on the short cut home that led round the south of Reading, streaking down deserted back roads, going fast for no reason except that speed had become a habit. This car was easily the best I'd ever had, the only one I had felt proud of. Mechanically a masterpiece and with looks to match. Even thirty thousand miles in the past year hadn't dulled the pleasure I got from driving it. Its only fault was that like so many other sports cars it had a totally inefficient heater, which in spite of coaxing and overhauls stubbornly refused to do more than demist the windscreen and raise my toes one degree above frostbite. If kicked, it retaliated with a smell of exhaust.

I had gone to the dance without a coat, and the night was frosty. I shivered and switched on the heater to maximum. As usual, damn all.

There was a radio in the car, which I seldom listened to, and a spare crash helmet, and my five-pound racing saddle which I'd been going to take to Wetherby races.

Depression flooded back. Fierce though the evening had been, in many ways I had forgotten for a while the dreariness of being banned. It could be a long slog now, after what I had said to the Lords Gowery and Ferth. A very long slog indeed. Cranfield wouldn't like the gamble. I wasn't too sure that I could face telling him, if it didn't come off.

Lord Ferth . . . would he or wouldn't he? He'd be torn between loyalty to an equal and a concept of justice. I didn't know him well enough to be sure which would win. And maybe anyway he would shut everything I'd said clean out of his mind, as too far-fetched and preposterous to bother about.

Bobbie had been great, I thought. I wondered who he was. Maybe one day I'd ask Roberta.

Mrs Roxford . . . poor dear Grace. What a life Jack must lead . . . Hope he liked vodka . . .

I took an unexpectedly sharp bend far too fast. The wheels screeched when I wrenched the nose round and the car went weaving and skidding for a hundred yards before I had it in control again. I put my foot gingerly back on the accelerator and still had in my mind's eye the solid trunks of the row of trees I had just missed by centimetres.

God, I thought, how could I be so careless. It rocked me. I was a careful driver, even if fast, and I'd never had an accident. I could feel myself sweating. It was something to sweat about.

How stupid I was, thinking about the dance, not concentrating on driving, and going too fast for these small roads. I rubbed my forehead, which felt tense and tight, and kept my speed down to forty.

Roberta had looked beautiful ... keep your mind on the road, Kelly, for God's sake ... Usually I drove semi-automatically without having to concentrate every yard of the way. I found myself going slower still, because both my reactions and my thoughts were growing sluggish. I'd drunk a total of about half a glass of champagne all evening, so it couldn't be that.

I was simply going to sleep.

I stopped the car, got out, and stamped about to wake myself up. People who went to sleep at the wheels of sports cars on the way home from dances were not a good risk.

Too many sleepless nights, grinding over my sorry state. Insulting the lions seemed to have released the worst of that. I felt I could now fall unconscious for a month.

I considered sleeping there and then, in the car. But the car was cold and couldn't be heated. I would drive on, I decided, and stop for good if I felt really dozy again. The fresh air had done the trick; I was wide awake and irritated with myself.

The beam of my headlights on the cats' eyes down the empty road was soon hypnotic. I switched on the radio to see if that would hold my attention, but it was all soft and sweet late-night music. Lullaby. I switched it off.

Pity I didn't smoke. That would have helped.

It was a star-clear night with a bright full moon. Ice crystals sparkled like diamond dust on the grass verges, now that I'd left the wooded part behind. Beautiful but unwelcome, because a hard frost would mean no racing tomorrow at Sandown ... With a jerk I realized that that didn't matter to me any more.

I glanced at the speedometer. Forty. It seemed very fast. I slowed down still further to thirty-five, and nodded owlishly to myself. Anyone would be safe at thirty-five.

The tightness across my forehead slowly developed into a headache. Never mind, only an hour to home, then sleep ... sleep ... sleep ...

It's no good, I thought fuzzily. I'll have to stop and black out for a bit, even if I do wake up freezing, or I'll black out without stopping first, and that will be that.

The next layby, or something like tha ...

I began looking, forgot what I was looking for, took

my foot still farther off the accelerator and reckoned that thirty miles an hour was quite safe. Maybe twenty five . . . would be better.

A little farther on there were some sudden bumps in the road surface and my foot slipped off the accelerator altogether. The engine stalled. Car stopped.

Oh well, I thought. That settles it. Ought to move over to the side though. Couldn't see the side. Very odd.

The headache was pressing on my temples, and now that the engine had stopped I could hear a faint ringing in my ears.

Never mind. Never mind. Best to go to sleep. Leave the lights on . . . no one came along that road much . . . not at two in the morning . . . but have to leave the lights on just in case.

Ought to pull in to the side.

Ought to . . .

Too much trouble. Couldn't move my arms properly, anyway, so couldn't possibly do it.

Deep, deep in my head a tiny instinct switched itself to emergency.

Something was wrong. Something was indistinctly but appallingly wrong.

Sleep. Must sleep.

Get out, the flickering instinct said. Get out of the car.

171

Ridiculous.

Get out of the car.

Unwillingly, because it was such an effort, I struggled weakly with the handle. The door swung open. I put one leg out and tried to pull myself up, and was swept by a wave of dizziness. My head was throbbing. This wasn't ... it couldn't be ... just ordinary sleep.

Get out of the car ...

My arms and legs belonged to someone else. They had me on my feet ... I was standing up ... didn't remember how I got there. But I was out.

Out.

Now what?

I took three tottering steps towards the back of the car and leant against the rear wing. Funny, I thought, the moonlight wasn't so bright any more.

The earth was trembling.

Stupid. Quite stupid. The earth didn't tremble.

Trembling. And the air was wailing. And the moon was falling on me. Come down from the sky and rushing towards me ...

Not the moon. A great roaring wailing monster with a blinding moon eye. A monster making the earth tremble. A monster racing to gobble me up, huge and dark and faster than the wind and unimaginably terrifying ...

I didn't move. Couldn't.

ENQUIRY

The one-thirty mail express from Paddington to Plymouth ploughed into my sturdy little car and carried its crumpled remains half a mile down the track.

CHAPTER TEN

I didn't know what had happened. Didn't understand. There was a tremendous noise of tearing metal and a hundred-mile-an-hour whirl of ninety-ton diesel engine one inch away from me, and a thudding catapulting scrunch which lifted me up like a rag doll and toppled me somersaulting through the air in a kaleidoscopic black arc.

My head crashed against a concrete post. The rest of my body felt mangled beyond repair. There were rainbows in my brain, blue, purple, flaming pink, with diamond-bright pin stars. Interesting while it lasted. Didn't last very long. Dissolved into an embracing inferno in which colours got lost in pain.

Up the line the train had screeched to a stop. Lights and voices were coming back that way.

The earth was cold, hard, and damp. A warm stream ran down my face. I knew it was blood. Didn't care much. Couldn't think properly, either. And didn't really want to.

More lights. Lots of lights. Lots of people. Voices.
A voice I knew.

'Roberta, my dear girl, don't look.'

'It's Kelly!' she said. Shock. Wicked, unforgettable
shock. 'It's Kelly.' The second time, despair.

'Come away, my dear girl.'

She didn't go. She was kneeling beside me. I could
smell her scent, and feel her hand on my hair. I was
lying on my side, face down. After a while I could see
a segment of honey silk dress. There was blood on it.

I said, 'You're ruining . . . your dress.'

'It doesn't matter.'

It helped somehow to have her there. I was grateful
that she had stayed. I wanted to tell her that. I tried . . .
and meant . . . to say 'Roberta'. What in fact I said
was . . . 'Rosalind'.

'Oh Kelly . . .' Her voice held a mixture of pity and
distress.

I thought groggily that she would go away, now that
I'd made such a silly mistake, but she stayed, saying
small things like, 'You'll be all right soon,' and sometimes not talking at all, but just being there. I didn't
know why I wanted her to stay. I remembered that I
didn't even like the girl.

All the people who arrive after accidents duly
arrived. Police with blue flashing lights. Ambulance
waking the neighbourhood with its siren. Bobbie took
Roberta away, telling her there was no more she could

175

do. The ambulance men scooped me unceremoniously on to a stretcher and if I thought them rough it was only because every movement brought a scream up as far as my teeth and heaven knows whether any of them got any farther.

By the time I reached the hospital the mists had cleared. I knew what had happened to my car. I knew that I wasn't dying. I knew that Bobbie and Roberta had taken the backroads detour like I had, and had reached the level crossing not long after me.

What I didn't understand was how I had come to stop on the railway. That crossing had drop-down-fringe gates, and they hadn't been shut.

A young dark-haired doctor with tired dark-ringed eyes came to look at me, talking to the ambulance men.

'He'd just come from a dance,' they said. 'The police want a blood test.'

'Drunk?' said the doctor.

The ambulance men shrugged. They thought it possible.

'No,' I said. 'It wasn't drink. At least . . .'

They didn't pay much attention. The young doctor stooped over my lower half, feeling the damage with slender gentle fingers. 'That hurts? Yes.' He parted my hair, looking at my head. 'Nothing much up there. More blood than damage.' He stood back. 'We'll get your pelvis X-rayed. And that leg. Can't tell what's what until after that.'

A nurse tried to take my shoes off. I said very loudly, 'Don't.'

She jumped. The doctor signed to her to stop. 'We'll do it under an anaesthetic. Just leave him for now.'

She came instead and wiped my forehead.

'Sorry,' she said.

The doctor took my pulse. 'Why ever did you stop on a level crossing?' he said conversationally. 'Silly thing to do.'

'I felt ... sleepy. Had a headache.' It didn't sound very sensible.

'Had a bit to drink?'

'Almost nothing.'

'At a dance?' He sounded sceptical.

'Really,' I said weakly. 'I didn't.'

He put my hand down. I was still wearing my dinner jacket, though someone had taken off my tie. There were bright scarlet blotches down my white shirt and an unmendable tear down the right side of my black trousers.

I shut my eyes. Didn't do much good. The screaming pain showed no signs of giving up. It had localized into my right side from armpit to toes, with repercussions up and down my spine. I'd broken a good many bones racing, but this was much worse. Much. It was impossible.

'It won't be long now,' the doctor said comfortingly. 'We'll have you under.'

'The train didn't hit me,' I said. 'I got out of the car . . . I was leaning against the back of it . . . the train hit the car . . . not me.'

I felt sick. How long? . . .

'If it had hit you, you wouldn't be here.'

'I suppose not . . . I had this thumping headache . . . needed air . . .' Why couldn't I pass out, I thought. People always passed out, when it became unbearable. Or so I'd always believed.

'Have you still got the headache?' he asked clinically.

'It's gone off a bit. Just sore now.' My mouth was dry. Always like that, after injuries. The least of my troubles.

Two porters came to wheel me away, and I protested more than was stoical about the jolts. I felt grey. Looked at my hands. They were quite surprisingly red.

X-ray department. Very smooth, very quick. Didn't try to move me except for cutting the zip out of my trousers. Quite enough.

'Sorry,' they said.

'Do you work all night?' I asked.

They smiled. On duty, if called.

'Thanks,' I said.

Another journey. People in green overalls and white masks, making soothing remarks. Could I face taking my coat off? No? Never mind then. Needle into vein in back of hand. Marvellous. Oblivion rolled through me in grey and black and I greeted it with a sob of welcome.

The world shuffled back in the usual way, bit by uncomfortable bit, with a middle-aged nurse patting my hand and telling me to wake up dear, it was all over.

I had to admit that my wildest fears were not realized. I still had two legs. One I could move. The other had plaster on. Inside the plaster it gently ached. The scream had died to a whisper. I sighed with relief.

What was the time? Five o'clock, dear.

Where was I? In the recovery ward, dear. Now go to sleep again and when you wake up you'll be feeling much better, you'll see.

I did as she said, and she was quite right.

Mid-morning, a doctor came. Not the same one as the night before. Older, heavier, but just as tired looking.

'You had a lucky escape,' he said.

'Yes, I did.'

'Luckier than you imagine. We took a blood test. Actually we took two blood tests. The first one alcohol. With practically negative results. Now this interested us, because who except a drunk would stop a car on a level crossing and get out and lean against it? The casualty doctor told us you swore you hadn't been drinking and that anyway you seemed sober enough to him ... but that you'd had a bad headache which was now better ... We gave you a bit of thought, and we looked at those very bright scarlet stains on your shirt ... and tested your blood again ... and there it was!' He paused triumphantly.

'What?'

'Carboxyhaemoglobin.'

'*What*?'

'Carbon monoxide, my dear chap. Carbon-monoxide poisoning. Explains everything, don't you see?'

'Oh ... but I thought ... with carbon monoxide ... one simply blacked out.'

'It depends. If you got a large dose all at once that would happen, like it does to people who get stuck in snow drifts and leave their engines running. But a trickle, that would affect you more slowly. But it would all be the same in the end, of course. The haemoglobin in the red corpuscles has a greater affinity for carbon monoxide than for oxygen, so it mops up any carbon monoxide you breathe in, and oxygen is disregarded. If the level of carbon monoxide in your blood builds up gradually ... you get gradual symptoms. Very insidious they are too. The trouble is that it seems that when people feel sleepy they light a cigarette to keep themselves awake, and tobacco smoke itself introduces significant quantities of carbon monoxide into the body, so the cigarette may be the final knock out. Er . . . do you smoke?'

'No.' And to think I'd regretted it.

'Just as well. You obviously had quite a dangerous concentration of CO in any case.'

'I must have been driving for half an hour . . . maybe forty minutes. I don't really know.'

'It's a wonder you stopped safely at all. Much more likely to have crashed into something.'

'I nearly did . . . on a corner.'

He nodded. 'Didn't you smell exhaust fumes?'

'I didn't notice. I had too much on my mind. And the heater burps out exhaust smells sometimes. So I wouldn't take much heed, if it wasn't strong.' I looked down at myself under the sheets. 'What's the damage?'

'Not much now,' he said cheerfully. 'You were lucky there too. You had multiple dislocations . . . hip, knee, and ankle. Never seen all three before. Very interesting. We reduced them all successfully. No crushing or fractures, no severed tendons. We don't even think there will be a recurring tendency to dislocate. One or two frayed ligaments round your knee, that's all.'

'It's a miracle.'

'Interesting case, yes. Unique sort of accident, of course. No direct force involved. We think it might have been air impact . . . that it sort of blew or stretched you apart. Like being on the rack, eh?' He chuckled. 'We put plaster on your knee and ankle, to give them a chance to settle, but it can come off in three or four weeks. We don't want you to put weight on your hip yet, either. You can have some physiotherapy. But take it easy for a while when you leave here. There was a lot of spasm in the muscles, and all your ligaments and so on were badly stretched. Give everything time to subside properly before you run a mile.' He smiled, which turned halfway through into a yawn. He smothered it apologetically. 'It's been a long night . . .'

'Yes,' I said.

I went home on Tuesday afternoon in an ambulance with a pair of crutches and instructions to spend most of my time horizontal.

Poppy was still sick. Tony followed my slow progress up the stairs apologizing that she couldn't manage to have me stay, the kids were exhausting her to distraction.

'I'm fine on my own.'

He saw me into the bedroom, where I lay down in my clothes on top of the bedspread, as per instructions. Then he made for the whisky and refreshed himself after my labours.

'Do you want anything? I'll fetch you some food, later.'

'Thanks,' I said. 'Could you bring the telephone in here?'

He brought it in and plugged the lead into the socket beside my bed.

'OK?'

'Fine,' I said.

'That's it, then.' He tossed off his drink quickly and made for the door, showing far more haste than usual and edging away from me as though embarrassed.

'Is anything wrong?' I said.

He jumped. 'No. Absolutely nothing. Got to get the kids their tea before evening stables. See you later, pal. With the odd crust.' He smiled sketchily and disappeared.

I shrugged. Whatever it was that was wrong, he would tell me in time, if he wanted to.

I picked up the telephone and dialled the number of the local garage. Its best mechanic answered.

'Mr Hughes . . . I heard . . . Your beautiful car.' He commiserated genuinely for half a minute.

'Yes,' I said. 'Look, Derek, is there any way that exhaust gas could get into the car through the heater?'

He was affronted. 'Not the way I looked after it. Certainly not.'

'I apparently breathed in great dollops of carbon monoxide,' I said.

'Not through the heater . . . I can't understand it.' He paused, thinking. 'They take special care not to let that happen, see? At the design stage. You could only get exhaust gas through the heater if there was a loose

183

or worn gasket on the exhaust manifold *and* a crack or break in the heater tubing *and* a tube connecting the two together, and you can take it from me, Mr Hughes, there was nothing at all like that on your car. Maintained perfect, it is.'

'The heater does sometimes smell of exhaust. If you remember, I did mention it, some time ago.'

'I give the whole system a thorough check then, too. There wasn't a thing wrong. Only thing I could think of was the exhaust might have eddied forwards from the back of the car when you slowed down, sort of, and got whirled in through the fresh-air intake, the one down beside the heater.'

'Could you possibly go and look at my car? At what's left of it? . . .'

'There's a good bit to do here,' he said dubiously.

'The police have given me the name of the garage where it is now. Apparently all the bits have to stay there until the insurance people have seen them. But you know the car . . . it would be easier for you to spot anything different with it from when you last serviced it. Could you go?'

'D'you mean,' he paused. 'You don't mean . . . there might be something . . . well . . . *wrong* with it?'

'I don't know,' I said. 'But I'd like to find out.'

'It would cost you,' he said warningly. 'It would be working hours.'

'Never mind. If you can go, it will be worth it.'

'Hang on, then.' He departed to consult. Came back. 'Yes, all right. The Guvnor says I can go first thing in the morning.'

'That's great,' I said. 'Call me when you get back.'

'It couldn't have been a gasket,' he said suddenly.

'Why not?'

'You'd have heard it. Very noisy. Unless you had the radio on?'

'No.'

'You'd have heard a blown gasket,' he said positively. 'But there again, if the exhaust was being somehow fed straight into the heater ... perhaps not. The heater would damp the noise, same as a silencer ... but I don't see how it could have happened. Well ... all I can do is take a look.'

I would have liked to have gone with him. I put down the receiver and looked gloomily at my right leg. The neat plaster casing stretched from well up my thigh down to the base of my toes, which were currently invisible inside a white hospital theatre sock. A pair of Tony's slacks, though too long by six inches, had slid up easily enough over the plaster, decently hiding it, and as far as looks went, things were passable.

I sighed. The plaster was a bore. They'd designed it somehow so that I found sitting in a chair uncomfortable. Standing and lying down were both better. It wasn't going to stay on a minute longer than I could help, either. The muscles inside it were doing themselves no good in immobility. They would be getting flabby, unfit, wasting away. It would be just too ironic if I got my licence back and was too feeble to ride.

Tony came back at eight with half a chicken. He didn't want to stay, not even for a drink.

'Can you manage?' he said.

'Sure. No trouble.'

'Your leg doesn't hurt, does it?'

'Not a flicker,' I said. 'Can't feel a thing.'

'That's all right then.' He was relieved: wouldn't look at me squarely: went away.

Next morning, Roberta Cranfield came.

'Kelly?' she called. 'Are you in?'

'In the bedroom.'

She walked across the sitting-room and stopped in the doorway. Wearing the black-and-white striped fur coat, hanging open. Underneath it, black pants and a stagnant-pond-coloured sweater.

'Hullo,' she said. 'I've brought you some food. Shall I put it in the kitchen?'

'That's pretty good of you.'

She looked me over. I was lying, dressed, on top of the bedspread, reading the morning paper. 'You look comfortable enough.'

'I am. Just bored. Er ... not now you've come, of course.'

'Of course,' she agreed. 'Shall I make some coffee?'

'Yes, do.'

She brought it back in mugs, shed her fur, and sat loose limbed in my bedroom armchair.

'You look a bit better today,' she observed.

'Can you get that blood off your dress?'

She shrugged. 'I chucked it at the cleaners. They're trying.'

'I'm sorry about that . . .'

'Think nothing of it.' She sipped her coffee. 'I rang the hospital on Saturday. They said you were OK.'

'Thanks.'

'Why on earth did you stop on the railway?'

'I didn't know it was the railway, until too late.'

'But how did you get there, anyway, with the gates down?'

'The gates weren't down.'

'They were when we came along,' she said. 'There were all those lights and people shouting and screaming and we got out of the car to see what it was all about, and someone said the train had hit a car . . . and then I saw you, lying spark out with your face all covered in blood, about ten feet up the line. Nasty. Very nasty. It was, really.'

'I'm sorry . . . I'd had a couple of lungfuls of carbon monoxide. What you might call diminished responsibility.'

She grinned. 'You're some moron.'

The gates must have shut after I'd stopped on the line. I hadn't heard them or seen them. I must, I supposed, have been more affected by the gas than I remembered.

'I called you Rosalind,' I said apologetically.

'I know.' She made a face. 'Did you think I was her?'

'No . . . It just came out. I meant to say Roberta.'

She unrolled herself from the chair, took a few steps, and stood looking at Rosalind's picture. 'She'd have been glad . . . knowing she still came first with you after all this time.'

The telephone rang sharply beside me and interrupted my surprise. I picked up the receiver.

'Is that Kelly Hughes?' The voice was cultivated, authoritative, loaded indefinably with power. 'This is Wykeham Ferth speaking. I read about your accident in the papers . . . a report this morning says you are now home. I hope . . . you are well?'

'Yes, thank you, my lord.'

It was ridiculous, the way my heart had bumped. Sweating palms, too.

'Are you in any shape to come to London?'

'I'm . . . I've got plaster on my leg . . . I can't sit in a car very easily, I'm afraid.'

'Hm.' A pause. 'Very well. I will drive down to Corrie instead. It's Harringay's old place, isn't it?'

'That's right. I live in a flat over the yard. If you walk into the yard from the drive, you'll see a green door with a brass letter box in the far corner. It won't be locked. There are some stairs inside. I live up there.'

'Right,' he said briskly. 'This afternoon? Good. Expect me at . . . er . . . four o'clock. Right?'

'Sir . . .' I began.

'Not now, Hughes. This afternoon.'

I put the receiver down slowly. Six hours' suspense. Damn him.

'What an absolutely heartless letter,' Roberta exclaimed.

I looked at her. She was holding the letter from my parents, which had been under Rosalind's photograph.

'I dare say I shouldn't have been so nosey as to read it,' she said unrepentantly.

'I dare say not.'

'How *can* they be so beastly?'

'They're not really.'

'This sort of thing always happens when you get one bright son in a family of twits,' she said disgustedly.

'Not always. Some bright sons handle things better than others.'

'Stop clobbering yourself.'

'Yes, ma'am.'

'Are you going to stop sending them money?'

'No. All they can do about that is not spend it . . . or give it to the local cats' and dogs' home.'

'At least they had the decency to see they couldn't take your money *and* call you names.'

'Rigidly moral man, my father,' I said. 'Honest to

189

the last farthing. Honest for its own sake. He taught me a lot that I'm grateful for.'

'And that's why this business hurts him so much?'

'Yes.'

'I've never ... Well. I know you'll despise me for saying it ... but I've never thought about people like your father before as ... well ... *people*.'

'If you're not careful,' I said, 'those chains will drop right off.'

She turned away and put the letter back under Rosalind's picture.

'Which university did you go to?'

'London. Starved in a garret on a grant. Great stuff.'

'I wish ... how odd ... I wish I'd trained for something. Learned a job.'

'It's hardly too late,' I said, smiling.

'I'm nearly twenty. I didn't bother much at school with exams ... no one made us. Then I went to Switzerland for a year, to a finishing school ... and since then I've just lived at home ... What a waste!'

'The daughters of the rich are always at a disadvantage,' I said solemnly.

'Sarcastic beast.'

She sat down again in the armchair and told me that her father really seemed to have snapped out of it at last, and had finally accepted a dinner invitation the night before. All the lads had stayed on. They spent most of their time playing cards and football, as the only horses left in the yard were four half-broken two-year-olds and three old 'chasers recovering from injuries. Most of the owners had promised to bring their horses back at once, if Cranfield had his licence restored in the next few weeks.

'What's really upsetting Father now is hope. With the big Cheltenham meeting only a fortnight away, he's biting his nails about whether he'll get Breadwinner back in time for him to run in his name in the Gold Cup.'

'Pity Breadwinner isn't entered in the Grand National. That would give us a bit more leeway.'

'Would your leg be right in time for the Gold Cup?'

'If I had my licence, I'd saw the plaster off myself.'

'Are you any nearer . . . with the licences?'

'Don't know.'

She sighed. 'It was a great dream while it lasted. And you won't be able to do much about it now.'

She stood up and came over and picked up the crutches which were lying beside the bed. They were black tubular metal with elbow supports and hand grips.

'These are much better than those old fashioned under-the-shoulder affairs,' she said. She fitted the crutches round her arms and swung around the room a bit with one foot off the floor. 'Pretty hard on your hands, though.'

She looked unselfconscious and intent. I watched

191

her. I remembered the revelation it had been in my childhood when I first wondered what it was like to be someone else.

Into this calm sea Tony appeared with a wretched face and a folded paper in his hand.

'Hi,' he said, seeing Roberta. A very gloomy greeting.

He sat down in the armchair and looked at Roberta standing balanced on the crutches with one knee bent. His thoughts were not where his eyes were.

'What is it, then?' I said. 'Out with it.'

'This letter . . . came yesterday,' he said heavily.

'It was obvious last night that something was the matter.'

'I couldn't show it to you then, not straight out of hospital. And I don't know what to do, Kelly pal, sure enough I don't.'

'Let's see, then.'

He handed me the paper worriedly. I opened it up. A brief letter from the racing authorities. Bang bang, both barrels.

Dear Sir,

It has been brought to our attention that a person warned off Newmarket Heath is living as a tenant in your stable yard. This is contrary to the regulations, and you should remedy the situation as soon as possible. It is perhaps not necessary to warn you that your own training licence might have to be reviewed if you should fail to take the steps suggested.

'Sods,' Tony said forcefully. 'Bloody sods.'

CHAPTER ELEVEN

Derek from the garage came while Roberta was clearing away the lunch she had stayed to cook. When he rang the door bell she went downstairs to let him in.

He walked hesitatingly across the sitting-room looking behind him to see if his shoes were leaving dirty marks and out of habit wiped his hands down his trousers before taking the one I held out to him.

'Sit down,' I suggested. He looked doubtfully at the khaki velvet armchair, but in the end lowered himself gingerly into it. He looked perfectly clean. No grease, no filthy overalls, just ordinary slacks and sports jacket. He wasn't used to it.

'You all right?' he said.

'Absolutely.'

'If you'd been in that car . . .' He looked sick at what he was thinking, and his vivid imagination was one of the things which made him a reliable mechanic. He didn't want death on his conscience. Young, fair haired, diffident, he kept most of his brains in his fingertips and outside of cars used the upstairs lot sparingly.

'You've never seen nothing like it,' he said. 'You wouldn't know it was a car, you wouldn't straight. It's all in little bits . . . I mean, like, bits of metal that don't look as if they were ever part of anything. Honestly. It's like twisted shreds of stuff.' He swallowed. 'They've got it collected up in tin baths.'

'The engine too?'

'Yeah. Smashed into fragments. Still, I had a look. Took me a long time, though, because everything is all jumbled up, and honest you can't tell what anything used to be. I mean, I didn't think it was a bit of exhaust manifold that I'd picked up, not at first, because it wasn't any shape that you'd think of.'

'You found something?'

'Here.' He fished in his trouser pocket. 'This is what it was all like. This is a bit of the exhaust manifold. Cast iron, that is, you see, so of course it was brittle, sort of, and it had shattered into bits. I mean, it wasn't sort of crumpled up like all the aluminium and so on. It wasn't bent, see, it was just in bits.'

'Yes, I do see,' I said. The anxious lines on his forehead dissolved when he saw that he had managed to tell me what he meant. He came over and put the small black jagged-edged lump into my hands. Heavy for its size. About three inches long. Asymmetrically curved. Part of the side wall of a huge tube.

195

'As far as I can make out, see,' Derek said, pointing, 'it came from about where the manifold narrows down to the exhaust pipe, but really it might be anywhere. There were quite a few bits of manifold, when I looked, but I couldn't see the bit that fits into this, and I dare say it's still rusting away somewhere along the railway line. Anyway, see this bit here . . .' He pointed a stubby finger at a round dent in part of one edge. 'That's one side of a hole that was bored in the manifold wall. Now don't get me wrong, there's quite a few holes might have been drilled through the wall. I mean, some people have exhaust-gas temperature gauges stuck into the manifold . . . and other gauges too. Things like that. Only, see, there weren't no gauges in your manifold, now, were there?'

'You tell me,' I said.

'There weren't, then. Now you couldn't really say what the hole was for, not for certain you couldn't. But as far as I know, there weren't any holes in your manifold last time I did the service.'

I fingered the little semi-circular dent. No more than a quarter of an inch across.

'However did you spot something so small?' I asked.

'Dunno, really. Mind you, I was there a good couple of hours, picking through those tubs. Did it methodical, like. Since you were paying for it and all.'

'Is it a big job . . . drilling a hole this size through an exhaust manifold? Would it take long?'

'Half a minute, I should think.'

'With an electric drill?' I asked.

'Oh yeah, sure. If you did it with a hand drill, then it would take five minutes. Say nearer eight or ten, to be on the safe side.'

'How many people carry drills around in their tool kits?'

'That, see, it depends on the chap. Now some of them carry all sorts of stuff in their cars. Proper work benches, some of them. And then others, the tool kit stays strapped up fresh from the factory until the car's dropping to bits.'

'People do carry drills, then?'

'Oh yeah, sure. Quite a lot do. Hand drills, of course. You wouldn't have much call for an electric drill, not in a tool kit, not unless you did a lot of repairs, like, say on racing cars.'

He went and sat down again. Carefully, as before.

'If someone drilled a hole this size through the manifold, what would happen?'

'Well, honestly, nothing much. You'd get exhaust gas out through the engine, and you'd hear a good lot of noise, and you might smell it in the car, but it would sort of blow away, see, it wouldn't come in through the heater. To do that, like I said before, you'd have to put some tubing into the hole there and then stick the other end of the tubing into the heater. Mind you that would be pretty easy, you wouldn't need a drill. Some heater tubes are really only cardboard.'

'Rubber tubing from one end to the other?' I suggested.

He shook his head. 'No. Have to be metal. Exhaust gas, that's very hot. It'd melt anything but metal.'

'Do you think anyone could do all that on the spur of the moment?'

He put his head on one side, considering. 'Oh sure, yeah. If he'd got a drill. Like, say the first other thing he needs is some tubing. Well, he's only got to look around for that. Lots lying about, if you look. The other day, I used a bit of a kiddy's old cycle frame, just the job it was. Right, you get the tube ready first and then you fit a drill nearest the right size, to match. And Bob's your uncle.'

'How long, from start to finish?'

'Fixing the manifold to the heater? Say, from scratch, including maybe having to cast around for a bit of tube, well, at the outside half an hour. A quarter, if you had something all ready handy. Only the drilling would take any time, see? The rest would be like stealing candy from a baby.'

Roberta appeared in the doorway shrugging herself into the stripy coat. Derek stood up awkwardly and didn't know where to put his hands. She smiled at him sweetly and unseeingly and said to me, 'Is there anything else you want, Kelly?'

'No. Thank you very much.'

'Think nothing of it. I'll see ... I might come over again tomorrow.'

'Fine,' I said.

'Right.'

She nodded, smiled temperately, and made her usual poised exit. Derek's comment approached, 'Cor.'

'I suppose you didn't see any likely pieces of tube in the wreckage?' I asked.

'Huh?' He tore his eyes away with an effort from the direction Roberta had gone. 'No, like it was real bad. Lots of bits, you couldn't have told what they were. I never seen anything like it. Sure, I seen crashes, stands to reason. Different, this was.' He shivered.

'Did you have any difficulty with being allowed to search?'

'No, none. They didn't seem all that interested in what I did. Just said to help myself.' Course, I told them it was my car, like. I mean, that I looked after it. Mind you, they were right casual about it, anyway, because when I came away they were letting this other chap have a good look too.'

'Which other chap?'

'Some fellow. Said he was an insurance man, but he didn't have a notebook.'

I felt like saying Huh? too. I said, 'Notebook?'

'Yeah, sure, insurance men, they're always crawling

round our place looking at wrecks and never one without a notebook. Write down every blessed detail, they do. But this other chap, looking at your car, he didn't have any notebook.'

'What did he look like?'

He thought.

'That's difficult, see. He didn't look like anything, really. Medium, sort of. Not young and not old really either. A nobody sort of person, really.'

'Did he wear sunglasses?'

'No. He had a hat on, but I don't know if he had ordinary glasses. I can't actually remember. I didn't notice that much.'

'Was he looking through the wreckage as if he knew what he wanted?'

'Uh ... don't know, really. Strikes me he was a bit flummoxed, like, finding it was all in such small bits.'

'He didn't have a girl with him?'

'Nope.' He brightened. 'He came in a Volkswagen, an oldish grey one.'

'Thousands of those about,' I said.

'Oh yeah, sure. Er ... was this chap important?'

'Only if he was looking for what you found.'

He worked it out.

'Cripes,' he said.

*

Lord Ferth arrived twenty minutes after he'd said, which meant that I'd been hopping round the flat on my crutches for half an hour, unable to keep still.

He stood in the doorway into the sitting-room holding a briefcase and bowler hat in one hand and unbuttoning his short fawn overcoat with the other.

'Well, Hughes,' he said. 'Good afternoon.'

'Good afternoon, my lord.'

He came right in, shut the door behind him, and put his hat and case on the oak chest beside him.

'How's the leg?'

'Stagnating,' I said. 'Can I get you some tea ... coffee ... or a drink?'

'Nothing just now ...' He laid his coat on the chest and picked up the briefcase again, looking round him with the air of surprise I was used to in visitors. I offered him the green armchair with a small table beside it. He asked where I was going to sit.

'I'll stand,' I said. 'Sitting's difficult.'

'But you don't stand all day!'

'No. Lie on my bed, mostly.'

'Then we'll talk in your bedroom.'

We went through the door at the end of the sitting-room and this time he murmured aloud.

'Whose flat is this?' he asked.

'Mine.'

He glanced at my face, hearing the dryness in my voice. 'You resent surprise?'

'It amuses me.'

'Hughes ... it's a pity you didn't join the Civil Service. You'd have gone all the way.'

I laughed. 'There's still time ... Do they take in warned-off jockeys at the Administrative Grade?'

'So you can joke about it?'

'It's taken nine days. But yes, just about.'

He gave me a long straight assessing look, and there was a subtle shift somewhere in both his manner to me and in his basic approach, and when I shortly understood what it was I was shaken, because he was taking me on level terms, level in power and understanding and experience: and I wasn't level.

Few men in his position would have thought that this course was viable, let alone chosen it. I understood the compliment. He saw, too, that I did, and I knew later that had there not been this fundamental change of ground, this cancellation of the Steward-jockey relationship, he would not have said to me all that he did. It wouldn't have happened if he hadn't been in my flat.

He sat down in the khaki velvet armchair, putting the briefcase carefully on the floor beside him. I took the weight off my crutches and let the bed springs have a go.

'I went to see Lord Gowery,' he said neutrally. 'And I can see no reason not to tell you straight away that you and Dexter Cranfield will have your warning off rescinded within the next few days.'

'Do you mean it?' I exclaimed. I tried to sit up. The plaster intervened.

Lord Ferth smiled. 'As I see it, there is no alternative. There will be a quiet notice to that effect in next week's Calendar.'

'That is, of course,' I said, 'all you need to tell me.'

He looked at me levelly. 'True. But not all you want to know.'

'No.'

'No one has a better right . . . and yet you will have to use your discretion about whether you tell Dexter Cranfield.'

'All right.'

He sighed, reached down to open the briefcase, and pulled out a neat little tape-recorder.

'I did try to ignore your suggestion. Succeeded, too, for a while. However . . .' He paused, his fingers hovering over the controls. 'This conversation took place late on Monday afternoon, in the sitting-room of Lord Gowery's flat near Sloane Square. We were alone . . . you will see that we were alone. He knew, though, that I was making a recording.' He still hesitated. 'Compassion. That's what you need. I believe you have it.'

'Don't con me,' I said.

He grimaced. 'Very well.'

The recording began with the self-conscious platitudes customary in front of microphones, especially when no one wants to take the first dive into the deep end. Lord Ferth had leapt, eventually.

'Norman, I explained why we must take a good look at this Enquiry.'

'Hughes is being ridiculous. Not only ridiculous, but downright slanderous. I don't understand why you should take him seriously.' Gowery sounded impatient.

'We have to, even if only to shut him up.' Lord Ferth looked across the room, his hot eyes gleaming ironically. The recording ploughed on, his voice like honey. 'You know perfectly well, Norman, that it will be better all round if we can show there is nothing whatever in these allegations he is spreading around. Then we can emphatically confirm the suspension and squash all the rumours.'

Subtle stuff. Lord Gowery's voice grew easier, assured now that Ferth was still an ally. As perhaps he was. 'I do assure you, Wykeham, that if I had not sincerely believed that Hughes and Dexter Cranfield were guilty, I would not have warned them off.'

There was something odd about that. Both Ferth and Gowery had thought so too, as there were several seconds of silence on the tape.

'But you do still believe it?' Ferth said eventually.

'Of course.' He was emphatic. 'Of course I do.' Much too emphatic.

'Then . . . er . . . taking one of Hughes' questions

first . . . How did it come about that Newtonnards was called to the Enquiry?'

'I was informed that Cranfield had backed Cherry Pie with him.'

'Yes . . . but who informed you?'

Gowery didn't reply.

Ferth's voice came next, with absolutely no pressure in it.

'Um . . . Have you any idea how we managed to show the wrong film of Hughes racing at Reading?'

Gowery was on much surer ground. 'My fault, I'm afraid. I asked the Secretaries to write off for the film of the last race. Didn't realize there were seven races. Careless of me, I'll admit. But of course, as it was the wrong film, it was irrelevant to the case.'

'Er . . .' said Lord Ferth. But he hadn't yet been ready to argue. He cleared his throat and said, 'I suppose you thought it would be relevant to see how Hughes had ridden Squelch last time out.'

After another long pause Gowery said, 'Yes.'

'But in the event we didn't show it.'

'No.'

'Would we have shown it if, after having sent for it, we found that the Reading race bore out entirely Hughes' assertion that he rode Squelch in the Lemonfizz in exactly the same way as he always did?'

More silence. Then he said quietly, 'Yes,' and he sounded very troubled.

'Hughes asked at the Enquiry that we should show the right film,' Ferth said.

'I'm sure he didn't.'

'I've been reading the transcript. Norman, I've been reading and re-reading that transcript all weekend and frankly, that is why I'm here. Hughes did in fact suggest that we should show the right film, presumably because he knew it would support his case . . .'

'Hughes was guilty!' Gowery broke in vehemently. 'Hughes was guilty. I had no option but to warn him off.'

Lord Ferth pressed the stop button on the tape-recorder.

'Tell me,' he said, 'what you think of that last statement?'

'I think,' I said slowly, 'that he did believe it. Both from that statement and from what I remember of the Enquiry. His certainty that day shook me. He believed me guilty so strongly that he was stone deaf to anything which looked even remotely likely to assault his opinion.'

'That was your impression?'

'Overpowering,' I said.

Lord Ferth took his lower lip between his teeth and shook his head, but I gathered it was at the general situation, not at me. He pressed the start button again. His voice came through, precise, carefully without emotion, gentle as vaseline.

'Norman, about the composition of the Enquiry . . . the members of the Disciplinary Committee who sat with you . . . What guided you to choose Andrew Tring and old Plimborne?'

'What guided me?' He sounded astonished at the question. 'I haven't any idea.'

'I wish you'd cast back.'

'I can't see that it has any relevance . . . but let's see . . . I suppose I had Tring in my mind anyway, as I'm in the middle of some business negotiations with him. And Plimborne . . . well, I just saw him snoozing away in the Club. I was talking to him later in the lobby, and I asked him just on the spur of the moment to sit with me. I don't see the point of your asking.'

'Never mind. It doesn't matter. Now . . . about Charlie West. I can see that of course you would call the rider of the third horse to give evidence. And it is clear from the transcript that you knew what the evidence would be. However, at the preliminary enquiry at Oxford West said nothing at all about Hughes having pulled his horse back. I've consulted all three of the Oxford Stewards this morning. They confirm that West did not suggest it at the time. He asserted it, however, at the Enquiry, and you knew what he was going to say, so . . . er . . . how did you know?'

More silence.

Ferth's voice went on a shade anxiously. 'Norman, if you instructed a Stipendiary Steward to interview

West privately and question him further, for heaven's sake say so. These jockeys stick together. It is perfectly reasonable to believe that West wouldn't speak up against Hughes to begin with, but might do so if pressed with questions. Did you send a Stipendiary?'

Gowery said faintly, 'No.'

'Then how did you know what West was going to say?'

Gowery didn't answer. He said instead, 'I did instruct a Stipendiary to look up all the races in which Cranfield had run two horses and compile me a list of all the occasions when the lesser-backed had won. And as you know, it is the accepted practice to bring up everything in a jockey's past history at an Enquiry. It was a perfectly normal procedure.'

'I'm not saying it wasn't,' Ferth's voice said, puzzled.

Ferth stopped the recorder and raised his eyebrows at me.

'What d'you make of *that*?'

'He's grabbing for a rock in a quicksand.'

He sighed, pressed the starter again and Gowery's voice came back.

'It was all there in black and white . . . It was quite true . . . they'd been doing it again and again.'

'What do you mean, it was quite true? Did someone *tell* you they'd been doing it again and again?'

More silence. Gowery's rock was crumbling.

Again Ferth didn't press him. Instead he said in the same unaccusing way, 'How about David Oakley?'

'Who?'

'David Oakley. The enquiry agent who photographed the money in Hughes' flat. Who suggested that he should go there?'

No answer.

Ferth said with the first faint note of insistence, 'Norman, you really must give some explanation. Can't you see that all this silence just won't do? We *have* to have some answers if we are going to squash Hughes' rumours.'

Gowery reacted with defence in his voice. 'The evidence against Cranfield and Hughes was collected. What does it matter who collected it?'

'It matters because Hughes asserts that much of it was false.'

'No,' he said fiercely. 'It was not false.'

'Norman,' Ferth said, 'is that what you believe . . . or what you *want* to believe?'

'Oh . . .' Gowery's exclamation was more of anguish than surprise. I looked sharply across at Ferth. His dark eyes were steady on my face. His voice went on, softer again. Persuasive.

'Norman, was there any reason why you *wanted* Cranfield and Hughes warned off?'

'No.' Half a shout. Definitely a lie.

'Any reason why you should go so far as to manufacture evidence against them, if none existed?'

'Wykeham!' He was outraged. 'How can you say that! You are suggesting . . . You are suggesting . . . something so dishonourable . . .'

Ferth pressed the stop button. 'Well?' he said challengingly.

'That was genuine,' I said. 'He didn't manufacture it himself. But then I never thought he did. I just wanted to know where he got it from.'

Ferth nodded. Pressed the start again.

His voice. 'My dear Norman, you lay yourself open to such suggestions if you will not say how you came by all the evidence. Do you not see? If you will not explain how you came by it, you cannot be too surprised if you are thought to have procured it yourself.'

'The evidence was genuine!' he asserted. A rearguard action.

'You are still trying to convince yourself that it was.'

'No! It was.'

'Then where did it come from?'

Gowery's back was against the wall. I could see from the remembered emotion twisting Ferth's face that this had been a saddening and perhaps embarrassing moment.

'I was sent,' said Gowery with difficulty, 'a package. It contained . . . various statements . . . and six copies of the photograph taken in Hughes' flat.'

'Who sent it to you?'

Gowery's voice was very low. 'I don't know.'

'You don't know?' Ferth was incredulous. 'You warned two men off on the strength of it, and you don't know where it came from?'

A miserable assenting silence.

'You just accepted all that so-called evidence on its face value?'

'It was all true.' He clung to it.

'Have you still got that package?'

'Yes.'

'I'd like to see it.' A touch of iron in Ferth's voice.

Gowery hadn't argued. There were sounds of moving about, a drawer opening and closing, a rustling of papers.

'I see,' Ferth said slowly. 'These papers do, in fact, look very convincing.'

'Then you see why I acted on them,' Gowery said eagerly, with a little too much relief.

'I can see why you should consider doing so . . . after making a careful check.'

'I did check.'

'To what extent?'

'Well . . . the package only came four days before the Enquiry. On the Thursday before. I had the Secretaries send out the summonses to Newtonnards, Oakley, and West immediately. They were asked to confirm by telegram that they would be attending, and

211

they all did so. Newtonnards was asked to bring his records for the Lemonfizz Cup. And then of course I asked a Stipendiary to ask the Totalizator people if anyone had backed Cherry Pie substantially, and he collected those affidavits ... the ones we produced at the Enquiry. There was absolutely no doubt whatsoever that Cranfield had backed Cherry Pie. He lied about it at the Enquiry. That made it quite conclusive. He was entirely guilty, and there was no reason why I should not warn him off.'

Ferth stopped the recorder. 'What do you say to that?' he asked.

I shrugged. 'Cranfield did back Cherry Pie. He was stupid to deny it, but admitting it was, as he saw it, cutting his own throat. He told me that he backed him – through this unidentified friend – with Newtonnards and on the Tote, and not with his normal bookmaker, because he didn't want Kessel to know, as Kessel and the bookmaker are tattleswapping buddies. He in fact put a hundred pounds on Cherry Pie because he thought the horse might be warming up to give everyone a surprise. He also put two hundred and fifty pounds on Squelch, because reason suggested that *he* would win. And where is the villainy in that?'

Ferth looked at me levelly. 'You didn't know he had backed Cherry Pie, not at the Enquiry.'

'I tackled him with it afterwards. It had struck me by then that that had to be true, however hard he had denied it. Newtonnards might have lied or altered his books, but no one can argue against Tote tickets.'

'That was one of the things which convinced me too,' he admitted.

He started the recorder. He himself was speaking and now there was a distinct flavour in his voice of cross examination. The whole interview moved suddenly into the shape of an Enquiry of its own. 'This photograph . . . didn't it seem at all odd to you?'

'Why should it?' Gowery said sharply.

'Didn't you ask yourself how it came to be taken?'

'No.'

'Hughes says Oakley took the money and the note with him and simply photographed them in his flat.'

'No.'

'How can you be sure?' Ferth pounced on him.

'No!' Gowery said again. There was a rising note in his voice, the sound of pressure approaching blow-up.

'Who sent Oakley to Hughes' flat?'

'I've told you, I don't know.'

'But you're sure that is a genuine photograph?'

'Yes. Yes it is.'

'You are sure beyond doubt?' Ferth insisted.

'Yes!' The voice was high, the anxiety plain, the panic growing. Into this screwed up moment Ferth dropped one intense word, like a bomb.

'*Why?*'

CHAPTER TWELVE

The tape ran on for nearly a minute. When Gowery finally answered his voice was quite different. Low, broken up, distressed to the soul.

'It had . . . to be true. I said at first . . . I couldn't warn them off if they weren't guilty . . . and then the package came . . . and it was such a relief . . . they really were guilty . . . I could warn them off . . . and everything would be all right.'

My mouth opened. Ferth watched me steadily, his eyes narrowed with the pity of it.

Gowery went on compulsively. Once started, he needed to confess.

'If I tell you . . . from the beginning . . . perhaps you will understand. It began the day after I was appointed to substitute for the Disciplinary Steward at the Cranfield-Hughes Enquiry. It's ironic to think of it now, but I was quite pleased to be going to do it . . . and then . . . and then . . .' He paused and took an effortful control of his voice. 'Then, I had a telephone call.' Another pause. 'This man said . . . said . . . I must warn Cranfield off.' He cleared his throat. 'I told him I would do no such thing, unless Cranfield was guilty. Then he said . . . then he said . . . that he knew things about me . . . and he would tell everyone . . . if I didn't warn Cranfield off. I told him I couldn't warn him off if he wasn't guilty . . . and you see I didn't think he *was* guilty. I mean, racehorses are so unpredictable, and I saw the Lemonfizz myself and although after that crowd demonstration it was obvious the Stewards would have Cranfield and Hughes in, I was surprised when they referred it to the Disciplinary Committee . . . I thought that there must have been circumstances that I didn't know of . . . and then I was asked to take the Enquiry . . . and I had an open mind . . . I told the man on the telephone that no threats could move me from giving Cranfield a fair judgement.'

Less jelly in his voice while he remembered that first strength. It didn't last.

'He said . . . in that case . . . I could expect . . . after the Enquiry . . . if Cranfield got off . . . that my life wouldn't be worth living . . . I would have to resign from the Jockey Club . . . and everyone would know . . . And I said again that I would not warn Cranfield off unless I was convinced of his guilt, and that I would not be blackmailed, and I put down the receiver and cut him off.'

'And then,' Ferth suggested, 'you began to worry?'

'Yes.' Little more than a whisper.

'What exactly did he threaten to publish?'

'I can't ... can't tell you. Not criminal ... not a matter for the police ... but ...'

'But enough to ruin you socially?'

'Yes ... I'm afraid so ... yes, completely.'

'But you stuck to your guns?'

'I was desperately worried ... I couldn't ... how could I? ... take away Cranfield's livelihood just to save myself ... It would have been dishonourable ... and I couldn't see myself living with it ... and in any case I couldn't just warn him off, just like that, if there was no proof he was guilty ... So I did worry ... couldn't sleep ... or eat ...'

'Why didn't you ask to be relieved of the Enquiry?'

'Because he told me ... if I backed out ... it would count the same with him as letting Cranfield off ... so I had to go on, just in case some proof turned up.'

'Which it did,' Ferth said drily. 'Conveniently.'

'Oh ...' Again the anguish. 'I didn't realize ... I didn't indeed ... that it might have been the black-mailer who had sent the package. I didn't wonder very much who had sent it. It was release ... that's all I could see ... it was a heaven-sent release from the most unbearable ... I didn't question ... I just believed it ... believed it absolutely ... and I was so grateful ... so grateful ...'

Four days before the Enquiry, that package had

come. He must have been sweating for a whole week, taking a long bleak look at the wilderness. Send a St Bernard to a dying mountaineer and he's unlikely to ask for the dog licence.

'When did you begin to doubt?' Ferth said calmly.

'Not until afterwards. Not for days. It was Hughes . . . at the dance. You told me he was insisting he'd been framed and was going to find out who . . . and then he asked me directly who had sent Oakley to his flat . . . and it . . . Wykeham, it was *terrible*. I realized . . . what I'd done. Inside, I did know . . . but I couldn't admit it to myself . . . I shut it away . . . they *had* to be guilty . . .'

There was another long silence. Then Gowery said, 'You'll see to it . . . that they get their licences back?'

'Yes,' Ferth said.

'I'll resign . . .' He sounded desolate.

'From the Disciplinary Committee, I agree,' Ferth said reasonably. 'As to the rest . . . we will see.'

'Do you think the . . . the blackmailer . . . will tell . . . everyone . . . anyway, when Cranfield has his licence back?'

'He would have nothing to gain.'

'No, but . . .'

'There are laws to protect you.'

'They couldn't.'

'What does he in fact have over you?'

'I . . . I . . . oh, God.' The tape stopped abruptly, cutting off words that were disintegrating into gulps.

Ferth said, 'I switched it off. He was breaking down. One couldn't record that.'

'No.'

'He told me what it was he was being blackmailed about. I think I am prepared to tell you also, although he would hate it if he knew. But you only.'

'Only,' I said. 'I won't repeat it.'

'He told me . . .' His nose wrinkled in distaste. 'He told me that he has . . . he suffers from . . . unacceptable sexual appetites. Not homosexual. Perhaps that would have been better . . . simpler . . . he wouldn't now-adays have been much reviled for that. No. He says he belongs to a sort of club where people like him can gratify themselves fairly harmlessly, as they are all there because they enjoy . . . in varying forms . . . the same thing.' He stopped. He was embarrassed.

'Which is what?' I said matter-of-factly.

He said, as if putting a good yard of clean air between himself and the world, 'Flagellation.'

'That old thing!' I said.

'What?'

'The English disease. Shades of Fanny Hill. Sex tang-led up with self-inflicted pain, like nuns with their little disciplines and sober citizens paying a pound a lash to be whipped.'

'Kelly!'

'You must have read their coy little advertisements? "Correction given". That's what it's all about. More

218

widespread than most people imagine. Starts with husbands spanking their wives regularly before they bed
them, and carries right on up to the parties where they
all dress up in leather and have a right old orgy. I don't
actually understand why anyone should get fixated on
leather or rubber or hair, or on those instead of anything else. Why not coal, for instance . . . or silk? But
they do, apparently.'

'In this case . . . leather.'

'Boots and whips and naked bosoms?'

Ferth shook his head in disbelief. 'You take it so
coolly.'

'Live and let live,' I said. 'If that's what they feel
compelled to do . . . why stop them? As he said, they're
not harming anyone, if they're in a club where everyone
else is the same.'

'But for a Steward,' he protested. 'A member of the
Disciplinary Committee!'

'Gives you pause,' I agreed.

He looked horrified. 'But there would be nothing
sexual in his judgement on racing matters.'

'Of course not. Nothing on earth as unsexual as
racing.'

'But one can see . . . he would be finished in the
racing world, if this got out. Even I . . . I cannot think
of him now without this . . . this perversion . . . coming
into my mind. It would be the same with everyone.
One can't respect him any more. One can't like him.'

219

'Difficult,' I agreed.

'It's . . . horrible.' In his voice, all the revulsion of the normal for the deviation. Most racing men were normal. The deviation would be cast out. Ferth felt it. Gowery knew it. And so did someone else . . .

'Don't they wear masks, at this club?' I asked.

Ferth looked surprised. 'Why, yes, they do. I asked him who could know about him . . . in order to black-mail him . . . and he said he didn't know, they all wore masks. Hoods, actually, was the word he used. Hoods . . . and aprons . . .' He was revolted.

'All leather?'

He nodded. 'How can they?'

'They do less harm than the ones who go out and rape small children.'

'I'm glad I . . . ' he said passionately.

'Me too,' I said. 'But it's just luck.' Gowery had been unlucky, in more ways than one. 'Someone may have seen him going in, or leaving afterwards.'

'That's what he thinks. But he says he doesn't know the real names of any of his fellow members. They all call each other by fanciful made-up names, apparently.'

'There must be a secretary . . . with a list of members?'

Ferth shook his head. 'I asked him that. He said he'd never given his own name to anyone there. It wasn't expected. There's no annual subscription, just ten pounds in cash every time he attends. He says he goes about once a month, on average.'

'How many other members are there?'

'He didn't know the total number. He says there are never fewer than ten, and sometimes thirty or thirty-five. More men than women, usually. The club isn't open every day; only Mondays and Thursdays.'

'Where is it?'

'In London. He wouldn't tell me exactly where.'

'He wants . . . needs . . . to keep on going,' I said.

'You don't think he will!'

'After a while. Yes.'

'Oh no . . .'

'Who introduced him to the club, do you know?'

'He said it couldn't be the person who introduced him to the club. She was a prostitute . . . he'd never told her his real name.'

'But she understood his needs.'

He sighed. 'It would seem so.'

'Some of those girls make more money out of whipping men than sleeping with them.'

'How on earth do you know?'

'I had digs once in the next room to one. She told me.'

'Good Lord.' He looked as if he'd turned over a stone and found creepy-crawlies underneath. He had plainly no inkling of what it was like to *be* a creepy-crawly. His loss.

'Anyway,' he said slowly, 'you will understand why he accepted that package at its face value.'

'And why he chose Lord Plimborne and Andy Tring.'

Lord Ferth nodded. 'At the end, when he'd recovered a little, he understood that he'd chosen them for the reasons you said, but he believed at the time that they were impulsive choices. And he is now, as you would expect, a very worried and troubled man.'

'Was he,' I asked, 'responsible for this?'

I held out to him the letter Tony had received from the Stewards' Secretaries. He stood up, came to take it, and read its brief contents with exasperation.

'I don't know,' he said explosively. 'I really don't know. When did this arrive?'

'Tuesday. Postmarked noon on Monday.'

'Before I saw him . . . He didn't mention it.'

'Could you find out if it was his doing?'

'Do you mean . . . it will be all the more impossible to forgive him?'

'No. Nothing like that. I was just wondering if it was our little framer-blackmailer at work again. See those words "It has been brought to our attention"? . . . What I'd like to know is who brought it.'

'I'll find out,' he agreed positively. 'That shouldn't be difficult. And of course, disregard the letter. There won't be any question now of your having to move.'

'How are you going to work it? Giving our licences back. How are you going to explain it?'

He raised his eyebrows. 'We never have to give reasons for our decisions.'

I smothered a laugh. The system had its uses.

Lord Ferth sat down in the chair again and put the letter in his briefcase. Then he packed up the tape-recorder and tucked that away too. Then with an air of delicately choosing his words he said, 'A scandal of this sort would do racing a great deal of harm.'

'So you want me to take my licence back and shut up?'

'Er . . . yes.'

'And not chase after the blackmailer, in case he blows the gaffe?'

'Exactly.' He was relieved that I understood.

'No.' I said.

'Why not?' Persuasion in his voice.

'Because he tried to kill me.'

'*What?*'

I showed him the chunk of exhaust manifold, and explained. 'Someone at the dance,' I said. 'That means that our blackmailer is one of about six hundred people, and from there it shouldn't be too hard. You can more or less rule out the women, because few of them would drill through cast iron wearing an evening dress. Much too conspicuous, if anyone saw them. That leaves three hundred men.'

'Someone who knew your car,' he said. 'Surely that would narrow it down considerably?'

'It might not. Anyone could have seen me getting out of it at the races. It was a noticeable car, I'm afraid. But I arrived late at the dance. The car was parked right at the back.'

'Have you . . .' he cleared his throat. 'Are the police involved in this?'

'If you mean are they at present investigating an attempted murder, then no, they are not. If you mean, am I going to ask them to investigate, et cetera, then I haven't decided.'

'Once you start the police on something, you can't stop them.'

'On the other hand if I don't start them the blackmailer might have another go at me, with just a fraction of an inch more success. Which would be quite enough.'

'Um.' He thought it over. 'But if you made it clear to everyone now that you are not any longer trying to find out who framed you . . . he might not try again.'

I said curiously, 'Do you really think it would be best for racing if we just leave this blackmailing murderer romping around free?'

'Better than a full-blown scandal.'

The voice of Establishment diplomacy.

'And if he doesn't follow your line of reasoning . . . and he does kill me . . . how would that do for a scandal?'

He didn't answer. Just looked at me levelly with the hot eyes.

'All right, then,' I said. 'No police.'

'Thank you.'

'Us, though. We'll have to do it ourselves. Find him and deal with him.'

'How do you mean?'

'I'll find him. You deal with him.'

'To your satisfaction, I suppose,' he said ironically.

'Absolutely.'

'And Lord Gowery?'

'He's yours entirely. I shan't tell Dexter Cranfield anything at all.'

'Very well.' He stood up, and I struggled off the bed on to the crutches.

'Just one thing,' I said. 'Could you arrange to have that package of Lord Gowery's sent to me here?'

'I have it with me.' Without hesitation he took a large manila envelope out of the briefcase and put it on the bed. 'You'll understand how he fell on it with relief.'

'Things being as they were,' I agreed. He walked across the sitting-room to the way out, stopping by the chest to put on his coat.

'Can Cranfield tell his owners to shovel their horses back?' I said. 'The sooner the better, you see, if they're to come back in time for Cheltenham.'

'Give me until tomorrow morning. There are several other people who must know first.'

'All right.'

He held out his hand. I transferred the right crutch to the left, and shook it.

He said, 'Perhaps one day soon . . . when this is over . . . you will dine with me?'

'I'd like to,' I said.

'Good.' He picked up his bowler and his briefcase, swept a last considering glance round my flat, nodded to me as if finalizing a decision, and quietly went away.

I telephoned to the orthopod who regularly patched me up after falls.

'I want this plaster off.'

He went into a long spiel of which the gist was two or three more weeks.

'Monday,' I said.

'I'll give you up.'

'Tuesday I start getting it off with a chisel.'

I always slept in shirt-and-shorts pyjamas, which had come in very handy in the present circs. Bedtime that day I struggled into a lime-green and white checked lot I had bought in an off moment at Liverpool the year before with my mind more on the imminent Grand National than on what they would do to my yellow complexion at six on a winter's morning.

Tony had gloomily brought me some casseroled beef and had stayed to celebrate when I told him I wouldn't have to leave. I was out of whisky again in consequence.

When he'd gone I went to bed and read the pages which had sent me to limbo. And they were, indeed, convincing. Neatly typed, well set out, written in authoritative language. Not at first, second, or even third sight the product of malevolence. Emotionless. Cool. Damaging.

'Charles Richard West is prepared to testify that during the course of the race, and in particular at a spot six furlongs from the winning post on the second circuit, he heard Hughes say that he (Hughes) was about to ease his horse so that it should be in no subsequent position to win. Hughes' precise words were, "OK. Brakes on chaps".'

The four other sheets were equally brief, equally to the point. One said that through an intermediary Dexter Cranfield had backed Cherry Pie with Newtonnards. The second pointed out that an investigation of the past form would show that on several other occasions Cranfield's second string had beaten his favourite. The third suggested watching the discrepancies in Hughes' riding in the Lemonfizz and in the last race at Reading . . . and there it was in black and white, 'the last race at Reading.' Gowery hadn't questioned it or checked; had simply sent for the last race at Reading. If he had shown it privately to Plimborne and Tring only, and not to me as well, no one might ever have realized it was the wrong race. This deliberate piece of misleading had in fact gone astray, but only just. And the rest hadn't. Page four stated categorically that Cranfield had bribed Hughes not to win, and photographic evidence to prove it was hereby attached.

There was also a short covering note of explanation.

'These few facts have come to my notice. They should clearly be laid before the appropriate authorities, and I am therefore sending them to you, sir, as Steward in command of the forthcoming Enquiry.'

The typewriting itself was unremarkable, the paper medium-quality quarto. The paper clip holding the sheets together was sold by the hundred million, and the buff envelope in which they'd been sent cost a penny or two in any stationer's in the country.

There were two copies only of the photograph. On the back, no identifications.

I slid them all back into the envelope, and put it in the drawer of the table beside my bed. Switched out the light. Lay thinking of riding races again with a swelling feeling of relief and excitement. Wondered how poor old Gowery was making out, going fifteen rounds with his conscience. Thought of Archie and his mortgage ... Kessel having to admit he'd been wrong ... Roberta stepping off her dignity ... the blackmailer biting his nails in apprehension ... sweet dreams every one ... slid into the first easy sleep since the Enquiry.

*

I woke with a jolt, knowing I'd heard a sound which had no business to be there.

A pen-sized flashlight was flickering round the inside of one of the top drawers of the dressing chest. A dark shape blocked off half of its beam as an arm went into the drawer to feel around. Cautious. Very quiet, now.

I lay watching through slit-shut eyes, wondering how close I was this time to the pearly gates. Inconveniently my pulse started bashing against my eardrums as fear stirred up the adrenals, and inside the plaster all the hairs on my leg fought to stand on end.

Trying to keep my breathing even and make no rustle with the sheets I very cautiously slid one arm over the side of the bed and reached down to the floor for a crutch. Any weapon handy was better than none.

No crutches.

I felt around, knowing exactly where I'd laid them beside me, feeling nothing but carpet under my fingers.

The flashlight moved out of the drawer and swung in a small arc while the second top drawer was opened, making the same tiny crack as it loosened which had woken me with the other. The scrap of light shone fractionally on my two crutches propped up against the wall by the door.

I drew the arm very slowly back into bed and lay still. If he'd meant just to kill me, he would have done it by now: and whatever he intended I had little chance of avoiding. The plaster felt like a ton, chaining me immobile.

A clammy crawling feeling all over my skin. Jaw tight, clenched with tension. Dryness in the mouth. Head feeling as if it were swelling. I lay and tried to beat the physical sensations, tried to will them away.

No noticeable success.

He finished with the drawers. The flashlight swung over the khaki chair and steadied on the polished oak chest behind it, against the wall. He moved over there soundlessly and lifted the lid. I almost cried out to him not to, it would wake me. The lid always creaked loudly. I really didn't want him to wake me, it was much too dangerous.

The lid creaked sharply. He stopped dead with it six inches up. Lowered it back into place. It creaked even louder.

He stood there, considering. Then there were quick soft steps on the carpet, a hand fastening in my hair and yanking my head back, and the flashlight beam full in my eyes.

'Right, mate. You're awake. So you'll answer some questions.'

I knew the voice. I shut my eyes against the light and spoke in as bored a drawl as I could manage.

'Mr Oakley, I presume?'

'Clever Mr Hughes.'

He let go of my hair and stripped the bedclothes off

with one flick. The flashlight swung away and fell on top of them. I felt his grip on my neck and the front of my shirt as he wrenched me off the bed and on to the floor. I fell with a crash

'That's for starters,' he said.

CHAPTER THIRTEEN

He was fast, to give him his due. Also strong and ruthless and used to this sort of thing.

'Where is it?' he said.

'What?'

'A chunk of metal with a hole in it.'

'I don't know what you're talking about.'

He swung his arm and hit me with something hard and knobbly. When it followed through to the tiny light I could see what it was. One of my own crutches. Delightful.

I tried to disentangle my legs and roll over and stand up. He shone the light on me to watch. When I was half up he knocked me down again.

'Where is it?'

'I told you . . .'

'We both know, chum, that you have this chunk of metal. I want it. I have a customer for it. And you're going to hand it over like a good little warned-off crook.'

'Go scratch yourself.'

I rolled fast and almost missed the next swipe. It landed on the plaster. Some flakes came off. Less work for Tuesday.

'You haven't a hope,' he said. 'Face facts.'

The facts were that if I yelled for help only the horses would hear.

Pity.

I considered giving him the chunk of metal with the hole in it. Correction, half a hole. He didn't know it was only half a hole. I wondered whether I should tell him. Perhaps he'd be only half as savage.

'Who wants it?' I said.

'Be your age.' He swung the crutch.

Contact.

I cursed.

'Save yourself, chum. Don't be stupid.'

'What is this chunk of metal?'

'Just hand it over.'

'I don't know what you're looking for.'

'Chunk of metal with a hole in it.'

'What chunk of metal?'

'Look, chum, what does it matter what chunk of metal? The one you've got.'

'I haven't.'

'Stop playing games.' He swung the crutch. I grunted. 'Hand it over.'

'I haven't . . . got . . . any chunk of metal.'

233

'Look chum, my instructions are as clear as glass. You've got some lump of metal and I've come to fetch it. Understand? Simple. So save yourself, you stupid crumb.'

'What is he paying for it?'

'You still offering more?'

'Worth a try.'

'So you said before. But nothing doing.'

'Pity.'

'Where's the chunk? . . .'

I didn't answer, heard the crutch coming, rolled at the right instant, and heard it thud on the carpet, roughly where my nose had been.

The little flashlight sought me out. He didn't miss the second time, but it was only my arm, not my face.

'Didn't you ask what it was?' I said.

'None of your bloody business. You just tell me' . . . bash . . . 'where' . . . bash . . . 'it is.'

I'd had about enough. Too much, in fact. And I'd found out all I was likely to, except how far he was prepared to go, which was information I could do without.

I'd been trying to roll towards the door. Finally made it near enough. Stretched backwards over my head and felt my fingers curl round the bottom of the other crutch still propped against the wall.

The rubber knob came into my hand, and with one

scything movement I swept the business end round viciously at knee level.

It caught him square and unexpected on the back of the legs just as he himself was in mid swing, and he overbalanced and crashed down half on top of me. I reached out and caught something, part of his coat, and gripped and pulled, and tried to swing my plaster leg over his body to hold him down.

He wasn't having any. We scrambled around on the floor, him trying to get up and me trying to stop him, both of us scratching and punching and gouging in a thoroughly unsportsmanlike manner. The flashlight had fallen away across the far side of the room and shone only on the wall. Not enough light to be much good. Too much for total evasion of his efficient fists.

The bedside table fell over with a crash and the lamp smashed. Oakley somehow reached into the ruins and picked up a piece of glass, and I just saw the light shimmer on it as he slashed it towards my eyes. I dodged it by a millimetre in the last half-second.

'You bugger,' I said bitterly.

We were both gasping for breath. I loosed the grip I had on his coat in order to have both hands free to deal with the glass, and as soon as he felt me leave go he was heaving himself back on to his feet.

'Now,' he said, panting heavily, 'where bloody is it?'

I didn't answer. He'd got hold of a crutch again. Back to square one. On the thigh, that time.

I was lying on the other crutch. The elbow supports were digging into my back. I twisted my arm underneath me and pulled out the crutch, hand-swung it at him just as he was having a second go. The crutches met and crashed together in the air. I held on to mine for dear life and rolled towards the bed.

'Give ... up ...' he said.

'Get ... stuffed.'

I made it to the bed and lay in the angle between it and the floor. He couldn't get a good swing at me there. I turned the crutch round, and held it by the elbow and hand grips with both of my own. To hit me where I was lying he had to come nearer.

He came. His dark shadow was above me, exaggerated by the dim torchlight. He leant over, swinging. I shoved the stick end of the crutch hard upwards. It went into him solidly and he screeched sharply. The crutch he had been swinging dropped harmlessly on top of me as he reeled away, clutching at his groin.

'I'll ... kill you ... for that ...' His voice was high with pain. He groaned, hugging himself.

'Serves ... you ... right,' I said breathlessly.

I pulled myself across the floor, dragging the plaster, aiming for the telephone which had crashed on to the floor with the little table. Found the receiver. Pulled the cord. The telephone bumped over the carpet into my hand.

Put my finger on the button. Small ting. Dialling tone. Found the numbers. Three . . . nine . . . one . . .

'Yeah?' Tony's voice, thick with sleep.

Dead careless, I was. Didn't hear a thing. The crutch swung wickedly down on the back of my head and I fell over the telephone and never told him to gallop to the rescue.

I woke where Oakley had left me, still lying on the floor over the telephone, the receiver half in and half out of my hand.

It was daylight, just. Grey and raw and raining. I was stiff. Cold. Had a headache.

Remembered bit by bit what had happened. Set about scraping myself off the carpet.

First stop, back on to the bed, accompanied by bed-clothes. Lay there feeling terrible and looking at the mess he had made of my room.

After he'd knocked me out, he had nothing to be quiet about. Everything had been pulled out of the closet and drawers and flung on the floor. Everything smashable was smashed. The sleeves of some of my suits were ripped and lying in tatters. Rosalind's picture had been torn into four pieces and the silver frame twisted and snapped. It had been revenge more than a search. A bad loser, David Oakley.

What I could see of the sitting-room through the

open door seemed to have received the same treatment.

I lay and ached in most places you could think of.

Didn't look to see if Oakley had found the piece of manifold because I knew he wouldn't have. Thought about him coming, and about what he'd said.

Thought about Cranfield.

Thought about Gowery.

Once I got the plaster off and could move about again, it shouldn't take me too long now to dig out the enemy. A bit of leg work. Needed two legs.

Oakley would shortly be reporting no success from the night's work. I wondered if he would be sent to try again. Didn't like that idea particularly.

I shifted on the bed, trying to get comfortable. I'd been concussed twice in five days once before, and got over it. I'd been kicked along the ground by a large field of hurdlers, which had been a lot worse than the crutches. I'd broken enough bones to stock a cemetery and this time they were all whole. But all the same I felt sicker than after racing falls, and in the end realized my unease was revulsion against being hurt by another man. Horses, hard ground, even express trains, were impersonal. Oakley had been a different type of invasion. The amount you were mentally affected by a pain always depended on how you got it.

I felt terrible. Had no energy at all to get up and tidy the mess.

Shut my eyes to blot it out. Blotted myself out, too. Went to sleep.

A voice said above my head, 'Won't you ever learn to keep your door shut?'

I smiled feebly. 'Not if you're coming through it.'

'Finding you flat out is becoming a habit.'

'Try to break it.'

I opened my eyes. Broad daylight. Still raining.

Roberta was standing a foot from the bed wearing a blinding yellow raincoat covered in trickling drops. The copper hair was tied up in a pony tail and she was looking around her with disgust.

'Do you realize it's half past ten?' she said.

'No.'

'Do you always drop your clothes all over the place when you go to bed?'

'Only on Wednesdays.'

'Coffee?' she said abruptly, looking down at me.

'Yes, please.'

She picked her way through the mess to the door, and then across the sitting-room until she was out of sight. I rubbed my hand over my chin. Bristly. And there was a tender lump on the back of my skull and a sore patch all down one side of my jaw, where I hadn't dodged fast enough. Bruises in other places set up a morning chorus. I didn't listen.

She came back minus the raincoat and carrying two steaming mugs which she put carefully on the floor.

Then she picked up the bedside table and transferred the mugs to its top.

The drawer had fallen out of the table, and the envelope had fallen out of the drawer. But Oakley hadn't apparently looked into it: hadn't known it was there to find.

Roberta picked up the scattered crutches and brought them over to the bed.

'Thanks,' I said.

'You take it very calmly.'

'I've seen it before,' I pointed out.

'And you just went to sleep?'

'Opted out,' I agreed.

She looked more closely at my face and rolled my head over on the pillow. I winced. She took her hand away.

'Did you get the same treatment as the flat?'

'More or less.'

'What for?'

'For being stubborn.'

'Do you mean,' she said incredulously, 'that you could have avoided all this . . . and didn't?'

'If there's a good reason for backing down, you back down. If there isn't, you don't.'

'And all this . . . isn't a good enough reason?'

'No.'

'You're crazy,' she said.

'You're so right,' I sighed, pushed myself up a bit, and reached for the coffee.

'Have you called the police?' she asked.

I shook my head. 'Not their quarrel.'

'Who did it, then?'

I smiled at her. 'Your father and I have got our licences back.'

'*What?*'

'It'll be official some time today.'

'Does Father know? How did it happen? Did you do it?'

'No, he doesn't know yet. Ring him up. Tell him to get on to all the owners. It'll be confirmed in the papers soon, either today's evening editions, or tomorrow's dailies.'

She picked the telephone off the floor and sat on the edge of my bed, and telephoned to her father with real joy and sparkling eyes. He wouldn't believe it at first.

'Kelly says it's true,' she said.

He argued again, and she handed the telephone to me.

'You tell him.'

Cranfield said, 'Who told you?'

'Lord Ferth.'

'Did he say why?'

'No,' I lied. 'Just that the sentences had been

reviewed ... and reversed. We're back, as from today. The official notice will be in next week's Calendar.'

'No explanation at all?' he insisted.

'They don't have to give one,' I pointed out.

'All the same ...'

'Who cares why?' I said. 'The fact that we're back ... that's all that matters.'

'Did you find out who framed us?'

'No.'

'Will you go on trying?'

'I might do,' I said. 'We'll see.'

He had lost interest in that. He bounded into a stream of plans for the horses, once they were back. 'And it will give me great pleasure to tell Henry Kessel ...'

'I'd like to see his face,' I agreed. But Pat Nikita would never part with Squelch, nor with Kessel, now. If Cranfield thought Kessel would come crawling apologetically back, he didn't know his man. 'Concentrate on getting Breadwinner back,' I suggested. 'I'll be fit to ride in the Gold Cup.'

'Old Strepson promised Breadwinner would come back at once ... and Pound Postage of his ... that's entered in the National, don't forget.'

'I haven't,' I assured him, 'forgotten.'

He ran down eventually and disconnected, and I could imagine him sitting at the other end still wondering whether to trust me.

Roberta stood up with a spring, as if the news had filled her with energy.

'Shall I tidy up for you?'

'I'd love some help.'

She bent down and picked up Rosalind's torn picture.

'They didn't have to do that,' she said in disgust.

'I'll get the bits stuck together and re-photographed.'

'You'd hate to lose her . . .'

I didn't answer at once. She looked at me curiously, her eyes dark with some unreadable expression.

'I lost her,' I said slowly. 'Rosalind . . . Roberta . . . you are so unalike.'

She turned away abruptly and put the pieces on the chest of drawers where they had always stood.

'Who wants to be a carbon copy?' she said, and her voice was high and cracking. 'Get dressed . . . while I start on the sitting-room.' She disappeared fast and shut the door behind her.

I lay there looking at it.

Roberta Cranfield. I'd never liked her.

Roberta Cranfield. I couldn't bear it . . . I was beginning to love her.

She stayed most of the day, helping me clear up the mess.

Oakley had left little to chance: the bathroom and

kitchen both looked as if they'd been gutted by a whirlwind. He'd searched everywhere a good enquiry agent could think of, including in the lavatory cistern and the refrigerator; and everywhere he'd searched he'd left his trail of damage.

After midday, which was punctuated by some scrambled eggs, the telephone started ringing. Was it true, asked the *Daily Witness* in the shape of Daddy Leeman, that Cranfield and I? . . . 'Check with the Jockey Club,' I said.

The other papers had checked first. 'May we have your comments?' they asked.

'Thrilled to bits,' I said gravely. 'You can quote me.'

A lot of real chums rang to congratulate, and a lot of pseudo chums rang to say they'd never believed me guilty anyway.

For most of the afternoon I lay flat on the sitting-room floor with my head on a cushion talking down the telephone while Roberta stepped around and over me nonchalantly, putting everything back into place.

Finally she dusted her hands off on the seat of her black pants, and said she thought that that would do. The flat looked almost as good as ever. I agreed gratefully that it would do very well.

'Would you consider coming down to my level?' I asked.

She said calmly, 'Are you speaking literally, metaphorically, intellectually, financially, or socially?'

'I was suggesting you might sit on the floor.'

'In that case,' she said collectedly, 'yes.' And she sank gracefully into a cross-legged sprawl.

I couldn't help grinning. She grinned companionably back.

'I was scared stiff of you when I came here last week,' she said.

'You were *what*?'

'You always seemed so aloof. Unapproachable.'

'Are we talking about me ... or you?'

'You, of course,' she said in surprise. 'You always made me nervous. I always get sort of ... strung up ... when I'm nervous. Put on a bit of an act, to hide it, I suppose.'

'I see,' I said slowly.

'You're still a pretty good cactus, if you want to know ... but ... well, you see people differently when they've been bleeding all over your best dress and looking pretty vulnerable ...'

I began to say that in that case I would be prepared to bleed on her any time she liked, but the telephone interrupted me at halfway. And it was old Strepson, settling down for a long cosy chat about Breadwinner and Pound Postage.

Roberta wrinkled her nose and got to her feet.

'Don't go,' I said, with my hand over the mouthpiece.

'Must. I'm late already.'

'Wait.' I said. But she shook her head, fetched the

yellow raincoat from the bath, where she'd put it, and edged herself into it.

''Bye,' she said.

'Wait . . .'

She waved briefly and let herself out of the door. I struggled up on to my feet, and said, 'Sir . . . could you hold on a minute . . .' into the telephone, and hopped without the crutches over to the window. She looked up when I opened it. She was standing in the yard, tying on a headscarf. The rain had eased to drizzle.

'Will you come tomorrow?' I shouted down.

'Can't tomorrow. Got to go to London.'

'Saturday?'

'Do you want me to?'

'Yes.'

'I'll try, then.'

'Please come.'

'Oh . . .' She suddenly smiled in a way I'd never seen before. 'All right.'

Careless I might be about locking my front door, but in truth I left little about worth stealing. Five hundred pounds would never have been lying around on my chest of drawers for enquiry agents to photograph.

When I'd converted the flat from an old hay loft I'd built in more than mod cons. Behind the cabinet in the kitchen which housed things like fly killer and soap powder, and tucked into a crafty piece of brickwork, lay a maximum security safe. It was operated not by keys or combinations, but by electronics. The manufacturers had handed over the safe itself and also the tiny ultrasonic transmitter which sent out the special series of radio waves which alone would release the lock mechanism, and I'd installed them myself: the safe in the wall and the transmitter in a false bottom to the cabinet. Even if anyone found the transmitter, they had still to find the safe and to know the sequence of frequencies which unlocked it.

A right touch of the Open Sesame. I'd always liked gadgets.

Inside the safe there were, besides money and some racing trophies, several pieces of antique silver, three paintings by Houthuesen, two Chelsea figures, a Meissen cup and saucer, a Louis XIV snuff box, and four uncut diamonds totalling twenty-eight carats. My retirement pension, all wrapped in green baize and appreciating nicely. Retirement for a steeplechase jockey could lurk in the very next fall: and the ripe age of forty, if one lasted that long, was about the limit.

There was also a valueless lump of cast iron, with a semi-circular dent in it. To these various treasures I added the envelope which Ferth had given me, because it wouldn't help if I lost that either.

Bolting my front door meant a hazardous trip down the stairs, and another in the morning to open it. I decided it could stay unlocked as usual. Wedged a chair under the door into my sitting-room instead.

During the evening I telephoned to Newtonnards in his pink washed house in Mill Hill.

'Hallo,' he said. 'You've got your licence back then. Talk of the meeting it was at Wincanton today, soon as the Press Association chaps heard about it.'

'Yes, it's great news.'

'What made their lordships change their minds?'

'I've no idea . . . Look, I wondered if you'd seen that man again yet, the one who backed Cherry Pie with you.'

'Funny thing,' he said, 'but I saw him today. Just after I'd heard you were back in favour, though, so I didn't think you'd be interested any more.'

'Did you by any chance find out who he is?'

'I did, as a matter of fact. More to satisfy my own curiosity, really. He's the Honourable Peter Foxcroft. Mean anything to you?'

'He's a brother of Lord Middleburg.'

'Yeah. So I'm told.'

I laughed inwardly. Nothing sinister about Cranfield refusing to name his mysterious pal. Just another bit of ladder climbing. He might be one rung up being in a position to use the Hon. P. Foxcroft as a runner: but he would certainly be five rungs down involving him in a messy Enquiry.

'There's one other thing...' I hesitated. 'Would you ... could you ... do me a considerable favour?'

'Depends what it is.' He sounded cautious but not truculent. A smooth, experienced character.

'I can't offer much in return.'

He chuckled. 'Warning me not to expect tip offs when you're on a hot number?'

'Something like that,' I admitted.

'OK then. You want something for strictly nothing. Just as well to know where we are. So shoot.'

'Can you remember who you told about Cranfield backing Cherry Pie?'

'Before the Enquiry, you mean?'

'Yes. Those bookmaker colleagues you mentioned.'

'Well...' he sounded doubtful.

'If you can,' I said, 'could you ask *them* who *they* told?'

'Phew.' He half breathed, half whistled down the receiver. 'That's some favour.'

'I'm sorry. Just forget it.'

'Hang on, hang on. I didn't say I wouldn't do it. It's a bit of a tall order, though, expecting them to remember.'

'I know. Very long shot. But I still want to know who told the Stewards about the bet with you.'

'You've got your licence back. Why don't you let it rest?'

'Would you?'

He sighed. 'I don't know. All right then, I'll see what I can do. No promises, mind. Oh, and by the way, it can be just as useful to know when one of your mounts is *not* fit or likely to win. If you take my meaning.'

'I take it,' I said smiling. 'It's a deal.'

I put down the receiver reflecting that only a minority of bookmakers were villains, and that most of them were more generous than they got credit for. The whole tribe were reviled for the image of the few. Like students.

CHAPTER FOURTEEN

Oakley didn't come. No one came. I took the chair from under the door knob to let the world in with the morning. Not much of the world accepted the invitation.

Made some coffee. Tony came while I was standing in the kitchen drinking it and put whisky into a mug of it for himself by way of breakfast. He'd been out with one lot of horses at exercise and was waiting to go out with the other, and spent the interval discussing their prospects as if nothing had ever happened. For him the warning off was past history, forgotten. His creed was that of newspapers; today is important, tomorrow more so, but yesterday is nothing.

He finished the coffee and left, clapping me cheerfully on the shoulder and setting up a protest from an Oakley bruise. I spent most of the rest of the day lying flat on my bed, answering the telephone, staring at the ceiling, letting Nature get on with repairing a few ravages, and thinking.

Another quiet night. I had two names in my mind, juggling them. Two to work on. Better than three hundred. But both could be wrong.

Saturday morning the postman brought the letters right upstairs, as he'd been doing since the era of plaster. I thanked him, sorted through them, dropped a crutch, and had the usual awkward fumble picking it up. When I opened one of the letters I dropped both the crutches again in surprise.

Left the crutches on the floor. Leant against the wall and read.

Dear Kelly Hughes,

I have seen in the papers that you have had your licence restored, so perhaps this information will be too late to be of any use to you. I am sending it anyway because the friend who collected it is considerably out of pocket over it, and would be glad if you could reimburse him. I append also his list of expenses.

As you will see he went to a good deal of trouble over this, though to be fair he also told me that he had enjoyed doing it. I hope it is what you wanted.

Sincerely,
Teddy Dewar.
Great Stag Hotel, Birmingham.

Clipped behind the letter were several other sheets of varying sizes. The top one was a schematic presentation of names which looked at first glance like an inverted family tree. There were clumps of three or four names inside two-inch circles. The circles led via arrows to other circles below and sometimes beside them, but the eye was led downwards continually until all the arrows had converged to three circles, and then to two, and finally to one. And the single name in the bottom circle was David Oakley.

Behind the page was an explanatory note.

I knew one contact, the J.L. Jones underlined in the third row of circles. From him I worked in all directions, checking people who knew of David Oakley. Each clump of people heard about him from one of the people in the next clump. Everyone on the page, I guarantee, has heard either directly or indirectly that Oakley is the man to go to if one is in trouble. I posed as a man in trouble, as you suggested, and nearly all that I talked to either mentioned him of their own accord, or agreed when I brought him up as a possibility.

I only hope that one at least of these names has some significance for you, as I'm afraid the expenses were rather high. Most of the investigation was conducted in pubs or hotels, and it was sometimes necessary to get the contact tight before he would divulge.

Faithfully,

B.R.S. Timieson.

The expense list was high enough to make me whistle. I turned back to the circled names, and read them carefully through.

Looking for one of two.

One was there.

Perhaps I should have rejoiced. Perhaps I should have been angry. Instead, I felt sad.

I doubled the expenses and wrote out a cheque with an accompanying note:

'This is really magnificent. Cannot thank you enough. One of the names has great significance, well worth all your perseverance. My eternal thanks.'

I wrote also a grateful letter to Teddy Dewar saying the information couldn't have been better timed, and enclosing the envelope for his friend Timieson.

As I was sticking on the stamp the telephone rang. I hopped over to it and lifted the receiver.

George Newtonnards.

'Spent all last evening on the blower. Astronomical phone bill, I'm going to have.'

'Send me the account,' I said resignedly.

'Better wait to see if I've got results,' he suggested. 'Got a pencil handy?'

'Just a sec.' I fetched a writing pad and ballpoint. 'OK. Go ahead.'

'Right then. First, here are the chaps I told.' He dictated five names. 'The last one, Pelican Jobberson, is the one who holds a fierce grudge against you for that bum steer you gave him, but as it happens he didn't tell the Stewards or anyone else because he went off to Casablanca the next day for a holiday. Well . . . here are the people Harry Ingram told . . .' He read out three names. 'And these are the people Herbie Subbing told . . .' Four names. 'These are the people Dimmie Ovens told . . .' Five names. 'And Clobber Mackintosh, he really spread it around . . .' Eight names. 'That's all they can remember. They wouldn't swear there was no one else. And of course, all those people they've mentioned could have passed the info on to someone else . . . I mean, things like this spread out in ripples.'

'Thanks anyway,' I said sincerely. 'Thank you very much indeed for taking so much trouble.'

'Has it been any help?'

'Oh yes, I think so. I'll let you know, some time.'

'And don't forget. The obvious non-winner . . . give me the wink.'

'I'll do that,' I promised. 'If you'll risk it, after Pelican Jobberson's experience.'

'He's got no sense,' he said. 'But I have.'

255

He rang off, and I studied his list of names. Several were familiar and belonged to well-known racing people: the bookmakers' clients, I supposed. None of the names were the same as those on Timieson's list of Oakley contacts, but there was something . . .

For ten minutes I stood looking at the paper wondering what was hovering around the edge of consciousness, and finally, with a thud, the association clicked.

One of the men Herbie Subbing had told was the brother-in-law of the person I had found among the Oakley contacts.

I thought for a while, and then opened the newspaper and studied the programme for the day's racing, which was at Reading. Then I telephoned to Lord Ferth at his London house, and reached him via a plummy-voiced manservant.

'Well, Kelly? . . .' There was something left of Wednesday's relationship. Not all, but something.

'Sir,' I said, 'are you going to Reading races?'

'Yes, I am.'

'I haven't yet had any official notice of my licence being restored . . . Will it be all right for me to turn up there? I would particularly like to talk to you.'

'I'll make sure you have no difficulty, if it's important.' There was a faint question in his tone, which I answered.

'I know,' I said, 'who engineered things.'

'Ah . . . Yes. Then come. Unless the journey would

be too uncomfortable for you? I could, you know, come on to Corrie after the races. I have no engagements tonight.'

'You're very thoughtful. But I think our engineer will be at the races too ... or at least there's a very good chance of it.'

'As you like,' he agreed. 'I'll look out for you.'

Tony had two runners at the meeting and I could ask him to take me. But there was also Roberta ... she was coming over, probably, and she too might take me. I smiled wryly to myself. She might take me anywhere. Roberta Cranfield. Of all people.

As if by telepathy the telephone rang, and it was Roberta herself on the other end. She sounded breathless and worried.

'Kelly! I can't come just yet. In fact ...' The words came in a rush. 'Can you come over here?'

'What's the matter?'

'Well ... I don't really know if *anything's* the matter ... seriously, that is. But Grace Roxford has turned up here.'

'Dear Grace?'

'Yes ... look, Kelly, she's just sitting in her car outside the house sort of glaring at it. Honestly, she looks a bit mad. We don't know quite what to do. Mother wants to call the police, but, I mean, one *can't* ...

Supposing the poor woman has come to apologize or something, and is just screwing herself up?'

'She's still sitting in the car?'

'Yes. I can see her from here. Can you come? I mean ... Mother's useless and you know how dear Grace feels about *me* ... She looks pretty odd, Kelly.' Definite alarm in her voice.

'Where's your father?'

'Out on the gallops with Breadwinner. He won't be back for about an hour.'

'All right then. I'll get Tony or someone to drive me over. As soon as I can.'

'That's great,' she said with relief. 'I'll try and stall her till you come.'

It would take half an hour to get there. More, probably. By then dear Grace might not still be sitting in her car ...

I dialled three nine one.

'Tony,' I said urgently. 'Can you drop everything instantly and drive me to Cranfield's? Grace Roxford has turned up there and I don't like the sound of it.'

'I've got to go to Reading,' he protested.

'You can go on from Cranfield's when we've sorted Grace out ... and anyway, I want to go to Reading too, to talk to Lord Ferth. So be a pal, Tony. Please.'

'Oh all right. If you want it that much. Give me five minutes.'

He took ten. I spent some of them telephoning to

Jack Roxford. He was surprised I should be calling him.

'Look, Jack,' I said, 'I'm sorry to be upsetting you like this, but have you any idea where your wife has gone?'

'Grace?' More surprise, but also anxiety. 'Down to the village, she said.'

The village in question was roughly forty miles from Cranfield's house.

'She must have gone some time ago,' I said.

'I suppose so ... what's all this about?' The worry was sharp in his voice.

'Roberta Cranfield has just telephoned to say that your wife is outside their house, just sitting in her car.'

'Oh God,' he said. 'She can't be.'

'I'm afraid she is.'

'Oh *no* ...' he wailed. 'She seemed better this morning ... quite her old self ... it seemed safe to let her go and do the shopping ... she's been so upset, you see ... and then you and Dexter got your licences back ... it's affected her ... it's all been so awful for her.'

'I'm just going over there to see if I can help,' I said. 'But ... can you come down and collect her?'

'Oh *yes*,' he said. 'I'll start at once. Oh poor dear Grace ... Take care of her, till I come.'

'Yes,' I said reassuringly, and disconnected.

I made it without mishap down the stairs and found

259

Tony had commandeered Poppy's estate car for the journey. The back seat lay flat so that I could lie instead of sit, and there were even cushions for my shoulders and head.

'Poppy's idea,' Tony said briefly, helping me climb in through the rear door. 'Great girl.'

'She sure is,' I said gratefully, hauling in the crutches behind me. 'Lose no time, now, friend.'

'You sound worried.' He shut the doors, switched on and drove away with minimum waste of time.

'I am, rather. Grace Roxford is unbalanced.'

'But surely not dangerous?'

'I hope not.'

I must have sounded doubtful because Tony's foot went heavily down on the accelerator. 'Hold on to something,' he said. We rocked round corners. I couldn't find any good anchorage: had to wedge my useful foot against the rear door and push myself off the swaying walls with my hands.

'OK?' he shouted.

'Uh . . . yes,' I said breathlessly.

'Good bit of road just coming up.' We left all the other traffic at a standstill. 'Tell me if you see any cops.'

We saw no cops. Tony covered the eighteen miles through Berkshire in twenty-three minutes. We jerked to a stop outside Cranfield's house, and the first thing I saw was that there was no one in the small grey Volkswagen standing near the front door.

Tony opened the back of the car with a crash and unceremoniously tugged me out.

'She's probably sitting down cosily having a quiet cup of tea,' he said.

She wasn't.

Tony rang the front-door bell and after a lengthy interval Mrs Cranfield herself opened it.

Not her usual swift wide-opening fling. She looked at us through a nervous six inches.

'Hughes. What are you doing here? Go away.'

'Roberta asked me to come. To see Grace Roxford.'

'Mrs Roxford is no longer here.' Mrs Cranfield's voice was as strung up as her behaviour.

'Isn't that her car?' I pointed to the Volkswagen.

'No,' she said sharply.

'Whose is it, then?'

'The gardener's. Now Hughes, go away at once. Go away.'

'Very well,' I said, shrugging. And she instantly shut the door.

'Help me back into the car,' I said to Tony.

'Surely you're not just *going*?'

'Don't argue,' I said. 'Get me into the car, drive away out through the gates, then go round and come back in through the stable entrance.'

'That's better.' He shuffled me in, threw in the crutches, slammed the door and hustled round to the driving seat.

'Don't rush so,' I said. 'Scratch your head a bit. Look disgusted.'

'You think she's watching?' He didn't start the car: looked at me over his shoulder.

'I think Mrs Cranfield would never this side of doomsday allow her gardener to park outside her front door. Mrs Cranfield was doing her best to ask for help.'

'Which means,' he added slowly, 'that Grace Roxford is very dangerous indeed.'

I nodded with a dry mouth. 'Drive away, now.'

He went slowly. Rolled round into the back drive, accelerated along that, and stopped with a jerk beside the stables. Yet again he helped me out.

'There's a telephone in the small office in the yard,' I said. 'Next to the tackroom. Look up in the classified directory and find a local doctor. Tell him to come smartish. Then wait here until Dexter Cranfield comes back with the horses, and stop him going into the house.'

'Kelly, couldn't you be exaggerating? . . .'

'I'll never be able to stop Cranfield.'

'Tell him no one ever believes anything tragic will happen until it has.'

He looked at me for two seconds, then wheeled away into the yard.

I peg-legged up the back drive and tried the back door. Open. It would be. For Cranfield to walk easily through it. And to what?

I went silently along into the main hall, and listened. There was no sound in the house.

Tried the library first, juggling the crutches to get a good grip on the door handle, sweating lest I should drop one with a crash. Turned the handle, pressed the door quietly inwards.

The library was uninhabited. A large clock on the mantel ticked loudly. Out of time with my heart.

I left the door open. Went slowly, silently towards the small sitting-room beside the front door. Again the meticulously careful drill with the handle. If they'd seen me come, they would most probably be in this room.

The door swung inwards. Well oiled. No creaks. I saw the worn chintz covers on the armchairs, the elderly rugs, the debris of living, scattered newspapers, a pair of spectacles on some letters, a headscarf and a flower basket. No people.

On the other side of the hall there were the double doors into the large formal drawing-room, and at the back, beyond the staircase, the doors to the dining-room and to Dexter Cranfield's own study, where he kept his racing books and did all his paper work.

I swung across to the study, and opened the door. It was quiet in there. Dust slowly gravitated. Nothing else moved.

That left only the two large rooms downstairs, and the whole of upstairs. I looked at the long broad flight uneasily. Wished it were an escalator.

The dining-room was empty. I shifted back through the hall to the double doors of the drawing-room. Went through the crutch routine with more difficulty, because if I were going in there I would need both doors open, and to open both doors took both hands. I managed it in the end by hooking both crutches over my left arm like walking sticks, and standing on one leg.

The doors parted and I pushed them wide. The quarter-acre of drawing-room contained chairs of gold brocade upholstery, a pale cream Chinese carpet and long soft blue curtains. A delicate, elegant, class-conscious room designed for Cranfield's glossiest aspirations.

Everything in there was motionless. A tableau.

I hitched the crutches into place, and walked forwards. Stopped after a very few paces. Stopped because I had to.

Mrs Cranfield was there. And Roberta. And Grace Roxford. Mrs Cranfield was standing by the fireplace, hanging on to the shoulder-high mantel as if needing support. Roberta sat upright in an armless wooden chair set out of its usual place in a large clear area of carpet. Behind her and slightly to one side, and with one hand firmly grasping Roberta's shoulder, stood Grace Roxford.

Grace Roxford held the sort of knife used by fishmongers. Nearly a foot long, razor sharp, with a point like a needle. She was resting the lethal end of it against Roberta's neck.

'Kelly!' Roberta said. Her voice was high and a trifle wavery, but the relief in it was overwhelming. I feared it might be misplaced.

Grace Roxford had a bright colour over her taut cheekbones and a piercing glitter in her eyes. Her body was rigid with tension. The hand holding the knife trembled in uneven spasms. She was as unstable as wet gelignite; but she still knew what she was doing.

'You went away, Kelly Hughes,' she said. 'You went away.'

'Yes, Grace,' I agreed. 'But I came back to talk to Roberta.'

'You come another step,' she said, 'and I'll cut her throat.'

Mrs Cranfield drew a breath like a sob, but Roberta's expression didn't change. Grace had made that threat already. Several times, probably. Especially when Tony and I had arrived at the front door.

She was desperately determined. Neither I nor the Cranfields had room to doubt that she wouldn't do as she said. And I was twenty feet away from her and a cripple besides.

'What do you want, Grace?' I said, as calmly as possible.

'Want? Want?' Her eyes flickered. She seemed to be trying to remember what she wanted. Then her rage sharpened on me like twin darts, and her purpose came flooding back.

'Dexter Cranfield ... bloody snob ... I'll see he doesn't get those horses ... I'm going to kill him, see, kill him ... then he can't get them, can he? No ... he can't.'

Again there was no surprise either in Roberta or her mother. Grace had told them already what she'd come for.

'Grace, killing Mr Cranfield won't help your husband.'

'Yes. Yes. Yes. Yes.' She nodded sharply between each yes, and the knife jumped against Roberta's neck. Roberta shut her eyes for a while and swayed on the chair.

I said, 'How do you hope to kill him, Grace?'

She laughed. It got out of control at halfway and ended in a maniacal high-pitched giggle. 'He'll come here, won't he? He'll come here and stand beside me, because he'll do just what I say, won't he? Won't he?'

I looked at the steel blade beside Roberta's pearly skin and knew that he would indeed do as she said. As I would.

'And then, see,' she said, 'I'll just stick the knife into *him*, not into her. See? See?'

'I see,' I said.

She nodded extravagantly and her hand shook.

'And then what?' I asked.

'Then what?' She looked puzzled. She hadn't got any further than killing Cranfield. Beyond that lay only darkness and confusion. Her vision didn't extend to consequences.

'Edwin Byler could send his horses away to someone else,' I said.

'No. No. Only Dexter Cranfield. Only him. Telling him he ought to have a more snobbish trainer. Taking him away from us, I'm going to kill him. Then he can't have those horses.' The words tumbled out in a vehement monotone, all the more frightening for being clearly automatic. These were thoughts she'd had in her head for a very long time.

'It would have been all right, of course,' I said slowly. 'If Mr Cranfield hadn't got his licence back.'

'Yes!' It was a bitterly angry shriek.

'I got it back for him,' I said.

'They just gave it back. They just gave it back. They shouldn't have done that. They shouldn't.'

'They didn't just give it back,' I said. 'They gave it back because I made them.'

'You couldn't . . .'

'I told everyone I was going to. And I did.'

'No. No. No.'

'Yes,' I said flatly.

Her expression slowly changed, and highly frightening it was too. I waited while it sank into her disorganized brain that if Byler sent his horses to Cranfield after all it was me alone she had to thank for it. I watched the intention to kill widen to embrace me too.

The semi-cautious restraint in her manner towards me was transforming itself into a vicious glare of hate.

I swallowed. I said again, 'If I hadn't made the Stewards give Mr Cranfield's licence back, he would still be warned off.'

Roberta said in horror, 'No, Kelly. Don't. Don't do it.'

'Shut up,' I said. 'Me or your father ... which has more chance? And run, when you can.'

Grace wasn't listening. Grace was grasping the essentials and deciding on a course of action.

There was a lot of white showing round her eyes.

'I'll kill you,' she said. 'I'll kill you.'

I stood still. I waited. The seconds stretched like centuries.

'Come here,' she said. 'Come here, or I'll cut her throat.'

CHAPTER FIFTEEN

I took myself crutch by crutch towards her. When I was halfway there Mrs Cranfield gave a moaning sigh and fainted, falling awkwardly on the rug and scattering the brass fire irons with a nerve-shattering crash.

Grace jumped. The knife snicked into Roberta's skin and she cried out. I stood half unbalanced, freezing into immobility, trying to will Grace not to disintegrate into panic, not to go over the edge, not to lose the last tiny grip she had on her reason. She wasn't far off stabbing everything in sight.

'Sit still,' I said to Roberta with dreadful urgency and she gave me a terrified look and did her best not to move. She was trembling violently. I had never thought I could pray. I prayed.

Grace was moving her head in sharp birdlike jerks. The knife was still against Roberta's neck. Grace's other hand still grasped Roberta's shoulder. A thread of blood trickled down Roberta's skin and was blotted up in a scarlet patch by her white jersey.

No one went to help Roberta's mother. I didn't even dare to look at her, because it meant turning my eyes away from Grace.

'Come here,' Grace said. 'Come here.'

Her voice was husky, little more than a loud whisper. And although she was watching me come with unswerving murder in her eyes, I was inexpressibly thankful that she could still speak at all, still think, still hold a purpose.

During the last few steps I wondered how I was going to dodge, since I couldn't jump, couldn't bend my knees, and hadn't even my hands free. A bit late to start worrying. I took the last step short so that she would have to move to reach me and at the same time eased my elbow out of the right-hand crutch.

She was almost too fast. She struck at me instantly, in a flashing thrust directed at my throat, and although I managed to twist the two inches needed to avoid it, the hissing knife came close enough, through the collar of my coat. I brought my right arm up and across, crashing crutch against her as she prepared to try again.

Out of the corner of my eye I saw Roberta wrench herself out of Grace's clutching grasp, and half stumble, half fall as she got away from the chair.

'Kill you,' Grace said. The words were distorted. The meaning clear. She had no thought of self-defence. No thought at all, as far as I could see. Just one single burning obsessive intention.

I brought up the left-hand crutch like a pole to push her away. She dived round it and tried to plunge her knife through my ribs, and in throwing myself away from that I over-balanced and half fell down, and she was standing over me with her arm raised like a priest at a human sacrifice.

I dropped one crutch altogether. Useless warding off a knife with a bare hand. I tried to shove the other crutch round into her face, but got it tangled up against an armchair.

Grace brought her arm down. I fell right to the floor as soon as I saw her move and the knife followed me harmlessly, all the impetus gone by the time it reached me. Another tear in my coat.

She came down on her knees beside me, her arm going up again.

From nowhere my lost crutch whistled through the air and smashed into the hand which held the knife. Grace hissed like a snake and dropped it, and it fell point down into my plaster. She twisted round to see who had hit her and spread out her hands towards the crutch that Roberta was aiming at her again.

She caught hold of it and tugged. I wriggled round on the floor, stretched until I had my fingers round the handle of the knife, and threw it as hard as I could towards the open door into the hall.

Grace was too much for Roberta. Too much for me. She was appallingly, insanely, strong. I heaved myself

271

up on to my left knee and clasped my arms tight round her chest from behind, trying to pin her arms down to her sides. She shook me around like a sack of feathers, struggling to get to her feet.

She managed it, lifting me with her, plaster and all. She knew where I'd thrown the knife. She started to go that way, dragging me with her still fastened to her back like a leech.

'Get that knife and run to the stables,' I gasped to Roberta. A girl in a million. She simply ran and picked up the knife and went on running, out into the hall and out of the house.

Grace started yelling unintelligibly and began trying to unclamp the fingers I had laced together over her thin breastbone. I hung on for everyone's dear life, and when she couldn't dislodge them she began pinching wherever she could reach with fierce hurting spite.

The hair which she usually wore screwed into a fold up the back of her neck had come undone and was falling into my face. I could see less and less of what was going on. I knew only that she was still headed towards the doorway, still unimaginably violent, and mumbling now in a continuous flow of senseless words interspersed with sudden shrieks.

She reached the doorway and started trying to get free of me by crashing me against the jamb. She had a hard job of it, but she managed it in the end, and when she felt my weight fall off her she turned in a flash, sticking out her hands with rigid fingers towards my neck.

Her face was a dark congested crimson. Her eyes were stretched wide in a stark screaming stare. Her lips were drawn back in a tight line from her teeth.

I had never in all my life seen anything so terrifying. Hadn't imagined a human could look like that, had never visualized homicidal madness.

She would certainly have killed me if it hadn't been for Tony, because her strength made a joke of mine. He came tearing into the hall from the kitchen and brought her down with a rugger tackle about the knees, and I fell too, on top of her, because she was trying to tear my throat out in handfuls, and she didn't leave go.

It took all Tony could do, all Archie could do, all three other lads could do to unlatch her from me and hold her down on the floor. They sat on her arms and legs and chest and head, and she threshed about convulsively underneath them.

Roberta had tears streaming down her face and I hadn't any breath left to tell her to cheer up, there was no more danger, no more . . . no more . . . I leant weakly against the wall and thought it would be too damned silly to pass out now. Took three deep breaths instead. Everything steadied again, reluctantly.

Tony said, 'There's a doctor on his way. Don't think he's expecting this, though.'

'He'll know what to do.'

'Mother!' exclaimed Roberta suddenly. 'I'd forgotten about her.' She hurried past me into the drawing-room and I heard her mother's voice rising in a disturbed, disorientated question.

Grace was crying out, but her voice sounded like seagulls and nothing she said made sense. One of the lads said sympathetically. 'Poor thing, oughtn't we to let her get up?' and Tony answered fiercely, 'Only under a tiger net.'

'She doesn't know what's happening,' I said wearily. 'She can't control what she does. So don't for God's sake let go of her.'

Except for Tony's resolute six foot they all sat on her gingerly and twice she nearly had them off. Finally and at long last the front door bell rang, and I hopped across the hall to answer it.

It was the local doctor, looking tentative, wondering no doubt if it were a hoax. But he took one look at Grace and was opening his case while he came across the hall. Into her arm he pushed a hypodermic needle and soon the convulsive threshing slackened, and the high-pitched crying dulled to murmurs and in the end to silence.

The five men slowly stood up and stepped away from her, and she lay there looking shrunk and crumpled, her greying hair falling in streaks away from her flaccidly relaxing face. It seemed incredible that such thin limbs, such a meagre body, could have put out such strength.

We all stood looking down at her with more awe than pity, watching while the last twitches shook her and she sank into unconscious peace.

Half an hour later Grace still lay on the floor in the hall, but with a pillow under her head and a rug keeping her warm.

Dexter Cranfield had come back from watching the horses work and walked unprepared into the aftermath of drama. His wife's semi-hysterical explanations hadn't helped him much.

Roberta told him that Grace had come to kill him because he had his licence back and that she was the cause of his losing it in the first place, and he stamped around in a fury which I gathered was mostly because the source of our troubles was a woman. He basically didn't like women. She should have been locked up years ago, he said. Spiteful, petty minded, scheming, interfering . . . just like a woman, he said. I listened to him gravely and concluded he had suffered from a bossy nanny.

The doctor had done some intensive telephoning, and presently an ambulance arrived with two com-passionate-looking men and a good deal of special equipment. The front door stood wide open and the prospect of Grace's imminent departure was a relief to everyone.

Into this active bustling scene drove Jack Roxford.

He scrambled out of his car, took a horrified look at the ambulance, and ploughed in through the front door. When he saw Grace lying there with the ambulance men preparing to lift her on to a stretcher, he went down on his knees beside her.

'Grace dear . . .' He looked at her more closely. She was still unconscious, very pale now, looking wizened and sixty. 'Grace dear!' There was anguish in his voice. 'What's the matter with her?'

The doctor started to break it to him. Cranfield interrupted the gentle words and said brutally. 'She's raving mad. She came here trying to kill me and she could have killed my wife and daughter. It's absolutely disgraceful that she should have been running around free in that state. I'm going to see my solicitors about it.'

Jack Roxford only heard the first part. His eyes went to the cut on Roberta's neck and the blood-stain on her jersey, and he put his hand over his mouth and looked sick.

'Grace,' he said. 'Oh, Grace . . .'

There was no doubt he loved her. He leant over her, stroking the hair away from her forehead, murmuring to her, and when he finally looked up there were tears in his eyes and on his cheeks.

'She'll be all right, won't she?'

The doctor shifted uncomfortably and said one

would have to see, only time would tell, there were marvellous treatments nowadays . . .

The ambulance men loaded her gently on to the stretcher and picked it up.

'Let me go with her,' Jack Roxford said. 'Where are you taking her? Let me go with her.'

One of the ambulance men told him the name of the hospital and advised him not to come.

'Better try this evening, sir. No use you waiting all day, now, is it?' And the doctor added that Grace would be unconscious for some time yet and under heavy sedation after that, and it was true, it would be better if Roxford didn't go with her.

The uniformed men carried Grace out into the sunshine and loaded her into the ambulance, and we all followed them out into the drive. Jack Roxford stood there looking utterly forlorn as they shut the doors, consulted finally with the doctor, and with the minimum of fuss, drove away.

Roberta touched his arm. 'Can't I get you a drink, Mr Roxford?'

He looked at her vaguely, and then his whole face crumpled and he couldn't speak.

'Don't, Mr Roxford,' Roberta said with pity. 'She isn't in any pain, or anything.'

He shook his head. Roberta put her arm across his shoulders and steered him back into the house.

'Now what?' Tony said. 'I've really got to get to

Reading, pal. Those runners of mine have to be declared for the second race.'

I looked at my watch. 'You could spare another quarter of an hour. I think we should take Jack Roxford with us. He's got a runner too, incidentally, though I imagine he doesn't much care about that ... Except that it's one of Edwin Byler's. But he's not fit to drive anywhere himself, and the races would help to keep him from brooding too much about Grace.'

'Yeah. A possible idea,' Tony grinned.

'Go into the house and see if you can persuade him to let you take him.'

'OK.' He went off amiably, and I passed the time swinging around the drive on my crutches and peering into the cars parked there. I'd be needing a new one ... probably choose the same again, though.

I leant against Tony's car and thought about Grace. She'd left on me a fair legacy of bruises from her pinches to add to the crop grown by Oakley. Also my coat would cost a fortune at the invisible menders, and my throat felt like a well-developed case of septic tonsils. I looked gloomily down at my plastered leg. The dangers of detection seemed to be twice as high as steeplechasing. With luck, I thought with a sigh, I could now go back to the usual but less frequent form of battery.

Tony came out of the house with Roberta and Jack Roxford. Jack looked dazed, and let Tony help him into the front of the estate car as if his thoughts were miles away. As indeed they probably were.

I scrunched across the gravel towards Roberta.

'Is your neck all right?' I asked.

'Is yours?'

I investigated her cut more closely. It wasn't deep. Little more than an inch long.

'There won't be much of a scar,' I said.

'No,' she agreed.

Her face was close to mine. Her eyes were amber with dark flecks.

'Stay here,' she said abruptly. 'You don't have to go to the races.'

'I've an appointment with Lord Ferth . . . Best to get this business thoroughly wrapped up.'

'I suppose so.' She looked suddenly very tired. She'd had a wearing Saturday morning.

'If you've nothing better to do,' I suggested, 'would you come over tomorrow . . . and cook me some lunch?'

A small smile tugged at her mouth and wrinkled her eyes.

'I fell hopelessly in love with you,' she said, 'when I was twelve.'

'And then it wore off?'

'Yes.'

'Pity,' I said.

Her smile broadened.

'Who is Bobbie?' I asked.

'Bobbie? Oh . . . he's Lord Iceland's son.'

'He would be.'

She laughed. 'Father wants me to marry him.'

'That figures.'

'But Father is going to be disappointed.'

'Good,' I said.

'Kelly,' yelled Tony. 'Come on, for Hell's sakes, or I'll be late.'

'Goodbye,' she said calmly. 'See you tomorrow.'

Tony drove to Reading races with due care and attention and Jack Roxford sat sunk in gloomy silence from start to finish. When we stopped in the car park he stepped out of the car and walked dazedly away towards the entrance without a word of thanks or explanation.

Tony watched him go and clicked his tongue. 'That woman isn't worth it.'

'She is, to him,' I said.

Tony hurried off to declare his horses, and I went more slowly through the gate looking out for Lord Ferth.

It felt extraordinary being back on a racecourse. Like being let out of prison. The same people who had looked sideways at me at the Jockey's Fund dance now slapped me familiarly on the back and said they were delighted to see me. Oh yeah, I thought ungratefully. Never kick a man once he's up.

Lord Ferth was standing outside the weighing-room in a knot of people from which he detached himself when he saw me coming.

'Come along to the Steward's dining-room,' he said. 'We can find a quiet corner there.'

'Can we postpone it until after the third race?' I asked. 'I want my cousin Tony to be there as well, and he has some runners . . .'

'Of course,' he agreed. 'Later would be best for me too, as it happens. After the third, then.'

I watched the first three races with the hunger of an exile returned. Tony's horse, my sometime mount, finished a fast fourth, which augured well for next time out, and Byler's horse won the third. As I hurried round to see how Jack Roxford would make out in the winner's enclosure I almost crashed into Kessel. He looked me over, took in the plaster and crutches, and said nothing at all. I watched his cold expressionless face with one to match. After ramming home the point that he had no intention of apologizing he turned brusquely on his heel and walked away.

'Get that,' Tony said in my ear. 'You could sue him for defamation.'

'He's not worth the effort.'

From Charlie West, too, I'd had much the same reaction. Defiance, slightly sullen variety. I shrugged resignedly. That was my own fault, and only time would tell.

Tony walked with me to the winner's enclosure. Byler was there, beaming. Jack Roxford still looked lost. We watched Byler suggest a celebration drink, and Jack shake his head vaguely as if he hadn't understood.

'Go and fish Jack out,' I said to Tony. 'Tell him you're still looking after him.'

'If you say so, pal.' He obligingly edged through the crowd, took Jack by the elbow, said a few explanatory words to Byler, and steered Jack out.

I joined them and said neutrally, 'This way,' and led them along towards the Stewards' dining-room. They both went through the door, taking off their hats and hanging them on the pegs inside.

The long tables in the Stewards' dining-room had been cleared from lunch and laid for tea, but there was no one in there except Lord Ferth. He shook hands with Tony and Jack and invited them to sit down around one end of a table.

'Kelly? . . .' he suggested.

'I'll stand,' I said. 'Easier.'

'Well now,' Ferth said, glancing curiously at Tony and Jack, 'you told me, Kelly, that you knew who had framed you and Dexter Cranfield.'

I nodded.

Tony said regretfully, 'Grace Roxford. Jack's wife.'

Jack looked vaguely down at the tablecloth and said nothing at all.

Tony explained to Lord Ferth just what had happened at Cranfield's and he looked more and more upset.

'My dear Roxford,' he said uncomfortably, 'I'm so sorry. So very sorry.' He looked up at me. 'One could never have imagined that she ... that Grace Roxford of all people ... could have framed you.'

'That's right,' I said mildly. 'She didn't.'

CHAPTER SIXTEEN

Both Tony and Jack sat up as if electrified.

Lord Ferth said, 'But you said...' And Tony answered, 'I thought there was no doubt... She tried to kill Kelly... she was going to kill Cranfield too.'

'She tried to kill me this time,' I agreed. 'But not the time before. It wasn't she who fiddled with my car.'

'Then *who*?' Lord Ferth demanded.

'Her husband.'

Jack stood up. He looked a lot less lost.

I poked Tony on the shoulder with my crutch, and he took the hint and stood up too. He was sitting between Jack and the door.

'Sit down, Mr Roxford,' Ferth said authoritatively, and after a pause, slowly, he obeyed.

'That's nonsense,' he said protestingly. 'I didn't touch Kelly's car. No one could have arranged that accident.'

'You couldn't have imagined I would be hit by a train,' I agreed. 'But some sort of smash, yes, definitely.'

'But Grace...' began Tony, still bewildered.

'Grace,' I said prosaically, 'has in most respects displayed exactly opposite qualities to the person who engineered Cranfield's and my suspension. Grace has been wild, accusing, uncontrolled, and emotional. The planning which went into getting us warned off was cool, careful, efficient, and brutal.'

'Mad people are very cunning,' Tony said doubtfully.

'It wasn't Grace,' I said positively. 'It was Jack.'

There was a pause. Then Jack said in a rising wail, 'Why ever did she have to go to Cranfield's this morning? Why ever couldn't she leave things alone?'

'It wouldn't have done any good,' I said, 'I already knew it was you.'

'That's impossible.'

Ferth cleared his throat. 'I think ... er ... you'd better tell us, Kelly, what your grounds are for making this very serious accusation.'

'It began,' I said, 'when Dexter Cranfield persuaded Edwin Byler to take his horses away from Roxford and send them to him. Cranfield did no doubt persuade Byler, as Grace maintained, that he was a more highly regarded trainer socially than Roxford. Social standing means a great deal to Mr Cranfield, and he is apt to expect that it does to everyone else. And in Edwin Byler's case, he was very likely right. But Jack had trained Byler's horses from the day he bought his first, and as Byler's fortune and string grew, so did Jack's prosperity and prestige. To lose Byler was to him a

total disaster. A return to obscurity. The end of everything. Jack isn't a bad trainer, but he hasn't the person-
ality to make the top ranks. Not without an accident . . .
a gift from Heaven . . . like Byler. And you don't find
two Bylers in your yard in one lifetime. So almost
from the start I wondered about Jack; from as soon as
Cranfield told me, two days after the Enquiry, that
Byler had been going to transfer his horses. Because I
felt such a wrench of regret, you see, that I was not
going to ride them . . . and I realized that that was
nothing compared to what Jack would have felt if he'd
lost them.'

'I didn't feel so bad as that,' said Jack dully.

'I had an open mind,' I said, 'because Pat Nikita had
much the same motive, only the other way round. He
and Cranfield detest each other. He had been trying to
coax Kessel away from Cranfield for years, and getting
Cranfield warned off was one way of clinching things.
Then there were various people with smaller motives,
like Charlie West, who might have hoped to ride
Squelch for Nikita if I were out of the way. And there
was a big possibility that it was someone else altogether,
someone I hadn't come across, whose motive I couldn't
even suspect.'

'So why must it be Mr Roxford?' Ferth said.

I took the paper Teddy Dewar had sent me out of
my pocket and handed it to him, explaining what it
meant.

'That shows a direct link between Oakley and the people in the circles. One of those people is Jack Roxford. He did, you see, know of Oakley's existence. He knew Oakley would agree to provide faked evidence.'

'But . . .' Lord Ferth began.

'Yes, I know,' I said. 'Circumstantial. Then there's this list of people from George Newtonnards.' I gave him the list, and pointed. 'These are the people who definitely knew that Cranfield had backed Cherry Pie with Newtonnards. Again this is not conclusive, because other people might have known, who are not on this list. But that man,' I pointed to the name in Herbie Subbings' list of contacts, 'that man is Grace Roxford's brother. Jack's brother-in-law.'

Ferth looked at me levelly. 'You've taken a lot of trouble.'

'It was taken for me,' I said, 'by Teddy Dewar and his friend, and by George Newtonnards.'

'They acted on your suggestions, though.'

'Yes.'

'Anything else?'

'Well.' I said. 'There are those neatly typed sheets of accusations which were sent to Lord Gowery. So untypical, by the way, of Grace. We could compare the typewriter with Jack's . . . Typewriters are about as distinctive as finger prints. I haven't had an opportunity to do that yet.'

Jack looked up wildly. The typewriter made sense to him. He hadn't followed the significance of the lists.

Ferth said slowly, 'I obtained from the Stewards' Secretaries the letter which pointed out to them that a disqualified person was living in a racing stable. As far as I remember, the typing is the same as in the original accusations.'

'Very catty, that,' I said. 'More like Grace. Revengeful, and without much point.'

'I never wrote to the Stewards' Secretaries,' Jack said.

'Did Grace?'

He shook his head. I thought perhaps he didn't know. It didn't seem to be of any great importance. I said instead: 'I looked inside the boot of Jack's car this morning, while he was in Mr Cranfield's house. He carries a great big tool kit, including a hand drill.'

'No,' Jack said.

'Yes, indeed. Also you have an old grey Volkswagen, the one Grace drove today. That car was seen by the mechanic from my garage when you went to pick over the remains of my car. I imagine you were hoping to remove any tell-tale drill holes which might have led the insurance company to suspect attempted murder, but Derek was there before you. And you either followed him or asked the garage whether he'd taken anything from the wreckage, because you sent David Oakley to my flat to get it back. Oakley didn't know the significance of what he was looking for. A chunk of metal with a hole in it. That was all he knew. He was there to earn a fee.'

'Did he find it?' Ferth asked.

'No. I still have it. Can one prove that a certain drill made a certain hole?'

Ferth didn't know. Jack didn't speak.

'When you heard, at the dance,' I said, 'that I was trying to find out who had framed Cranfield and me, you thought you would get rid of me, in case I managed it. Because if I managed it, you'd lose far more than Byler's horses . . . so while I was talking to Lord Ferth and dancing with Roberta, you were out at the back of the car park rigging up your booby trap. Which,' I added calmly, remembering the blazing hell of the dislocations, 'I find hard to forgive.'

'I'll strangle him,' Tony said forcefully.

'What happens to him,' I shook my head, 'depends on Lord Ferth.'

Ferth regarded me squarely. 'You find him. I deal with him.'

'That was the agreement.'

'To your satisfaction.'

'Yes.'

'And what *is* your satisfaction?'

I didn't know.

Tony moved restlessly, looking at his watch. 'Lord

Ferth, Kelly, look, I'm sorry, but I've got a horse to saddle for the last race . . . I'll have to go now.'

'Yes, of course,' said Lord Ferth. 'But we'd all be obliged if you wouldn't talk about what you've learned in here.'

Tony looked startled. 'Sure. If you say so. Not a word.' He stood up and went over to the door. 'See you after,' he said to me. 'You secretive so-and-so.'

As he went out a bunch of Stewards and their wives came in chattering for their tea. Lord Ferth went over to them and exerted the flashing eyes, and they all went into reverse. A waiter who had materialized behind them was stationed outside the door with instructions to send all customers along to the members' tea room.

While this was going on Jack looked steadfastly down at the tablecloth and said not a word. I didn't feel like chatting to him idly either. He'd cost me too much.

Lord Ferth came briskly back and sat down.

'Now then, Roxford,' he said in his most businesslike way, 'we've heard Kelly's accusations. It's your turn now to speak up in your defence.'

Jack slowly lifted his head. The deep habitual lines of worry were running with sweat.

'It was someone else.' His voice was dead.

'It certainly wasn't Grace,' I said, 'because Lord Gowery was quite clear that the person who tried to blackmail him on the telephone was a man.' So was the person who had got at Charlie West a man, or so he'd said.

Jack Roxford jerked.

'Yes, Roxford, we know about Lord Gowery,' Ferth said.

'You *can't* . . .'

'You belong to the same club,' I said assertively, as if I knew.

For Jack Roxford, too, the thought of that club was the lever which opened the floodgates. Like Gowery before him he broke into wretched pieces.

'You don't understand . . .'

'Tell us then,' Ferth said. 'And we'll try.'

'Grace . . . we . . . I . . . Grace didn't like . . .' He petered out.

I gave him a shove. 'Grace liked her sex natural and wouldn't stand for what you wanted.'

He gulped. 'Soon after we were married we were having rows all the time, and I hated that. I loved her, really I did. I've always loved her. And I felt . . . all tangled up . . . she didn't understand that when I beat her it was because of love . . . she said she'd leave me and divorce me for cruelty . . . so I asked a girl I'd known . . . a street girl, who didn't mind . . . I mean . . . she let you, if you paid well enough . . . if I could go on seeing her . . . but she said she'd given that up now . . . but there was a club in London . . . and I went there . . . and it was a terrific relief . . . and then I was

291

all right with Grace ... but of course we didn't ... well,
hardly ever ... but somehow ... we could go on being
married.'

Lord Ferth looked revolted.

'I couldn't believe it at first,' Jack said more coher-
ently, 'when I saw Lord Gowery there. I saw him in
the street, just outside. I thought it was just a coincidence. But then, one night, inside the club, I was sure
it was him, and I saw him again in the street another
time ... but I didn't say anything. I mean, how could
I? And anyway, I knew how he felt ... you don't go
there unless you must ... and you can't keep away.'

'How long have you known that Lord Gowery went
to the same club?' I asked.

'Oh ... two or three years. A long time. I don't know
exactly.'

'Did he know you were a member?'

'No. He hadn't a clue. I spoke to him once or twice
on the racecourse about official things ... He didn't
have any idea.'

'And then,' Ferth said thoughtfully, 'you read that
he had been appointed in Colonel Midgley's place to
officiate at the Cranfield-Hughes Enquiry, and you saw
what you thought was a good chance of getting Cranfield out of racing, and keeping Byler's horses yourself.'

Jack sat huddled in his chair, not denying it.

'And when Lord Gowery declined to be blackmailed,

you couldn't bear to give up the idea, and you set about faking evidence that would achieve your ends.'

A long silence. Then Jack said in a thick disjointed voice. 'Grace minded so much... about Cranfield taking our horses. She went on and on about it... morning, noon, and night. Couldn't stop. Talk, talk, talk. All the time. Saying she'd like to kill Cranfield... and things like that. I mean... she's always been a bit nervy... a bit strung up... but Cranfield was upsetting her... I got a bit frightened for her sometimes, she was that violent about him... Well, it was really because of that that I tried to get Cranfield warned off... I mean, he was better warned off than Grace trying to kill him.'

'Did you truly believe she would?' I asked.

'She was ranting about it all the time... I didn't know if she really would... but I was so afraid... I didn't want her to get into trouble... dear dear Grace... I wanted to help her... and make things right again... so I set about it... and it wasn't too difficult really, not once I'd set my mind to it.'

Ferth gave me a twisted smile. I gave him a similar one back and reflected that marriage could be a deadly institution. Grace's strung-up state would have been aggravated by the strain of living with a sexually odd man, and Jack would have felt guilty about it and wanted to make it up to her. Neither of them had been rationally inclined, and the whole situation had boiled up claustrophobically inside their agonized private world. Having dear Grace harping on endlessly would have driven many a stronger man to explosive action: but Jack couldn't desert her, because he had to stay with his horses, and he couldn't drive her away because he loved her. The only way he'd seen of silencing his wife had been to ruin Cranfield.

'Why me?' I said, trying to keep out the bitterness. 'Why me too?'

'Eh?' He squinted at me, half focussing. 'You ... well ... I haven't anything against you personally ... But I thought it was the only way to make it a certainty ... Cranfield couldn't have swindled that race without Squelch's jockey being in the know.'

'That race was no swindle,' I said.

'Oh ... I know that. Those stupid Oxford Stewards ... still, they gave me such an opportunity ... when I heard about Lord Gowery being in charge. And then, when I'd fixed up with Charlie West and Oakley ... Grace's brother told me, just told me casually, mind you, that his bookmaker had told him that Cranfield had backed Cherry Pie, and do you know what, I couldn't stop laughing. Just like Grace, I felt ... dead funny, it was, that he really had backed Cherry Pie ...'

'What was that about Charlie West?' Ferth said sharply.

'I paid him ... to say Kelly pulled Squelch back. I

telephoned and asked him . . . if Kelly ever did anything like that . . . and he said once, in a novice 'chase, Kelly had said, "OK. Brakes on, chaps," and I told him to say Kelly had said that in the Lemonfizz Cup because it sounded so convincing, didn't it, saying something Kelly really had said . . .'

Ferth looked at me accusingly. 'You shielded West.'

I shrugged ruefully. Jack paid no attention: didn't hear.

He went on miserably: 'Grace was all right before the dance. She was wonderfully calm again, after Cranfield was warned off. And then Edwin Byler said that we would be keeping his horses for always . . . and we were happy . . . in our way . . . and then we heard . . . that Kelly was at the dance . . . saying he'd been framed . . . and was just on the point of finding out who . . . and Grace saw Cranfield's daughter and just boiled over all over again, nearly as bad as before . . . and I thought . . . if Kelly was dead . . . it would be all right again . . .'

Ferth slowly shook his head. The reasoning which had led Jack Roxford step by step from misfortune to crime defeated him.

'I thought he wouldn't feel anything,' Jack said. 'I thought that you just blacked out suddenly from carbon monoxide. I thought it would be like going to sleep . . . he wouldn't know about it. Just wouldn't wake up.'

'You didn't drill a big enough hole,' I said without

irony. 'Not enough gas came through at once to knock me out.'

'I couldn't find a large enough tube,' he said with macabre sense. 'Had to use a piece I had. It was a bit narrow. That was why.'

'I see,' I said gravely. So close. Not a few inches from the express train. One eighth of an inch extra in the tube's diameter would have done it.

'And you went to look for the pieces of manifold, afterwards?'

'Yes . . . but you know about that. I was furious with Oakley for not finding it . . . he said he tried to make you tell, but you wouldn't . . . and I said it didn't surprise me . . .'

'Why didn't you ask *him* to kill me?' I said matter-of-factly.

'Oh, I did. He said he didn't kill. He said he would dispose of the body if I did it, but he never did the job himself. Not worth it, he said.'

That sounded like the authentic Oakley. Straight from the agent's mouth.

'But you couldn't risk it?' I suggested.

'I didn't have any chance. I mean . . . I didn't like to leave Grace alone much . . . she was so upset . . . and then, you were in hospital . . . and then you went back to your flat . . . and I did try to shift you out into the open somewhere . . .'

'You did write to the Stewards' Secretaries,' Ferth exclaimed. 'After all.'

'Yes . . . but it was too late . . . wasn't it . . . She really meant it . . . poor Grace, poor Grace . . . why did I let her go out . . . But she seemed so much better this morning . . . and now . . . and now . . .' His face screwed up and turned red as he tried not to cry. The thought of Grace as he'd last seen her was too much for him. The tears rolled. He sniffed into a handkerchief.

I wondered how he would have felt if he'd seen Grace as I'd seen her. But probably the uncritical love he had would have survived even that.

'Just sit here quietly a moment, Roxford,' Lord Ferth directed, and he himself stood up and signed for me to walk with him over to the door.

'So what do we do with him?' he said.

'It's gone too far now,' I said reluctantly, 'to be entirely hushed up. And he's if anything more dangerous than Grace . . . She will live, and he will very likely see everything for ever in terms of her happiness. Anyone who treats her badly in any way could end up as a victim of his scheming. End up ruined . . . or dead. People like nurses . . . or relations . . . or even people like me, who did her no harm at all. Anybody . . .'

Ferth said, 'You seem to understand his mind. I must say that I don't. But what you say makes sense. We cannot just take away his licence and leave it at that . . . It isn't a racing matter any more. But Lord Gowery . . .'

'Lord Gowery will have to take his chance,' I said
without satisfaction. 'Very likely you can avoid busting
open his reputation ... but it's much more important
to stop Jack Roxford doing the same sort of thing
again.'

'Yes,' he said. 'It is.' He spread out his hands sideways in a pushing gesture as if wanting to step away
from the decision. 'All this is so *distressing*.'

I looked down the room at Jack, a huddled defeated
figure with nervous eyes and an anxious forehead. He
was picking at the tablecloth with his fingers, folding it
into senseless little pleats. He didn't look like a villain.
No hardened criminal. Just a tenacious little man with
a fixed idea, to make up to dear Grace for being what
he was.

Nothing was more useless than sending him to
prison, and nothing could do him more harm: yet that,
I imagined, was where he would go. Putting his body
in a little cage wouldn't straighten the kinks in his mind.
The system, for men like him, was screwy.

He stood up slowly and walked unsteadily towards
us.

'I suppose,' he said without much emotion, 'that
you are going to get the police. I was wondering ...
please ... don't tell them about the club ... I won't
say Lord Gowery goes there ... I won't tell anybody
ever ... I never really wanted to ... it wouldn't have
done any good, would it? I mean, it wouldn't have kept

those horses in my yard . . . wouldn't have made a scrap of difference . . . So do you think anyone need know about . . . the club?'

'No,' said Ferth with well-disguised relief. 'They need not.'

A faint smile set up a rival set of creases to the lines of anxiety. 'Thank you.' The smile faded away. The lost look deepened. 'How long . . . do you think I'll get?'

Ferth moved uncomfortably. 'No point in worrying about that until you have to.'

'You could probably halve it,' I said.

'How?' He was pathetically hopeful. I flung him the rope.

'By giving evidence at another trial I have in mind, and taking David Oakley down with you.'

PART THREE

MARCH

EPILOGUE

Yesterday I rode Breadwinner in the Cheltenham Gold Cup.

A horse of raw talent with more future than past. A shambling washy chestnut carrying his head low. No one's idea of equine beauty.

Old Strepson watched him slop around the parade ring and said with a sigh, 'He looks half asleep.'

'Hughes will wake him up,' Cranfield said condescendingly.

Cranfield stood in the chill March sunshine making his usual good stab at arrogance. The mean calculating lines round his mouth seemed to have deepened during the past month, and his manner to me was if anything more distant, more master-servant, than ever before. Roberta said she had told him that I had in some way managed to get our licences back, but he saw no reason to believe her and preferred the thought of divine intervention.

Old Strepson said conversationally, 'Kelly says

Breadwinner was a late foal and a late developer, and won't reach his true strength until about this time next year.'

Cranfield gave me a mouth-tightening mind-your-own-business glare, and didn't seem to realize that I'd given him an alibi if the horse didn't win and built him up into one heck of a good trainer if it did. Whatever low opinion Cranfield held of me, I reciprocated it in full.

Farther along the parade ring stood a silent little group of Kessel, Pat Nikita, and their stable jockey, Al Roach. They were engaged in running poor old Squelch, and their interest lay not so fiercely in winning as in finishing at all costs in front of Breadwinner. Kessel himself radiated so much hatred that I thought it was probably giving him a headache. Hating did that. The day I found it out, I gave up hating.

Grace's hatred-headache must have been unbearable . . .

Grace's recovery was still uncertain. Ferth had somehow wangled the best available psychiatrist on to her case, and had also arranged for him to see Jack. Outside the weighing-room when I had arrived, he had jerked his head for me to join him, and told me what the psychiatrist had reported.

'He says Jack is sane according to legal standards, and will have to stand trial. He wouldn't commit himself about Grace's chances. He did say, though, that from all points of view their enforced separation was a godsend. He said he thought their only chance of leading fairly normal lives in the future was to make the separation total and permanent. He said a return to the same circumstances could mean a repeat of the whole cycle.'

I looked at Ferth gloomily. 'What a cold, sad, depressing solution.'

'You never know,' he said optimistically, 'once they get over it, they might both feel . . . well . . . released.'

I smiled at him. He said abruptly, 'Your outlook is catching, dammit . . . How about that dinner?'

'Any time,' I said.

'Tomorrow, then? Eight o'clock. The Caprice, round the corner from the Ritz . . . The food's better there than at my club.'

'Fine,' I said.

'And you can tell me how the police are getting on with David Oakley . . .'

I'd had the Birmingham police on my telephone and doorstep for much of the past week. They had almost fallen on my neck and sobbed when I first went to them with enough to make an accusation stick, and had later promised to deliver to me, framed, one of the first fruits of their search warrant: a note from Cranfield to Jack Roxford dated two years earlier, thanking him for not bidding him up at an auction after a selling race and enclosing a cheque for fifty pounds. Across the bottom of the page Cranfield had written:

As agreed. Thanks. D.C.

It was the note Oakley had photographed in my flat. Supplied by Roxford, who had suggested the photograph.

Kept by Oakley, as a hold over Roxford.

The police also told me that Jack Roxford had drawn six hundred pounds in new notes out of his bank during the two weeks before the Enquiry, and David Oakley had paid three hundred of the same notes into his own account five days later.

Clever, slippery Mr Oakley had been heard to remark that he regretted not having slaughtered Kelly Hughes.

The bell rang for the jockeys to mount, and Cranfield and old Strepson and I walked over to where Breadwinner waited.

The one jockey missing from the day's proceedings was Charlie West, whose licence had been suspended for the rest of the season. And it was only thanks to Hughes' intervention, Ferth had told him forcefully, that he hadn't got his deserts and been warned off for life. Whether Charlie West would feel an atom of gratitude was another matter.

I swung up easily on to Breadwinner and fitted my right foot carefully into the stirrup. A compromise between me and the orthopod had seen the plaster off seven days previously, but the great surgeon's kind parting words had been, 'You haven't given that leg enough time and if it dislocates again it's your own bloody fault.'

I had told him that I couldn't afford to have Cranfield engage another jockey for Breadwinner with all the horse's future races at stake. Old Strepson was the grateful type who didn't dislodge a jockey who had won for him, and if some other jockey won the Gold Cup on Breadwinner I would lose the mount for life: and it was only this argument which had grudgingly brought out the saw.

I gathered up the reins and walked the horse quietly round the ring while everyone sorted themselves out into the right order for the parade down the course. Apart from the Grand National, the Cheltenham Gold Cup was the biggest steeplechase of the year. In prestige, probably the greatest of all. All the stars turned out for it, meeting each other in level terms. Bad horses hadn't a hope.

There were nine runners. Breadwinner was the youngest, Squelch the most experienced, and a bad-tempered grey called Ironclad, the favourite.

Al Roach, uninfected by Kessel, lined up beside me at the start and gave me his usual wide friendly Irish grin. 'Now Kelly my bhoy,' he said, 'tell me how you ride this little fellow, now.'

'You want to be warned off?' I said.

He chuckled. 'What's the owner got against you, Kelly me bhoy?'

'I was right and he was wrong, and he can't forgive that.'

'Peculiar fellow, he is, that Kessel . . .'

The tapes went up and we were away. Three and a quarter miles, twenty-one jumps, two whole circuits of the course.

Nothing much happened on the first circuit. No horses fell and no jockeys got excited, and going past the stands and outward bound for the second time a fair-sized sheet would have covered the lot. The next mile sorted the men from the boys, and the bunch flattened out into a relentless, thundering, muscle-straining procession in which hope and sweat and tactics merged into a rushing private world of conflict. Speed . . . jumping at near-disaster rate . . . gambling on the horse's coordination . . . stretching your own . . . a race like the Gold Cup showed you what you were made of . . .

Coming to the second last fence, Ironclad was leading Squelch by three lengths which could have been ten, and he set himself right with all the time in the world. Squelch followed him over, and four lengths behind Breadwinner strained forwards to be third.

Between the last two fences the status quo was unchanged, Breadwinner making no impression on Squelch, nor Squelch on Ironclad. Oh well, I thought resignedly. Third. That wasn't really too bad for such a young horse. One couldn't have everything. And there was always Pound Postage in the Grand National, two weeks on Saturday ...

Ironclad set himself right for the last fence, launched himself muscularly into the air, crossed the birch with a good foot of air beneath him ... and pitched forwards on to his nose on landing.

I couldn't believe it. Shook up Breadwinner with a bang of renewed hope and drove him into the last fence for the jump of his young life.

Squelch was over it first, of course. Squelch the sure-footed trained-to-the-minute familiar old rascal ... Irony of ironies, to be beaten to the Gold Cup by Squelch.

Breadwinner did the best he could to catch him, and I saw that as in the Lemonfizz, Squelch was dying from tiredness. Length by length my gangling chestnut pegged back the gap, straining, stretching, quivering to get past ... but the winning post was too near ... it was no good ... there wasn't time ...

Al Roach looked round to see who was pressing him. Saw me. Knew that Breadwinner was of all others the one he had to beat. Was seized with panic. If he had sat still, he would have won by two lengths. Instead, he picked up his whip and hit Squelch twice down the flank.

You stupid ass, I thought breathlessly. He hates that. He'll stop. He always stops if you hit him . . .

Squelch's tail swished in fury. His rhythmic stride broke up into bumps. He shook his head violently from side to side.

I saw Al's desperate face as Breadwinner caught him . . . and the winning post was there and gone in a flash . . . and neither of us knew even then which had won.

The photograph gave it to Breadwinner by a nostril. And if I got booed by the crowd after the Lemonfizz they made up for it after the Gold Cup.

Kessel, predictably, was purple with fury, and he seemed on the brink of explosion when someone remarked loudly that Squelch would have won if Hughes had been riding him. I laughed. Kessel looked almost as murderous as Grace.

Old Strepson was pale with emotion but even the Gold Cup did not raise much observable joy in Cranfield; and I found out later that Edwin Byler had just told him he wouldn't be sending him his horses after all. Grace's psychiatrist had written to say that Grace's ultimate sanity might depend on Cranfield not having the horses, and Byler said he felt he owed the Roxfords something ... sorry and all that, but there it was.

Roberta with her mother had been there patting Breadwinner in the winner's enclosure, and when I came out of the weighing-room twenty minutes later after changing into street clothes, she was leaning against the rails there, waiting.

'You're limping,' she said calmly.

'Unfit, that's all.'

'Coffee?' she suggested.

'Yes,' I said.

She walked sedately ahead of me into the coffee room. Her copper hair still shone after she'd stepped out of the sunshine, and I liked the simple string-coloured coat which went underneath it.

I bought her some coffee and sat at a little plastic-topped table and looked at the litter left by the last occupants; empty coffee cups, plates with crumbs, cigarette butts, and a froth-lined beer glass. Roberta packed them coolly to one side and ignored them.

'Winning and losing,' she said. 'That's what it's all about.'

'Racing?'

'Life.'

I looked at her.

She said, 'Today is marvellous, and being warned off was terrible. I suppose everything goes on like that ... up and down ... always.'

'I suppose so,' I agreed.

'I've learned a lot, since the Enquiry.'

'So have I . . . about you.'

'Father says I must remember your background . . .'

'That's true,' I said. 'You must.'

'Father's mind has chains on. Iron bars in his soul. His head's chock-a-block with ideas half a century out of date.' She mimicked my own words with pompous mischief.

I laughed. 'Roberta . . .'

'Please tell me . . .'

She hesitated. ' . . . At the level crossing . . . when you called me Rosalind . . . was it her you wanted?'

'No,' I said slowly, 'it was you . . . In her place.'

She sighed contentedly.

'That's all right, then,' she said. 'Isn't it?'

REFLEX

My thanks to the Photographers
Bernard Parkin and David Hastings
and especially RON MASSEY
who made me the puzzles.

CHAPTER ONE

Winded and coughing, I lay on one elbow and spat out a mouthful of grass and mud. The horse I'd been riding raised its weight off my ankle, scrambled untidily to its feet and departed at an unfeeling gallop. I waited for things to settle: chest heaving, bones still rattling from the bang, sense of balance recovering from a thirty-mile-an-hour somersault and a few tumbling rolls. No harm done. Nothing broken. Just another fall.

Time and place: sixteenth fence, three-mile steeplechase, Sandown Park racecourse, Friday, November, in thin, cold, persistent rain. At the return of breath and energy I stood wearily up and thought with intensity that this was a damn silly way for a grown man to be spending his life.

The thought itself was a jolt. Not one I'd ever thought before. Riding horses at high speed over various jumps was the only way I knew of making a living, and it was a job one couldn't do if one's heart wasn't in it. The chilling flicker of disillusion nudged like the first twinge of toothache, unexpected, unwelcome, an uneasy hint of possible trouble.

I repressed it without much alarm. Reassured myself that I loved the life, of course I did, the way I always had. Believed quite easily that nothing was wrong except the weather, the fall, the lost race ... minor, everyday stuff, business as usual.

Squelching uphill to the stands in paper-thin racing boots unsuitable for hiking, I thought only and firmly about the horse I'd started out on, sorting out what I might and might not say to its trainer. Discarded 'How do you expect it to jump if you don't school it properly?' in favour of 'The experience will do him good.' Thought better of 'useless, panicky, hard-mouthed, underfed dog', and decided on 'might try him in blinkers'. The trainer, anyway, would blame me for the fall and tell the owner I'd misjudged the pace. He was that sort of trainer. Every crash was a pilot error.

I thanked heaven in a mild way that I didn't ride often for that stable, and had been engaged on that day only because Steve Millace, its usual jockey, had gone to his father's funeral. Spare rides, even with disaster staring up from the form books, were not lightly to be turned down. Not if you needed the money, which I did. And not if, like me, you needed your name up on the number boards as often as possible, to show you were useful and wanted and *there*.

The only good thing, I supposed, about my descent at the fence was that Steve Millace's father hadn't been there to record it. George Millace, pitiless photographer of moments all jockeys preferred to ignore, was safe in his box and approximately at that moment being lowered underground to his long sleep. And good riddance, I thought uncharitably. Goodbye to the snide sneering pleasure George got from delivering to owners the irrefutable evidence of their jockeys' failings. Goodbye to the motorised camera catching at three and a half frames per second one's balance in the wrong place, one's arms in the air, one's face in the mud.

Where other sports photographers played fair and shot you winning from time to time, George trafficked exclusively in ignominy and humiliation. George was a natural-born dragger-down. Newspapers might mourn the passing of his snigger-raising pictures, but there had been little sorrow in the changing room the day Steve told us his father had driven into a tree.

Out of liking for Steve himself, no one had said much. He had listened to the silence, though, and he knew. He had been anxiously defending his father for years; and he knew.

Trudging back in the rain it seemed odd to me still that we wouldn't actually be seeing George Millace again. His image, too familiar for too long, rose sharply in the mind: bright clever eyes, long nose, drooping moustache, twisted mouth sourly smiling. A terrific photographer, one had to admit, with an exceptional talent for anticipation and timing, his lens always pointing in the right direction at the right moment. A

3

comic, too, in his way, showing me less than a week ago a black and white glossy of me taking a dive, nose to ground, bottom up, with a caption written on the back, 'Philip Nore, arse high to a grasshopper.' One would have laughed but for the genuine ill-will which had prompted his humour. One might always have at least tolerated his debunking approach but for the cruelty sliding out of his eyes. He had been a mental thrower of banana skins, lying in wait to scoff at the hurt; and he would be missed with thankfulness.

When I finally reached the shelter of the verandah outside the weighing room, the trainer and owner were waiting there with the expected accusing expressions.

'Misjudged things pretty badly, didn't you?' said the trainer aggressively.

'He took off a stride too soon.'

'Your job to put him right.'

No point in saying that no jockey on earth could get every horse to jump perfectly always, and particularly not a badly schooled rogue. I simply nodded, and smiled a shade ruefully at the owner.

'Might try him in blinkers,' I said.

'*I'll* decide about that,' said the trainer sharply.

'Not hurt, are you?' asked the owner timidly.

I shook my head. The trainer brusquely stamped on this humane jockey-orientated enquiry and wheeled his money-source away from the danger that I might say something truthful about why the horse wouldn't jump when asked. I watched them go without rancour and turned towards the weighing room door.

'I say,' said a young man, stepping in front of me, 'are you Philip Nore?'

'That's right.'

'Well . . . could I have a word with you?'

He was about twenty-five, tall as a stork and earnest, with office-coloured skin. Charcoal flannel suit, striped tie, no binoculars, and no air of belonging where he stood, in the business-only section of the racecourse.

'Sure,' I said. 'If you'll wait while I check with the doctor and get into something dry.'

'Doctor?' He looked alarmed.

'Oh . . . routine. After a fall. I shan't be long.'

When I went out again, warmed and in street clothes, he was still waiting; and he was more or less alone on the verandah, as nearly everyone else had gone to watch the last race, already in progress.

'I . . . er . . . my name is Jeremy Folk.' He produced a card from inside the charcoal jacket and held it out to me. I took it, and read: *Folk, Langley, Son and Folk.*

Solicitors. Address in St Albans, Hertfordshire.

'That last Folk,' said Jeremy, pointing diffidently, 'is me.'

'Congratulations,' I said.

He gave me an anxious half smile and cleared his throat.

'I've been sent . . . er . . . I've come to ask you to . . .

er . . .' He stopped, looking helpless and not in the least like a solicitor.

'To what?' I said encouragingly.

'They said you wouldn't like . . . but well . . . I've been sent to ask you . . . er . . .'

'Do get on with it,' I said.

'To come and see your grandmother.' The words came out in a nervous rush, and he seemed relieved to be rid of them.

'No,' I said.

He scanned my face and seemed to take heart from its calmness.

'She's dying,' he said. 'And she wants to see you.'

Death all around, I thought. George Millace and my mother's mother. Negative grief in both cases.

'Did you hear?' he said.

'I heard.'

'Now, then? I mean, today?'

'No,' I said. 'I'm not going.'

'But you must.' He looked troubled. 'I mean . . . she's old . . . and she's dying . . . and she wants you . . .'

'Too bad.'

'And if I don't persuade you, my uncle . . . that's Son . . .' He pointed to the card again, getting flustered. 'Er. Folk is my grandfather and Langley is my great-uncle, and . . . er . . . they sent me . . .' He swallowed. 'They think I'm frightfully useless, to be honest.'

'And that's blackmail,' I said.

6

A faint glint in his eyes told me that he wasn't basically as silly as he made out.

'I don't want to see her,' I said.

'But she is dying.'

'Have you yourself seen her . . . dying?'

'Er . . . no . . .'

'I'll bet she isn't. If she wants to see me, she would say she was dying just to fetch me, because she'd guess nothing else would.'

He looked shocked. 'She's seventy-eight, after all.'

I looked gloomily out at the non-stop rain. I had never met my grandmother and I didn't want to, dying or dead. I didn't approve of death-bed repentances, last minute insurances at the gates of hell. It was too damned late.

'The answer,' I said, 'is still no.'

He shrugged dispiritedly and seemed to give up. Walked a few steps out into the rain, bareheaded, vulnerable, with no umbrella. Turned round after ten paces and came tentatively back again.

'Look . . . she really needs you, my uncle says.' He was as earnest, as intense, as a missionary. 'You can't just let her die.'

'Where is she?' I said.

He brightened. 'In a nursing home.' He fished in another pocket. 'I've got the address. But I'll lead you there, straight away, if you'll come. It's in St Albans. You live in Lambourn, don't you? So it isn't terribly far out of your way, is it? I mean, not a hundred miles, or anything like that.'

'A good fifty, though.'

'Well . . . I mean . . . you always do drive around an awful lot.'

I sighed. The options were rotten. A choice between meek capitulation or a stony rejection. Both unpalatable. That she had dished out to me the stony rejection from my birth gave me no excuse, I supposed, for doing it to her at her death. Also I could hardly go on smugly despising her, as I had done for years, if I followed her example. Irritating, that.

The winter afternoon was already fading, with electric lights growing brighter by the minute, shining fuzzily through the rain. I thought of my empty cottage; of nothing much to fill the evening, of two eggs, a piece of cheese and black coffee for supper, of wanting to eat more and not doing so. If I went, I thought, it would at least take my mind off food, and anything which helped with the perennial fight against weight couldn't be wholly bad. Not even meeting my grandmother.

'All right,' I said, resignedly, 'lead on.'

The old woman sat upright in bed staring at me, and if she was dying it wasn't going to be on that evening, for sure. The life force was strong in the dark eyes and there was no mortal weakness in her voice.

'Philip,' she said, making it a statement and looking me up and down.

'Yes.'

'Hah.'

The explosive sound contained both triumph and contempt and was everything I would have expected. Her ramrod will had devastated my childhood and done worse damage to her own daughter, and there was to be, I was relieved to see, no maudlin plea for forgiveness. Rejection, even if in a moderated form, was still in operation.

'I knew you'd come running,' she said, 'when you heard about the money.' As a cold sneer it was pretty unbeatable.

'What money?'

'The hundred thousand pounds, of course.'

'No one,' I said, 'has mentioned any money.'

'Don't lie. Why else would you come?'

'They said you were dying.'

She gave me a startled and malevolent flash of the eyes and a baring of teeth which had nothing to do with smiling. 'So I am. So are we all.'

'Yeah,' I said, 'and all at the same rate. One day at a time.'

She was no one's idea of a sweet little pink-cheeked grannie. A strong stubborn face with disapproval lines cut deep around the mouth. Iron grey hair still vigorous, clean and well shaped. Blotchy freckles of age showing brown on an otherwise pale skin, and dark ridged veins on the backs of the hands. A thin woman, almost gaunt; and tall, as far as I could judge.

The large room where she lay was furnished more as a sitting room with a bed in it than as a hospital, which was all of a piece with what I'd seen of the place on the way in. A country house put to new use: hotel with nurses. Carpets everywhere, long chintz curtains, armchairs for visitors, vases of flowers. Gracious dying, I thought.

'I instructed Mr Folk,' she said, 'to make you the offer.'

I reflected. 'Young Mr Folk? About twenty-five? Jeremy?'

'Of course not.' She was impatient. 'Mr Folk, my solicitor. I told him to get you here. And he did. Here you are.'

'He sent his grandson.'

I turned away from her and sat unasked in an armchair. Why, I wondered, had Jeremy not mentioned a hundred thousand pounds? It was the sort of trifle, after all, that one didn't easily forget.

My grandmother stared at me steadily with no sign of affection, and I stared as steadily back. I disliked her certainty that she could buy me. I was repelled by her contempt, and mistrusted her intentions.

'I will leave you a hundred thousand pounds in my will, upon certain conditions,' she said.

'No, you won't,' I said.

'I beg your pardon?' Icy voice, stony look.

10

'I said no. No money. No conditions.'

'You haven't heard my proposition.'

I said nothing. I felt in fact the first stirrings of curiosity, but I was definitely not going to let her see it. Since she seemed in no hurry, the silence lengthened. More stocktaking on her part, perhaps. Simple patience, on mine. One thing my haphazard upbringing had given me was an almost limitless capacity for waiting. Waiting for people to come, who didn't; and for promises to be fulfilled, that weren't.

Finally she said, 'You're taller than I expected. And tougher.'

I waited some more.

'Where is your mother?' she said.

My mother, her daughter. 'Scattered on the winds,' I said.

'What do you mean?'

'I think she's dead.'

'*Think!*' She looked more annoyed than anxious. 'Don't you *know*?'

'She didn't exactly write to me to say she'd died; no.'

'Your flippancy is disgraceful.'

'Your behaviour since before my birth,' I said, 'gives you no right to say so.'

She blinked. Her mouth opened, and stayed open for fully five seconds. Then it shut tight with rigid muscles showing along the jaw, and she stared at me darkly in a daunting mixture of fury and ferocity. I saw, in that expression, what my poor young mother had had to

11

face, and felt a great uprush of sympathy for the feckless butterfly who'd borne me.

There had been a day, when I was quite small, that I had been dressed in new clothes and told to be exceptionally good as I was going with my mother to see my grandmother. My mother had collected me from where I was living and we had travelled by car to a large house, where I was left alone in the hall, to wait. Behind a white painted closed door there had been a lot of shouting. Then my mother had come out, crying, and had grabbed me by the hand, and pulled me after her to the car.

'Come on, Philip. We'll never ask her for anything, ever again. She wouldn't even see you. Don't you ever forget, Philip, that your grandmother's a hateful *beast*.'

I hadn't forgotten. I'd thought of it rarely, but I still clearly remembered sitting in the chair in the hall, my feet not touching the ground, waiting stiffly in my new clothes, listening to the shouting.

I had never actually lived with my mother, except for a traumatic week or two now and then. We had had no house, no address, no permanent base. Herself always on the move, she had solved the problem of what to do with me by simply dumping me for varying periods with a long succession of mostly astonished married friends, who had been, in retrospect, remarkably tolerant.

'Do look after Philip for me for a few days, darling,' she would say, giving me a push towards yet another strange lady. 'Life is so unutterably *cluttered* just now and I'm at my wits' end to know what to do with him, you know how it is, so, darling Deborah ... (or Miranda, or Chloe, or Samantha, or anyone else under the sun) ... do be an absolute *sweetie*, and I'll pick him up on Saturday, I promise.' And mostly she would have soundly kissed darling Deborah or Miranda or Chloe or Samantha and gone off with a wave in a cloud of joy.

Saturdays came and my mother didn't, but she always turned up in the end, full of flutter and laughter and gushing thanks, retrieving her parcel, so to speak, from the left luggage office. I could remain uncollected for days or for weeks or for months: I never knew which in advance, and nor, I suspect, did my hosts. Mostly, I think, she paid something towards my keep, but it was all done with a giggle.

She was, even to my eyes, deliciously pretty, to the extent that people hugged her and indulged her and lit up when she was around. Only later, when they were left literally holding the baby, did the doubts creep in. I became a bewildered silent child forever tiptoeing nervously around so as not to give offence, perennially frightened that someone, one day, would abandon me altogether out in the street.

Looking back, I knew I owed a great deal to Samantha, Deborah, Chloe, *et al.* I never went hungry, was never ill-treated, nor was ever, in the end, totally rejected. Occasionally people took me in twice or three times, sometimes with welcome, mostly with resignation. When I was three or four someone in long hair and bangles and an ethnic smock taught me to read and write, but I never stayed anywhere long enough to be formally sent to school. It was an extraordinary, disorientating and rootless existence from which I emerged at twelve, when I was dumped in my first long-stay home, able to do almost any job around the house and unable to love.

She left me with two photographers, Duncan and Charlie, standing in their big bare-floored studio that had a darkroom, a bathroom, a gas ring and a bed behind a curtain.

'Darlings, look after him until Saturday, there's a sweet pair of lambs...' And although birthday cards arrived, and presents at Christmas, I didn't see her again for three years. Then when Duncan departed she swooped in one day and took me away from Charlie, and drove me down to a racehorse trainer and his wife in Hampshire, telling those bemused friends, 'It's only until Saturday, darlings, and he's fifteen and strong, he'll muck out the horses for you, and things like that...'

Cards and presents arrived for two years or so, always without an address to reply to. On my eighteenth birthday there was no card, and no present the following Christmas, and I'd never heard from her again.

She must have died, I had come to understand, from

drugs. There was a great deal, as I grew older, that I'd sorted out and understood.

The old woman glared across the room, as unforgiving and destructive as ever, and still angry at what I'd said.

'You won't get far with me if you talk like that,' she said.

'I don't want to get far.' I stood up. 'This visit is pointless. If you wanted to find your daughter you should have looked twenty years ago. And as for me . . . I wouldn't find her for you, even if I could.'

'I don't want you to find Caroline. I dare say you're right, that she's dead.' The idea clearly caused her no grief. 'I want you to find your sister.'

'My . . . *what*?'

The hostile dark eyes assessed me shrewdly. 'You didn't know you had a sister? Well, you have. I'll leave you a hundred thousand pounds in my will if you find her and bring her here to me. And don't think,' she went on caustically, before I had time to utter, 'that you can produce any little imposter and expect me to believe it. I'm old but I'm far from a fool. You would have to prove to Mr Folk's satisfaction that the girl was my grandchild. And Mr Folk would not be easy to convince.'

I scarcely heard the acid words, but felt only a curiously intense thrust of shock. There had been only one of me. One single fruit of the butterfly. I felt an unreasonable but stinging jealousy that she had had

15

another. She had been mine alone, and now I had to share her: to revise and share her memory. I thought in confusion that it was ridiculous to be experiencing at thirty the displacement emotions of two.

'Well?' my grandmother said sharply.

'No,' I said.

'It's a lot of money,' she snapped.

'If you've got it.'

She was again outraged. 'You're insolent!'

'Oh, sure. Well, if that's all, I'll be going.' I turned and went towards the door.

'Wait,' she said urgently. 'Don't you even want to see her picture? There's a photograph of your sister over there on the chest.'

I glanced over my shoulder and saw her nodding towards a chest of drawers across the room. She must have seen the hesitation that slowed my hand on the doorknob because she said with more confidence, 'Just look at her, then. Why don't you look?'

Without positively wanting to but impelled by undeniable curiosity I walked over to the chest and looked. There was a snapshot lying there, an ordinary postcard-sized family-album print. I picked it up and tilted it towards the light.

A little girl, three or four years old, on a pony.

The child, with shoulder-length brown hair, wore a red and white striped T-shirt and a pair of jeans. The pony was an unremarkable Welsh grey, with clean-looking tack. Photographed in what was evidently a

16

stable yard, they both looked contented and well fed, but the photographer had been standing too far away to bring out much detail in the child's face. Enlargement would help to some extent.

I turned the print over, but there was nothing on the back of it to indicate where it had come from, or who had held the camera.

Vaguely disappointed, I put it down again on the chest and saw, with a wince of nostalgia, an envelope lying there addressed in my mother's handwriting. Addressed to my grandmother, Mrs Lavinia Nore, at the old house in Northamptonshire where I'd had to wait in the hall.

In the envelope, a letter.

'What are you doing?' said my grandmother in alarm.

'Reading a letter from my mother.'

'But I . . . That letter shouldn't be out. Put it down at once. I thought it was in the drawer.'

I ignored her. The loopy, extravagant, extrovert writing came as freshly to me off the paper as if she'd been there in the room, gushing and half laughing, calling out as always for help.

That letter, dated only October 2nd, was no joke.

Dear Mother,

I know I said I would never ask you for anything ever again but I'm having one more try because I still hope, silly me, that one day you might change your mind. I am sending you a photograph of my daughter Amanda, your granddaughter. She is very sweet and darling and she's three now, and she needs a proper home and to go to school and everything, and I know you wouldn't want a child around but if you'd just give her an allowance or even do one of those covenant things for her, she could live with some perfectly angelic people who love her and want to keep her but simply can't afford everything for another child as they've three of their own already. If you could pay something regularly into their bank account you wouldn't even notice it and it would mean your granddaughter was brought up in a happy home and I am so desperate to get that for her that I'm writing to you now.

She hasn't the same father as Philip, so you couldn't hate her for the same reasons, and if you'd see her you'd love her, but even if you won't see her, please, Mother, look after her. I'll hope to hear from you soon. Please, please, Mother, answer this letter.

Your daughter,
Caroline,

Staying at Pine Woods Lodge,
Mindle Bridge, Sussex.

I looked up and across at the hard old woman.
  'When did she write this?'

'Years ago.'

'And you didn't reply,' I said flatly.

'No.'

I supposed it was no good getting angry over so old a tragedy. I looked at the envelope to try to see the date of the letter from the postmark, but it was smudged and indecipherable. How long, I wondered, had she waited at Pine Woods Lodge, hoping and caring and desperate. Desperation, of course, when it concerned my mother, was always a relative term. Desperation was a laugh and an outstretched hand – and the Lord (or Deborah or Samantha or Chloe) would provide. Desperation wouldn't be grim and gritty: but it must have been pretty deep to make her ask her own mother for help.

I put the letter, the envelope and the photograph in my jacket pocket. It seemed disgusting to me that the old woman had kept them all these years when she had ignored their plea, and I felt in an obscure way that they belonged to me, and not her.

'So you'll do it,' she said.

'No.'

'But you're taking the photograph.'

'Yes.'

'Well, then.'

'If you want ... Amanda ... found, you should hire a private detective.'

'I did,' she said impatiently. 'Naturally. Three detectives. They were all useless.'

'If three failed, she can't be found,' I said. 'There's no way I could succeed.'

'More incentive,' she said triumphantly. 'You'll try your damnedest, for that sort of money.'

'You're wrong.' I stared bitterly at her across the room and from her pillow-piled bed she stared unsmilingly back. 'If I took any money from you I'd vomit.'

I walked over to the door and this time opened it without hesitation.

To my departing back, she said, 'Amanda shall have my money . . . if you find her.'

CHAPTER TWO

When I went back to Sandown Park the following day the letter and photograph were still in my pocket but the emotions they had engendered had subsided. The unknown half-sister could be contemplated without infantile rage, and yet another chunk of the past had fallen into place.

It was the present, in the shape of Steve Millace, which claimed everyone's attention. He came steaming into the changing room half an hour before the first race with drizzle on his hair and righteous fury in his eyes.

His mother's house, he said, had been burgled while they were all out at his father's funeral.

We sat in rows on the benches, half changed into riding clothes, listening with shock. I looked at the scene – jockeys in all stages of undress, in underpants, bare-chested, in silks and pulling on nylon tights and boots, and all of them suddenly still, as if in suspended animation, listening with open mouths and eyes turned towards Steve.

Almost automatically I reached for my Nikon, twiddled the controls, and took a couple of photographs: and they were all so accustomed to me doing that sort of thing that no one took any notice.

'It was awful,' Steve said. 'Bloody disgusting. She'd made some cakes and things, Mum had, for the aunts and everyone, for when we got back from the cremation, and they were all thrown around the place, squashed flat, jam and such, onto the walls, and stamped into the carpet. And there was more mess everywhere, in the kitchen . . . bathroom . . . It looked as if a herd of mad children had rampaged round the whole house making it as filthy as they could. But it wasn't children . . . children wouldn't have stolen all that was taken, the police said.'

'Your mother have a load of jewels, did she?' said someone, teasing.

One or two laughed and the first tension was broken, but the sympathy for Steve was genuine enough, and he went on talking about it to anyone who cared to listen: and I did listen, not only because his peg at Sandown was next to mine, which gave me little choice, but also because we always got on well together in a day-to-day, superficial way.

'They stripped Dad's darkroom,' he said. 'Just ripped everything out. And it was senseless . . . like I told the police . . . because they didn't just take things you could sell, like the enlarger and the developing stuff, but all his work, all those pictures taken over all those years, they're all gone. It's such a bloody shame. There's Mum with all that mess, and Dad dead, and now she hasn't even got what he spent his life doing. Just *nothing*. And they took her fur jacket and even the scent Dad gave her for her birthday, that she hadn't opened, and she's just sitting there crying . . .'

He stopped suddenly and swallowed, as if it was all too much for him too. At twenty-three, although he no longer lived with them, he was still very much his parents' child, attached to them with a difficult loyalty most people admired. George Millace himself might have been widely disliked, but he had never been belittled by his son.

Small-boned, slight in build, Steve had bright dark eyes and ears that stuck out widely, giving him an overall slightly comic look: but in character he was more intense than humorous, and was apt, even without so much cause as on that day, to keep on returning obsessively to things which upset him.

'The police said that burglars do it for spite,' Steve said ' . . . mess up people's houses and steal their photographs. They told Mum it's always happening. They said to be thankful there wasn't urine and shit over everything, which there often was, and she was lucky she didn't have the chairs and settee slashed and all the furniture scratched.' He went on compulsively talking to all comers, but I finished changing and went out to ride in the first race, and more or less forgot the Millace burglary for the rest of the afternoon.

It was a day I had been looking forward to, and trying not to, for nearly a month. The day that Daylight was to run in the Sandown Handicap Pattern 'Chase. A big race, a good horse, moderate opposition, and a great chance of winning. Such combinations came my way rarely enough to be prized, but I never liked to believe in them until I was actually on my way down to the post. Daylight, I'd been told, had arrived at the course safe and sound, and for me there was just the first race, a novice hurdle, to come back unscathed from, and then, perhaps, I would win the big Pattern 'Chase and half a dozen people would fall over themselves to offer me the favourite for the Gold Cup.

Two races a day was about my usual mark, and if I ended a season in the top twenty on the jockeys' list, I was happy. For years I'd been able to kid myself that the modesty of my success was due to being taller and heavier than was best for the job. Even with constant semi-starvation I weighed ten stone seven stripped, and was cut off, consequently, from the countless horses running at ten stone or less. Most seasons I rode in about two hundred races with forty or so winners, and I knew that I was considered 'strong', 'reliable', 'good over fences', and 'not first class in a close finish'.

Most people think, when they're young, that they're going to the top of their chosen world, and that the climb up is only a formality. Without that faith, I suppose, they might never start. Somewhere on the way they lift their eyes to the summit and know they aren't going to reach it; and happiness then is looking down and enjoying the view they've got, not envying the one they haven't. At around twenty-six I'd come to terms with the view I'd reached, and with knowing I wasn't going any further: and oddly, far from depressing me, the realization had been a relief. I'd never been graspingly ambitious, but only willing to do anything as well as I could. If I couldn't do better, well, I couldn't, and that was that. All the same, I'd no positive objection to having Gold Cup winners thrust upon me, so to speak.

On that afternoon at Sandown I completed the novice hurdle in an uneventful way ('useful but uninspired'), finishing fifth out of eighteen runners. Not too bad. Just the best that I and the horse could do on the day, same as usual.

I changed into Daylight's colours and in due course walked out to the parade ring, feeling nothing but pleasure for the coming race. Daylight's trainer, for whom I rode regularly, was waiting there, and also Daylight's owner.

Daylight's owner waved away my cheerful opener about it being splendid the drizzle had stopped and said without preamble, 'You'll lose this one today, Philip.'

I smiled. 'Not if I can help it.'

'Indeed you will,' he said sharply. 'Lose it. My money's on the other way.'

I don't suppose I kept much of the dismay and anger out of my face. He had done this sort of thing before, but not for about three years, and he knew I didn't like it.

Victor Briggs, Daylight's owner, was a sturdily built man in his forties, about whose job and background I knew almost nothing. Unsociable, secretive, he came to the races with a closed unsmiling face, and never talked to me much. He always wore a heavy navy-blue overcoat, a black broad-brimmed hat, and thick black leather gloves. He had been, in the past, an aggressive gambler, and in riding for him I had had the choice of doing what he said or losing my job with the stable. Harold Osborne, the trainer, had said to me plainly, soon after I'd joined him, that if I wouldn't do what Victor Briggs wanted, I was out.

I had lost races for Victor Briggs that I might have won. It was a fact of life. I needed to eat and to pay off the mortgage on the cottage. For that I needed a good big stable to ride for, and if I had walked out of the one that was giving me a chance I might easily not have found another. There weren't so very many of them, and apart from Victor Briggs the Osborne set-up was just right. So, like many another rider in a like fix, I had done what I was told, and kept quiet.

Back at the beginning Victor Briggs had offered me a fair-sized cash present for losing. I'd said I didn't want it: I would lose if I had to, but I wouldn't be paid. He said I was a pompous young fool, but after I'd refused his offer a second time he'd kept his bribes in his pocket and his opinion of me to himself.

'Why don't you take it?' Harold Osborne had said. 'Don't forget you're passing up the 10 per cent you'd get for winning. Mr Briggs is making it up to you, that's all.'

I'd shaken my head, and he hadn't persevered. I thought that probably I was indeed a fool, but somewhere along the line it seemed that Samantha or Chloe or the others had given me this unwelcome uncomfortable conviction that one should pay for one's sins. As for three years or more I'd been let off the dilemma it was all the more infuriating to be faced with it again.

'I can't lose,' I protested. 'Daylight's the best of the bunch. Far and away. You know he is.'

'Just do it,' Victor Briggs said. 'And lower your voice, unless you want the Stewards to hear you.'

I looked at Harold Osborne. He was busy watching the horses plod around the ring and pretending not to listen to what Victor Briggs was saying.

'Harold,' I said.

He gave me a brief unemotional glance. 'Victor's right. The money's on the other way. You'll cost us a packet if you win, so don't.'

'Us?'

He nodded. 'Us. That's right. Fall off, if you have to. Come in second, if you like. But not first. Understood?'

I nodded. I understood. Back in the old pincers, three years on.

I cantered Daylight down to the start with reality winning out over rebellion, as before. If I hadn't been

27

able to afford to lose the job at twenty-three, still less could I at thirty. I was known as Osborne's jockey. I'd been with him seven years. If he chucked me out, all I'd get would be other stables' odds and ends; ride second string to other jockeys; be on a one-way track to oblivion. He wouldn't say to the Press that he'd got rid of me because I wouldn't any longer lose to order. He would tell them (regretfully, of course) that he was looking for someone younger ... had to do what was best for the owners ... terribly sad, but an end came to every jockey's career ... naturally sorry, and all that, but time marches on, don't you know?

God damn it, I thought. I didn't want to lose that race. I hated to be dishonest ... and the 10 per cent I would lose this time was big enough to make me even angrier. Why the bloody hell had Briggs gone back to this caper, after this long time? I'd thought that he'd stopped it because I'd got just far enough as a jockey for him to think it likely I would refuse. A jockey who got high enough on the winners' list was safe from that sort of pressure, because if his own stable was silly enough to give him the kick, another would welcome him in. And maybe he thought I'd gone past that stage now that I was older, and was back again in the danger area: and he was right.

We circled around while the starter called the roll, and I looked apprehensively at the four horses ranged against Daylight. There wasn't a good one among them. Nothing that on paper could defeat my own powerful gelding; which was why people were at that moment staking four pounds on Daylight to win one.

Four to one on . . .

Far from risking his own money at those odds, Victor Briggs in some subterranean way had taken bets from other people, and would have to pay out if his horse won. And so, it seemed, would Harold also: and however I might feel I did owe Harold some allegiance.

After seven years of a working relationship that had a firmer base than many a trainer-jockey alliance, I had come to regard him if not with close personal warmth at least with active friendship. He was a man of rages and charms, of black moods and boisterous highs, of tyrannical decisions and generous gifts. His voice could out-shout and out-curse any other on the Berkshire Downs, and stable lads with delicate sensibilities left his employ in droves. On the first day that I rode work for him his blistering opinion of my riding could be heard fortissimo from Wantage to Swindon, and, in his house immediately afterwards, at ten in the morning, he had opened a bottle of champagne, and we had drunk to our forthcoming collaboration.

He had trusted me always and entirely, and had defended me against criticism where many a trainer would not. Every jockey, he had said robustly, had bad patches; and he had employed me steadily through mine. He assumed that I would be, for my part, totally committed to himself and his stable, and for the past three years that had been easy.

The starter called the horses into line, and I wheeled Daylight round to point his nose in the right direction.

No starting stalls. They were never used for jump racing. A gate of elastic tapes instead.

In cold angry misery I decided that the race, from Daylight's point of view, would have to be over as near the start as possible. With thousands of pairs of binoculars trained my way, with television eyes and patrol cameras and perceptive pressmen acutely focussed, losing would be hard enough anyway, and practically suicidal if I left it until it was clear that Daylight would win. Then, if I just fell off in the last half mile for not much reason, there would be an enquiry and I might lose my licence; and it would be no comfort to know that I deserved to.

The starter put his hand on the lever and the tapes flew up, and I kicked Daylight forward into his business. None of the other jockeys wanted to make the running, and we set off in consequence at a slow pace, which compounded my troubles. Daylight, with all the time in the world, wouldn't stumble at any fence. A fluent jumper always, he hardly ever fell. Some horses couldn't be put right on the approach to a fence: Daylight couldn't be put wrong. All he accepted were the smallest indications from his jockey, and he would do the rest himself. I had ridden him many times. Won six races on him. Knew him well.

Cheat the horse. Cheat the public.

Cheat.

Damn it, I thought. *Damn and damn and damn.*

I did it at the third fence, on the decline from the top of the hill, round the sharpish bend, going away from the stands. It was the best from the credibility angle as it was the least visible to the massed watchers, and it had a sharp downhill slope on the approach side: a fence that claimed many a victim during the year.

Daylight, confused by getting the wrong signals from me, and perhaps feeling some of my turmoil and fury in the telepathic way that horses do, began to waver in the stride before take-off, putting in a small jerky extra stride where none was needed.

God, boy, I thought, I'm bloody sorry, but down you go, if I can make you: and I kicked him at the wrong moment and twitched hard on the bit in his mouth while he was in mid-air, and shifted my weight forward in front of his shoulder.

He landed awkwardly and stumbled slightly, dipping his head down to recover his balance. It wasn't really enough . . . but it would have to do. I whisked my right foot out of the stirrup and over his back, so that I was entirely on his left side, out of the saddle, clinging onto his neck.

It's almost impossible to stay on, from that position. I clung to him for about three bucking strides and then slid down his chest, irrevocably losing my grip and bouncing onto the grass under his feet. A flurry of thuds from his hooves, and a roll or two, and the noise and the galloping horses were gone.

I sat on the quiet ground and unbuckled my helmet, and felt absolutely wretched.

'Bad luck,' they said briefly in the weighing room. 'Rotten luck', and got on with the rest of the day. I wondered if any of them guessed, but maybe they didn't. No one nudged or winked or looked sardonic. It was my own embarrassed sense of shame which kept me staring mostly at the floor.

'Cheer up,' Steve Millace said, buttoning some orange and blue colours. 'It's not the end of the world.' He picked up his whip and his helmet. 'Always another day.'

'Yeah.'

He went off to ride and I changed gloomily back into street clothes. So much, I thought, for the sense of excitement in which I'd arrived. So much for winning, for half a dozen mythical trainers climbing over themselves to secure my services for the Gold Cup. So much for a nice boost to the finances, which were wilting a bit after buying a new car. On all fronts, depression.

I went out to watch the race.

Steve Millace, with more courage than sense, drove his horse at leg-tangling pace into the second last fence and crashed on landing. It was the sort of hard fast fall which cracked bones, and one could see straight away that Steve was in trouble. He struggled up as far as his knees, and then sat on his heels with his head bent forward and his arms wrapped round his body, as if he was hugging himself. Arm, shoulder, ribs . . . something had gone.

His horse, unhurt, got up and galloped away, and I stood for a while watching while two first aid men gingerly helped Steve into an ambulance. A bad day for him, too, I thought, on top of all his family troubles. What on earth made us do it? Whatever drove us to persist, disregarding injury and risk and disappointment? What lured us continually to speed, when we could earn as much sitting in an office?

I walked back to the weighing room feeling the bits of me that Daylight had trodden on beginning to stiffen with bruises. I'd be crimson and black the next day, which was nothing but usual. The biffs and bangs of the trade had never bothered me much and nothing I'd so far broken had made me frightened about the next lot. I normally had, in fact, a great feeling of physical well-being, of living in a strong and supple body, of existing as an efficient coordinated athletic whole. Nothing obtrusive. It was there. It was health.

Disillusion, I thought, would be the killer. If the job no longer seemed worth it, if people like Victor Briggs soured it beyond acceptance, at that point one would give up. But not yet. It was still the life I wanted; still the life I was far from ready to leave.

Steve came into the changing room in boots, breeches, undervest, clavicle rings, bandage and sling, with his head inclined stiffly to one side.

'Collar bone,' he said crossly. 'Bloody nuisance.' Discomfort was making his thin face gaunt, digging hollows in his cheeks and round his eyes, but what he clearly felt most was annoyance.

His valet helped him to change and dress, touching him with the gentleness of long practice, and pulling off his boots smoothly so as not to jar the shoulder. A crowd of other jockeys around us jostled and sang and made jokes, drank tea and ate fruit cake, slid out of colours and pulled on trousers, laughed and cursed and hurried. Knocking-off time, the end of the working week, back again Monday.

'I suppose,' Steve said to me, 'you couldn't possibly drive me home?' He sounded tentative, as if not sure if our friendship stretched that far.

'Yes, I should think so,' I said.

'To my mother's house? Near Ascot.'

'OK.'

'I'll get someone to fetch my car tomorrow,' he said. 'Sodding nuisance.'

I took a photograph of him and his valet, who was pulling off the second boot.

'What do you ever do with all them snaps?' the valet said.

'Put them in a drawer.'

He gave a heaven-help-us jerk of the head. 'Waste of time.'

Steve glanced at the Nikon. 'Dad said once he'd

seen some of your pics. You would put him out of business one of these days, he said.'

'He was laughing at me.'

'Yeah. Maybe. I don't know.' He inched one arm into his shirt and let the valet fasten the buttons over the other. 'Ouch,' he said, wincing.

George Millace had seen some pictures I'd had in my car, catching me looking through them as I sat in the car park at the end of a sunny spring day, waiting for the friend I'd given a lift to, to come out of the racecourse.

'Proper little Cartier Bresson,' George had said, faintly smiling. 'Let's have a look.' He'd put his arm through the open window and grasped the stack, and short of a tug-o'-war I couldn't have prevented him. 'Well, well,' he said, going through them methodically. 'Horses on the Downs, coming out of a mist. Romantic muck.' He handed them back. 'Keep it up, kid. One of these days you might take a photograph.'

He'd gone off across the car park, the heavy camera bag hanging from his shoulder, with him hitching it from time to time to ease its weight: the only photographer I knew with whom I didn't feel at home.

Duncan and Charlie, in the three years I'd lived with them, had patiently taught me all I could learn. No matter that when I was first dumped on them I was only twelve: Charlie had said from the start that as I was there I could sweep the floors and clean up in the darkroom, and I'd been glad to. The rest had come gradually and thoroughly, and I'd finished by regularly doing all of Duncan's printing, and the routine half of Charlie's. 'Our lab assistant' Charlie called me. He mixes our chemicals,' he would say. 'A dab hand with a hypodermic. Mind now, Philip, only one point four millilitres of benzol alcohol.' And I'd suck the tiny amounts accurately into the syringe and add them to the developer, and feel as if I were perhaps of some use in the world after all.

The valet helped Steve into his jacket and gave him his watch and wallet, and we went at Steve's tender pace out to my car.

'I promised to give Mum a hand with clearing up that mess, when I got back. What a bloody hope.'

'She's probably got neighbours.' I eased him into the modern Ford and went round to the driving seat. Started up in the closing dusk, switched on the lights and drove off in the direction of Ascot.

'I can't get used to the idea of Dad not being there,' Steve said.

'What happened?' I asked. 'I mean, you said he drove into a tree . . .'

'Yes.' He sighed. 'He went to sleep. At least, that's what everyone reckons. There weren't any other cars, nothing like that. There was a bend, or something, and he didn't go round it. Just drove straight ahead. He must have had his foot on the accelerator . . . The front of the car was smashed right in.' He shivered. 'He was on his way home from Doncaster. Mum's always warned him about driving on the motorway at night when he's had a long day, but this wasn't the motorway . . . he was much nearer home.'

He sounded tired and depressed, which no doubt he was, and in brief sideways glances I could see that for all my care the car's motion was hurting his shoulder.

'He'd stopped for half an hour at a friend's house,' Steve said. 'And they'd had a couple of whiskies. It was all so stupid. Just going to sleep . . .'

We drove for a long way in silence, he with his problems, and I with mine.

'Only last Saturday,' Steve said. 'Only a week ago.'

Alive one minute, dead the next . . . the same as everybody.

'Turn left here,' Steve said.

We turned left and right and left a few times and came finally to a road bordered on one side by a hedge and on the other by neat detached houses in shadowy gardens.

In the middle distance along there things were happening. There were lights and people. An ambulance with its doors open, its blue turret flashing on top. A police car. Policemen. People coming and going from one of the houses, hurrying. Every window uncurtained, spilling out light.

'My *God*,' Steve said. 'That's *their* house. Mum's and Dad's.'

I pulled up outside, and he sat unmoving, staring, stricken.

'It's Mum,' he said. 'It must be. It's Mum.'

There was something near cracking point in his voice. His face was twisted with terrible anxiety and his eyes in the reflected light looked wide and very young.

'Stay here,' I said practically. 'I'll go and see.'

CHAPTER THREE

His mum lay on the sofa in the sitting room, quivering and coughing and bleeding. Someone had attacked his mum pretty nastily, splitting her nose and mouth and eyelid and leaving her with bright raw patches on cheek and jaw. Her clothes were torn here and there, her shoes were off, and her hair stuck out in straggly wisps.

I had seen Steve's mother at the races from time to time: a pleasant well-dressed woman nearing fifty, secure and happy in her life, plainly proud of her husband and son. As the grief-stricken, burgled, beaten-up person on the sofa, she was unrecognizable.

There was a policeman sitting on a stool beside her, and a policewoman, standing, holding a bloodstained cloth. Two ambulance men hovered in the background, with a stretcher propped upright against one wall. A neighbourly looking woman stood around looking grave and worried. The room itself was a shambles, with papers and smashed furniture littering the floor. On the wall, the signs of jam and cakes, as Steve had said.

When I walked in the policeman turned his head. 'Are you the doctor?'

'No . . .' I explained who I was.

'Steve!' his mother said. Her mouth trembled, and her hands. 'Steve's hurt.' She could hardly speak, yet the fear for her son came across like a fresh torment, overshadowing anything she'd yet suffered.

'It's not bad, I promise you,' I said hastily. 'He's here, outside. It's just his collar bone. I'll get him straight away.'

I went outside and told him, and helped him out of the car. He was hunched and stiff, but seemed not to feel it.

'Why?' he said, uselessly, going up the path. 'Why did it happen? What for?'

The policeman indoors was asking the same question, and others as well.

'You were just saying, when your son came home, that there were two of them, with stockings over their faces. Is that right?'

She nodded slightly. 'Young,' she said. The word came out distorted through her cut, swollen lips. She saw Steve and held her hand out to him, to hold his own hand tight. He himself, at the sight of her, grew still paler and even more gaunt.

'White youths or black?' the policeman said.

'White.'

'What were they wearing?'

'Jeans.'

'Gloves?'

She closed her eyes. The cut one looked puffed and angry. She whispered, 'Yes.'

'Mrs Millace, please try to answer,' the policeman said. 'What did they want?'

'Safe,' she said, mumbling.

'What?'

'Safe. We haven't got a safe. I told them.' A pair of tears rolled down her cheeks. 'Where's the safe, they said. They hit me.'

'There isn't a safe here,' Steve said furiously. 'I'd like to kill them.'

'Yes, sir,' the policeman said. 'Just keep quiet, sir, if you wouldn't mind.'

'One . . . smashed things,' Mrs Millace said. 'The other just hit me.'

'Bloody *animals*,' Steve said.

'Did they say what they wanted?' the policeman asked.

'Safe.'

'Yes, but is that all? Did they say they wanted money? Jewellery? Silver? Gold coins? What exactly did they say they wanted, Mrs Millace?'

She frowned slightly, as if thinking. Then forming the words with difficulty, she said, 'All they said was "where is the safe?" '

'I suppose you do know,' I said to the policeman, 'that this house was also burgled yesterday?'

'Yes, I do, sir. I was here yesterday myself.' He

looked at me assessingly for a few seconds and turned back to Steve's mother.

'Did these two young men in stocking masks say anything about being here yesterday? Try to remember, Mrs Millace.'

'I don't . . . think so.'

'Take your time,' he said. 'Try to remember.'

She was silent for a long interval, and two more tears appeared. Poor lady, I thought. Too much pain, too much grief, too much outrage: and a good deal of courage.

At last she said, 'They were . . . like bulls. They shouted. They were rough. Rough voices. They . . . shoved me. Pushed. I opened the front door. They shoved in. Pushed me . . . in here. Started . . . smashing things. Making this mess. Shouting . . . Where is the safe. Tell us, where is the safe . . . Hit me.' She paused. 'I don't think . . . they said anything . . . about yesterday.'

'I'd like to *kill* them,' Steve said.

'Third time,' mumbled his mother.

'What was that, Mrs Millace?' the policeman said.

'Third time burgled. Happened . . . two years ago.'

'You can't just let her lie here,' Steve said violently. 'Asking all these questions . . . Haven't you got a doctor?'

'It's all right, Steve dear,' the neighbourly woman said, moving forward as if to give comfort. 'I've rung Dr Williams. He said he would come at once.' Caring and bothered, she was nonetheless enjoying the drama, and I could envisage her looking forward to telling it all to the locals. 'I was over here helping your mother earlier, Steve dear,' she said rushing on, 'but of course I went home – next door, as you know, dear – to get tea for my family, and then I heard all this shouting and it seemed all wrong, dear, so I was just coming back to see, and calling out to your mother to ask if she was all right, and those two dreadful young men just burst out of the house, dear, just *burst* out, so of course I came in here ... and well ... your poor mother ... so I rang for the police and for the ambulance, and Dr Williams ... and everybody.' She looked as if she would like at least a pat on the back for all this presence of mind, but Steve was beyond such responses.

The policeman was equally unappreciative. He said to her, 'And you still can't remember any more about the car they drove off in?'

Defensively she said, 'It was dark.'

'A lightish-coloured car, medium sized. Is that all?'

'I don't notice cars much.'

No one suggested that this was a car she should have noticed. Everyone thought it.

I cleared my throat and said diffidently to the policeman, 'I don't know if it would be of any use, and of course you may want your own man or something, but I've a camera in my car, if you could do with any photographs of all this.'

He raised his eyebrows and considered and said yes:

so I fetched both cameras and took two sets of pictures, in colour and in black and white, with close-ups of the damaged face and wide-angle shots of the room. Steve's mother bore the flashlight without complaint, and none of it took very long.

'Professional, are you, sir?' the policeman said.

I shook my head. 'Just had a lot of practice.'

He told me where to send the photographs when they were printed, and the doctor arrived.

'Don't go yet,' Steve said to me, and I looked at the desperation in his overstretched face, and stayed with him through all the ensuing bustle, sitting on the stairs out in the hall.

'I don't know what to do,' he said, joining me there. 'I can't drive like this, and I'll have to go and see that she's all right. They're taking her to hospital for the night. I suppose I can get a taxi . . .'

He didn't actually ask it, but the question was there. I stifled a small sigh and offered my services, and he thanked me as if I'd thrown him a lifebelt.

I found myself finally staying the night, because when we got back from the hospital he looked so exhausted that one simply couldn't drive away and leave him. I made us a couple of omelettes as by that time, ten o'clock, we were both starving, neither of us having eaten since breakfast; and after that I picked up some of the mess.

He sat on the edge of the sofa looking white and strained and not mentioning that his fracture was hurting quite a bit. Perhaps he hardly felt it, though one could see the pain in his face. Whenever he spoke it was of his mother.

'I'll kill them,' he said. 'Those *bastards*.'

More guts than sense, I thought; same as usual. By the sound of things, if nine-stone-seven Steve met up with the two young bulls, it would be those bastards who'd do the killing.

I started at the far end of the room, picking up a lot of magazines, newspapers, and old letters, and also the base and lid of a flat ten-by-eight-inch box which had once held photographic printing paper. An old friend.

'What shall I do with all this?' I asked Steve.

'Oh, just pile it anywhere,' he said vaguely. 'Some of it came out of that rack over there by the television.'

A wooden-slatted magazine rack, empty, lay on its side on the carpet.

'And that's Dad's rubbish box, that battered old orange thing. He kept it in that rack with the papers. Never threw it away. Just left it there, year after year. Funny really.' He yawned. 'Don't bother too much. Mum's neighbour will do it.'

I picked up a small batch of oddments; a transparent piece of film about three inches wide by eight long, several strips of 35 mm colour negatives, developed but blank, and an otherwise pleasant picture of Mrs Millace spoilt by splashes of chemical down the hair and neck.

'Those were in Dad's rubbish box, I think,' Steve said, yawning again. 'You might as well throw them away.'

I put them in the wastepaper basket, and added to them a nearly black black-and-white print which had been torn in half, and some more colour negatives covered in magenta blotches.

'He kept them to remind himself of his worst mistakes,' Steve said. 'It doesn't seem *possible* that he isn't coming back.'

There was another very dark print in a paper folder, showing a shadowy man sitting at a table. 'Do you want this?' I asked.

He shook his head. 'Dad's junk.'

I put some feminine magazines and a series on woodwork back in the magazine rack, and piled the letters on the table. The bulk of the mess left on the floor seemed to be broken china ornaments, the remnants of a spindly-legged sewing box which had been thoroughly smashed, and a small bureau, tipped on its side, with cascades of writing paper falling out of the drawers. None of the damage seemed to have had any purpose beyond noise and speed and frightening power, all of a piece with the pushing, shoving and shouting that Mrs Millace had described. A rampage designed to confuse and bewilder: and when they got no results from attacking her possessions, they'd started on her face.

I stood the bureau up again and shovelled most of

the stuff back into it, and collected together a heap of scattered tapestry patterns and dozens of skeins of wool. One began at last to see clear stretches of carpet.

'*Bastards*,' Steve said. 'I hate them. I'll kill them.'

'Why would they think your mother had a safe?'

'God knows. Perhaps they just go round ripping off new widows, screaming "safe" at them on the off-chance. I mean, if she'd had one, she'd have told them where it was, wouldn't she? After losing Dad like that. And yesterday's burglary, while we were at the funeral. Such dreadful shocks. She'd have told them. I know she would.'

I nodded.

'She can't take any more,' he said. There were tears in his voice, and his eyes were dark with the efforts of trying not to cry. It was he, I thought, who was closest to the edge. His mother would be tucked up with sympathy and sedation.

'Time for bed,' I said abruptly. 'Come on. I'll help you undress. She'll be better tomorrow.'

I woke early after an uneasy night and lay watching the dingy November dawn creep through the window. There was a good deal about life that I didn't want to get up and face; a situation common, no doubt, to the bulk of mankind. Wouldn't it be marvellous, I thought dimly, to be pleased with oneself, to look forward to the day ahead, to not have to think about mean-minded

dying grandmothers and one's own depressing dis-
honesty. Normally fairly happy-go-lucky, a taking-
things-as-they-come sort of person, I disliked being
backed into uncomfortable corners from which escape
meant action.

Things had happened to me, had arrived, all my life.
I'd never gone out looking. I had learned whatever had
come my way, whatever was there. Like photography,
because of Duncan and Charlie. And like riding,
because of my mother dumping me in a racing stable:
and if she'd left me with a farmer I would no doubt be
making hay.

Survival for so many years had been a matter of
accepting what I was given, of making myself useful,
of being quiet and agreeable and no trouble, of
repression and introversion and self-control, that I was
now, as a man, fundamentally unwilling to make a fuss
or fight.

I had taught myself for so long not to want things
that weren't offered to me that I now found very little
to want. I had made no major decisions. What I had,
had simply come.

Harold Osborne had offered me the cottage, along
with the job of stable jockey. I'd accepted. The bank
had offered a mortgage. I'd accepted. The local
garage had suggested a certain car. I'd bought it.

I understood why I was as I was. I knew why I just
drifted along, going where the tide took me. I knew
why I was passive, but I felt absolutely no desire to

change things, to stamp about and insist on being the master of my own fate.

I didn't want to look for my half-sister, and I didn't want to lose my job with Harold. I could simply drift along as usual doing nothing very positive ... and yet for some obscure reason that instinctive course was seeming increasingly *wet*.

Irritated, I put my clothes on and went downstairs, peering in at Steve on the way and finding him sound asleep.

Someone had perfunctorily swept the kitchen floor since the funeral-day burglary, pushing into a heap a lot of broken crockery and spilled groceries. The coffee and sugar had turned out the evening before to be down there in the dust, but there was milk along with the eggs in the refrigerator, and I drank some of that. Then, to pass the time, I wandered round the downstairs rooms, just looking.

The room which had been George Millace's dark-room would have been far and away the most interesting, had there been anything there: but it was in there that the original burglary had been the most thorough. All that was left was a wide bench down one side, two large deep sinks down the other, and rows of empty shelves across the end. Countless grubby out-lines and smudges on the walls showed where the loads of equipment had stood, and stains on the floor marked where he'd stored his chemicals.

He had, I knew, done a lot of his own colour

developing and printing, which most professional photographers did not. The development of colour slides and negatives was difficult and exacting, and it was safer, for consistent results, to entrust the process to commercial large-scale labs. Duncan and Charlie had sent all their colour developing out: it was only the printing from negatives, much easier, which they had done themselves.

George Millace had been a craftsman of the first order. Pity about his unkind nature.

From the looks of things he had had two enlargers, one big and one smaller, enlargers being machines which held the negatives in what was basically a box up a stick, so that a bright light could shine through the negative onto a baseboard beneath.

The head of the enlarger, holding the light and the negative, could be wound up and down the stick. The higher one wound the head above the baseboard, the larger one saw the picture. The lower head, the smaller the picture. An enlarger was in fact a projector, and the baseboard was the screen.

To take a print from a negative one wound the enlarger head up or down to get the size required, then sharpened the focus, then in darkness put a piece of photographic paper on the baseboard, then shone the light through the negative onto the photographic paper for a few seconds, then put the photographic paper through developer, fixer, washer and stabilizer, and hey presto, if one hadn't stuck thumb marks all over it, one ended up with a clear print, enlarged to the size one wanted.

Besides the enlargers, George would have had an electric box of tricks for regulating the length of exposures, and a mass of developing equipment, and a drier for drying the finished prints. He would have had dozens of sheets of various types of photographic paper in different sizes, and light-tight dispensers to store them in. He would have had rows of files holding all his past work in reference order, and safe-lights and measuring jugs and paper-trimmers and filters.

The whole lot, every scrap, had gone.

Like most serious photographers he had kept his unexposed films in the refrigerator. They too had gone, Steve had said, and were presumably at the root of the vandalism in the kitchen.

I went aimlessly into the sitting room and switched on the lights, wondering how soon I could decently wake Steve and say I was going. The half-tidied room looked cold and dreary, a miserable sight for poor Mrs Millace when she got home. From habit and from having nothing else to do I slowly carried on from where I'd stopped the night before, picking up broken scraps of vases and ornaments and retrieving reels of cotton and bits of sewing from under the chairs.

Half under the sofa itself lay a large black light-proof envelope, an unremarkable object in a photographer's house. I looked inside, but all it seemed to contain was a piece of clear thickish plastic about eight inches square, straight cut on three sides but wavy along the fourth. More rubbish. I put it back in the envelope and threw it in the wastepaper basket.

George Millace's rubbish box lay open and empty on the table. For no reason in particular, and certainly impelled by nothing more than photographic curiosity, I picked up the wastepaper basket and emptied it again on the carpet. Then I put all of George's worst mistakes back in the box where he'd kept them, and returned the broken bits of glass and china to the waste basket.

Why, I wondered, looking at the spoiled prints and pieces of film, had George ever bothered to keep them. Photographers, like doctors, tended to be quick to bury their mistakes, and didn't usually leave them hanging around in magazine racks as permanent mementoes of disasters. I had always been fond of puzzles. I thought it would be quite interesting to find out why such an expert as George should have found these particular things interesting.

Steve came downstairs in his pyjamas looking frail and hugging his injured arm, wanly contemplating the day.

'Good Lord,' he said. 'You've tidied the lot.'

'Might as well.'

'Thanks, then.' He saw the rubbish box on the table, with all its contents back inside. 'He used to keep that lot in the freezer,' he said. 'Mum told me there was a terrible fuss one day when the freezer broke down and all the peas and stuff unfroze. Dad didn't care a damn about the chickens and things and all the pies she'd made which had spoiled. All he went on and on about, she said, was that some ice-cream had melted all over his rubbish.' Steve's tired face lit into a remembering smile. 'It must have been quite a scene. She thought it was terribly funny, and when she laughed he got crosser and crosser . . .' He broke off, the smile dying. 'I can't believe he isn't coming back.'

'Did your father often keep things in the freezer?'

'Oh sure. Of course. Masses of stuff. You know what photographers are like. Always having fits about colour dyes not being permanent. He was always raving on about his work deteriorating after twenty years. He said the only way to posterity was through the deep freeze, and even that wasn't certain.'

'Well . . .' I said. 'Did the burglars also empty the freezer?'

'Good Lord.' He looked startled. 'I don't know. I never thought of that. But why should they want his films?'

'They stole the ones that were in the darkroom.'

'But the policeman said that that was just spite. What they really wanted was the equipment, which they could sell.'

'Um,' I said. 'Your father took a lot of pictures which people didn't like.'

'Yes, but only as a joke.' He was defending George, the same as ever.

'We might look in the freezer,' I suggested.

'Yes. All right. It's out at the back, in a sort of shed.'

He picked a key out of the pocket of an apron hanging in the kitchen and led the way through the back door into a small covered yard, where there were dustbins and stacks of logs and a lot of parsley growing in a tub.

'In there,' Steve said, giving me the key and nodding to a green painted door set into a bordering wall; and I went in and found a huge chest freezer standing between a motor lawn mower and about six pairs of gum boots.

I lifted the lid. Inside, filling one end and nestling next to joints of lamb and boxes of beefburgers, was a stack of three large grey metal cash boxes, each one closely wrapped in transparent polythene sheeting. Taped to the top one was a terse message:

DO NOT STORE ICE CREAM NEAR THESE BOXES

I laughed.

Steve looked at the boxes and the message and said, 'There you are. Mum said he went berserk when it all melted, but in the end nothing of his was really damaged. The food was all spoilt, but his best transparencies were OK. It was after that that he started storing them in these boxes.'

I shut the lid, and we locked the shed and went back into the house.

'You don't really think,' Steve said doubtfully, 'that the burglars were after Dad's pictures? I mean, they stole all sorts of things. Mum's rings, and his cuff-links, and her fur coat, and everything.'

'Yes . . . so they did.'

'Do you think I should mention to the police that all that stuff's in the freezer? I'm sure Mum's forgotten it's there. We never gave it a thought.'

'You could talk it over with her,' I said. 'See what she says.'

'Yes, that's best.' He looked a shade more cheerful. 'One good thing, she may have lost all the indexes and the dates and places saying where all the pictures were taken, but she has at least still got some of his best work. It hasn't all gone. Not all of it.'

I helped him to get dressed and left soon afterwards, as he said he felt better, and looked it; and I took with me George Millace's box of disasters, which Steve had said to throw in the dustbin.

'But you don't mind if I take it?' I said.

'Of course not. I know you like messing about with films, the same as he does . . . same as he did. He liked that old rubbish. Don't know why. Take it, if you want, by all means.'

He came out into the drive and watched me stow the box in the boot, alongside my two camera bags.

'You never go anywhere without a camera, do you?' he said. 'Just like Dad.'

'I suppose not.'

'Dad said he felt naked without one.'

'It gets to be part of you.' I shut the boot and locked

it from long habit. 'It's your shield. Keeps you a step away from the world. Makes you an observer. Gives you an excuse not to feel.'

He looked extremely surprised that I should think such things, and so was I surprised, not that I'd thought them, but that I should have said them to him. I smiled to take the serious truth away and leave only an impression of satire, and Steve, photographer's son, looked relieved.

I drove the hour from Ascot to Lambourn at a Sunday morning pace and found a large dark car standing outside my front door.

The cottage was one of a terrace of seven built in the Edwardian era for the not-so-rich and currently inhabited, apart from me, by a schoolteacher, a horsebox driver, a curate, a vet's assistant, sundry wives and children, and two hostels-ful of stable lads. I was the only person living alone. It seemed almost indecent, among such a crowd, to have so much space to myself.

My house was in the centre: two up, two down, with a modern kitchen stuck on at the back. A white painted brick front, nothing fancy, facing straight out onto the road, with no room for garden. A black door, needing paint. New aluminium window frames replacing the original wood, which had rotted away. An old thing patched up. Not impressive, but home.

I drove slowly past the visiting car and turned into

the muddy drive at the end of the row, continuing round to the back and parking under the corrugated plastic roof of the carport next to the kitchen. As I went I caught a glimpse of a man getting hastily out of the car, and knew he had seen me; and for my part thought only that he had no business to be pursuing me on a Sunday.

I went through the house from the back and opened the front door. Jeremy Folk stood there, tall, thin, physically awkward, using earnest diffidence as a lever, as before.

'Don't solicitors sleep on Sundays?' I said.

'Well, I say, I'm awfully sorry . . .'

'Yeah,' I said. 'Come on in, then. How long have you been waiting?'

'Nothing to . . . ah . . . worry about.'

He stepped through the door with a hint of expectancy and took the immediate disappointment with a blink. I had rearranged the interior of the cottage so that what had once been the front parlour was now divided into an entrance hall and dark-room, and in the hall section there was only a filing cabinet and the window which looked out to the street. White walls, white floor tiles; uninformative.

'This way,' I said amused, and led him past the dark-room to what had once been the back kitchen but was now mostly bathroom and in part a continuation of the hall. Beyond lay the new kitchen, and to the left, the narrow stairs.

'Which do you want,' I said. 'Coffee or talk?'

'Er . . . talk.'

'Up here, then.'

I went up the stairs, and he followed. I used one of the two original bedrooms as the sitting room, because it was the largest room in the house and had the best view of the Downs; and the smaller room next to it was where I slept.

In the sitting room, white walls, brown carpet, blue curtains, track lighting, bookshelves, sofa, low table and floor cushions. My guest looked around with small flickering glances, making assessments.

'Well?' I said neutrally.

'Er . . . that's a nice picture.' He walked over to take a closer look at the only thing hanging on the wall, a view of pale yellow sunshine falling through some leafless silver birches onto snow. 'It's . . . er . . . a print?'

'It's a photograph,' I said.

'Oh! Is it really? It looks like a painting.' He turned away and said, 'Where would you live if you had a hundred thousand pounds?'

'I told her I didn't want it.' I looked at the angular helpless way he was standing there, dressed that day not in working charcoal flannel but in a tweed jacket with decorative leather patches on the elbows. The brain under the silly ass act couldn't be totally disguised, and I wondered vaguely whether he had developed that surface because he was embarrassed by his own acuteness.

58

'Sit down,' I said, gesturing to the sofa, and he folded his long legs as if I'd given him a gift. I sat on a bean-bag floor cushion and said, 'Why didn't you mention the money when I saw you at Sandown?'

He seemed almost to wriggle. 'I just . . . ah . . . thought I'd try you first on blood-stronger-than-water, don't you know?'

'And if that failed, you'd try greed?'

'Sort of.'

'So that you would know what you were dealing with?'

He blinked.

'Look,' I sighed. 'I do understand thoughts of one syllable, so why don't you just . . . drop the waffle?'

His body relaxed for the first time into approximate naturalness and he gave me a small smile that was mostly in the eyes.

'It gets to be a habit,' he said.

'So I gathered.'

He cast a fresh look around the room, and I said, 'All right, say what you see.'

He did so, without squirming and without apology. 'You like to be alone. You're emotionally cold. You don't need props. And unless you took that photo-graph, you've no vanity.'

'I took it.'

'Tut tut.'

'Yes,' I said. 'So what did you come for?'

59

'Well, obviously, to persuade you to do what you don't want to.'

'To try to find the half-sister I didn't know I had?'

He nodded.

'Why?'

After a very short pause into which I could imagine him packing a lot of pros and cons he said, 'Mrs Nore is insisting on leaving a fortune to someone who can't be found. It is . . . unsatisfactory.'

'Why is she insisting?'

'I don't know. She instructs my grandfather. She doesn't take his advice. He's old and he's fed up with her, and so is my uncle, and they've shoved the whole mess onto me.'

'Three detectives couldn't find Amanda.'

'They didn't know where to look.'

'Nor do I,' I said.

He considered me. 'You'd know.'

'No.'

'Do you know who your father is?' he said.

CHAPTER FOUR

I sat with my head turned towards the window, looking out at the bare calm life of the Downs. A measurable silence passed. The Downs would be there for ever.

I said, 'I don't want to get tangled up in a family I don't feel I belong to. I don't like their threads falling over me like a web. That old woman can't claw me back just because she feels like it, after all these years.'

Jeremy Folk didn't answer directly, and when he stood up some of the habitual gaucheness had come back into his movements, though not yet into his voice.

'I brought the reports we received from the three firms of detectives,' he said. 'I'll leave them with you.'

'No, don't.'

'It's useless,' he said. He looked again around the room. 'I see quite plainly that you don't want to be involved. But I'm afraid I'm going to plague you until you are.'

'Do your own dirty work.'

He smiled. 'The dirty work was done about thirty

61

years ago, wasn't it? Before either of us was born. This is just the muck floating back on the tide.'

'Thanks a bunch.'

He pulled a long bulging envelope out of the inside pocket of his country tweed and put it carefully down on the table. 'They're not very long reports. You could just read them, couldn't you?'

He didn't expect an answer, or get one. He just moved vaguely towards the door to indicate that he was ready to leave, and I went downstairs with him and saw him out to his car.

'By the way,' he said, pausing awkwardly halfway into the driving seat, 'Mrs Nore really is dying. She has cancer of the spine. Secondaries, they say. Nothing to be done. She'll live maybe six weeks, or maybe six months. They can't tell. So . . . er . . . no time to waste, don't you know?'

I spent the bulk of the day contentedly in the dark-room, developing and printing the black-and-white shots of Mrs Millace and her troubles. They came out clear and sharp so that one could actually read the papers on the floor, and I wondered casually just where the borderline fell between positive vanity and simple pleasure in a job efficiently done. Perhaps it had been vanity to mount and hang the silver birches . . . but apart from the content the large size of the print had been a technical problem, and it had all come out right . . . and what did a sculptor do, throw a sack over his best statue?

Jeremy Folk's envelope stayed upstairs on the table where he'd put it; unopened, contents unread. I ate some tomatoes and some muesli when I grew hungry, and cleared up the darkroom, and at six o'clock locked my doors and walked up the road to see Harold Osborne.

Sundays at six o'clock he expected me for a drink, and each Sunday from six to seven we talked over what had happened in the past week and discussed plans for the week ahead. For all his unpredictable up-and-down moods Harold was a man of method and he hated anything to interrupt these sessions, which he referred to as our military briefings. His wife during that hour answered the telephone and took messages for him to ring back as requested, and they had once had a blazing row with me there because she had burst in to say their dog had been run over and killed.

'You could have told me in twenty minutes,' he yelled. 'Now how the hell am I going to concentrate on Philip's orders for the Schweppes?'

'But the dog,' she wailed.

'Damn the dog.' He'd ranted at her for several minutes and then he'd gone out into the road and wept over the body of his mangled friend. Harold, I supposed, was everything I wasn't: moody, emotional, flamboyant, bursting with peaks of feeling, full of rage and love and guile and gusto. Only in our basic belief in getting things right were we alike, and that tacit agreement stuck us together in underlying peace. He might scream at me violently, but he didn't expect me to mind, and because I knew him well, I didn't. Other jockeys and trainers and several pressmen had said to me often in varying degrees of exasperation or humour, 'I don't know how you put up with it,' and the answer was always the true one . . . 'Easily.'

On that particular Sunday the sacrosanct hour had been interrupted before it could begin, because Harold had a visitor. I walked through his house from the stable entrance and went into the comfortable cluttered sitting room-office, and there in one of the armchairs was Victor Briggs.

'Philip!' Harold said, welcoming and smiling. 'Pour yourself a drink. We're just going to run through the videotape of yesterday. Sit down. Are you ready? I'll switch on.'

Victor Briggs gave me several nods of approval and a handshake. No gloves, I thought. Cold pale dry hands with nothing aggressive in the grasp. Without the broadrimmed hat he had thick glossy straight black hair which was receding slightly above the eyebrows to leave a centre peak: and without the heavy navy overcoat, a plain dark suit. Indoors he still wore the close-guarded expression as if afraid his thoughts might show, but there was overall a distinct air of satisfaction. Not a smile, just an atmosphere.

I opened a can of Coca-Cola and poured some into a glass.

'Don't you drink?' Victor Briggs asked.

'Champagne,' Harold said. 'That's what he drinks, don't you, Philip?' He was in great good humour, his voice and presence amplifying the warm russet colours of the room, resonant as brass.

Harold's reddish-brown hair sprang in wiry curls all over his head, as untamable as his nature. He was fifty-two at that time and looked ten years younger, a big burly six feet of active muscle commanded by a strong but ambiguous face, his features more rounded than hawkish.

He switched on the video machine and sat back in his armchair to watch Daylight's débâcle in the Sandown Pattern 'Chase, as pleased as if he'd won the Grand National. A good job no Stewards were peering in, I thought. There was no mistaking the trainer's joy in his horse's failure.

The recording showed me on Daylight going down to the start, and lining up, and setting off: odds-on favourite at four to one on, said the commentator; only got to jump round to win. Immaculate leaps over the first two fences. Strong and steady up past the stands. Daylight just in the lead, dictating the pace, but all five runners closely bunched. Round the top bend, glued to the rails . . . faster downhill. The approach to the third fence . . . everything looking all right . . . and then the screw in the air and the stumbling landing, and the figure in red and blue silks going over the horse's neck and down under the feet. A groaning roar from the crowd, and the commentator's unemotional voice. 'Daylight's down at that fence, and now in the lead is Little Moth ...'

The rest of the race rolled on into a plodding undistinguished finish, and then came a re-run of Daylight's departure, with afterthought remarks from the commentator. 'You can see the horse try to put in an extra stride, throwing Philip Nore forward ... the horse's head ducks on landing, giving his jockey no chance ... poor Philip Nore clinging on ... but hopeless ... horse and jockey both unhurt.'

Harold stood up and switched the machine off. 'Artistic,' he said, beaming down. 'I've run through it twenty times. It's impossible to tell.'

'No one suspected,' Victor Briggs said. 'One of the Stewards said to me "what rotten bad luck".' There was a laugh somewhere inside Victor Briggs, a laugh not quite breaking the surface but quivering in the chest. He picked up a large envelope which had lain beside his gin and tonic, and held it out to me. 'Here's my thank you, Philip.'

I said matter-of-factly, 'It's kind of you, Mr Briggs. But nothing's changed. I don't like to be paid for losing ... I can't help it.'

Victor Briggs put the envelope down again without comment, and it wasn't he who was immediately angry, but Harold.

'Philip,' he said loudly, towering above me. 'Don't be such a bloody prig. There's a great deal of money in that envelope. Victor's being very generous. Take it and thank him, and shut up.'

'I'd ... rather not.'

'I don't care what you'd bloody rather. You're not so squeamish when it comes to committing the crime, are you, it's just the thirty pieces of silver you turn your pious nose up at. You make me sick. And you'll take that bloody money if I have to ram it down your throat.'

'Well, you will,' I said.

'I will what?'

'Have to ram it down my throat.'

Victor Briggs actually laughed, though when I glanced at him his mouth was tight shut as if the sound had escaped without his approval.

'And,' I said slowly, 'I don't want to do it any more.'

'You'll do what you're bloody told,' Harold said.

Victor Briggs rose purposefully to his feet, and the two of them, suddenly silent, stood looking down at me.

It seemed that a long time passed, and then Harold said in a quiet voice which held a great deal more threat than his shouting. 'You'll do what you're told, Philip.'

I stood up in my turn. My mouth had gone dry, but I made my voice sound as neutral, as calm, as unprovoking as possible.

'Please ... don't ask me for a repeat of yesterday.'

Victor Briggs narrowed his eyes. 'Did the horse hurt you? He trod on you . . . you can see it on the video.'

I shook my head. 'It's not that. It's the losing. You know I hate it. I just . . . don't want you to ask me . . . again.'

More silence.

'Look,' I said. 'There are degrees. Of course I'll give a horse an easy ride if he isn't a hundred per cent fit and a hard race would ruin him for next time out. Of course I'll do that, it only makes sense. But no more like Daylight yesterday. I know I used to . . . but yesterday was the last.'

Harold said coldly, 'You'd better go now Philip. I'll talk to you in the morning,' and I nodded, and left, and there were none of the warm handshakes which had greeted my arrival.

What would they do? I wondered. I walked in the windy dark down the road from Harold's house to mine as I had on hundreds of Sundays, and wondered if it would be for the last time. If he wanted to he could put other jockeys up on his horses from that day onwards. He was under no obligation to give me rides. I was classed as self-employed, because I was paid per race by the owners, and not per week by the trainer; and there was no such thing as 'unfair dismissal' inquiries for the self-employed.

I suppose it was too much to hope that they would let me get away with it. Yet for three years they had run the Briggs horses honestly, so why not in future?

And if they insisted on fraud, couldn't they get some other poor young slob just starting his career, and put the squeezers on him when they wanted a race lost? Foolish wishes, all of them. I'd put my job down at their feet like a football and at that moment they were probably kicking it out of the ground.

It was ironic. I hadn't known I was going to say what I had. It had just forced its own way out, like water through a new spring.

All those races I'd thrown away in the past, not liking it, but doing it . . . Why was it so different now? Why was the revulsion so strong now that I didn't think I *could* do a Daylight again, even if to refuse meant virtually the end of being a jockey?

When had I changed . . . and how could it have happened without my noticing? I didn't know. I just had a sense of having already travelled too far to turn back. Too far down a road where I didn't want to go.

I went upstairs and read the three detectives' reports on Amanda because it was better, on the whole, than thinking about Briggs and Harold.

Two of the reports had come from fairly large firms and one from a one-man outfit, and all three had spent a lot of ingenuity padding out very few results. Justifying their charges, no doubt. Copiously explaining what they had all spent so long not finding out: and all three, not surprisingly, had not found out approximately the same things.

None of them, for a start, could find any trace of her birth having been registered. They all expressed doubt and disbelief over this discovery, but to me it was no surprise at all. I had discovered that I myself was unregistered when I tried to get a passport, and the fuss had gone on for months.

I knew my name, my mother's name, my birth date, and that I'd been born in London. Officially, however, I didn't exist. 'But here I am,' I'd protested, and I'd been told, 'Ah yes, but you don't have a piece of paper to prove it, do you?' There had been affidavits by the ton and miles of red tape, and I'd missed the race I'd been offered in France by the time I got permission to go there.

The detectives had all scoured Somerset House for records of Amanda Nore, aged between ten and twenty-five, possibly born in Sussex. In spite of the fairly unusual name, they had all completely failed.

I sucked my teeth, thinking that I could do better than that about her age.

She couldn't have been born before I went to live with Duncan and Charlie, because I'd seen my mother fairly often before that, about five or six times a year, and often for a week at a time, and I would have known if she'd had a child. The people she left me with used to talk about her when they thought I wasn't listening, and I gradually understood what I remembered them saying, though sometimes not for years afterwards: but none of them, ever, had hinted that she was pregnant.

That meant that I was at least twelve when Amanda was born; and consequently she couldn't at present be older than eighteen.

At the other end of things she couldn't possibly be as young as ten. My mother, I was sure, had died sometime between Christmas and my eighteenth birthday. She might have been desperate enough at that time to write to her own mother and send her the photograph. Amanda in the photograph had been three . . . so Amanda, if she was still alive, would be at least fifteen.

Sixteen or seventeen, most likely. Born during the three years when I hadn't seen my mother at all, when I'd lived with Duncan and Charlie.

I went back to the reports . . .

All three detectives had been given the last known address of Caroline Nore, Amanda's mother: Pine Woods Lodge, Mindle Bridge, Sussex. All three had trekked there 'to make enquiries'.

Pine Woods Lodge, they rather plaintively reported, was not as the name might suggest a small private hotel complete with guest register going back umpteen years, forwarding addresses attached. Pine Woods Lodge was an old Georgian mansion gone to ruin and due to be demolished. There were trees growing in what had been the ballroom. Large sections had no roof.

It was owned by a family which had largely died out

twenty-five years earlier, leaving distant heirs who had no wish and no money to keep the place up. They had let the house at first to various organizations (list attached, supplied by Estate Agents) but of latter years it had been inhabited by squatters and vagrants. The dilapidation was now so advanced that even such as they had moved out, and the five acres the house was built on were to come up for auction within three months; but as whoever bought the land was going to have to demolish the mansion, it was not expected to fetch much of a price.

I read through the list of tenants, none of whom had stayed long. A nursing home. A sisterhood of nuns. An artists' commune. A boys' youth club adventure project. A television film company. A musicians' cooperative. Colleagues of Supreme Grace. The Confidential Mail Order Corporation.

One of the detectives, persevering, had investigated the tenants as far as he could, and had added unflattering comments.

Nursing home	– euthanasia for all. Closed by council.
Nuns	– disbanded through bitchiness.
Artists	– left disgusting murals.
Boys	– broke everything still whole.
T.V.	– needed a ruin to film.

Musicians	– fused all the electricity.
Colleagues	– religious nutters.
Mail order	– perverts' delights.

There were no dates attached to the tenancies, but presumably if the Estate Agents could still furnish the list, they would have kept some other details. If I was right about when my mother had written her desperate letter, I should at least be able to find out which bunch of kooks she had been staying with.

If I wanted to, of course.

Sighing, I read on.

Copies of the photograph of Amanda Nore had been extensively displayed in public places (newsagents' shop windows) in the vicinity of the small town of Mindle Bridge, but no one had come forward to identify either the child or the stable yard or the pony.

Advertisements had been inserted (accounts attached) in various periodicals and one national Sunday newspaper (for six weeks) stating that if Amanda Nore wished to hear something to her advantage she should write to Folk, Langley, Son and Folk, solicitors, of St Albans, Herts.

One of the detectives, the one who had persisted with the tenants, had also enterprisingly questioned the Pony Club, but to no avail. They had never had a member called Amanda Nore. He had furthermore written to the British Show Jumping Association, with the same result.

A canvass of schools in a wide area round Mindle Bridge had produced no one called Amanda Nore on the registers, past or present.

She had not come into council care in Sussex. She was on no official list of any sort. No doctor or dentist had heard of her. She had not been confirmed, married, buried or cremated within the county.

The reports came to the same conclusions: that she had been, or was being, brought up elsewhere (possibly under a different name), and was no longer interested in riding.

I shuffled the typed sheets together and returned them to the envelope. They had tried, one had to admit. They had also indicated their willingness to continue to search through each county in the land, if the considerable expenditure should be authorized: but they couldn't in any way guarantee success.

Their collective fee must already have been fearful. The authorization, anyway, seemed not to have been forthcoming. I wondered sardonically if the old woman had thought of me to look for Amanda because it would cost so much less. A promise, a bribe . . . no foal, no fee.

I couldn't understand her late interest in her long ignored grandchildren. She'd had a son of her own, a boy my mother had called 'my hateful little brother'. He would have been about ten when I was born, which made him now about forty, presumably with children of his own.

Uncle. Cousins. Half-sister. Grandmother.

I didn't want them. I didn't want to know them or be drawn into their lives. I was in no way whatever going to look for Amanda.

I stood up with decision and went down to the kitchen to do something about cheese and eggs: and to stave off the thought of Harold a bit longer I fetched George Millace's box of trash in from the car and opened it on the kitchen table, taking out the items and looking at them one by one.

On a closer inspection it still didn't seem to make much sense that he should have kept those particular odds and ends. They didn't have the appearance of interesting or unique mistakes. Sorting my way through them I concluded with disappointment that it had been a waste of time after all to bring them home.

I picked up the folder which contained the dark print of a shadowy man sitting at a table and thought vaguely that it was odd to have bothered to put such an over-exposed mess into a mount.

Shrugging, I slid the dark print out onto my hand . . . and it was then that I found George's private pot of gold.

CHAPTER FIVE

It was not, at first sight, very exciting.

Sellotaped onto the back of the print there was an envelope made of the special sort of sulphur-free paper used by careful professionals for the long-term storage of developed film. Inside the envelope, a negative.

It was the negative from which the print had been made, but whereas the print was mostly black and elsewhere very dark greys, the negative itself was clear and sharp with many details and highlights.

I looked at the print and at the negative, side by side.

I had no quickening of the pulse. No suspicions, no theories, merely curiosity. As I also had the means and the time, I went back into the darkroom and made four five-by-four inch prints, each at a different exposure, from one second to eight seconds.

Not even the longest exposure looked exactly like George's dark print, so I started again with the most suitable exposure, six seconds, and left the photograph in the developer too long, until the sharp outlines first went dark and then mostly disappeared, leaving a grey man sitting at a table against blackness. At that point I lifted the paper from the tray of developer and transferred it to the one containing fixer; and what I had then was another print almost exactly like George's.

Leaving a print too long in the developing fluid had to be one of the commonest mistakes on earth. If George's attention had been distracted and he'd left a print too long in developer, he'd simply have cursed and thrown the ruin away. Why, then, had he kept it? And mounted it. And stuck the clear sharp negative onto the back?

It wasn't until I switched on a bright light and looked more closely at the best of the four original exposures I'd made that I understood why: and I stood utterly still in the darkroom, taking in the implications in disbelief.

With something approaching a whistle I finally moved. I switched off the white light, and, when my eyes had accustomed themselves again to the red safelight, I made another print, four times as large, and on higher contrast grade of paper, to get as clear a result as I could possibly manage.

I switched on the white light again and fed the finished print through the drier, and then I looked at what I'd got.

What I'd got was a picture of two people talking together who had sworn on oath in a court of law that they had never met.

There wasn't the slightest possibility of a mistake.

The shadowy man was now revealed as a customer sitting at a table outside a café somewhere in France. The man himself was a Frenchman with a moustache who had merely happened to be sitting there, a plate and a glass by his hand. The café had a name: Le Lapin d'Argent. There were advertisements for beer and lottery tickets in its half-curtained window, and a waiter in an apron standing in the doorway. A woman some way inside was sitting at a cash desk in front of a mirror, looking out to the street. The detail was sharp throughout, with remarkable depth of focus. George Millace at his usual expert best.

Sitting together at a table outside the café window were two men, both of them facing the camera but with their heads turned towards each other, unmistakably deep in conversation. A wine glass stood in front of each of them, half full, with a bottle to one side. There were coffee cups also, and an ashtray with a half-smoked cigar balanced on the edge. All the signs of a lengthy meeting.

Both men had been involved in an affair which had shaken the racing world like a thunderclap eighteen months earlier. Elgin Yaxley, the one on the left of the photograph, had owned five expensive steeplechasers which had been trained in Lambourn. At the end of the 'chasing season all five had been sent to a local farmer for a few weeks' summer break out at grass; and then, out in the fields, they had all been shot dead with a rifle. Terence O'Tree, the man on the right in the photograph, had shot them.

Some smart police work (aided by two young boys out at dawn when their parents thought them safe in bed) had tracked down and identified O'Tree, and brought him to court.

All five horses had been heavily insured. The insurance company, screeching with disbelief, had tried their damnedest to prove that Yaxley himself had hired O'Tree to do the killing, but both men had consistently denied it, and no link between them had been found.

O'Tree, saying he'd shot the horses just because he'd felt like it . . . 'for a bit o' target practice, like, your honour, and how was I to know they was valuable racehorses' . . . had been sent to jail for nine months with a recommendation that he should see a psychiatrist.

Elgin Yaxley, indignantly proclaiming his virtue and threatening to sue the insurance company for defamation of character if they didn't instantly pay up, had wrung out of them the whole insured amount and had then faded out of the racing scene.

The insurance company, I thought, would surely have paid George Millace a great deal for his photograph, if they had known it existed. Probably 10 per cent of what they would not have had to pay Yaxley. I couldn't remember the exact sums, but I knew the total insured value of the five horses had been getting on for a hundred and fifty thousand pounds. It had been, in fact, the very size of the pay-out which had infuriated the insurers into suspecting fraud.

So why hadn't George asked for a reward ... and why had he so carefully hidden the negative ... and why had his house been burgled three times? For all that I'd never liked George Millace, it was the obvious answer to those questions that I disliked even more.

In the morning I walked up to the stables and rode out at early exercise as usual. Harold behaved in his normal blustery fashion, raising his voice over the scouring note of the November wind. The lads scowled and sulked as the vocal lash landed, and one or two, I reckoned, would be gone by the week's end. When lads left any stable nowadays they tended simply not to turn up one morning, nor ever again. They would sidle off to some other stable and the first news their old masters would have would be requests for references from the new. Notice, for many of the modern breed of lads, was something they never gave. Notice led to arguments and aggro, and who wanted that, man, when ducking out was so much easier? The lad population washed in and out of British stables like a swirling endless river, with long-stayers being an exception rather than the rule.

'Breakfast,' Harold bellowed at me at one point. 'Be there.'

I nodded. I usually went home for breakfast even

if I were riding out second lot, which I did only on non-racing days, and not always even then. Breakfast, in Harold's wife's view, consisted of a huge fry-up accompanied by mountains of toast served on the big kitchen table with generosity and warmth. It always smelled and looked delicious, and I always fell.

'Another sausage, Philip?' Harold's wife said, lavishly shovelling straight from the pan. 'And some hot fried potatoes?'

'You're destroying him, woman,' Harold said, reaching for the butter.

Harold's wife smiled at me in her special way. She thought I was too thin; and she thought I needed a wife. She told me so, often. I disagreed with her on both counts, but I dare say she was right.

'Last night,' Harold said. 'We didn't discuss the week's plans.'

'No.'

'There's Pamphlet at Kempton on Wednesday,' he said. 'In the two mile hurdle; and Tishoo and Sharpener on Thursday . . .'

He talked about the races for some time, munching vigorously all the while, so that I got my riding instructions out of the side of his mouth accompanied by crumbs.

'Understood?' he said finally.

'Yes.'

It appeared that after all I had not been given the instant sack, and for that I was relieved and grateful, but it was clear all the same that the precipice wasn't all that far away.

Harold glanced across the big kitchen to where his wife was stacking things in the dishwasher and said, 'Victor doesn't like your attitude.'

I didn't answer.

Harold said, 'The first thing one demands from a jockey is loyalty.'

That was rubbish. The first thing one demanded from a jockey was value for money.

'My Füehrer, right or wrong?' I said.

'Owners won't stand for jockeys passing moral judgements on them.'

'Owners shouldn't defraud the public, then.'

'Have you finished eating?' he demanded.

I sighed regretfully. 'Yes.'

'Then come into the office.'

He led the way into the russet-coloured room which was filled with chill bluish Monday morning light and had no fire yet in the grate.

'Shut the door,' he said.

I shut it.

'You'll have to choose, Philip,' he said. He stood by the fireplace with one foot on the hearth, a big man in riding clothes, smelling of horses and fresh air and fried eggs.

I waited non-committally.

'Victor will eventually want another race lost. Not at once, I grant you, because it would be too obvious.

But in the end, yes. He says if you really mean you won't do it, we'll have to get someone else.'

'For those races only?'

'Don't be stupid. You're not stupid. You're too bloody smart for your own good.'

I shook my head. 'Why does he want to start this caper again? He's won a lot of prize money playing it straight these last three years.'

Harold shrugged. 'I don't know. What does it matter? He told me on Saturday when we got to Sandown that he'd laid his horse and that I was on to a big share of the profit. We've all done it before . . . why not again? Just what has got into you, Philip, that you're swooning over a little fiddle like a bloody virgin?'

I didn't know the answer. He swept on anyway before I'd thought of a reply. 'Well, you just work it out, boy. Whose are the best horses in the yard? Victor's. Who buys good new horses to replace the old? Victor. Who pays his training bills on the nose, bills for usually five horses? Victor. Who owns more horses in this yard than anyone else? Victor. And which owner can I least afford to lose, particularly as he has been with me for more than ten years and has provided me with a large proportion of the winners I've trained in the past, and is likely to provide most of those I train in the future? Just who, do you think, my business most depends on?'

I stared at him. I supposed that I hadn't realized

until then that he was in perhaps the same position as myself. Do what Victor wanted, or else.

'I don't want to lose you, Philip,' he said. 'You're a prickly bastard, but we've got on all right all these years. You won't go on for ever, though. You've been racing ... what ... ten years?'

I nodded.

'Three or four more, then. At the most, five. Pretty soon you won't bounce back from those falls the way you do now. And at any time a bad one might put you out of action for good. So look at it straight, Philip. Who do I need most in the long term, you or Victor?'

In a sort of melancholy we walked into the yard, where Harold shouted, but half-heartedly, at a couple of dawdling lads.

'Let me know,' he said, turning towards me.

'All right.'

'I want you to stay.'

I was surprised, but also pleased.

'Thanks,' I said.

He gave me a clumsy buffet on the shoulder, the nearest he'd ever come to the slightest show of affection. More than all the threatening and screaming on earth it made me want to agree to do what he asked; a reaction, I acknowledged flickeringly, as old as the hills. It was often kindness that finally broke the prisoner's spirit, not torture. One's defences were always defiantly angled outward to withstand aggression: it was kindness which crept round behind and stabbed you in the back, so that your will evaporated into tears and gratitude. Defences against kindness were much harder to build. And not the defences I would ever have thought I needed against Harold.

I sought instinctively to change the subject, and came up with the nearest thought to hand, which was George Millace and his photograph.

'Um,' I said, as we stood a shade awkwardly. 'Do you remember those five horses of Elgin Yaxley's, that were shot?'

'What?' He looked bewildered. 'What's that got to do with Victor?'

'Nothing at all,' I said. 'I was just thinking about them, yesterday.'

Irritation immediately cancelled out the passing moment of emotion, which was probably a relief to us both.

'For God's sake,' he said sharply. 'I'm serious. Your career's at stake. You can do what you damn well like. You can bloody well go to hell. It's up to you.'

I nodded.

He turned away abruptly and took two purposeful steps. Then he stopped, looked back, and said, 'If you're so bloody interested in Elgin Yaxley's horses, why don't you ask Kenny?' He pointed to one of the lads, who was filling two buckets by the tap. 'He looked after them.'

He turned his back again and firmly strode away, outrage and anger thumping down with every foot.

I walked irresolutely over to Kenny, not sure what questions I wanted to ask, or even if I wanted to ask questions at all.

Kenny was one of those people whose defences were the other way round: impervious to kindness, open to fright. Kenny was a natural near-delinquent who had been treated with so much understanding by social workers that he could shrug off pleasant approaches with contempt.

He watched me come with an expression wilfully blank to the point of insolence, his habitual expression. Skin reddened by the wind; eyes slightly watering; spots.

'Mr Osborne said you used to work for Bart Underfield,' I said.

'So what?'

The water splashed over the top of the first bucket. He bent to remove it, and kicked the second one forward under the tap.

'And looked after some of Elgin Yaxley's horses?'

'So what?'

'So were you sorry when they were shot?'

He shrugged. 'Suppose so.'

'What did Mr Underfield say about it?'

'Huh?' His gaze rested squarely on my face. 'He didn't say nothing.'

'Wasn't he angry?'

'Not as I noticed.'

'He must have been,' I said.

Kenny shrugged again.

'At the very least,' I said. 'He was five horses short, and no trainer with his size stable can afford that.'

'He didn't say nothing.' The second bucket was nearly full, and Kenny turned off the tap. 'He didn't seem to care much about losing them. Something cheesed him off a bit later, though.'

'What did?'

Kenny looked uninterested and picked up the buckets. 'Don't know. He was right grumpy. Some of the owners got fed up and left.'

'So did you,' I said.

'Yeah.' He started walking across the yard with water sloshing gently at each step. I went with him, warily keeping a dry distance. 'What's the point of staying when a place is going down the drain?'

'Were Yaxley's horses in good shape when they went off to the farm?' I asked.

'Sure.' He looked slightly puzzled. 'Why are you asking?'

'No real reason. Someone mentioned those horses . . . and Mr Osborne said you looked after them. I was just interested.'

'Oh.' He nodded. 'They had the vet in court, you know, to say the horses were fine the day before they died. He went to the farm to give one of them some anti-tetanus jabs, and he said he looked them all over, and they were OK.'

'Did you go to the trial?'

'No. Read it in the *Sporting Life*.' He reached the row of boxes and put the buckets down outside one of the doors. 'That all, then?'

'Yes. Thanks, Kenny.'

'Tell you something . . .' He looked almost surprised at his own sudden helpfulness.

'What?'

'That Mr Yaxley,' he said. 'You'd've thought he'd been pleased getting all that lolly, even if he had lost his horses, but he came into Underfield's yard one day in a right proper rage. Come to think of it, it was after that that Underfield went sour. And Yaxley, of course, he buggered off out of racing and we never saw no more of him. Not while I was there, we didn't.'

I walked thoughtfully home, and when I got there the telephone was ringing.

'Jeremy Folk,' a familiar voice said.

'Oh, not again,' I protested.

'Did you read those reports?'

'Yes, I did. And I'm not going looking for her.'

'Be a good fellow,' he said.

'No.' I paused. 'To get you off my back, I'll help you a bit. But you must do the looking.'

'Well . . .' He sighed. 'What sort of help?'

I told him my conclusions about Amanda's age, and also suggested he should get the dates of the various tenancies of Pine Woods Lodge from the estate agents.

'My mother was probably there thirteen years ago,' I said. 'And now it's all yours.'

'But I *say* . . .' he almost wailed. 'You simply can't stop there.'

'I simply can.'

'I'll get back to you.'

'Just leave me alone,' I said.

I drove into Swindon to take the colour film to the processors, and on the way thought about the life and times of Bart Underfield.

I knew him in the way one got to know everyone in racing if one lived long enough in Lambourn. We met occasionally in the village shops and in other people's houses, as well as at the races. We exchanged 'Good mornings' and 'Hard lucks' and a variety of vague nods. I had never ridden for him because he had never asked me; and he'd never asked me, I thought, because he didn't like me.

He was a small busy man full of importance, given to telling people confidentially what other more successful trainers had done wrong. 'Of course Walwyn shouldn't have run such-and-such at Ascot,' he would say. 'The distance was all wrong, one could see it a mile off.'

Strangers thought him very knowledgeable. Lambourn thought him an ass.

No one had suggested, however, that he was such an ass as to deliver his five best horses to the slaughter. Everyone had undoubtedly felt sorry for him, particularly as Elgin Yaxley had not spent the insurance money on buying new and equal animals, but had merely departed altogether, leaving Bart a great deal worse off.

Those horses, I reflected, had undoubtedly been good, and must always have earned more than their keep, and could have been sold for high prices. They had been insured above their market value, certainly, but not by impossible margins if one took into account the prizes they couldn't win if they were dead. It was the fact that there seemed to be little profit in killing them that had finally baffled the suspicious insurers into paying up.

That . . . and no trace of a link between Elgin Yaxley and Terence O'Tree.

In Swindon the processors, who knew me well, said I was lucky, they were just going to feed a batch through, and if I cared to hang about I could have my negatives back in a couple of hours. I did some oddments of shopping and in due course picked up the developed films, and went home.

In the afternoon I printed the coloured versions of Mrs Millace, and sent them off with the black-and-white lot to the police; and in the evening I tried –

and failed – to stop thinking in uncomfortable circles about Amanda and Victor Briggs and George Millace.

By far the worst was Victor Briggs and Harold's ultimatum. The jockey life suited me fine in every way, physically, mentally, financially. I'd put off for years the thought that one day I would have to do something else: the 'one day' had always been in the mists of the future, not staring me brutally in the face.

The only thing I knew anything about besides horses was photography, but there were thousands of photographers all over the place ... everyone took photographs, every family had a camera, the whole western world was awash with photographers ... and to make a living at it one had to be exceptionally good.

One also had to work exceptionally hard. The photographers I knew on the racecourse were always running about: scurrying from the start to the last fence and from there up to the unsaddling enclosures before the winner got there, and then down the course again for the next race, and six times, at least, every after-noon, five or six days a week. Some of their pictures they rushed off to news agencies who might offer them to newspapers, and some they sent to magazines, and some they flogged to the owners of the horses, and some to sponsors handing over cups.

If you were a racing photographer the pictures didn't come to you, you had to go out looking. And when you'd got them, the customers didn't flock to your door, you had to go out selling. It was all a lot different from

91

Duncan and Charlie, who had mostly done still-life things like pots and pans and clocks and garden furniture for advertisements.

There were very few full-time successful racing photographers. Fewer than ten, probably. Of those perhaps four were outstanding; and one of those four had been George Millace.

If I tried to join their ranks the others wouldn't hinder me, but they wouldn't help me either. I'd be out there on my own, stand or fall.

I wouldn't mind the running about, I thought: it was the selling part that daunted. Even if I considered my pictures good enough, I couldn't push.

And what else?

Setting up as a trainer was out. I hadn't the capital, and training racehorses was no sort of life for someone who liked stretches of silent time and being alone. Trainers talked to people from dawn to bedtime and lived in a whirl.

What I wanted, and instinctively knew that I would always need, was to continue to be self-employed. A regular wage packet looked like chains. An illogical feeling, but overwhelming. Whatever I did, I would have to do it on my own.

The habit of never making decisions would have to be broken. I could drift, I saw, into jobs which had none of the terrific satisfactions of being a jockey. I had been lucky so far, but if I wanted to find contentment in the next chapter I would have for once to be positive.

Damn Victor Briggs, I thought violently.

Inciting jockeys to throw races was a warning-off offence, but even if I could manage to get Victor Briggs warned-off the person who would most suffer would be Harold. And I'd lose my job anyway, as Harold would hardly keep me on after that, even if we didn't both lose our licences altogether because of the races I'd thrown in the past. I couldn't prove Victor Briggs's villainy without having to admit Harold's and my own.

Cheat or retire. A stark choice . . . absolutely bloody.

Nothing changed much on the Tuesday, but when I went to Kempton on Wednesday to ride Pamphlet the weighing room was electric with two pieces of gossip.

Ivor den Relgan had been made a Member of the Jockey Club, and Steve Millace's mother's house had burned down.

CHAPTER SIX

'Ivor den Relgan!' I heard the name on every side, repeated in varying tones of astonishment and disbelief. 'A Member of the Jockey Club! Incredible!'

The Jockey Club, that exclusive and gentlemanly body, had apparently that morning voted into its fastidious ranks a man they had been holding at arm's length for years, a rich self-important man from no one knew where, who had spread his money about in racing and done a certain amount of good in a way that affronted the recipients.

He was supposed to be of Dutch extraction. Extraction, that is, from some unspecified ex-Dutch colony. He spoke with an accent that sounded like a mixture of South African, Australian and American, a conglomerate mid-globe amalgam of vowels and consonants which could have been attractive but came out as patronizing. He, the voice seemed to say, was a great deal more sophisticated than the stuffy British upper crust. He sought not favours from the entrenched powers, but admiration. It was they, he implied, who would prosper if they took his advice. He offered it to them free, frequently, in letters to the *Sporting Life*.

Until that morning the Jockey Club had indeed observably taken his advice on several occasions while steadfastly refusing to acknowledge he had given it. I wondered fleetingly what had brought them to such a turnaround; what had caused them suddenly to embrace the anathema.

Steve Millace was in the changing room, waiting by my peg.

The strain in him that was visible from the doorway was at close quarters overpowering. White-faced, vibrating, he stood with his arm in a black webbing sling and looked at me from sunken desperate eyes.

'Have you heard?' he said.

I nodded.

'It happened on Monday night. Well, yesterday morning, I suppose . . . about three o'clock. By the time anyone noticed the whole place had gone.'

'Your mother wasn't there?'

'They'd kept her in hospital. She's still there. It's too much for her. I mean . . .' He was trembling ' . . . too much.'

I made some sincerely sympathetic noises.

'Tell me what to do,' he said; and I thought, he's elected me as some sort of elder brother, an unofficial advice bureau.

'Didn't you say something about aunts?' I asked. 'At the funeral?'

He shook his head impatiently. 'They're Dad's sisters. Older sisters. They've never liked Mum.'

'All the same . . .'

'They're *cats*,' he said, exploding. 'I rang them . . . they said what a shame.' He mimicked their voices venomously. ' "Tell poor dear Marie she can get quite a nice little bungalow near the seaside with the insurance money." They make me sick.'

I began taking off my street clothes to change into colours, aware that to Steve the day's work was irrelevant.

'Philip,' he said imploringly. 'You saw her. All bashed about . . . and without Dad . . . and now the whole house . . . Please . . . *please* . . . help me.'

'All right,' I said resignedly. What else could one say? 'When I've finished riding, we'll work something out.'

He sat down on the bench as if his legs wouldn't hold him and just stayed there staring into space while I finished changing and went to weigh out.

Harold was by the scales as usual, waiting to take my saddle when I'd been weighed. Since Monday he'd made no reference to the life-altering decision he'd handed me, and perhaps he took my silence not for spirit-tearing indecision but tacit acceptance of a return to things past. At any rate it was with a totally normal manner that he said, as I put the saddle over his arm, 'Did you hear who's been elected to the Jockey Club?'

'Yeah.'

'They'll take Genghis Khan next.'

He walked out with the saddle to go and put it on Pamphlet, and in due course I joined him in the parade ring, where the horse walked nonchalantly round and his pop star owner bit his nails with concentration.

Harold had gleaned some more news. 'I hear that it was the Great White Chief who insisted on den Relgan joining the Club.'

'Lord White?' I was surprised.

'Old Driven Snow himself.'

Pamphlet's youngish owner flicked his fingers and said, 'Hey, man, how's about a little sweet music on this baby?'

'A tenner each way,' Harold suggested, having learnt the pop star's language. The pop star was using the horse for publicity and would only let it run when its race would be televised: and he was, as usual, wholly aware of the positions of the cameras, so that if they should chance to point his way he would not be care-lessly obscured behind Harold or me. I admired his expertise in this respect, and indeed his whole perform-ance, because off-stage, so to speak, he was apt to relapse into middle-class suburban. The jazzed-up working-class image was all a fake.

He had come to the races that day with dark blue hair. The onset of a mild apoplexy could be observed in the parade ring all about us, but Harold behaved as if he hadn't noticed, on the basis that owners who paid their bills could be as eccentric as they liked.

'Philip, darling,' said the pop star, 'bring this baby back for Daddy.'

He must have learned it out of old movies, I thought. Surely not even pop musicians talked like that any more. He reverted to biting his nails and I got up on Pamphlet and rode out to see what I could do about the tenner each way.

I was not popularly supposed to be much good over hurdles, but maybe Pamphlet had winning on his mind that day as much as I did. He soared round the whole thing with bursting *joie de vivre*, even to the extent of passing the favourite on the run-in, and we came back to bear hugs from the blue hair (for the benefit of television) and an offer to me of a spare ride in the fifth race, from a worried-looking small-time trainer. Stable jockey hurt ... would I mind? I wouldn't mind, I'd be delighted. Fine, the valet has the colours, see you in the parade ring. Great.

Steve was still brooding by my peg.

'Was the shed burnt?' I asked.

'What?'

'The shed. The deep freeze. Your Dad's photos.'

'Oh, well, yes it was ... but Dad's stuff wasn't in there.'

I stripped off the pop star's orange and pink colours and went in search of the calmer green and brown of the spare ride.

'Where was it, then?' I said, returning.

'I told Mum what you said about people maybe not

98

liking Dad's pictures of them, and she reckoned that
you thought all the burglaries were really aimed at the
photos, not at her fur and all that, and that if so she
didn't want to leave those transparencies where they
could still be stolen, so on Monday she got me to move
them next door, to her neighbours. And that's where
they are now, in a sort of outhouse.'

I buttoned the green and brown shirt, thinking it
over.

'Do you want me to visit her in the hospital?' I said.

Almost on my direct route home. No great shakes.
He fell on it, though, with embarrassing fervour. He
had come to the races, he said, with the pub-keeper
from the Sussex village where he lived in digs near the
stable he rode for, and if I would visit his mother he
could go home with the pub-keeper, because otherwise
he had no transport, because of his collarbone. I hadn't
exactly meant I would see Mrs Millace alone, but on
reflection I didn't mind.

Having shifted his burden Steve cheered up a bit
and asked if I would telephone him when I got home.

'Yes,' I said absently. 'Did your father often go to
France?'

'France?'

'Ever heard of it?' I said.

'Oh . . .' He was in no mood to be teased. 'Of course
he did. Longchamps, Auteuil, St Cloud. Everywhere.'

'And round the world?' I said, packing lead into my
weight cloth.

'Huh?' He was decidedly puzzled. 'What do you mean?'

'What did he spend his money on?'

'Lenses, mostly. Telephotos as long as your arm. Anything new.'

I took my saddle and weight-cloth over to the trial scales and added another flat pound of lead. Steve got up and followed me.

'What do you mean, what did he spend his money on?'

I said, 'Nothing. Nothing at all. Just wondered what he liked doing, away from the races.'

'He just took pictures. All the time, everywhere. He wasn't interested in anything else.'

In time I went out to ride the green-and-brown horse and it was one of those days, which happened so seldom, when absolutely everything went right. In unqualified euphoria I dismounted once again in the winners' enclosure, and thought that I couldn't possibly give up the life; I couldn't *possibly*. Not when winning put you higher than heroin.

My mother had likely died of heroin.

Steve's mother lay alone in a glass-walled side-ward, isolated but indecently exposed to the curious glances of any stranger walking past. There were curtains which might have shielded her from public gaze, but they were not pulled across. I hated the system which denied privacy to people in hospital: who on earth, if they were ill or injured, wanted their indignities gawped at?

Marie Millace lay on her back with two flat pillows under her head and a sheet and a thin blue blanket covering her. Her eyes were shut. Her brown hair, greasy and in disarray, straggled on the pillow. Her face was dreadful.

The raw patches of Saturday night were now covered by extensive dark scabs. The cut eyelid, stitched, was monstrously swollen and black. The nose was crimson under some shaping plaster of Paris, which had been stuck onto forehead and cheeks with white sticky tape. Her mouth, open and also swollen, looked purple. All the rest showed deep signs of bruising: crimson, grey, black and yellow. Fresh, the injuries had looked merely nasty: it was in the healing process that their true extent showed.

I'd seen people in that state before, and worse than that, damaged by horses' galloping hooves; but this, done out of malice to an inoffensive lady in her own home, was differently disturbing. I felt not sympathy but anger: Steve's 'I'll kill the bastards' anger.

She heard me come in, and opened her less battered eye a fraction as I approached. What I could see of an expression looked merely blank, as if I was the last person she would have expected.

'Steve asked me to come,' I said. 'He couldn't get here because of his shoulder. He can't drive . . . not for a day or two.'

The eye closed.

I fetched a chair from against the wall and put it by the bed, to sit beside her. The eye opened again; and then her hand, which had been lying on the blanket, slowly stretched out towards me. I took it, and she gripped me hard, holding on fiercely, seeking, it seemed, support and comfort and reassurance. The spirit of need ebbed after a while, and she let go of my hand and put her own weakly back on the blanket.

'Did Steve tell you,' she said, 'about the house?'

'Yes, he did. I'm so sorry.' It sounded feeble. Anything sounded feeble in the face of such knocks as she'd taken.

'Have you seen it?' she said.

'No. Steve told me about it at the races. At Kempton, this afternoon.'

Her speech was slurred and difficult to understand, as she moved her tongue as if it were stiff inside the swollen lips.

'My nose is broken,' she said, fluttering her fingers on the blanket.

'Yes,' I said. 'I broke mine once. They put a plaster on me, too, just like yours. You'll be as good as new in a week.'

Her silent response couldn't be interpreted as anything but dissent.

'You'll be surprised,' I said.

There was the sort of pause that occurs at hospital bedsides. Perhaps it was there that the ward system scored, I thought: when you'd run out of platitudes you could always discuss the gruesome symptoms in the next bed.

'George said you took photographs, like him,' she said.

'Not like him,' I said. 'George was the best.'

No dissent at all, this time. Discernibly the intentions of a smile.

'Steve told me you'd had George's boxes of transparencies moved out before the fire,' I said. 'That was lucky.'

Her smile, however, disappeared, and was slowly replaced by distress.

'The police came today,' she said. A sort of shudder shook her, and her breathing grew more troubled. She could get no air through her nose so the change was audible and rasped in her throat.

'They came here?' I asked.

'Yes. They said . . . Oh God . . .' Her chest heaved and she coughed.

I put my hand flatly over hers on the blanket and said urgently. 'Don't get upset. You'll make everything hurt worse. Just take three slow deep breaths. Four or five, if you need them. Don't talk until you can make it cold.'

She lay silent for a while until the heavy breathing slackened. I watched the tightened muscles relax under the blanket, and eventually she said, 'You're much older than Steve.'

'Eight years,' I agreed, letting go of her hand.

'No. Much ... much older.' There was a pause. 'Could you give me some water?'

There was a glass on the locker beside her bed. Water in the glass, angled tube for drinking. I steered the tube to her mouth, and she sucked up a couple of inches.

'Thanks.' Another pause, then she tried again, this time much more calmly. 'The police said ... The police said it was arson.'

'Did they?'

'You're not ... surprised?'

'After two burglaries, no.'

'Paraffin,' she said. 'Five-gallon drum. Police found it in the hall.'

'Was it your paraffin?'

'No.'

Another pause.

'The police asked ... if George had any enemies.' She moved her head restlessly. 'I said of course not ... and they asked ... if he had anything someone would want ... enough ... enough ... oh ...'

'Mrs Millace,' I said matter-of-factly. 'Did they ask if George had any photographs worth burglary and burning?'

'George wouldn't ...' she said intensely.

George had, I thought.

'Look,' I said slowly, 'You might not want me to ... you might not trust me ... but if you like I could look through those transparencies for you, and I could tell you if I thought there were any which could possibly come into the category we're talking about.'

After a while she said only, 'Tonight?'

'Yes, certainly. Then if they're OK you can tell the police they exist . . . if you want to.'

'George isn't a blackmailer,' she said. Coming from the swollen mouth the words sounded extraordinary, distorted but passionately meant. She was not saying 'I don't want to believe George could blackmail anyone,' but 'George didn't.' Yet she hadn't been sure enough to give the transparencies to the police. Sure but not sure. Emotionally sure. Rationally unsure. In a nonsensical way, that made sense.

She hadn't much left except that instinctive faith. It was beyond me entirely to tell her it was misplaced.

I collected the three metal boxes from the neighbour, who had been told, it appeared, that they contained just odds and ends the burglars had missed, and I was given by her a conducted tour of the burned mess next door.

Even in the dark one could see that there was nothing to salvage. Five gallons of paraffin had made no mistake. The house was a shell, roofless, windowless, acrid and creaking: and it was to this savage destruction of her nest that Marie would have to return.

I drove home with George's life's work and spent

the rest of the evening and half of the night projecting his slides onto the flat white wall of my sitting room.

His talent had been stupendous. Seeing his pictures there together, one after the other, and not scattered in books and newspapers and magazines across a canvas of years, I was struck continually by the speed of his vision. He had caught life over and over and over again at the moment when a painter would have composed it: nothing left out, nothing disruptive let in. An absolute master.

The best of his racing pictures were there, some in colour, some in black and white, but there were also several stunning series on unexpected subjects like card players and alcoholics and giraffes and sculptors in action and hot Sundays in New York. These series stretched back almost to George's youth, the date and place being written on each mount in tiny fine-nibbed letters.

There were dozens of portraits of people: some posed in a studio, mostly not. Again and again he had caught the fleeting expression which exposed the soul, and even if he had originally taken twenty shots to keep but one, the ones he had kept were collectively breathtaking.

Pictures of France. Paris, St Tropez, cycle racing, fish docks. No pictures of people sitting outside cafés, talking to whom they shouldn't.

When I'd got to the end of the third box I sat for a

while thinking of what George hadn't photographed, or hadn't in any case kept.

No war. No riots. No horrors. No mangled bodies or starving children or executions or bombed-apart cars.

What had yelled from my wall for hours had been a satirical baring of the essence under the external; and perhaps George had felt the external satire of violence left him nothing to say.

I was rather deeply aware that I was never going to see the world in quite the same way again: that George's piercing view of things would intrude when I least expected it and nudge me in the ribs. But George had had no compassion. The pictures were brilliant. Objective, exciting, imaginative and revealing; but none of them kind.

None of them either, in any way that I could see, could have been used as a basis for blackmail.

I telephoned Marie Millace in the morning, and told her so. The relief in her voice when she answered betrayed the existence of her doubts, and she heard it herself and immediately began a cover-up.

'I mean,' she said, 'of course I knew George wouldn't . . .'

'Of course,' I said. 'What shall I do with the pictures?'

'Oh dear, I don't know. No one will try to steal them

now though, will they?' The mumbling voice was even less distinct over the wire. 'What do you think?'

'Well,' I said. 'You can't exactly advertise that although George's pictures still exist no one needs to feel threatened. So I do think they may still be at risk.'

'But that means . . . that means . . .'

'I'm terribly sorry. I know it means that I agree with the police. That George did have something which someone desperately wanted destroyed. But please don't worry. Please don't. Whatever it was has probably gone with the house . . . and it's all over.' And God forgive me, I thought.

'Oh dear . . . George didn't . . . I know he didn't . . .'

I could hear the distress rising again in the noise of her breathing.

'Listen,' I said quickly. 'About those transparencies. Are you listening?'

'Yes.'

'I think the best thing for now would be to put them into a cold store somewhere. Then when you feel better, you could get an agent to put on an exhibition of George's work. The collection is marvellous, it really is. An exhibition would celebrate his talent, and make you a bit of money . . . and also reassure anyone who might be worrying that there was nothing to . . . er . . . worry about.'

There was a silence, but I knew she was still there, because of the breathing.

'George wouldn't use an agent,' she said at last. 'How could I find one?'

'I know one or two. I could give you their names.'

'Oh . . .' She sounded weak and there was another long pause. Then she said, 'I know . . . I'm asking such a lot . . . but could you . . . put those transparencies into store? I'd ask Steve . . . but you seem to know . . . what to do.'

I said that I would, and when we had disconnected I wrapped the three boxes in their polythene sheets and took them along to the local butcher, who already kept a box of my own in his walk-in freezer room. He cheerfully agreed to the extra lodgers, suggested a reasonable rental, and gave me a receipt.

Back home I looked at the negative and the print of Elgin Yaxley talking to Terence O'Tree, and wondered what on earth I should do with them.

If George had extorted from Elgin Yaxley all the profits from the shot-horse affair – and it looked as if he must have done, because of Bart Underfield's gloominess and Yaxley's own disappearance from racing – then it had to be Elgin Yaxley who was now desperate to find the photograph before anyone else did.

If Elgin Yaxley had arranged the burglaries, the beating-up and the burning, should retribution not follow? If I gave the photograph to the police, with explanations, Elgin Yaxley would be in line for prosecution for most crimes on the statutes, not least perjury

109

and defrauding an insurance company of a hundred and fifty thousand.

If I gave the photograph to the police I was telling the world that George Millace had been a blackmailer.

Which would Marie Millace prefer, I thought: never to know who had attacked her, or to know for sure that George had been a villain . . . and to have everyone else know it too.

There was no doubt about the answer.

I had no qualms about legal justice. I put the negative back where I'd found it, in its envelope stuck onto the back of the dark print in its paper mount. I put the mount back into the box of rubbish which still lay on the kitchen dresser, and I put the clear big print I'd made into a folder in the filing cabinet in the hall.

No one knew I had them. No one would come looking. No one would burgle or burn my house, or beat me up. Nothing at all would happen from now on.

I locked my doors and went to the races to ride Tishoo and Sharpener and to agonize over that other thorny problem, Victor Briggs.

CHAPTER SEVEN

Ivor den Relgan was again the big news, and what was more, he was there.

I saw him immediately I arrived, as he was standing just outside the weighing room door talking to two pressmen. I was a face among many to him, but to me, as to everyone else whose business was racing, he was as recognizable as a poppy in corn.

He wore, as he often did, an expensively soft camel-coloured coat, buttoned and belted, and he stood bare-headed with greying hair neatly brushed, a stocky, slightly pugnacious-looking man with an air of expecting people to notice his presence. A lot of people considered it a plus to be in his favour, but for some reason I found his self-confidence repellent, and his strong gravitational pull was something I instinctively resisted.

I would have been more than happy never to have come into his focus, but as I was passing them one of the pressmen shot out a hand and fastened it on my arm.

'Philip,' he said, 'you can tell us. You're always on the business end of a camera.'

'Tell you what?' I said, hovering in mid-stride, and intending to walk on.

'How do you photograph a wild horse?'

'Point and click,' I said pleasantly.

'No, Philip,' he said, exasperated. 'You know Mr den Relgan, don't you?'

I inclined my head slightly and said, 'By sight.'

'Mr den Relgan, this is Philip Nore. Jockey, of course.' The pressman was unaccustomedly obsequious: I'd noticed den Relgan often had that effect. 'Mr den Relgan wants photographs of all his horses, but one of them rears up all the time when he sees a camera. How would you get him to stand still?'

'I know one photographer,' I said, 'who got a wild horse to stand still by playing a tape of a hunt in full cry. The horse just stood and listened. The pictures were great.'

Den Relgan smiled superciliously as if he didn't want to hear good ideas that weren't his own, and I nodded with about as much fervour and went on into the weighing room thinking that the Jockey Club must have been mad. The existing members of the Jockey Club were for the most part forward-looking people who put good will and energy into running a huge industry fairly. That they were also self-electing meant in practice that the members were almost all aristocrats or upper class, but the ideal of service bred into them worked pretty well for the good of racing. The old autocratic change-resistant bunch had died out, and there were fewer bitter jokes nowadays about bone-heads at the top. All the more surprising that they should have beckoned to a semi-phoney like den Relgan.

Harold was inside in the weighing room talking to Lord White, which gave me a frisson like seeing a traffic warden standing next to one's wrongly parked car: but it appeared that Lord White, powerful Steward of the Jockey Club, was not enquiring into the outcome of the Sandown Pattern 'Chase, nor into any other committed sins. He was telling Harold that there was a special trophy for Sharpener's race, and, should he happen to win it, both Harold and I, besides the owner, would be required to put in an appearance and receive our gifts.

'It wasn't advertised as a sponsored race,' Harold said, surprised.

'No . . . but Mr den Relgan has generously made this gesture. And incidentally it will be his daughter who does the actual presentations.' He looked directly at me. 'Nore, isn't it?'

'Yes, sir.'

'You heard all that? Good. Fine.' He nodded, turned, and left us, crossing to speak to another trainer with a runner in the same race.

'How many trophies does it take,' Harold said under his breath, 'to buy your way into the Jockey Club?' And in a normal voice he added, 'Victor's here.'

113

I said anxiously, 'But Sharpener will do his best.'

Harold looked amused. 'Yes, he will. This time. Win that pot if you can. It would really give Victor a buzz, taking Ivor den Relgan's cup. They can't stand each other.'

'I didn't know they knew . . .'

'Everyone knows everyone,' Harold said, shrugging. 'I think they belong to the same gaming club.' He lost interest and went out of the weighing room, and I stood for a few aimless moments watching Lord White make his way towards yet another trainer to pass on the instructions.

Lord White, in his fifties, was a well-built good-looking man with thick light-grey hair progressively turning the colour of his name. He had disconcertingly bright blue eyes and a manner that disarmed anyone advancing on him with a grievance; and it was he, although not Senior Steward, who was the true leader of the Jockey Club, elected not by votes but by the natural force born in him.

An upright man, widely respected, whose nickname Driven Snow (spoken only behind his back) had been coined, I thought, only partly through admiration and mostly to poke fun at the presence of so much notice-able virtue.

I went off to the changing room and on into the business of the day, and was guiltily relieved to find Steve Millace had not made the journey. No beseeching eyes and general helplessness to inveigle me into yet another round of fetching and carrying and visiting the sick. I changed into Tishoo's colours and thought only about the race he was due to start in, which was for novices over hurdles.

In the event there were no great problems but no repeat either of the previous day's joys. Tishoo galloped willingly enough into fourth place at the finish, which pleased his woman owner, and I carried my saddle to the scales to be weighed in, and so back to my changing-room peg to put on Victor Briggs's colours for Sharpener. Just another day's work. Each day unique in itself, but in essence the same. On two thousand days, or thereabouts, I had gone into changing rooms and put on colours and passed the scales and ridden the races. Two thousand days of hope and effort and sweat and just the unjust rewards. More than a job: part of my fabric.

I put on a jacket over Victor Brigg's colours, because there were two other races to be run before Sharpener's, and went outside for a while to see what was happening in general: and what was happening in particular was Lady White with a scowl on her thin aristocratic face.

Lady White didn't know me especially, but I, along with most other jump jockeys, had shaken her hand as she stood elegantly at Lord White's side at two parties they had given to the racing world. The parties had been large everyone-invited affairs three or four years apart, held at Cheltenham racecourse during the March meeting; and they had been Lord White's own idea, paid for by him, and given, one understood, because of his belief that everyone in jump racing belonged at heart to a brotherhood of friends, and should meet as such to enjoy themselves. Old Driven Snow at his priceless best, and like everyone else I'd gone to the parties and enjoyed them.

Lady White was hugging her mink around her and almost glaring forth from under a wide-brimmed brown hat. Her intensity was such that I followed her gaze and found it fixed on her paragon of a husband, who was himself talking to a girl.

Lord White was not simply talking to the girl but revelling in it, radiating flirtatious fun from his sparkling eyes to his gesturing fingertips. I looked sardonically back from this picture telling the old old story and found Lady White's attention still balefully fixed on it, and I thought in amusement 'Oh dear', as one does. The pure white lord, that evening, would be in for an unaristocratic ticking off.

Ivor den Relgan was still holding court to a clutch of journalists, among whom were two racing writers and three gossip columnists from the larger daily papers. Ivor den Relgan was definitely a gossip man's man.

Bart Underfield was loudly telling an elderly married couple that Osborne should know better than to run Sharpener in a three mile 'chase when any fool knew that the horse couldn't go further than two. The elderly couple nodded, impressed.

I gradually became aware that a man standing near me was also, like Lady White, intently watching Lord White and the girl. The man near me was physically unremarkable; an ordinary average man, no longer young, not quite middle-aged, with dark thinning hair and black-framed glasses. Grey trousers, olive green jacket, suede, not tweed, well-cut. When he realized that I was looking at him he gave me a quick annoyed glance and moved away: and I thought no more about him for another hour.

Victor Briggs, when I joined him in the parade ring before Sharpener's race, was heavily pleasant and made no reference to the issue hanging between us. Harold had boosted himself into a state of confidence and was standing with his long legs apart, his hat tipped back on his head, and his binoculars swinging rhythmically from one hand.

'A formality,' he was saying. 'Sharpener's never been better, eh, Philip? Gave you a good feel on the Downs, didn't he? Worked like a train.' His robust voice floated easily over several nearby owner-trainer-jockey groups who were all suffering from their own pre-race tensions and could have done without Harold's.

'Jumping out of his skin,' Harold said, booming. 'Never been better. He'll run the legs off 'em, today, eh, Victor?'

The only good thing one could say about Harold's

bursts of over-confidence was that if in the event they proved to be misplaced he would not relapse into acrimony and gloom. Failures were apt to be expansively forgiven with 'it was the weight that beat him, of course' and were seldom held to be the jockey's fault, even when they were.

Sharpener himself reacted to Harold's optimism in a thoroughly positive way, and encouraged also perhaps by my confidence left over from the two winners the day before, ran a faultless race with energy and courage, so that for the third time at that meeting my mount returned to applause.

Harold was metaphorically by this time two feet off the ground, and even Victor allowed his mouth a small smile.

Ivor den Relgan manfully shaped up to the fact that his fancy trophy had been won by a man he disliked, and Lord White fluttered around the girl he'd been talking to, clearing a passage for her through the throng.

When I'd weighed in and handed my saddle to my valet, and combed my hair and gone out to the prize-giving, the scene had sorted itself out into a square table with a blue cloth bearing one large silver object and two smaller ones surrounded by Lord White, the girl, Ivor den Relgan, Victor and Harold.

Lord White said through a hand microphone to the small watching crowd that Miss Dana den Relgan would present the trophies so kindly given by her father: and it cannot have been only in my mind that the cynical speculation arose. Was it the Dad that Lord White wanted in the Jockey Club, or Dad's daughter? Perish the thought. Lord White with a girlfriend? Impossible.

At close quarters it was clear that he was attracted beyond sober good sense. He touched her continually under the guise of arranging everyone suitably for the presentations, and he was vivacious where normally staid. It all remained just within the acceptable limits of roguishly avuncular behaviour, but discreet it was not.

Dana den Relgan was enough, I supposed, to excite any man she cared to respond to: and to Lord White she was responding with sweetness. Slender and graceful and not very tall, she had a lot of blonde-flecked hair curling casually onto her shoulders. There was also a curving mouth, very wide-apart eyes and excellent skin, and a quality of being not all dolly-bird in the brain. Her manner was observably more restrained than Lord White's, as if she didn't dislike his attentions but thought them too obvious, and she presented the trophies to Victor and Harold and myself without much conversation attached.

To me she said merely, 'Well done,' and gave me the small silver object (which turned out to be a saddle-shaped paperweight) with the bright surface smile of someone who isn't really looking at you and is going to forget you again within five minutes. Her voice, from what I heard of it, held the same modified American accent as her father's, but in her it lacked the patronizing quality and was, to me at least, attractive. A pretty girl, but not mine. Life was full of them.

While Victor and Harold and I compared trophies the average-looking man in spectacles reappeared, walking quietly up to Dana den Relgan's shoulder and speaking softly into her ear. She turned away from the presentation table and began slowly to move off with him, nodding and smiling a little, and listening to what he was saying.

This apparently harmless proceeding had the most extraordinary effect upon den Relgan, who stopped looking fatuously pleased with himself in one five-hundredth of a second and flung himself into action. He almost ran after his daughter, gripped the inoffensive-looking man by the shoulder and threw him away from her with such force that he staggered and went down on one knee.

'I've told you to keep away from her,' den Relgan said, looking as if kicking a man when he was down was something he had no reservations about; and Lord White muttered, 'I say' and 'Oh dear' and looked uncomfortable.

'Who is that man?' I asked of no one in particular, and it was Victor Briggs, surprisingly, who answered.

'Film director. Fellow called Lance Kinship.'

'And why the fuss?'

Victor Briggs knew the answer, but it took a fair

amount of internal calculation before he decided to part with it. 'Cocaine,' he said finally. 'White powder, for sniffing straight up the nose. Very fashionable. All these stupid little girls . . . their noses will collapse when the bone dissolves, and then where will they be?'

Both Harold and I looked at him with astonishment, as it was the longest speech I'd ever heard him make, and certainly the only one containing any private opinion.

'Lance Kinship supplies it,' he said. 'He gets asked to the parties for what he takes along.'

Lance Kinship was up on his feet and brushing dirt off his trousers; setting his glasses firmly on his nose and looking murderous.

'If I want to talk to Dana, I'll talk to her,' he said.

'Not while I'm there, you won't.'

Den Relgan's Jockey Club manners were in tatters and the bedrock under the camouflage was plainly on view. A bully, I thought; a bad enemy, even if his cause was just.

Lance Kinship seemed unintimidated. 'Little girls don't always have their daddies with them,' he said nastily; and den Relgan hit him; a hard sharp efficient crunch on the nose.

Noses bleed easily, and there was a good deal of blood. Lance Kinship tried to wipe it away with his hands and succeeded only in smearing it all over his face. It poured down on his mouth and chin, and fell in big splashing drops on his olive suede jacket.

Lord White, hating the whole thing, stretched out an arm towards Kinship and held out a huge white handkerchief as if in tongs. Kinship grabbed it without thanks and soaked it scarlet as he tried to staunch the flow.

'First aid room, don't you think?' Lord White said, looking round. 'Er . . . Nore,' he said, his gaze alighting. 'You know where the first aid room is, don't you? Take this gentleman there, would you? Awfully good of you . . .' He waved me towards the errand, but when I put a hand out towards the olive green sleeve, to guide Kinship in the direction of cold compresses and succour, he jerked away from me.

'Bleed, then,' I said.

Unfriendly eyes behind the black frames glared out at me, but he was too busy mopping to speak.

'I'll show you,' I said. 'Follow if you want.'

I set off past the parade ring towards the green-painted hut where the motherly ladies would be waiting to patch up the damaged, and not only did Kinship follow, but den Relgan also. I heard his voice as clearly as Kinship did, and there was no doubt about the message.

'If you come near Dana again, I'll break your neck.'

Kinship again didn't answer.

Den Relgan said, 'Did you hear, you vicious little ponce?'

We had gone far enough for there to be plenty of people blocking us from the view of the group outside the weighing room. I heard a scuffle behind me and looked over my shoulder in time to see Kinship aim a hard karate kick at den Relgan's crutch and land deftly on target. Kinship turned back to me and gave me another unfriendly stare over the reddening handkerchief, which he had held uninterruptedly to his nose.

Den Relgan was making choking noises and clutching himself. The whole fracas was hardly what one expected as the outcome of a decorous racecourse presentation on a Thursday afternoon.

'In there,' I said to Kinship, jerking my head, and he gave me a final reptilian glance as the first aid room opened its doors. Den Relgan said 'Aaah . . .' and walked round in a small circle half doubled over, one hand pressed hard under the lower front of his camel-hair coat.

A pity George Millace had gone to his fathers, I thought. He of all people would have relished the ding-dong, and he, unlike everyone else, would have been here with his lens sharply focussed, pointing the right way and taking inexorable notes at three point five frames a second. Den Relgan could thank George's couple of Scotches and a tree in the wrong place that he wouldn't find his tangle with Kinship illustrating in the daily papers the edifying news of his elevation to the Jockey Club.

Harold and Victor Briggs were still where I'd left them, but Lord White and Dana den Relgan had gone.

'His lordship took her off to calm her nerves,' Harold

said dryly. 'The old goat's practically dancing round her, silly fool.'

'She's pretty,' I said.

'Wars have been fought for pretty girls,' said Victor Briggs.

I looked at him with renewed astonishment and received in return the usual stonewall closed-in expression. Victor might have unexpected hidden depths, but that was just what they still were, hidden.

When I went out of the weighing room later to set off for home I was apologetically intercepted by the tall loitering figure of Jeremy Folk.

'I don't believe it,' I said.

'I did . . . er . . . warn you.'

'So you did.'

'Could I . . . um . . . have a word with you?'

'What do you want?'

'Ah yes . . . well . . .'

'The answer's no,' I said.

'But you don't know what I'm going to ask.'

'I can see that it's something I don't want to do.'

'Um,' he said. 'Your grandmother asks you to visit her.'

'Absolutely not,' I said.

There was a pause. People around us were going home, calling goodnights. It was four o'clock. Goodnights started early in the racing world.

'I went to see her,' Jeremy said. 'I told her you wouldn't look for your sister for money. I told her she would have to give you something else.'

I was puzzled. 'Give me what?'

Jeremy looked vaguely around from his great height and said, 'You could find her, couldn't you, if you really tried?'

'I don't think so.'

'But you might.'

I didn't answer, and his attention came gently back to my face.

'Your grandmother agreed,' he said, 'that she had a flaming row with Caroline . . . your mother . . . and chucked her out when she was pregnant.'

'My mother,' I said, 'was seventeen.'

'Um. That's right.' He smiled. 'Funny, isn't it, to think of one's mother being so *young*.'

Poor defenceless little butterfly . . . 'Yes,' I said.

'Your grandmother says . . . has agreed . . . that if you will look for Amanda she will tell you why she threw Caroline out. And also she will tell you who your father is.'

'My God!'

I took two compulsive steps away from him, and stopped, and turned, and stared at him.

'Is that what you said to her?' I demanded. 'Tell him who his father is, and he'll do what you want?'

'You don't know who your father is,' he said reasonably. 'But you'd want to know, wouldn't you?'

125

'No,' I said.

'I don't believe you.'

We practically glared at each other.

'You have to want to know,' he said. 'It's human nature.'

I swallowed. 'Did she tell you who he is?'

He shook his head. 'No. She didn't. She's apparently never told anyone. No one at all. If you don't go and find out, you'll never know.'

'You're a real bastard, Jeremy,' I said.

He wriggled his body with an embarrassment he didn't actually feel. The light in his eyes, which would have done a check-mating chess-player justice, was a far more accurate indicator of how he operated.

I said bitterly, 'I thought solicitors were supposed to sit behind desks and pontificate, not go tearing about manipulating old ladies.'

'This particular old lady is a . . . a challenge.'

I had an idea he had changed his sentence in mid-stride, but I said only, 'Why doesn't she leave her money to her son?'

'I don't know. She won't give reasons. She told my grandfather simply that she wanted to cancel her old will, which left everything to her son, and make a new one in favour of Amanda. The son will contest it, of course. We've told her that, but it makes no difference. She's . . . er . . . stubborn.'

'Have you met her son?'

'No,' he said. 'Have you?'

I shook my head. Jeremy took another long vague look around the racecourse and said, 'Why don't we get cracking on this together? We'd turn Amanda up in no time, wouldn't we? Then you could go back into your shell and forget the whole thing, if you want.'

'You couldn't forget . . . who your father was.'

His gaze sharpened instantly. 'Are you on, then?'

He would persevere, I thought, with or without my help. He would bother me whenever he wanted, catch me at the races any day he cared to read the programmes in the newspapers, and never let up, because he wanted, as he'd told me at the beginning, to prove to his grandfather and uncle that when he set his mind to sorting something out, it got sorted.

As for me . . . the mists round my birth were there for the parting. The cataclysm which had echoed like a storm receding over the horizon through my earliest memories could at last be explained and understood. I could know what the shouting had been about behind the white painted door, while I waited in the hall in my new clothes.

I might in the event detest the man who'd fathered me. I might be horrified. I might wish I hadn't been told anything about him. But Jeremy was right. Given the chance . . . one had to know.

'Well?' he said.

'All right.'

'Find her together?'

'Yes.'

He was visibly pleased. 'That's great.'

I wasn't so sure; but it was settled.

'Can you go this evening?' he said. 'I'll telephone and tell her you're coming.' He plunged lankily towards the public telephone box and disappeared inside with his eyes switched anxiously my way, watching all through his call to make sure I didn't go back on my decision and scram.

The call, however, gave him no joy.

'Blast,' he said, rejoining me. 'I spoke to a nurse. Mrs Nore had a bad day and they've given her an injection. She's asleep. No visitors. Ring tomorrow.'

I felt a distinct sense of relief, which he noticed.

'It's all very well for you,' I said. 'But how would you like to be on the verge of finding out that you owe your existence to a quickie in the bushes with the milkman?'

'Is that what you think?'

'Something like that. It has to be, doesn't it?'

'All the same . . .' he said doubtfully.

'All the same,' I agreed resignedly, 'one wants to know.'

I set off towards the car park thinking that Jeremy's errand was concluded, but it appeared not. He came in my wake, but slowly, so that I looked back and waited.

'About Mrs Nore's son,' he said. 'Her son James.'

'What about him?'

'I just thought you might visit him. Find out why he's been disinherited.'

'You just thought . . .'

'As we're working together,' he said hastily.

'You could go yourself,' I suggested.

'Er, no,' he said. 'As Mrs Nore's solicitor, I'd be asking questions I shouldn't.'

'And I can just see this James bird answering mine.'

He pulled a card out of his charcoal pocket. 'I brought his address,' he said, holding it out. 'And you've promised to help.'

'A pact is a pact,' I said, and took the card. 'But you're still a bastard.'

CHAPTER EIGHT

James Nore lived in London, and since I was more than halfway there I drove straight from the races to the house on Camden Hill. I hoped all the way there that he would be out, but when I'd found the street and the number and pressed the right bell, the door was opened by a man of about forty who agreed that James Nore was his name.

He was astounded, as well he might be, to find an unknown nephew standing unannounced on his mat, but with only a slight hesitation he invited me in, leading the way into a sitting room crammed with Victorian bric-à-brac and vibrant with colour.

'I thought Caroline had aborted you,' he said badly. 'Mother said the child had been got rid of.'

He was nothing like my memories of his sister. He was plump, soft-muscled and small-mouthed, and had a mournful droop to his eyes. None of her giggly lightness or grace of movement or hectic speed could ever have lived in his flaccid body. I felt ill at ease with him on sight, disliking my errand more by the minute.

He listened with his small lips pouted while I explained about looking for Amanda, and he showed more and more annoyance.

'The old bag's been saying for months that she's going to cut me off,' he said furiously. 'Ever since she came here.' He glanced round the room, but nothing there seemed to me likely to alienate a mother. 'Everything was all right as long as I went to Northamptonshire now and then. Then she came *here*. Uninvited. The old bag.'

'She's ill now,' I said.

'Of course she is.' He flung out his arms in an exaggerated gesture. 'I suggest visiting. She says no. Won't see me. Pig-headed old crone.'

A brass clock on the mantelshelf sweetly chimed the half hour, and I took note that everything there was of fine quality and carefully dusted. James Nore's bric-a-brac wasn't just junk but antiques.

'I'd be a fool to help you find this wretched second by-blow of Caroline's, wouldn't I?' he said. 'If no one can find her the whole estate reverts to me anyway, will or no will. But I'd have to wait years for it. Years and years. Mother's just being spiteful.'

'Why?' I said mildly.

'She loved Noël Coward,' he said resentfully, meaning, by the sound of it, if she loved Noël Coward she should have loved *him*.

'The abstract,' I said, enlightened, 'isn't always the same as the particular.'

'I didn't want her to come here. It would have saved all this fuss if she hadn't.' He shrugged. 'Are you going now? There's no point in your staying.'

He began to walk towards the door, but before he reached it it was opened by a man wearing a plastic cooking apron and limply carrying a wooden spoon. He was much younger than James, naturally camp, and unmistakable.

'Oh, hello, dear,' he said, seeing me. 'Are you staying for supper?'

'He's just going,' James said sharply. 'He's not . . . er . . .'

They both stood back to leave me room to pass, and as I went out into the hall I said to the man in the apron, 'Did you meet Mrs Nore when she came here?'

'Sure did, dear,' he said ruefully, and then caught sight of James shaking his head vigorously at him and meaning shut up. I smiled halfheartedly at a point in the air near their heads, and went to the front door.

'I wish you bad luck,' James said. 'That beastly Caroline, spawning all over the place. I never did like her.'

'Do you remember her?'

'Always laughing at me and tripping me up. I was glad when she went.'

I nodded, and opened the door.

'Wait,' he said suddenly.

He came towards me along the hall, and I could see he had had an idea that pleased him.

'Mother would never leave *you* anything, of course,' he began.

'Why not?' I said.

He frowned. 'There was a terrible drama, wasn't there, when Caroline got pregnant? Frightful scenes. Lots of screaming. I remember it . . . but no one would ever explain. All I do know is that everything changed because of you. Caroline went and Mother turned into a bitter old bag and I had beastly miserable years in that big house with her, before I left. She hated you . . . the thought of you. Do you know what she called you? "Caroline's disgusting foetus", that's what. Caroline's disgusting foetus.'

He peered at me expectantly, but in truth I felt nothing. The old woman's hatred hadn't troubled me for years.

'I'll give you some of the money, though,' he said, 'if you can prove that Amanda is dead.'

On Saturday morning Jeremy Folk telephoned.

'Will you be at home tomorrow?' he said.

'Yes, but . . .'

'Good. I'll pop over.' He put down his receiver without giving me a chance to say I didn't want him. It was an advance, I supposed, that he'd announced his visit and not simply turned up.

Also on Saturday I ran into Bart Underfield in the

post office and in place of our usual unenthusiastic 'good mornings' I asked him a question.

'Where is Elgin Yaxley these days, Bart?'

'Hong Kong,' he said. 'Why?'

'For a holiday?' I said.

'Of course not. He lives there.'

'But he's over here now, isn't he?'

'No, he isn't. He'd have told me.'

'But he must be,' I said insistently.

Bart said irritably, 'Why must he be? He isn't. He's working for a bloodstock agency and they don't give him much time off. And what's it to do with you?'

'I just thought . . . I saw him.'

'You couldn't have. When?'

'Oh . . . last week. A week ago yesterday.'

'Well, you're wrong,' Bart said triumphantly. 'That was the day of George Millace's funeral, and Elgin sent me a cable . . .' He hesitated and his eyes flickered, but he went on, ' . . . and the cable came from Hong Kong.'

'A cable of regrets, was it?'

'George Millace,' Bart said with venom, 'was a shit.'

'You didn't go to the funeral yourself, then?'

'Are you crazy? I'd have spat on his coffin.'

'Catch you bending with his camera, did he, Bart?'

He narrowed his eyes and didn't answer.

'Oh well,' I said, shrugging, 'I dare say a good many people will be relieved now he's gone.'

'More like down on their knees giving thanks.'

'Do you ever hear anything nowadays about that

chap who shot Elgin's horses? What's his name ...
Terence O'Tree?'

'He's still in jail,' Bart said.

'But,' I said, counting with my fingers, 'March, April,
May ... he should be out by now.'

'He lost his remission,' Bart said. 'He hit a warder.'

'How do you know?' I asked curiously.

'I ... er ... heard.' He had suddenly had too much
of this conversation, and began to move off, backing
away.

'And did you hear also that George Millace's house
had burned down?' I said.

He nodded. 'Of course. Heard it at the races.'

'And that it was arson?'

He stopped in mid-stride. 'Arson?' he said, looking
surprised. 'Why would anyone want ...? Oh!' He
abruptly at that point understood why; and I thought
that he couldn't possibly have achieved that revela-
tionary expression by art.

He hadn't known.

Elgin Yaxley was in Hong Kong and Terence O'Tree
was in jail, and neither they nor Bart Underfield had
burgled, or bashed, or burned.

The easy explanations were all wrong.

I had jumped, I thought penitently, to conclusions.

It was only because I'd disliked George Millace that
I'd been so ready to believe ill of him. He had taken

that incriminating photograph, but there was really nothing to prove that he'd used it, except that Elgin Yaxley had taken a paid job in Hong Kong instead of ploughing his insurance money back into racehorses. Any man had a right to do that. It didn't make him a villain.

Yet he had been a villain. He had sworn he'd never met Terence O'Tree; and he had. And it had to have been before the trial in February at least, since O'Tree had been in jail ever since. Not during the winter months just before the trial either, because it had been sitting-in-the-street weather; and there had been . . . I had unconsciously noticed and now remembered . . . there had been a newspaper lying on the table in front of the Frenchman, on which one might possibly see a date.

I walked slowly and thoughtfully home, and projected my big new print hugely onto the sitting room wall through an epidiascope.

The Frenchman's newspaper lay too flat on the table. Neither the date nor any useful headlines could be seen.

Regretfully I studied the rest of the picture for anything at all which might date it; and in the depths, beside Madame at her cash desk inside the café, there was a calendar hanging on a hook. The letters and numbers on it could be discerned by the general shape even if not with pin-sharp clarity, and they announced that it was Avril of the previous year.

Elgin Yaxley's horses had been sent out to grass late that April, and they had been shot on the fourth of May.

I switched off the projector and drove to Windsor races puzzling over the inconsistencies and feeling that I had gone round a corner in a maze confidently expecting to have reached the centre, only to find myself in a dead end surrounded by ten-foot hedges.

It was a moderate day's racing at Windsor, all the star names having gone to the more important meeting at Cheltenham, and because of the weak opposition one of Harold's slowest old 'chasers finally had his day. Half of the rest of the equally old runners obligingly fell, and my geriatric pal with his head down in exhaustion loped in first after three and a half miles of slog.

He stood with his chest heaving in the unsaddling enclosure as I, scarcely less tired, lugged at the girth buckles and pulled off my saddle, but the surprised delight of his faithful elderly lady owner made it all well worth the effort.

'I knew he'd do it one day,' she said enthusiastically. 'I knew he would. Isn't he a great old boy?'

'Great,' I agreed.

'It's his last season, you know. I'll have to retire him.' She patted his neck and spoke to his head. 'We're all getting on a bit, old boy, aren't we? Can't go on for ever, more's the pity. Everything ends, doesn't it, old boy? But today it's been great.'

I went in and sat on the scales and her words came

with me: everything ends, but today it's been great. Ten years had been great, but everything ends.

Most of my mind still rebelled against the thought of ending, particularly an ending dictated by Victor Briggs; but somewhere the frail seedling of acceptance was stretching its first leaf in the dark. Life changes, everything ends. I myself was changing. I didn't want it, but it was happening. My long contented float was slowly drifting to shore.

Outside the weighing room one wouldn't have guessed it. I had uncharacteristically won four races that week. I was the jockey in form. I had brought a no-hoper home. I was offered five rides for the following week by trainers other than Harold. The success-breeds-success syndrome was coming up trumps. Everything on a high note, with smiles all around. Seven days away from Daylight, and seven leagues in mood.

I enjoyed the congratulations and thrust away the doubt, and if anyone had asked me in that moment about retiring I'd have said 'Oh yes . . . in five years' time.'

They didn't ask me. They didn't expect me to retire. Retire was a word in my mind, not in theirs.

Jeremy Folk arrived the following morning, as he'd said he would, angling his stork-like figure apologetically through my front door and following me along to the kitchen.

'Champagne?' I said, picking a bottle out of the refrigerator.

'It's ... er ... only ten o'clock,' he said.

'Four winners,' I said, 'need celebrating. Would you rather have coffee?'

'Er ... actually ... no.'

He took his first sip all the same as if the wickedness of it would overwhelm him, and I thought that for all his wily ways he was a conformist at heart.

He had made an effort to be casual in his clothes: wool checked shirt, woolly tie, neat pale blue sweater. Whatever he thought of my unbuttoned collar, unbuttoned cuffs and unshaven jaw, he didn't say. He let his gaze do its usual inventorial travel-around from a great height and as usual return to my face when he'd shaped his question.

'Did you see ... ah ... James Nore?'

'Yes, I did.'

I gestured to him to sit on the leather-covered corner bench round the kitchen table, and joined him, with the bottle in reach.

'He's cohabiting happily on Camden Hill.'

'Oh,' Jeremy said. 'Ah.'

I smiled. 'Mrs Nore visited his house unexpectedly one day. She hadn't been there before. She met James's friend, and she realized, I suppose for the first time, that her son was 100 per cent homosexual.'

'Oh,' Jeremy said, understanding much.

I nodded. 'No descendants.'

'So she thought of Amanda.' He sighed and drank some pale gold fizz. 'Are you sure he's homosexual. I mean ... did he say so?'

'As good as. But anyway, I'm used to homosexuals. I lived with two of them for a while. You get to know, somehow.'

He looked slightly shocked and covered it with a relapse into the silly ass waffle.

'Did you? I mean ... are you ...? Er ... I mean ... living alone ...? I shouldn't ask. Sorry.'

'If I take someone to bed, she's female,' I said mildly. 'I just don't like permanence.'

He buried his nose and his embarrassment in his glass, and I thought of Duncan and Charlie who had hugged and kissed and loved each other all around me for three years. Charlie had been older than Duncan; a mature man in his forties, solid and industrious and kind. Charlie, to me, had been father, uncle, guardian, all in one. Duncan had been chatty and quarrelsome and very good company, and neither of them had tried to teach me their way.

Duncan had slowly grown less chatty, more quarrelsome and less good company, and one day he fell in love with someone else and walked out. Charlie's grief had been white-faced and desperately deep. He had put his arm round my shoulders and hugged me, and wept; and I'd wept for Charlie's unhappiness.

My mother had arrived within a week, blowing in like a whirlwind. Huge eyes, hollow cheeks, fluffy silk scarves.

'But you must see, Charlie darling,' she said, 'that I can't leave Philip with you now that Duncan's gone. Look at him, darling, he's hardly ugly, the way he's grown up. Darling Charlie, you must see that he can't stay here. Not any more.' She'd looked across at me, bright and more brittle than I remembered, and less beautiful. 'Go and pack, Philip darling. We're going down to the country.'

Charlie had come into the little box-like room he and Duncan had built for me in one corner of the studio, and I'd told him I didn't want to leave him.

'Your mother's right, boy,' he said. 'It's time you were off. We must do what she says.'

He'd helped me pack and given me one of his cameras as a goodbye present, and from the old life I'd been flung straight into the new in the space of a day. That evening I learned how to muck out a horse box, and the next morning I started to ride.

After a week I'd written to Charlie to say I was missing him, and he replied encouragingly that I'd soon get over it: and get over it I did, while Charlie himself pined miserably for Duncan and swallowed two hundred sleeping pills. Charlie made a will a week before the pills leaving all his possessions to me, including all his other cameras and darkroom equipment. He also left a letter saying he was sorry and wishing me luck.

'Look after your mother,' he wrote. 'I think she's sick. Keep on taking photographs, you already have the eye. You'll be all right, boy. So long now. Charlie.'

I drank some champagne and said to Jeremy, 'Did you get the list of the Pine Woods Lodge tenancies from the estate agents?'

'Oh gosh, yes,' he said, relieved to be back on firm ground. 'I've got it here somewhere.' He patted several pockets but stuck two fingers unerringly and only into the one where he'd stored the slip of paper he wanted: and I wondered how much energy he wasted each day in camouflage movements.

'Here we are ...' He spread the sheet of paper out, and pointed. 'If your mother was there thirteen years ago, the people she was with would have been the boy scouts, the television company, or the musicians. But the television people didn't live there, the agents say. They just worked there during the day. The musicians did live there, though. They were ... er ... experimental musicians, whatever that means.'

'More soul than success.'

He gave me a quick bright glance. 'A man in the estate agents' says he remembers they ruined the electric wiring and were supposed to be high all the time on drugs. Does any of that sound ... er ... like your mother?'

I pondered.

'Boy scouts don't sound like her a bit,' I said. 'We can leave them out. Drugs sounds like her, but musicians don't. Especially unsuccessful musicians. She never left me with anyone unsuccessful . . . or anyone musical, come to that.' I thought some more. 'I suppose if she was really drug-dependent by that time, she mightn't have cared. But she liked comfort.' I paused again. 'I think I'd try the television company first. They could at least tell us what programme they were making then, and who worked on it. They're bound to have kept the credits somewhere.'

Jeremy's face showed a jumble of emotions varying, I thought, from incredulity to bewilderment.

'Er . . .' he said, 'I mean . . .'

'Look,' I interrupted. 'Just ask the questions. If I don't like them I won't answer.'

'You're so frantically direct,' he complained. 'All right, then. What do you mean about your mother leaving you with people, and what do you mean about your mother and drugs?'

I outlined the dumping procedure and what I owed to the Deborahs, Samanthas and Chloes. Jeremy's shattered expression alone would have told me that this was not every child's experience of life.

'Drugs,' I said, 'are more difficult. I didn't understand about the drugs until I grew up, and I only saw her once after I was twelve . . . the day she took me away from the homosexuals and put me in the racing stable. But certainly she was taking drugs for as long as I remember. She kept me with her for a week, sometimes, and there would be a smell, an acrid distinctive smell. I smelled it again years later ... I must have been past twenty ... and it was marihuana. Cannabis. I smoked it when I was little. One of my mother's friends gave it to me when she was out, and she was furious. She did try, you know, in her way, to see I grew up properly. Another time a man she was with gave me some acid. She was absolutely livid.'

'Acid,' Jeremy said. 'Do you mean LSD?'

'Yeah. I could see all the blood running through my arteries and veins, just as if the skin was transparent. I could see the bones, like X-rays. It's extraordinary. You realize the limitations of our everyday senses. I could hear sounds as if they were three-dimensional. A clock ticking. Amazing. My mother came into the room and found me wanting to fly out of the window. I could see the blood going round in her, too.' I remembered it all vividly, though I'd been about five. 'I didn't know why she was so angry. The man was laughing, and she slapped him.' I paused. 'She did keep me away from drugs. She died from heroin, I think, but she kept me free of even the sight of it.'

'Why do you think she died of heroin?'

I poured refills of champagne.

'Something the racing people said. Margaret and Bill. Soon after I got there I went into the sitting room one day when they were arguing. I didn't realise at first that it was about me, but they stopped abruptly when they saw me, so then I did. Bill had been saying "his place is with his mother", and Margaret interrupted, "She's a heroin . . ." and then she saw me and stopped. It's ironic, but I was so pleased they should think my mother a heroine. I felt warmly towards them.' I smiled lop-sidedly. 'It wasn't for years that I realized what Margaret had really been going to say was "she's a heroin addict". I asked her later and she told me that she and Bill had known that my mother was taking heroin, but they didn't know, any more than I did, where to find her. They guessed, as I did, that she'd died, and of course, long before I did, they guessed why. They didn't tell me, to save me pain. Kind people. Very kind.'

Jeremy shook his head. 'I'm so sorry,' he said.

'Don't be. It was all long ago. I never grieved for my mother. I think perhaps now that I should have done, but I didn't.'

I had grieved for Charlie, though. For a short intense time when I was fifteen, and vaguely, sporadically, ever since. I used Charlie's legacy almost every day, literally in the case of photographic equipment and figuratively in the knowledge he'd given me. Any photograph I took was thanks to Charlie.

'I'll try the television people,' Jeremy said.

'OK.'

'And you'll see your grandmother?'

I said without enthusiasm, 'I suppose so.'

Jeremy half smiled. 'Where else can we look? For

Amanda, I mean. If your mother dumped you all over the place like that, she must have done the same for Amanda. Haven't you thought of that?'

'Yes, I have.'

'Well, then?'

I was silent. All those people. All so long in the past. Chloe, Deborah, Samantha ... all shadows without faces. I wouldn't know any of them if they walked into the room.

'What are you thinking?' Jeremy demanded.

'No one I was left with had a pony. I would have remembered a pony. I was never left where Amanda was in the photograph.'

'Oh, I see.'

'And I don't think,' I said, 'that the same friends would be pressed into looking after a second child. I very rarely went back to the same place myself. My mother at least spread the load.'

Jeremy sighed. 'It's all so irregular.'

I said slowly, unwillingly, 'I might find one place I stayed. Perhaps I could try. But even then ... there might be different people in the house after all this time, and anyway they're unlikely to know anything about Amanda ...'

Jeremy pounced on it. 'It's a chance.'

'Very distant.'

'Well worth trying.'

I drank some champagne and looked thoughtfully across the kitchen to where George Millace's box of rubbish lay on the dresser: and a hovering intention suddenly crystallized. Well worth trying. Why not?

'I've lost you,' Jeremy said.

'Yes.' I looked at him. 'You're welcome to stay, but I want to spend the day on a different sort of puzzle. Nothing to do with Amanda. A sort of treasure hunt . . . but there may be no treasure. I just want to find out.'

'I don't . . .' he said vaguely: and I got up and fetched the box and put it on the table.

'Tell me what you think of that lot,' I said.

He opened the box and poked through the contents, lifting things out and putting them back. From expectancy his face changed to disappointment, and he said, 'They're just . . . nothing.'

'Mm.' I stretched over and picked out the piece of clear-looking film which was about two and a half inches across by seven inches long. 'Look at that against the light.'

He took the piece of film and held it up. 'It's got smudges on it,' he said. 'Very faint. You can hardly see them.'

'They're pictures,' I said. 'Three pictures on one-twenty roll film.'

'Well . . . you can't see them.'

'No,' I agreed. 'But if I'm careful . . . and lucky . . . we might.'

He was puzzled. 'How?'

'With intensifying chemicals.'

'But what's the point? Why bother?'

I sucked my teeth. 'I found something of great interest in that box. All those things were kept by a great photographer who was also an odd sort of man. I just think that maybe some more of those bits aren't the rubbish they look.'

'But ... which ones?'

'That's the question. Which ones ... if any.'

Jeremy took a gulp of champagne. 'Let's stick to Amanda.'

'You stick to Amanda. I'm better at photographs.'

He watched with interest, however, while I rummaged in one of the cupboards in the darkroom.

'This all looks frightfully workmanlike,' he said, doing the eye-travel round the enlargers and print processor. 'I'd no idea you did this sort of thing.'

I explained briefly about Charlie and finally found what I was looking for, a tucked away bottle that I'd acquired on an American holiday three years earlier. It said Negative Intensifier on the label, followed by instructions. Most helpful. Many manufacturers printed their instructions on separate flimsy sheets of paper, which got wet or lost. I carried the bottle across to the sink, where there was a water filter fixed under the tap.

'What's that?' Jeremy asked, pointing at its round bulbous shape.

'You have to use ultra-clean soft water for photographic processing. And no iron pipes, otherwise you get a lot of little black dots on the prints.'

'It's all mad,' he said.

'It's precise.'

In a plastic measure I mixed water and intensifier into the strength of solution that the instructions said, and poured it into the developing tray.

'I've never done this before,' I said to Jeremy. 'It may not work. Do you want to watch, or would you rather stay with the bubbly in the kitchen?'

'I'm ... ah ... absolutely riveted, as a matter of fact. What exactly are you going to do?'

'I'm going to contact-print this clear strip of film with the ultra-faint smudges onto some ordinary black-and-white paper and see what it looks like. And then I'm going to put the negative into this intensifying liquid, and after that I'm going to make another black-and-white print to see if there's any difference. And after that ... well, we'll have to see.'

He watched while I worked in dim red light, peering into the developing tray with his nose right down to the liquid.

'Can't see anything happening,' he said.

'It's a bit trial-and-error,' I agreed. I tried printing the clear film four times at different exposures, but all we got on the prints was a fairly uniform black, or a uniform grey, or a uniform white.

'There's nothing there,' Jeremy said. 'It's useless.'

'Wait until we try the intensifier.'

With more hope than expectation I slid the clear film into the intensifying liquid and sloshed it about in there for a good deal longer than the required minimum time. Then I washed it and looked at it against the light: and the ultra-faint smudges were still ultra-faint.

'No good?' Jeremy asked, disappointed.

'I don't know. I don't really know what should happen. And maybe that intensifier is too old. Some photographic chemicals lose their power with age. Shelf life, and so on.'

I printed the negative again at the same variety of exposures as before, and as before we got a uniform black and a uniform dark grey, but this time on the light grey print there were patchy marks, and on the nearly white print, swirly shapes.

'Huh,' Jeremy said. 'Well, that's that.'

We retreated to the kitchen for thought and revivers.

'Too bad,' he said. 'Never mind, it was impossible to start with.'

I sipped a few bubbles and popped them round my teeth.

'I think,' I said reflectively, 'that we might get further if I print that negative not onto paper, but onto another film.'

'Print it onto a film? Do you mean the stuff you load into cameras? I didn't know it was possible.'

'Oh yes. You can print onto anything which has a photographic emulsion. And you can coat practically anything with photographic emulsion. I mean, it doesn't have to be paper, though that's the way everyone thinks of it, because of seeing snapshots in family albums, and all that. But you could coat canvas with emulsion, and print on that. Or glass. Or wood. On the back of your hand, I dare say, if you'd like to stand around in darkness for a while.'

'Good gracious.'

'Black-and-white, of course,' I said. 'Not colour.'

I popped a few more bubbles.

'Let's have another go, then,' I said.

'You really do love this sort of thing, don't you?' Jeremy said.

'Love it? Do you mean photography . . . or puzzles?'

'Both.'

'Well . . . I suppose so.'

I got up and went back to the darkroom, and he again followed to watch. In the dim red light I took a new roll of high-contrast Kodak 2556 film, pulling it off its spool into a long strip and cutting it into five pieces. Onto each separate piece I printed the almost-clear negative, exposing it under the white light of the enlarger for various exposure times: one second the shortest, up to ten seconds the longest. Each piece of high-contrast film after exposure went into the tray of developer, with Jeremy sloshing the liquid about and bending down to see the results.

The results, after taking each piece of film out of the developer at what looked like the best moment, and transferring it to the fixing tray, and finally washing it, were five new positives. From those positives I repeated the whole process, ending with negatives. Seen in bright light, all of the new negatives were much denser than the one I'd started with. On two of them there was a decipherable image ... and the smudges had come alive.

'What are you smiling at?' Jeremy demanded.

'Take a look,' I said.

He held the negative strip I gave him up to the light and said, 'I can see that you've got much clearer smudges. But they're still smudges, all the same.'

'No they're not. They're three pictures of a girl and a man.'

'How can you tell?'

'You get used to reading negatives, after a while.'

'And you look smug,' Jeremy complained.

'To be honest,' I said, 'I'm dead pleased with myself. Let's finish the champagne and then do the next bit.'

'What next bit?' he said, as we again drank in the kitchen.

'Positive prints from the new negatives. Black-and-white pictures. All revealed.'

'What's so funny?'

'The girl's nude, more or less.'

He nearly spilt his drink. 'Are you sure?'

'You can see her breasts.' I laughed at him. 'They're the clearest parts of the negatives, actually.'

'What ... I mean ... about her face?'

'We'll see better soon. Are you hungry?'

'Good heavens. It's one o'clock.'

We ate ham and tomatoes and brown toast, and

finished the bubbles: and then returned to the darkroom.

Printing onto paper from such faint negatives was still a critical business as again one had first to judge the exposures right and then stop the developing print at exactly the best instant and switch it to the fixer, or all that came out was a flat light or a dark grey sheet with no depth and no highlights. It took me several tries with each of the two best new strips to get truly visible results, but I finished with three pictures which were moderately clear, and more than clear enough to reveal what George had photographed. I looked at them with the bright lights on, and with a magnifying glass; and there was no chance of a mistake.

'What's the matter?' Jeremy said. 'They're wonderful. Unbelievable. Why aren't you blowing your trumpets and patting yourself on the back?'

I put the finished articles into the print drier, and silently cleared up the developing trays.

'What is it?' Jeremy asked. 'What's the matter?'

'They're bloody dynamite,' I said.

153

CHAPTER NINE

I took Jeremy and the new pictures upstairs and switched on the epidiascope, which hummed slightly in its idiosyncratic way as it warmed up.

'What's that?' Jeremy said, looking at the machine.

'You must have seen one,' I said, surprised. 'It's pretty old, I know. I inherited it from Charlie. But all the same, they must still be around. You put things in here on this baseboard and their image is projected large and bright onto a screen – or in my case, a wall. You can project anything. Pages of books, illustrations, photographs, letters, dead leaves. All done by mirrors.'

The photograph of Elgin Yaxley and Terence O'Tree still lay in position, and at the flick of a switch came into sharp focus as before, calendar and dates and all.

I drew the curtains against the fading afternoon light and let the picture shine bright in the dark room. After a minute I unclamped it and took it out, and put in instead the best strip I'd made downstairs, adjusting the lens, and enlarging each third separately, showing each of the three pictures on its own.

Even in their unavoidably imperfect state, even in shades of white to dark grey, they pulsated off the wall. The first one showed the top half of a girl as far down as the waist, and also the head and shoulders of a man. They were facing each other, the girl's head higher than the man's. Neither of them wore clothes. The man had his hands under the girl's breasts, lifting them up, with his mouth against the nipple furthest away from the camera.

'Good heavens,' Jeremy said faintly.

'Mm,' I said. 'Do you want to see the others?'

'They didn't look so bad in snapshot size.'

I projected the second picture, which was of much the same pose, except that the camera had been at a different angle, showing less of the girl's front and nearly all of the man's face.

'It's just pornography,' Jeremy said.

'No, it isn't.'

I unclamped the second picture and showed the third, which was different entirely. Events had moved on. The girl, whose own face this time was clearly visible, seemed to be lying on her back. The picture now stretched down to her knees, which were apart. Over her lay the man, his head turned to one side, showing his profile. His hand cupped the one visible breast, and there wasn't much doubt about the activity they were engaged in.

There was nothing to indicate where the pictures had been taken. No distinguishable background. The faint smudges on the transparent film had turned into people, but behind them there was nothing but grey.

I switched off the epidiascope and put on the room lights.

'Why do you say it isn't pornography?' Jeremy said. 'What else is it?'

'I've met them,' I said. 'I know who they are.'

He stared.

'As you're a lawyer,' I said. 'You can tell me. What do you do if you find out after a man's death that he may have been a blackmailer while he was alive?'

'Are you serious?'

'Absolutely.'

'Well ... ah ... he can't be prosecuted, exactly.'

'So one does nothing?'

He frowned. 'Are you ... um ... going to tell me what you're on about?'

'Yes, I think so.'

I told him about George Millace. About the burglaries, the attack on Marie Millace, and the burning of their house. I told him about Elgin Yaxley and Terence O'Tree and the five shot horses: and I told him about the lovers.

'George very carefully kept those oddments in that box,' I said. 'I've deciphered two of them. What if some of the others are riddles? What if they all are?'

'And all ... the basis for blackmail?'

'Heaven knows.'

'Heaven knows ... and you want to find out.'

I slowly nodded. 'It's not so much the blackmail angle, but the photographic puzzles. If George made them, I'd like to solve them. Just to see if I can. You were quite right. I do enjoy that sort of thing.'

Jeremy stared at the floor. He shivered as if he were cold. He said abruptly, 'I think you should destroy the whole lot.'

'That's instinct, not reason.'

'You have the same instinct. You said . . . dynamite.'

'Well . . . someone burgled and burnt George Millace's house. When I found the first picture I thought it must have been Elgin Yaxley who'd done it, but he was in Hong Kong, and it doesn't seem likely . . . And now one would think the lovers did it . . . but it might not be them either.'

Jeremy stood up and moved restlessly around the room in angular uncoordinated jerks.

'I don't like the feel of it,' he said. 'It could be dangerous.'

'To me?'

'Of course to you.'

'No one knows what I've got,' I said. 'Except, of course, you.'

His movements grew even more disturbed, his elbows bending and flapping almost as if he were imitating a bird. Agitation in his mind, I thought: real agitation, not camouflage.

'I suppose . . .' he said. 'Um . . . ah . . .'

'Ask the question.'

He shot me a glance. 'Oh yes . . . Well . . . Was there any doubt . . . about the way George Millace died?'

'Dear . . . God,' I said. I felt as if he'd punched the air out of my lungs. 'I don't think so.'

'What happened exactly?'

'He was driving home from Doncaster, and he went to sleep and ran into a tree.'

'Is that all? Precisely all?'

'Um . . .' I thought back. 'His son said his father stopped at a friend's house for a drink. Then he drove on towards home. Then he hit a tree.'

Jeremy jerked around a little more and said, 'How did anyone know he had stopped at the friend's house? And how does anyone know he went to sleep?'

'These are true lawyers' questions,' I said. 'I don't know the answer to the first, and as to the second, of course nobody knows; it's just what everyone supposes. Going to sleep in the dark towards the end of a long drive isn't all that uncommon. Deadly. Tragic. But always happening.'

'Did they do an autopsy?' he said.

'I don't know. Do they usually?'

He shrugged. 'Sometimes. They'd have tested his blood for the alcohol level. They might have checked for heart attack or stroke, if he wasn't too badly damaged. If there were no suspicious circumstances, that would be all.'

'His son would have told me – have told everyone

on the racecourse – if there had been any odd questions asked. I'm sure there weren't any.'

'Those burglaries must have made the police think a bit, though,' he said frowning.

I said weakly, 'The first serious burglary occurred actually during the funeral.'

'Cremation?'

I nodded. 'Cremation.' I pondered. 'The police might have wondered . . . in fact they did hint very broadly to Marie Millace, and upset her considerably . . . about George possessing photographs other people might not want found. But they don't *know* he had them.'

'Like we do.'

'As you say.'

'Give it up,' he said abruptly. 'Burn those pictures. Stick to looking for Amanda.'

'You're a lawyer. I'm surprised you want to suppress incriminating evidence.'

'You can damn well stop laughing,' he said. 'You could end up like George Millace. Splat on a tree.'

Jeremy left at six, and I walked along to the military briefing with Harold. He had six runners planned for me during the week, and with those and the five spare rides I'd been offered at Windsor I looked like having an exceptionally busy time.

'Don't come crashing down on one of those hyenas

159

you've accepted,' Harold said. 'What you take them for when you've got all my horses to ride I don't know.'

'Money,' I said.

'Huh.'

He never liked me taking outside rides, although as I was self-employed he couldn't stop me. He never admitted that some of the biggest races I'd won had been for other stables. In those cases, he would point out, if pressed, I had been riding those stables' second strings, which had confounded the trainer's assessments and won when they weren't expected.

'Next Saturday at Ascot I'm running two of Victor's,' he said. 'Chainmail . . . and Daylight.'

I glanced at him quickly, but he didn't meet my eyes.

'He didn't have a proper race at Sandown, of course,' he said. 'He's still at his peak.'

'He'll have a harder job at Ascot. Much stronger opponents.'

He nodded, and after a pause he said casually, 'Chainmail might be the best bet. Depends what's left in at the four day stage, of course. And there's the overnights . . . We'll see better what the prospects are on Friday.'

There was a silence.

'Prospects for winning?' I said at last. 'Or for losing?'

'Philip . . .'

'I'm not going to,' I said.

'But . . .'

'You tell me, Harold,' I said. 'Tell me early Saturday

morning, if you've any feeling for me at all. I'll get acute stomach ache. Bilious. The trots. Won't be able to go racing.'

'But there's Daylight.'

I compressed my mouth and stifled the tremble of anger.

'We had four winners last week,' I said tightly. 'Isn't that enough for you?'

'But Victor . . .'

I said, 'I'll ride my bloody guts out for Victor as long as we're trying to win. You tell him that. Tell him just that.' I stood up, unable to sit calmly. 'And don't you forget, Harold, that Chainmail's still only four, and pretty wayward, for all that he's fast. He pulls like a train and tries to duck out at the hurdles, and he's not above sinking his teeth into any horse that bumps him. He's the devil of a hard ride, but he's brave and I like him . . . and I'm not going to help you ruin him. And you *will* damn well ruin him if you muck him about. You'll turn him sour. You'll make him a real rogue. Apart from dishonest, it's stupid.'

'Have you finished?'

'I guess so.'

'Then I agree with you about Chainmail. I'll say it all to Victor. But in the end it's Victor's horse.'

I stood without speaking. Anything I said, I thought, could prove too decisive. While I was still riding for the stable, there was hope.

'Do you want a drink?' Harold said; and I said

yes, coke; and the fraught moment passed. We talked normally about the chances and plans for the other three runners, and only when I was leaving did Harold make any reference to the awaiting chasm.

'If necessary,' he said heavily, 'I'll give you time to get sick.'

At Fontwell races the next day I rode one horse for Harold, which fell three from home, and two for other people, resulting in a second place and a third, and faint congratulatory noises but no avalanches of further work. An average sort of day; better than some. The fall had been slow and easy: a bruise but no damage.

No hot gossip in the weighing room.

No unseemly fighting between newly elected Jockey Club members and cocaine-pushing film directors. No elderly Lords drooling over delectable dollies. Not even any worried broken-collarboned jockeys agonizing over battered mothers.

No heavy-blue-overcoated owners putting pressure on their going-straight jockeys.

A quiet day at the office.

Tuesday, with no racing engagements, I rode out both lots with Harold's string and schooled some of the horses over training jumps. It was a raw damp morning, the sort to endure, not enjoy, and even Harold seemed to take no pleasure in the work. The mood of the Downs, I thought, walking my mount back through Lambourn, infected the whole village. On days like this the inhabitants scarcely said good morning.

From twelve o'clock onwards the day was my own.

Eating some muesli I contemplated George Millace's box of riddles, but felt too restless for another long spell in the dark-room.

Thought of my promised visit to my grandmother, and hastily sought a good reason for postponing it.

Decided to placate the accusing image of Jeremy Folk by seeing if I could find the house in my childhood. A nice vague expedition with no expectation of success. A drift-around day; undemanding.

I set off accordingly to London and cruised up and down a whole lot of little streets between Chiswick and Hammersmith. All of them looked familiar to me in a way: rows of tidy terraces of mostly three storeys and a basement, bow-fronted townhouses for middle-income people, misleadingly narrow frontages stretching far back to small enclosed gardens. I had lived in several houses like that at some time or another, and I couldn't remember even the name of a road.

The years, too, had brought a host of changes. Whole streets had obviously disappeared with the building of bigger roads. Little remaining blocks of houses stood in lonely islands, marooned. Cinemas had closed. Asian shops had moved in. The buses looked the same.

Bus routes.

The buses triggered the memory. The house I was looking for had been three or four from the end of the road, and just round the corner there had been a bus-stop. I had been on the buses often, catching them at that stop.

Going to where?

Going to the river, for walks.

The knowledge drifted quietly back across twenty-plus years. We'd gone down to the river in the afternoons, to look at the houseboats and the seagulls and the mud when the tide was out; and we'd looked across to the gardens at Kew.

I drove down to Kew Bridge and reversed, and started from there, following buses.

A slow business, because I stopped when the bus did. Unproductive also, because none of the stops anywhere seemed to be near the corners of roads. I gave it up after an hour and simply cruised around, resigned to not finding anything I recognized. Probably I'd got even the district wrong. Probably I should be looking in Hampstead, where I knew I'd been also.

It was a pub that finally orientated me. The Willing Horse. An old pub. Dark brown paint. Frosted glass in the windows with tracery patterns round the edges. I parked the car round the corner and walked back to the chocolate doors, and simply stood there, waiting.

After a while I seemed to know which way to go.

Turn left, walk three hundred yards, cross the road, first turning on the right.

I turned into a street of bow-fronted terrace houses, three storeys high, narrow and neat and typical. Cars lined both sides of the street, with many front gardens converted to parking places. There were a few bare-branched trees growing from earth-patches near the edge of the pavement, and hedges and shrubs by the houses. Three steps up to a small flat area outside each front door.

I crossed that road and walked slowly up it, but the impetus had gone. Nothing told me whether I was in the right place, or which house to try. I walked more slowly, indecisively, wondering what to do next.

Four houses from the end I went up the short foot-path, and up the steps, and rang the doorbell.

A woman with a cigarette opened the door.

'Excuse me,' I said. 'Does Samantha live here?'

'Who?'

'Samantha?'

'No.' She looked me up and down with the utmost suspicion, and closed the door.

I tried six more houses. Two no answers, one 'clear off', one 'no dear, I'm Popsy, like to come in?', one 'we don't want no brushes', and one 'is that a cat?'

At the eighth an old lady told me I was up to no good, she'd watched me go from house to house, and if I didn't stop it she would call the police.

'I'm looking for someone called Samantha,' I said. 'She used to live here.'

'I'm watching you,' she said. 'If you try to climb in through any windows, I'll call the police.'

I walked away from her grim little face and she came right out into the street to watch me.

It wasn't much good, I thought. I wouldn't find Samantha. She might be out, she might have moved, she might never have lived in the street in the first place. Under the old woman's baleful gaze I tried another house where no one answered, and another where a girl of about twenty opened the door.

'Excuse me,' I said. 'Does anyone called Samantha live here?' I'd said it so often it now sounded ridiculous. This is the last one, I thought. I may as well give it up and go home.

'Who?'

'Samantha?'

'Samantha what? Samantha who?'

'I'm afraid I don't know.'

She pursed her lips, not quite liking it.

'Wait a moment,' she said. 'I'll go and see.' She shut the door and went away. I walked down the steps to the front garden where a small red car stood on some tarmac. Hovered, waiting to see if the girl returned, aware of the old woman beadily watching from along the road.

The door behind me opened as I turned. There were two people there, the girl and an older woman. When

I took a step towards them the woman made a sharp movement of the arm, to keep me away. Raising her voice she said, 'What do you want?'

'Well . . . I'm looking for someone called Samantha.'

'So I hear. What for?'

'Are you,' I said slowly, 'Samantha?'

She looked me up and down with the suspicion I was by now used to. A comfortably sized lady, grey-brown wavy hair to her shoulders.

'What do you want?' she said again, unsmiling.

I said, 'Would the name Nore mean anything to you? Philip Nore, or Caroline Nore?'

To the girl the names meant nothing, but in the woman there was a fast sharpening of attention.

'What exactly do you want?' she demanded.

'I'm . . . Philip Nore.'

The guarded expression turned to incredulity. Not exactly to pleasure, but certainly to acknowledgement.

'You'd better come in,' she said. 'I'm Samantha Bergen.'

I went up the steps and through the front door, and didn't have, as I'd half-expected, the feeling of coming home.

'Downstairs,' she said, leading the way and looking over her shoulder, and I followed her through the hall and down the stairs which in all those London houses led to the kitchen and the door out to the garden. The girl followed after me, looking mystified and still wary.

'Sorry not to have been more welcoming,' Samantha

167

said, 'but you know what it is these days. So many burglaries. You have to be careful. And strange young men coming to the door asking for Samantha ...'

'Yes,' I said.

She went through a doorway into a large room which looked more like a country kitchen than most kitchens in the country. A row of pine-covered fitments on the right. A big table, with chairs. A red-tiled floor. French windows to the garden. A big basket-chair hanging on a chain from the ceiling. Beams. Inglenook with gas fire. Bits of gleaming copper.

Without thinking I walked across the red floor and sat in the hanging basket chair, beside the inglenook, tucking my feet up under me, out of sight.

Samantha Bergen stood there looking astounded.

'You are!' she said. 'You are Philip. Little Philip. He always used to sit there like that, with his feet up. I'd forgotten. But seeing you do it ... Good gracious heavens.'

'I'm sorry,' I said, half stammering and standing up again, steadying the swinging chair. 'I just ... did it.'

'My dear man,' she said. 'It's all right. It's extra-ordinary to see you, that's all.' She turned to the girl but said still to me, 'This is my daughter, Clare. She wasn't born when you stayed here.' And to her daughter she said, 'I looked after a friend's child now and then. Heavens ... it must be twenty-two years since the last time. I don't suppose I ever told you.'

The girl shook her head but looked less mystified

and a good deal more friendly. They were both of them attractive in an unforced sort of way, both of them wearing jeans and sloppy jerseys and unpainted Tuesday afternoon faces. The girl was slimmer and had darker and shorter hair, but they both had large grey eyes, straight noses, and unaggressive chins. Both were self-assured; and both undefinably intelligent.

The work I had interrupted lay spread out on the table. Galley proofs and drawings and photographs, the makings of a book. When I glanced at it Clare said, 'Mother's cookery book,' and Samantha said, 'Clare is a publisher's assistant,' and they invited me to sit down again.

We sat round the table, and I told them about looking for Amanda, and the off-chance which had brought me to their door.

Samantha regretfully shook her head. 'An off-chance is all it was,' she said. 'I never saw Caroline after she took you away the last time. I didn't even know she had a daughter. She never brought her here.'

'Tell me about her,' I said. 'What was she like?'

'Caroline? So pretty you wanted to hug her. Full of light and fun. She could get anyone to do anything. But . . .' she stopped.

'But what?' I said. 'And please do be frank. She's been dead for twelve years, and you won't hurt my feelings.'

'Well . . . she took drugs.' Samantha looked at me anxiously, and seemed relieved when I nodded.

'Cocaine. LSD. Cannabis. Almost anything. Poppers and uppers and downers. She tried the lot. She told me she didn't want you around when she and her friends were all high. She begged me to look after you for a few days ... it always turned into a few weeks ... and you were such a quiet little mouse ... you were quite good company, actually. I never minded, when she brought you.'

'How often?' I said slowly.

'How often did she bring you? Oh ... half a dozen times. You were about four the first time ... and about eight at the end, I suppose. I told her I couldn't take you again, as Clare was imminent.'

'I've always been grateful to you,' I said.

'Have you?' She seemed pleased. 'I wouldn't have thought you'd remember ... but I suppose you must have done, as you're here.'

'Did you know anyone called Chloe or Deborah or Miranda?' I said.

'Deborah Baederbeck? Went to live in Brussels?'

'I don't know.'

Samantha shook her head dubiously. 'She wouldn't know anything about your Amanda. She must have been in Brussels for ... oh ... twenty-five years.'

Clare made some tea and I asked Samantha if my mother had ever told her anything about my father.

'No, nothing,' she said positively. 'An absolutely taboo subject, I gathered. She was supposed to have an abortion, and didn't. Left it too late. Just like Caroline, absolutely irresponsible.' She made a comical face. 'I suppose you wouldn't be here if she'd done what she'd promised her old dragon of a mother.'

'She made up for it by not registering my birth.'

'Oh God.' She chuckled with appreciation. 'I must say that's typical Caroline. We went to the same school. I'd known her for years. We'd not long left when she got landed with you.'

'Did she take drugs then? At school?'

'Heavens, no.' She frowned, thinking. 'Afterwards. We all did. I don't mean she and I together. But our generation . . . we all tried it, I should think, some time or other, when we were young. Pot mostly.'

Clare looked surprised, as if mothers didn't do that sort of thing.

I said, 'Did you know the friends she got high with?'

Samantha shook her head. 'Never met any of them. Caroline called them friends in the plural, but I always thought of it as one friend, a man.'

'No,' I said. 'Sometimes there were more. People lying on floor cushions half asleep, with the room full of haze. All enormously peaceful.'

They were the people with words like 'skins' and 'grass' and 'joints', which never seemed to mean what my childish brain expected; and it was one of those who had given me a cigarette and urged me to suck in the smoke. Suck it into your lungs, he'd said, and then hold your breath while you count ten. I'd coughed all the smoke out before I'd counted two, and he'd laughed and told me to try again. Three or four small drags, I'd had.

The result, which I'd dreamed of occasionally afterwards rather than actively remembered, was a great feeling of tranquillity. Relaxed limbs, quiet breathing, slight lightness of head. My mother had come home and slapped me, which put paid to all that. The friend who'd initiated me never reappeared. I hadn't met hash again until I was twenty, when I'd been given a present of some greeny-yellow Lebanese resin to sprinkle like an OXO cube onto tobacco.

I'd smoked some, and given some away, and never bothered again. The results, to me, weren't worth the trouble and expense. They would have been, a doctor friend had told me, if I'd had asthma. Cannabis was terrific for asthmatics, he'd said, sadly. Pity they couldn't smoke it on the National Health.

We drank the tea Clare had made, and Samantha asked what I did in the way of a job.

'I'm a jockey.'

They were incredulous. 'You're too tall,' Samantha said, and Clare said, 'People just aren't jockeys.'

'People are,' I said. 'I am. And steeplechase jockeys don't have to be small. Six-footers have been known.'

'Extraordinary thing to be,' Clare said. 'Pretty pointless, isn't it?'

'Clare!' Samantha said, protesting.

'If you mean,' I said equably, 'that being a jockey contributes nothing useful to society, I'm not so sure.'

'Proceed,' Clare said.

'Recreation gives health. I provide recreation.'

'And betting?' she demanded. 'Is that healthy?'

'Sublimation of risk-taking. Stake your money, not your life. If everyone actually set out to climb Everest, just think of the rescue parties.'

She started to smile and converted it into a chewing motion with her lips. 'But you yourself . . . take the risks.'

'I don't bet.'

'Clare will tie you in knots,' her mother said. 'Don't listen to her.'

Clare, however, shook her head. 'I would think your little Philip is as easy to tie in knots as a stream of water.'

Samantha gave her a surprised glance and asked me where I lived.

'In Lambourn. It's a village in Berkshire. Out on the Downs.'

Clare frowned and looked at me with sharpened concentration.

'Lambourn . . . isn't that the village where there are a lot of racing stables, rather like Newmarket?'

'That's right.'

'Hm.' She thought for a minute. 'I think I'll just ring up my boss. He's doing a book on British villages and village life. He was saying this morning the book's still a bit thin – asked me if I had any ideas. He has a writer chap doing it. Going to villages, staying a week and writing a chapter. He's just done one on a village that produces its own operas ... Look, do you mind if I give him a call?'

'Of course not.'

She was on her feet and going across to a telephone extension on the kitchen worktop before I'd even answered. Samantha gave her a fond motherly look, and I thought how odd it was to find Samantha in her late forties, when I'd always imagined her perpetually young. From under the unrecognizable exterior, though, the warmth, the directness, the steady values and the basic goodness came across to me as something long known: and I was reassured to find that those half-buried impressions had been right.

'Clare will bully you into things,' she said. 'She bullied me into doing this cookery book. She's got more energy than a power station. She told me when she was about six that she was going to be a publisher, and she's well on her way. She's already second-in-command to the man she's talking to. She'll be running the whole firm before they know where they are.' She sighed with pleased resignation, vividly illuminating the trials and pride of mothering a prodigy.

The prodigy herself, who looked normal enough, finished talking on the telephone and came back to the table nodding.

'He's interested. He says we'll both go down and

look the place over, and then if it's OK he'll send the writer, and a photographer.'

I said diffidently, 'I've taken pictures of Lambourn ... If you'd like to ...'

She interrupted with a shake of the head. 'We'd need professional work. Sorry and all that. But my boss says if you don't mind we'll call at your digs or whatever, if you'd be willing to help us with directions and general info.'

'Yes ... I'd be willing.'

'That's great.' She gave me a sudden smile that was more like a pat on the back than a declaration of friendship. She knows she's bright, I thought. She's used to being brighter than most. She's not as good as Jeremy Folk at concealing that she knows it.

'Can we come on Friday?' she said.

CHAPTER TEN

Lance Kinship was wandering around at the head of a retinue of cameramen, sound recordists and general dogsbodies when I arrived at Newbury racecourse on the following day, Wednesday. We heard in the changing room that he was taking stock shots for a film with the blessing of the management and that jockeys were asked to cooperate. Not, it was said, to the point of grinning into the camera lens at every opportunity, but just to not treading on the crew if one found them underfoot.

I slung my Nikon round my neck inside my raincoat and unobtrusively took a few pictures of the men taking pictures.

Technically speaking, cameras were not welcome at race meetings except in the hands of recognized photographers, but most racecourses didn't fidget unduly about the general public taking snaps anywhere except in the Members' enclosure. Most racecourse managers, because I'd been doing it for so long, looked tolerantly upon my own efforts and let me get on with it. Only at Royal Ascot was the crack-down on amateurs complete: the one meeting where people had to park their shooters at the entrance, like gunslingers riding into a bullet-free town.

Lance Kinship looked as if he had tried hard not to look like a film director. In place of his olive suede jacket, now presumably having its bloodstains removed at the cleaners, he wore a brownish tweed suit topped by a brown trilby set at a conservative angle and accompanied by checked shirt, quiet tie, and raceglasses. He looked, I thought, as if he'd cast himself as an uppercrust extra in his own film.

He was telling his crew what to do with pomposity in his voice and with indecisive gestures. It was only in the tenseness with which they listened to him, their eyes sliding his way every time he spoke, that one saw any authority. I took a couple of shots of that reaction; the eyes all looking towards him from averted heads. I reckoned that when printed, those pictures might quite clearly show men obeying someone they didn't like.

At one point, round by the saddling boxes, where the crew were filming the trainers fitting on the saddles before the first race, Lance Kinship turned his head in the instant I pressed the button, and stared straight into my lens.

He strode across to me, looking annoyed.

'What are you doing?' he said, though it must have been obvious.

'I was just interested,' I said inoffensively.

177

He looked at my boots, my white breeches and the red and yellow shirt which I wore under the raincoat.

'A jockey,' he said, as to himself. He peered through his black framed spectacles at my camera. 'A Nikon.' He raised his eyes to my face and frowned with half-recognition.

'How's the nose?' I said politely.

He grunted, finally placing me.

'Don't get into shot,' he said. 'You're not typical. I don't want Nikon-toting jocks lousing up the footage. Right?'

'I'll be careful,' I said.

He seemed on the point of telling me to go away altogether, but he glanced from side to side and took note that a few race-goers were listening, and decided against it. With a brief disapproving nod he went back to his crew, and presently they moved off and began taking shots of the saddled horses walking into the parade ring.

The chief cameraman carried his big movie camera on his shoulder and mostly operated it from there. An assistant walked one step behind, carrying a tripod. One sound recorder carried the charcoal sausage-shaped boom and a second fiddled endlessly with knobs on an electric box. A young man with frizzy hair operated a clapper board, and a girl took copious notes. They trailed round all afternoon getting in everyone's way and apologizing like mad so that no one much minded.

They were down at the start when I lined up on a
scatty novice 'chaser for Harold, and thankfully absent
from the eighth fence, where the novice 'chaser put his
fore-feet into the open ditch on the take-off side and
crossed the birch almost upside down. Somewhere
during this wild somersault I fell out of the saddle, but
by the mercy of heaven when the half-ton of horse
crashed to the ground I was not underneath it.

He lay prostrate for a few moments, winded and
panting, giving me plenty of time to grasp hold of the
reins and save his lad the frustrating job of catching
him loose. Some horses I loved: and some I didn't. This
was a clumsy stubborn delinquent with a hard mouth,
just starting what was likely to be a long career of bad
jumping. I'd schooled him at home several times and
knew him too well. If he met a fence right, he was safe
enough, but if he met it wrong he ignored signals to
change his stride; and every horse met a fence wrong
now and then, however skilful his rider. I reckoned
every time he completed a race, I'd be lucky.

Resignedly I waited until he was on his feet and
prancing about a bit, then remounted him and trotted
him back to the stands, and made encouraging remarks
to the downcast owner and honest ones to Harold.

'Tell him to cut his losses and buy a better horse.'

'He can't afford it.'

'He's wasting the training fees.'

'I dare say,' Harold said, 'but we're not telling him,
are we?'

I grinned at him. 'No, I guess not.'

I took my saddle into the weighing room and Harold went off to join the owner in a consolatory drink. Harold needed the training fees. I needed the riding fees. The owner was buying a dream and kidding himself. It happened every day, all the time, in racing. It was only occasionally that the dream came superbly, soul-fillingly true, and when that happened you saw points of light like stars in the owner's eyes. Thank God for the owners, I thought. Without them racing wouldn't exist.

When I was changing back into street clothes someone came and told me there was a man outside asking for the jockey with the camera.

I went to see, and found Lance Kinship trudging up and down and looking impatient.

'Oh there you are,' he said, as if I'd seriously kept him waiting. 'What's your name?'

'Philip Nore.'

'Well, Phil, what do you say? You took some photographs today. If they're any good I'll buy them from you. How's that?'

'Well . . .' I was nonplussed. 'Yes, if you like.'

'Good. Where's your camera? Get it then, get it. The crew is over by the winning post. Take some photographs of them shooting the finish of the next race. Right? Right?'

'Yes,' I said dazedly.

'Come on then. Come on.'

I fetched the camera from the changing room and found him still waiting for me but definitely in a hurry. I would have to get over there and assess the best angles, he explained, and I'd only have one chance because the crew would be moving out to the car park presently to film the racegoers going home.

He had apparently tried to get the regular racing photographers to do the present job, but they had said they were too busy.

'I thought of you. Worth trying, I thought. With the camera, you at least have to be able to focus. Right?'

We were walking fast. He broke now and then into a sort of trotting stride, and his breathing gradually grew shorter. His mental energy, however, was unflagging.

'We need these pics for publicity. Right?'

'I see,' I said.

His words and manner were so much at variance with his appearance that the whole expedition seemed to me powerfully unreal. Urgent film producers (who might or might not provide cocaine for sniffing at parties) were surely not accustomed to look the country gentleman, nor tweeded country gentlemen to speak with slovenly vowels and glottal-stop consonants. The 'right?' he was so fond of was pronounced without its final 't'.

I would have thought, if he wanted publicity pictures, that he would have brought a photographer of his own; and I asked him.

'Sure,' he said. 'I had one lined up. Then he died. Didn't get around to it again. Then today, saw you. Reminded me. Asked the news photographers. No dice. Thought of you, right? Asked them about you. They said you were good, you could do it. You may be lousy. If your pics are no good, I don't buy, right?'

He panted across the course to the winning post on the far side, and I asked him which photographer had died.

'Fellow called Millace. Know him?'

'I knew him,' I said.

'He said he'd do it. Died in a crash. Here we are. You get on with it. Take what you want. Got colour film in there, have you?'

I nodded and he nodded, and he turned away to give instructions to the crew. They again listened to him with the slightly averted heads, and I wandered away. Lance Kinship was not immediately likeable, but I again had a strong feeling that his crew felt positive discontent. He wouldn't buy photographs showing that response, I thought dryly, so I waited until the crew were not looking at him, and shot them absorbed in their work.

Lance Kinship's breathing returned to normal and he himself merged again into the racing background as if he'd been born there. An actor at heart, I thought: but unlike an actor he was dressing a part in real life, which seemed odd.

'What film are you making?' I asked.

'Stock shots,' he said uninformatively. 'Background.'

I left it, and walked round the crew looking for useful angles for pictures. The horses came out onto the course and cantered down to the start, and the frizzy-haired boy with the clapper board, who happened to be close to me, said with sudden and unexpected fierceness, 'You'd think he was God Almighty. You'd think this was an epic, the way he frigs about. We're making commercials. Half a second on screen, flash off. Huh!'

I half smiled. 'What's the product?'

'Some sort of brandy.'

Lance Kinship came towards me and told me it was important that he should be included in my photographs, and that I should take them from where he would be prominently in shot.

The frizzy-haired boy surreptitiously raised his eyebrows into comical peaks, and I assured Lance Kinship with a trembling straight face that I would do my absolute best.

I did by good luck get one or two reasonable pictures, but no doubt George Millace with his inner eye and his motor-drive camera would have outstripped me by miles. Lance Kinship gave me a card with his address on and told me again that he would buy the pictures if he liked them, right?

He didn't say for how much, and I didn't like to ask.

I would never be a salesman.

Taking photographs for a living, I thought ruefully, would find me starving within a week.

Reaching home I switched on the lights and drew the curtains, and sat by the kitchen table going again through George Millace's rubbish box, thinking of his talents and his cruel mind, and wondering just how much profit he had made from his deadly photographs.

It was true that if he'd left any more pictures in that box I wanted to decipher them. The urge to solve the puzzles was overpowering. But if I learned any more secrets, what would I do with them . . . and what ought I to do with those I already had?

In a fairly typical manner I decided to do pretty well nothing. To let events take their course. To see what happened.

Meanwhile there were those tantalizing bits that looked so pointless. . . .

I lifted out the black plastic light-proof envelope which was of about the same size as the box and lying at the bottom of it, under everything else. I looked again at its contents, as I had in Steve Millace's house, and saw again the page-sized piece of clear plastic, and also, which hadn't registered before, two sheets of paper of about the same size.

I looked at them briefly and closed them again into their light-proof holder, because it had suddenly occurred to me that George might not have stored them like that unless it was necessary. That plastic and that paper might bear latent images . . . which I might already have destroyed by exposing them to light.

The piece of plastic and the sheets of paper didn't actually look to me like photographic materials at all. They looked like a piece of plastic and two sheets of typing paper.

If they bore latent images, I didn't know how to develop them. If they didn't, why had George kept them in a light-proof envelope?

I sat staring vaguely at the silent black plastic and thinking about developers. To bring out the image on any particular type of film or any type of paper one had to use the right type of developer, the matched mixture of chemicals made for the task. All of which meant that unless I knew the make and type of the plastic and of the two sheets of paper I couldn't get any further.

A little pensively I pushed the black envelope aside and took up the strips of blank negatives, which at least didn't have the built-in difficulty of being still sensitive to light. They had already been developed. They just looked as if when they had been developed there had been no latent images on them to bring out.

They were thirty-five millimetre colour film negatives, and there were a lot of them, some simply blank and others blank with uneven magenta blotches here and there. The negatives were in strips, mostly six to a strip. I laid them all out end to end and made the first interesting discovery.

All the plain blank negatives had come from one film, and those with magenta blotches from another. The frame numbers along the top of each strip ran consecutively from one to thirty-six in each case. Two films of thirty-six exposures each.

I knew what make of film they were, because each manufacturer placed the frame numbers differently, but I didn't suppose that that was important. What might be important, however, was the very nature of colour negatives.

While slide films – transparencies – appeared to the eye in their true lifelike colours, negative film appeared in the reciprocal colours: and to get back to the true colours one had of course to make a print from the negative.

The primary colours of light were blue, green, and red. The reciprocal colours, in which they appeared on a negative, were yellow, magenta and cyan. Negatives therefore would have looked like mixtures of yellow, deep pink (magenta) and greeny-blue (cyan), except that to get good whites and highlights all manufacturers gave their negatives an overall pale orange cast. Colour negatives therefore always looked a pale clear orange at the edges.

The overall orange colour also had the effect of masking the yellow sections so that they didn't show to the eye as yellow bits of negative, but as orange.

George Millace's negatives looked a pale clear transparent orange throughout.

Just suppose, I thought, that under the orange there was an image in yellow, which at the moment didn't show.

If I printed those negatives, the yellow would become blue.

An invisible yellow negative image could turn into a totally visible printed image in blue.

Worth trying, I thought. I went into the darkroom and mixed the developing chemicals, and set up the colour print processor. It meant waiting half an hour for the built-in thermostatic heaters to raise the various chemical baths to the correct temperatures, but after that the prints were conveyed automatically inside the closed processor from one bath to another on rollers, each sheet of photographic paper taking seven minutes to travel from entry to exit.

I found out almost at once, by making contact prints, that under the orange masking there was indeed blue: but not blue images. Just blue.

There were so many variables in colour printing that searching for an image on blank negatives was like walking blindfold through a forest, and although in the end I printed every negative separately and tried every way I knew, I was only partially successful.

I ended, in fact, with thirty-six solid blue oblongs, enlarged to four inches by five and printed four to a sheet, and thirty-six more with greenish blotches here and there.

The only thing one could say, I thought, as I let them wash thoroughly in running water, was that George wouldn't have taken seventy-two pictures of a blue oblong for nothing.

I dried some of the prints and looked at them closely, and it did seem to me that there were faint darker marks on some of them. Nothing one could plainly see, but something.

When it dawned on me far too late what George had done I was too tired to start all over again. I cleaned up the processor and everything else, and went to bed.

Jeremy Folk telephoned early the next morning and asked if I'd been to see my grandmother.

Give me time, I said, and he said I'd had time, and did I remember I had promised?

'Well . . . I'll go,' I said. 'Saturday, after Ascot.'

'What have you been doing?' he asked plaintively. 'You could have gone any day this week. Don't forget she really is dying.'

'I've been working,' I said. 'And printing.'

'From that box?' he said suspiciously.

'Uh huh.'

'Don't do it,' he said, and then, 'What have you got?'

'Blue prints. Blue pictures.'

'What?'

'Blue as in blue. Pure deep blue. Forty-seven B.'

'*What* did you say? Are you sober?'

'I am awake and yawning,' I said. 'So listen. George Millace screwed a deep blue filter onto his camera and pointed it at a black and white picture, and he photographed the black and white picture through the blue filter onto colour negative film. Forty-seven B is the most intense blue filter you can buy, and I bet that's what he used.'

'You're talking Chinese.'

'I'm talking Millace. Crafty double Millace. Second cousin to double Dutch.'

'You really are drunk.'

'Don't be silly. As soon as I work out how to unscramble the blue, and do it, the next riveting Millace instalment will fall into our hands.'

'I seriously think you should burn the lot.'

'Not a chance.'

'You think of it as a game. It isn't a game.'

'No.'

'For God's sake be careful.'

I said I would. One says things like that so easily.

I went to Wincanton races in Somerset and rode twice for Harold and three times for other people. The day was dry with a sharp wind that brought tears to the eyes, tears which the standard of racing did nothing to dispel, since all the good horses had cried off and gone to Newbury or Ascot instead, leaving chances for the blundering majority. I fumbled and booted my way around five times in safety, and in the novice 'chase, owing to most of the field having fallen over each other at the first open ditch, found myself finishing in front, all alone.

My mount's thin little trainer greeted my return with a huge grin, tear-filled eyes and a blue dripping nose.

'By gum, lad, well done. By gum, it's bloody cold. Get thee in and weighed. Don't stand about. By gum, then, that was a bit of all right, wasn't it, all them others falling?'

'You'd schooled yours a treat,' I said, pulling off the saddle. 'He jumped great.'

His mouth nearly split its sides with pleasure. 'By gum, lad, he'd jump Aintree, the way he went today. Get thee in. Get thee in.'

I went in and weighed, and changed and weighed out, and raced, and returned, and changed and weighed . . .

There had been a time, when it was all new, that my heart had pumped madly every time I walked from the changing room to the parade ring, every time I cantered to the start. After ten years my heart pumped above normal only for the big ones, the Grand National and so on, and then only if my horse had a reasonable chance. The once fiendish excitement had turned to routine.

Bad weather, long journeys, disappointment and injuries had at first been shrugged off as 'part of the job'. After ten years I saw that they *were* the job. The peaks, the winners, those were the bonuses. Extras.

The tools of my trade were a liking for speed and a liking for horses, and the power to combine those two feelings. Also strong bones, an ability to bounce, and a tendency to mend quickly when I didn't.

None of these tools, except probably the liking for horses, would be of the slightest use to me as a photographer.

I walked irritably out to my car at the end of that afternoon. I didn't want to be a photographer. I wanted to remain a jockey. I wanted to stay where I was, in the known: not to step irrevocably into the future. I wanted things to go on as they were, and not to change.

Early the following morning Clare Bergen appeared on my doorstep accompanied by a dark young man whose fingertips in a handshake almost tingled with energy. Publishers, I had vaguely supposed, were portly father-figures. Another out-of-date illusion gone bust.

Clare herself had come in a bright woolly hat, bright scarf, Afghan sheepskin jacket, yellow satin ski-pants and huge fleece-lined boots. Ah well, I thought, she would only frighten half of the horses. The nervous half.

I drove them up onto the Downs in the Land Rover

borrowed from Harold for the occasion, and we watched a few strings work. Then I drove them round the village, pointing out which trainers lived where. Then I took them back to the cottage for coffee and cogitation.

The publisher said he would like to poke round a little on foot, and walked off. Clare drank her second steaming cup and said how on earth did we bear it with a wind like that sawing everyone in half.

'It always seems to be windy here,' I agreed, thinking about it.

'All those naked hills.'

'Good for horses.'

'I don't think I've ever actually touched a horse.' She looked faintly surprised. 'Most of the people I know despise horse people.'

'Everyone likes to feel superior,' I said, uninsulted. 'Particularly when they aren't.'

'Ouch,' she said. 'That's a damned fast riposte.'

I smiled. 'You'd be surprised the sort of hate that gets aimed at horses. Anything from sneers to hysteria.'

'And you don't mind?'

'What those people feel is their problem, not mine.'

She looked at me straightly with the wide grey eyes. 'What hurts you?' she said.

'People saying I jumped overboard when I went down with the ship.'

'Er . . . what?'

'People saying I fell off when it was the horse which fell, and took me with it.'

'And there's a distinction?'

'Most important.'

'You're having me on,' she said.

'A bit.' I took her empty cup and put it in the dish-water. 'So what hurts you?'

She blinked, but after a pause she answered, 'Being held to be a fool.'

'That,' I said, 'is a piercingly truthful reply.'

She looked away from me as if embarrassed, and said she liked the cottage and the kitchen and could she borrow the bathroom. She emerged from there shortly minus the woolly hat and plus some fresh lip-stick and asked if the rest of the house was on a par.

'You want to see it?' I said.

'Love to.'

I showed her the sitting room, the bedroom, and finally the darkroom. 'And that's all,' I said.

She turned slowly from the darkroom to where I stood behind her in the hall.

'You said you took photographs.'

'Yes, I do.'

'But I thought you meant . . .' She frowned. 'Mother said I was short with you when you offered . . . but I'd no idea . . .'

'It doesn't matter,' I said. 'It's quite all right.'

'Well . . . can I see them?'

'If you like. They're in that filing cabinet over there.'

I pulled open one of the drawers and sorted through the folders. 'Here you are, Lambourn village.'

'What are all those others?' she said.

'Just pictures.'

'What of?'

'Fifteen years.'

She looked at me sharply as if I wasn't making sense, so I added, 'Since I owned my own camera.'

'Oh.' She looked along the tags on the folders, reading, aloud. 'America, France, Children, Harold's Place, Jockey's Life ... What's Jockey's Life?'

'Just everyday living, if you're a jockey.'

'Can I look?'

'Sure.'

She eased the well-filled holder out of the drawer and peered inside. Then she carried it away towards the kitchen and I followed with the pictures of Lambourn.

She laid the folder she carried on the kitchen table, and opened it, and went through the bulky contents picture by picture, steadily and frowning.

No comments.

'Can I see Lambourn?' she said.

I gave her Lambourn, and she looked through those also in silence.

'I know they're not marvellous,' I said mildly. 'You don't have to rack your brains for something kind to say.'

She looked up at me fiercely. 'You're lying. You know damned well they're good.'

She closed the Lambourn file and drummed her fingers on it. 'I can't see why we can't use these,' she said. 'But it's not my decision, of course.'

She fished into her large brown handbag and came up with cigarettes and a lighter. She put a cigarette to her mouth and lit it, and I noticed with surprise that her fingers were trembling. What on earth, I wondered, could have made her nervous. Something had disturbed her deeply, because all the glittery extrovert surface had vanished, and what I saw was a dark-haired young woman concentrating acutely on the thoughts in her head.

She took several deep inhaling breaths of smoke, and looked unseeingly at her fingers, which went on trembling.

'What's the matter?' I said at last.

'Nothing.' She gave me a quick glance and looked away, and said, 'I've been looking for something like you.'

'Something?' I echoed, puzzled.

'Mm.' She tapped off some ash. 'Mother told you, didn't she, that I wanted to be a publisher?'

'Yes, she did.'

'Most people smile, because I'm still young. But I've worked in publishing for five years . . . and I know what I'm doing.'

'I don't doubt it.'

'No . . . but I need . . . I want . . . I need to make a book that will establish my own personal reputation in publishing. I need to be known as the person who produced such-and-such a book. A very successful book. Then my whole future in publishing will be assured. Do you understand?'

'Yes.'

'So I've been looking for that book for a year or two now. Looking and despairing, because what I want is exceptional. And now . . .' she took a deep breath, 'now I've found it.'

'But,' I said, puzzled, 'Lambourn's not news, and anyway I thought it was your boss's book . . .'

'Not that, you fool,' she said. 'This.' She put her hand on the Jockey's Life folder. 'The pictures in here. They don't need a text. They tell the story on their own.' She drew on the cigarette. 'Arranged in the right order . . . presented as a way of living . . . as an autobiography, a social comment, an insight into human nature . . . as well as how an industry works . . . it'll make a spectacular change from flowers and fish.'

'The flowers sold about two million copies, didn't they?'

'You don't believe me, do you?' she demanded. 'You simply don't see . . .' She broke off and frowned. 'You haven't had any of these photographs published before, have you? In papers or magazines, or anywhere?'

I shook my head. 'Nowhere. I've never tried.'

'You're amazing. You have this talent, and you don't use it.'

'But . . . everyone takes photographs.'

'Sure they do. But not everyone takes a long series of photographs which illustrate a whole way of life.' She tapped off the ash. 'It's all there, isn't it? The hard work, the dedication, the bad weather, the humdrum, the triumphs, the pain . . . I've only looked through these pictures once, and in no sort of order, and I know what your life's like. I know it *intimately*. Because that's how you've photographed it. I know your life from inside. I see what you've seen. I see the enthusiasm in those owners. I see their variety. I see what you owe to the stable-lads. I see the worry of trainers, it's everywhere. I see the laughter in jockeys, and the stoicism. I see what you've felt. I see what you've understood about people. I see people in a way I hadn't before, because of what you've seen.'

'I didn't know,' I said slowly, 'that those pictures were quite so revealing.'

'Look at this last one,' she said, pulling it out. 'This picture of a man in an overall pulling the boot off this boy with the broken shoulder . . . you don't need any words to say the man is doing it as gently as he can, or that it hurts . . . you can see it all, in every line of their bodies and faces.' She replaced the picture in the folder and said seriously, 'It's going to take me some time to set things up the way I want. Will you give me your assurance that you won't go straight off and sell these pictures to someone else?'

'Of course,' I said.

'And don't mention any of this to my boss when he comes back. I want this to be my book, not his.'

I half smiled. 'All right.'

'You may have no ambition,' she said sharply, 'but I have.'

'Yes.'

'And my ambition won't do you any harm either,' she said. 'If the book's a seller . . . and it will be . . . you'll get royalties.' She paused. 'You can have an advance, anyway, as soon as the contracts are signed.'

'Contracts . . .'

'Contracts, naturally,' she said. 'And keep these pictures safe, will you? I'll come back for them soon, on my own.'

She thrust the folder into my hands and I replaced it in the filing cabinet, so that when her energetic young boss returned it was only the views of Lambourn that he saw. He said without too much excitement that they would do well enough, and shortly afterwards he and Clare bore them away.

When they'd gone I thought that Clare's certainty about her book would evaporate. She would remember that most of the people she knew despised horse people. She would work out that a book of pictures taken by a jockey about his life would have a very limited appeal, and she would write apologetically, or briskly, and say that after all, on reflection . . .

I shrugged. I had no expectations. When the letter came, that would be that.

CHAPTER ELEVEN

I went into Swindon to collect the films I'd left there for processing on my way to Wincanton the previous morning, and spent the rest of that Friday printing the shots of Lance Kinship and his crew.

Apart from those showing clearly the crew's unease in his company, which I didn't intend in any case to show him, I thought that quite likely he might approve. I'd been fortunate in the way the crew had arranged themselves often into natural patterns, and there was Kinship himself looking frantically upper-class in his racing tweeds directing them with a conductor's gestures, and in one sequence the horses behind them were all coming head on satisfactorily towards the winning post.

There were also several close-ups of Kinship with the crew in blurred focus behind him, and a couple of slightly surrealistic views which I'd taken from directly behind the cameraman, in which the camera itself looked large with Kinship's sharply focussed figure standing in a stray shaft of sunlight in the middle field.

The total effect, looking through them all, was a record of a substantial operator in command of his job, and that, I presumed, was what he'd wanted. No matter that the product had been two seconds in a commercial, the production itself looked an epic.

In the evening I captioned the dried prints with typed strips of thin paper sellotaped onto the backs, and feeling faintly foolish added the words *Copyright Philip Nore*, in the way I'd seen Charlie do, all those long years ago. Charlie seemed almost to be leaning over my shoulder, reminding me to keep control of my work.

Work.

The very word filled me with disquiet. It was the first time I'd actively thought of my photographs in those terms.

No, I thought, I'm a jockey.

When I woke early on Saturday morning I waited for Harold to telephone and tell me to get sick, and it wouldn't have been much trouble as I already felt sick with waiting.

He called at a quarter to ten.

'Are you well?' he said.

'Christ.'

'You'd better be,' he said. 'Victor rang just now. I didn't wait to hear what he meant to say. I told him straight away that Chainmail's future depended on his being handled right in all his races.'

'What happened?'

'Victor said an easy race wouldn't hurt him, so I told him what you said. Word for word. And I told him you'd said you would ride your bloody guts out for him as long as we're trying to win.' Harold's voice boomed down the wire with cheerfulness. 'And do you know what Victor said? He said tell that pious bastard that that's just what I'll expect.'

'Do you mean . . . ?'

'I mean,' Harold bellowed, 'he's changed his mind. You can win on Chainmail if you can. In fact you'd better.'

'But Chainmail isn't . . .'

'Dammit, do you want to ride the horse or don't you?'

'I do.'

'Right, then. See you at Ascot.' He slammed the receiver down, informing me that he didn't think I'd been properly grateful for his efforts with Victor: but if he had promised Victor that Chainmail would win – and it seemed only too likely that he had – I would be in a worse fix than ever.

At Ascot I sought out Harold's head travelling lad, who had as usual come with the horses, and asked how Chainmail was feeling that day.

'Bucking and kicking fit to murder.'

'And Daylight?'

'Placid as an old cow.'

'Where have the lads put their money?'

He gave me a sharp sideways look. 'A bit on both of them. Why, shouldn't they?'

'Sure,' I said casually. 'They should. But you know how it is ... sometimes the lads know more about a horse's chances than the trainer does.'

He grinned. 'I'll say. But today ...' He shrugged. 'A bit on both. Not the week's wages, mind. Just some beer money, like.'

'Thanks.' I nodded and went off to the weighing room with at least no added anxieties. The lads wouldn't be staking even beer money without what they considered to be good reason. The legs, stomachs and spirits of both horses could be held to be normal. One didn't ask more.

I saw Victor Briggs standing in a group of one on the area of grass outside the weighing room door. Always the same clothes: the broad-brimmed hat, the thick navy overcoat, the black leather gloves. Always the same expression: the wiped-clean slate. He saw me, and no doubt he also saw the falter in my stride as I wondered whether I could possibly walk right past him without speaking.

I couldn't.

'Good morning, Mr Briggs.'

'Morning.' His voice was curt, but no more. He didn't seem to want me to stop for conversation, so after a slight hesitation I went on towards the weighing room. As I passed him he said grittily, 'I'll see your guts.'

I stopped and turned my head. His face was still expressionless. His eyes looked cold and hard. I stopped myself from swallowing, and said merely 'All right', and went on again, wishing I'd never made that stupidly flamboyant promise.

Inside the changing room someone was telling a funny story about two statues, and Steve Millace was flexing his mending arm and complaining that the doctor wouldn't pass him fit to ride, and someone else was voicing the first rumours of a major racing upheaval. I took off my street clothes and listened to all three at once.

'So these two naked statues, the man and the woman, they had been standing looking at each other in this park for a hundred years . . .'

'I told him I'd got all the movement back. It's not fair . . .'

'Is it true the Jockey Club are forming a new committee . . .'

'So an angel comes to visit them, and says that as they've stood there patiently through such ages of summers and winters, they will be rewarded by half an hour of human life to do what they have been wanting to do most . . .'

'Look, I can swing my arm round in a circle. What do you think?'

'A committee for appointing paid Stewards, or something.'

'So these two statues come to life, and look at each other and laugh a bit, and say "Shall we?" and "Yes, let's", and then they nip off behind some bushes, and there's a lot of rustling . . .'

'I could hold any horse. I told him so, but the sod wouldn't listen.'

' . . . like paying the Senior Steward a salary.'

'After a quarter of an hour they come out from behind the bushes all hot and flustered and happy and the angel says they've only used half the time, why don't they start all over again . . .'

'How long do collar-bones usually take, anyway?'

'I heard Lord White has agreed to the scheme . . .'

'So the statues giggle a bit and the man statue says to the girl statue, "OK, let's do it again, only this time we'll do it the other way round. I'll hold down the effing pigeon, and you shit on it." '

Amid the burst of laughter I heard the rumour man say ' . . . and Ivor den Relgan is to be chairman.'

I turned to him. 'What did you say?'

'I don't know if it's true . . . one of the gossip writers told me Ivor den Relgan's been appointed to set up a committee to appoint paid Stewards.'

I frowned. 'That gives den Relgan an awful lot of power all of a sudden, doesn't it?'

He shrugged. 'Don't know.'

He might not, but others did. During the afternoon

one could almost see the onward march of the rumour as uneasy surprise spread from one Jockey Club face to the next. The only group seeming unaffected by the general reaction were the ill-assorted bunch of people attracting the glances of everyone else.

Lord White. Lady White. Ivor den Relgan. Dana den Relgan.

They stood outside the weighing room in weak November sunshine, the women both dressed in mink. Lady White, always thin, looked gaunt and plain and unhappy. Dana den Relgan glowed with health, laughed with bright teeth, twinkled her eyes at Lord White, and cast patronizing glances at his Lady.

Lord White basked in the light of Dana's smile, shedding years like snakeskins. Ivor den Relgan smirked at the world in general and smoked a cigar with proprietorial gestures, as if Ascot racecourse were his own. He wore again the belted camel overcoat and the swept back greyish hair, and commanded attention as his natural right.

Harold appeared at my elbow, following my gaze.

'Ghengis Khan,' he said, 'is setting out to rule the world.'

'This committee?'

'Wouldn't you say,' Harold asked acidly, 'that asking someone like den Relgan to chair a committee of his own choosing is a paint job?'

'Cosmetic . . . or camouflage?'

'Both. What they're really doing is saying to den

Relgan "OK you choose anyone you like as Stewards, and we'll pay them." It's incredible.'

'Yes, it is.'

'Old Driven Snow,' Harold said, 'is so besotted with that girl that he'll give her father *anything*.'

'Was it all Lord White's idea?'

Harold grimaced wolfishly. 'Be your age, Philip. Just who has been trying for years to muscle into the Jockey Club? And just who has a knock-out of a daughter who is now old enough to play up to old Driven Snow? Ivor den Relgan has at last got his lever into the door to power in racing, and once he's inside the citadel and making decisions the old guard will have a hopeless job trying to get him out.'

'You really care,' I said wonderingly.

'Of course I bloody do. This is a great sport, and at the moment, free. Who the hell wants the top management of racing to be carved up and manipulated and sold and *tainted* like some other sports we could mention. The health of racing is guaranteed by having unpaid aristocrats working for the love of it. Sure, they make stupid fuck-ups occasionally, but we get them put right. If den Relgan appoints paid Stewards, for whom do you think those Stewards will be working? For us? For racing? Or for the interests of Ivor den bloody Relgan?'

I listened to his passion and his conviction and felt the tremor of his extreme dismay.

'Surely,' I said, 'the Jockey Club won't let it happen.'

'It is happening. The ones at the top are all so used to being led by Lord White that they've agreed to his proposal for this committee without thinking it through. They take it for granted he's virtuous and well-meaning and dead honest. And so he is. But he's also infatuated. And that's damn bloody dangerous.'

We watched the group of four. Lord White made continual small gestures which involved laying his hand on Dana's arm, or across her shoulders, or against her cheek. Her father watched with an indulgent smile and a noticeable air of satisfaction: and poor Lady White seemed to shrink even further and more greyly into her mink. When she eventually walked away, not one of the others seemed to notice her go.

'Someone,' Harold said grimly, 'has got to do something to stop all this. And before it goes too far.'

He saw Victor Briggs standing as usual alone in the distance and strode off to join him, and I watched Lord White and Dana flirt together like two joyful humming birds, and thought that today she was responding to him with much less discretion than she had at Kempton.

I turned away, troubled, and found Lance Kinship coming slowly towards me, his gaze flicking rapidly from me to the den Relgans and back again. It struck me that he wanted to talk to me without den Relgan noticing he was there, and with an inward smile I went to meet him.

'I've got your pictures in the car,' I said. 'I brought them in case you were here.'

'Have you? Good, good. I want to talk to that girl.' He flicked another quick glance. 'Can you get near her? Give her a message? Without that man hearing. Without either of them hearing. Can you?'

'I might try,' I said.

'Right. Good. You tell her, then, that I'll meet her after the third race in one of the private boxes.' He told me the number. 'You tell her to come up there. Right?'

'I'll try,' I said again.

'Good. I'll watch you. From over there.' He pointed. 'When you've given her the message, you come and tell me. Right?'

I nodded, and with another quick peek at Dana he scuttled away. His clothes that day were much as they had been at Newbury, except that he'd ruined the overall true-blue impression with some pale green socks. A pathetic man, I thought. Making himself out to be what he wasn't. Neither a significant film producer nor bred in the purple. They ask him to parties, Victor Briggs had said, because of what he brings. A sad ineffectual man buying his way into the big time with little packets of white powder.

I looked from him to den Relgan, who was using Dana, instead, for much the same purpose. Nothing sad or pathetic, though, about Ivor den Relgan. A bully boy on the march, power hungry and complacent, a trampler of little men.

I went up to him, and in an ingratiating voice, which

after years of buttering-up owners I could regrettably do quite convincingly, thanked him again for the gifts he had scattered at Kempton.

'The silver saddle . . . thought I must tell you,' I said. 'Great to have around, just to look at.'

'So glad,' he said, his gaze passing over me without interest. 'My daughter selected it.'

'Splendid taste,' Lord White said fondly, and I said directly to Dana, 'Thank you very much.'

'So glad,' she murmured also with an almost identical lack of interest.

'Please do tell me,' I said, 'whether it is unique, or whether it is one of many.'

I moved a step or two so that to answer she had to turn away from the two men, and almost before she had finished replying that it was the only one she'd seen, but she couldn't be certain . . . I said to her quietly, 'Lance Kinship is here, wanting to see you.'

'Oh.' She glanced quickly to the two men, returned Lord White's automatic smile with a dazzling one of her own, and softly said to me, 'Where?'

'After the third race in a private box.' I gave her the number.

'So glad you liked the saddle,' she said clearly, turning back towards Lord White. 'Isn't it fun,' she said to him, 'to give pleasure?'

'My dear girl,' he said roguishly, 'you give pleasure just by being yourself.'

Enough to bring angels to tears, I thought.

I wandered away and by a roundabout route arrived at Lance Kinship's side.

'She's got the message,' I said, and he said 'Good,' and we arranged for me to give him his pictures outside the weighing room during the running of the last race.

Daylight's race was third on the card, and Chainmail's the fourth. When I went out for the third I was stopped on my way from weighing room to parade ring by a pleasant-mannered woman who I realized with delayed shock was Marie Millace.

Marie Millace with scarcely a trace showing of the devastation of her face. Mrs Millace on her feet, dressed in brown, pale and ill-looking, but healed.

'You said there wouldn't be a mark,' she said, 'and there isn't.'

'You look great.'

'Can I talk to you?'

I looked to where all the other jockeys I'd started out with were already filing into the parade ring. 'Well . . . how about later? How about . . . um . . . after the fourth race. After I've changed. In the warm somewhere.'

She mentioned a particular bar, and we agreed on it, and I went on to the ring where Harold and Victor Briggs waited. Neither of them said anything to me, nor I to them. Everything of importance had already been said and for the unimportant there was no appetite. Harold gave me a leg up onto Daylight, and I nodded to him and Victor and got a grade-one blank Briggs stare in return.

There was no certainty that day that Daylight would win. With much stronger opponents, he wasn't even favourite, let alone odds-on.

I cantered down to the starting gate thinking about courage, which was not normally a word I found much in my mind. The process of getting a horse to go fast over jumps seemed to me merely natural, and something I very much liked doing. One knew theoretically that there would be falls and injuries, but the risk of them seldom affected the way I rode. I had no constant preoccupation with my own safety.

On the other hand I'd never been reckless, as some were, as Steve Millace was, and perhaps my aim had been a little too much to bring myself and the horse back together, and not enough to throw my heart over a fence and let the horse catch up if he could.

It was the latter style of riding that Victor Briggs would expect on that day. My own fault, I thought. And moreover I'd have to do it twice.

On Daylight it turned out to be fairly easy, as his jumping style held good even though I could sense his surprise at the change of mental gears in his rider. The telepathic quality of horses, that remarkable extra sense, picked up instantaneously the strength of my intention, and although I knew horses did tune in in that way, it freshly amazed me. One got used to a certain response from horses, because it was to oneself they were responding. When one's own cast of mind changed radically, so did the horse's response.

Daylight and I therefore turned in what was for us a thoroughly uncharacteristic performance, leaving more to luck than judgement. He was accustomed to measure his distance from a fence and alter his stride accordingly; but infected by my urgency he began not to do that but simply to take-off when he was vaguely within striking distance of getting over. We hit the tops of three fences hard, which was unheard of for him, and when we came to the last and met it right we raced over it as if it had been but a shadow on the ground.

Hard as we tried, we didn't win the race. Although we persevered to the end, a stronger, faster, fitter, (whatever) horse beat us into second place by three lengths.

In the unsaddling enclosure I unbuckled the girths while Daylight panted and rocketed around in a highly excitable state which was a world away from his 'placid cow' image; and Victor Briggs watched without giving a thought surface life.

'Sorry,' I said to Harold, as he walked in with me to the scales.

He grunted, and said merely, 'I'll wait for your saddle.'

I nodded, went into the changing room for a change of lead weights in the weight cloth, and returned to the scales to check out for Chainmail.

'Don't kill yourself,' Harold said, taking my saddle.

'It won't prove anything except that you're a bloody fool.'

I smiled at him. 'People die crossing the road.'

'What you're doing is no accident.'

He walked off with the saddle and I noticed that he had not in fact instructed me to return to a more sober style for his second runner. Perhaps he too, I reflected, wanted Victor to run his horses straight, and if this was the only way to achieve that, well . . . so be it.

With Chainmail things were different to the extent that the four-year-old hurdler was unstable to begin with, and what I was doing to him was much like urging a juvenile delinquent to go mugging. The rage within him, which made him fight against his jockey and duck out at the jumps and bite other horses, needed to be controlled by a calm mind and steady handling: or so I'd always thought.

On that day he didn't get it. He got a rider prepared to overlook every aggressive act except that of ducking out, and when he tried that at the third hurdle he got such a fierce slash from my whip that I could almost feel him thinking resentfully, 'Hey, that's not like you'; and it wasn't.

He fought and scrambled and surged and flew. I went with him to his ultimate speed, to total disregard of good sense. I did without any reservation ride my bloody guts out for Victor Briggs.

It wasn't enough. Chainmail finished third in a field of fourteen. Undisgraced. Better, probably, than one

213

would realistically have expected. Beaten only by a length and a neck. But still third.

Victor Briggs unsmilingly watched me pull the saddle off his second stamping, tossing, hepped-up horse. I wrapped the girths round the saddle and paused for a moment face to face with him. He said nothing at all, and nor did I. We looked with equal blankness into each other's eyes for a space of seconds, and then I went on, past him, away to the scales.

When I had changed and come out again, he was nowhere in sight. I had needed two winners to save my job, and got none. Recklessness wasn't enough. He wanted winners. If he couldn't have certain winners, he'd want certain losers. Like before. Like three years ago. Like when I and my soul were young.

With a deep feeling of weariness I went to meet Marie Millace in the appointed bar.

CHAPTER TWELVE

She was sitting in an armchair deep in conversation with another woman, whom I found to my surprise to be Lady White.

'I'll come back later,' I said, preparing to retreat.

'No, no,' Lady White said, standing up. 'I know Marie wants to talk to you.' She smiled with all her own troubles showing in lines of anxiety, her eyes screwed up as if in permanent pain. 'She tells me you've been so helpful.'

'Nothing,' I said, shaking my head.

'Not what she says.'

The two women smiled and kissed cheeks, and said goodbye, and Lady White with a nod and another vague smile for me made her way out of the bar. I watched her go; a thin defeated lady trying to behave as if the whole racing world were not aware of her discomfiture, and not altogether succeeding.

'We were at school together,' Marie Millace said. 'We shared a bedroom, in our last year there. I'm very fond of her.'

'You know about ... er ...?'

'About Dana den Relgan? Yes.' She nodded. 'Would you like a drink?'

'Let me get you one.'

I fetched a gin and tonic for her and some coke for me, and sat in the armchair Lady White had left.

The bar itself, an attractive place of bamboo furniture and green and white colours, was seldom crowded and often, as on that day, almost empty. Tucked away up on the stands far away from the parade ring and the bookmakers, it was a better place for talking than for following the horses, and as such was also warm where most of the stands were not. Semi-invalids tended to spend a lot of time there, with nephews and nieces scurrying backwards and forwards with Tote tickets.

Marie Millace said, 'Wendy ... Wendy White ... was asking me if I thought her husband's affair with Dana den Relgan would just blow over. But I don't know. I couldn't tell her. How could I tell her? I said I was sure it would ...' She paused, and when I didn't answer, said, 'Do you think it will?'

'Not for a while, I wouldn't think.'

She gloomily swilled the ice around in her drink. 'Wendy says he's been away with her. He took her to some friends overnight. He told Wendy he was going to shoot, which she finds boring. She hasn't gone with him to shooting parties for years. But he took Dana den Relgan with him this week, and Wendy says when

the party went out with the guns, her husband and
Dana den Relgan stayed in the house ... I suppose I
shouldn't be telling you all this. She heard it from
someone who was there. You're not to repeat what I've
just said. You won't, will you?'

'Of course not.'

'It's so awful for Wendy,' Marie Millace said. 'She
thought it was all over long ago.'

'All over? I thought it had just started.'

She sighed. 'Wendy says her husband fell like a ton
of bricks for this Dana creature months ago, but then
the wretched girl faded off the scene and didn't go
racing at all, and Wendy thought that he'd stopped
seeing her. And now she's back in full view and it's
obvious to everyone. Wendy says that her husband is
more overpoweringly in love than ever, and also *proud*
of it. I'm sorry for Wendy. It's all so horrid.' She looked
genuinely sympathetic, and yet her own troubles, by
any standard, were much worse.

'Do you know Dana den Relgan yourself?' I asked.

'No, not at all. George knew her, I think. Or at least
he knew her by sight. He knew everyone. He said when
we were in St Tropez last summer that he thought he'd
seen her there one afternoon, but I don't know if he
meant it, he was laughing when he said it.'

I drank some coke and asked her conversationally
if she and George had enjoyed St Tropez, and if they
had been there often. Yes they had loved it, and no,
only once. George as usual had spent most of the time

glued to his camera, but he and Marie had lain on their balcony looking out to sea every afternoon and had tanned marvellously . . .

'Anyway,' she said, 'that's not what I wanted to talk to you about. I wanted to thank you for your kindness and ask you about that exhibition you suggested . . . and about how I might make some money out of those photographs. Because . . . and I know it's a sordid subject . . . I'm going to need . . . er . . .'

'Everyone needs,' I said comfortingly. 'But didn't George leave things like insurance policies?'

'Yes. Some. And I'll have the money for the house, though not its full value, unfortunately. But it won't be enough to live on, not with inflation and everything.'

'Didn't George,' I asked delicately, 'have any . . . well . . . savings . . . in any separate bank accounts?'

Her friendly expression began to change to suspicion. 'Are you asking me the same sort of things as the police?'

'Marie . . . Think of the burglaries, and your face, and the arson.'

'He wasn't,' she said explosively. 'George wouldn't . . . I told you before. Don't you believe me?'

I sighed and didn't answer, and asked her if she knew which friend George had stopped for a drink with, on his way back from Doncaster.

'Of course I know. He wasn't a friend. Barely an acquaintance. A man called Lance Kinship. George rang me from Doncaster in the morning, as he often did when he stayed away overnight, and he mentioned he'd be half an hour or so late as he was calling at this man's house, as it was on his way home. This Lance Kinship wanted George to take some pictures of him working. He's a film director, or something. George said he was a pernicious self-deluding little egotist, but if he flattered him he'd pay well. That was almost the last thing he said to me.' She took a deep breath and tried to control the tears which stood suddenly in her eyes. 'I'm so sorry . . .' She sniffed and straightened her face with an effort, fishing in her pocket for a handkerchief.

'It's natural to cry,' I said. It was only three weeks, after all, since George had died.

'Yes, but . . .' she tried to smile. 'Not at the races.' She wiped the edge of the handkerchief along under her lower eyelids and sniffed again. 'The very last thing he said,' she said, trying too hard, 'was to ask me to buy some Ajax window cleaner. It's stupid, isn't it? I mean, except for saying "See you," the last thing George ever said to me was "get some liquid Ajax, will you?" and I don't even know . . .' She gulped. The tears were winning. 'I don't even know what he wanted it for.'

'Marie . . .' I held my hand out towards her and she gripped it as fiercely as at the hospital.

'They say you always remember the last thing that someone you love says to you . . .' Her lips quivered hopelessly.

'Don't think about it now,' I said.

'No.'

She wiped her eyes again and held onto my hand, but presently the turmoil subsided and she loosened her grip and gave a small laugh of embarrassment: and I asked her if there had been an autopsy.

'Oh . . . alcohol, do you mean? Yes, they tested his blood. They said it was below the limit . . . he'd only had two small whiskies with that Kinship. The police asked him . . . Lance Kinship . . . after I told them about George planning to stop there. He wrote to me, you know, saying he was sorry. But it wasn't his fault. I'd told George over and over to be careful. He often got dozy when he'd been driving a long way.'

I told her how it had happened that it had been I who took the photographs of Lance Kinship that George had been going to do, and she was more interested than I had expected.

'George always said you'd wake up one day and pinch his market.' She produced a wavery smile to make it the joke it had undoubtedly been. 'I wish he knew. I wish . . . oh dear, oh dear.'

We just sat for a while until the fresh tears subsided, and she apologized again for them, and again I said one would expect them.

I asked for her address so that I could put her in touch with an agent for George's work, and she said she was staying with some friends who lived near Steve. She didn't know, she said forlornly, where she would be going from there. Because of the arson she had no clothes except the few new ones she was wearing. No furniture. Nothing to make a home of. Worse . . . much worse . . . she had no photograph of George.

By the time I left Marie Millace the fifth race had been run. I went straight out to the car to fetch Lance Kinship's pictures, and returned towards the weighing room to find Jeremy Folk standing outside the door on one leg.

'You'll fall over,' I said.

'Oh . . . er . . .' He put the foot down gingerly as if to stand on two legs made him more positively there. 'I thought . . . er . . .'

'You thought if you weren't here I might not do what you want.'

'Er . . . yes.'

'You may well be right.'

'I came here by train,' he said contentedly. 'So can you take me with you to St Albans?'

'I guess I'll have to.'

Lance Kinship, seeing me there, came over to collect his prints. I introduced him and Jeremy to each other out of habit, and added for Jeremy's sake that it was at Lance Kinship's house that George Millace had taken his last drink.

Lance Kinship, untucking the flap of the stiffened

221

envelope, gave each of us a sharp glance followed by
a sorrowful shake of the head.

'A great fellow, George,' he said. 'Too bad.'

He pulled the pictures out of the envelope and
looked through them with his eyebrows rising even
higher above his spectacle frames.

'Well, well,' he said. 'I like them. How much do you
want?'

I mentioned a figure which I thought exorbitant but
he merely nodded, pulled out a stuffed wallet, and paid
me there and then in cash.

'Reprints?' he said.

'Certainly. They'd be less.'

'Get me two sets,' he said. 'Right?'

As before, the last 't' of right stuck somewhere in
his throat.

'Complete sets?' I said surprised. 'All of them?'

'Sure. All of them. Very nice, they are. Want to see?'

He flicked them invitingly at Jeremy, who said he'd
like to see them very much: and he too inspected them
with his eyebrows rising.

'You must be,' he said to Kinship, 'a director of great
note.'

Kinship positively beamed and tucked his pictures
back into the envelope. 'Two more sets,' he said.
'Right?'

'Right.'

He nodded and walked away, and before he'd gone

ten paces he was pulling the pictures out again to show them to someone else.

'He'll get you a lot of work if you don't look out,' Jeremy said, watching.

I didn't know whether or not I wanted to believe him, and in any case my attention was caught by something much more extraordinary. I stood very still, and stared.

'Do you see,' I said to Jeremy, 'those two men over there, talking?'

'Of course I see them.'

'One of them is Bart Underfield, who trains in Lambourn. And the other is one of the men in that photograph of the French café. That's Elgin Yaxley ... come home from Hong Kong.'

Three weeks after George's death, two weeks after the burning of his house; and Elgin Yaxley back on the scene.

I had jumped to conclusions before, but surely this time it was reasonable to suppose that Elgin Yaxley believed the incriminating photograph had safely gone up in smoke.

Reasonable to suppose, watching him standing there expansively smiling and full of confidence, that he felt freed and secure.

When a blackmailer and all his possessions were cremated, his victims rejoiced.

Jeremy said, 'It can't be coincidence.'

'No.'

'He looks pretty smug.'

'He's a creep.'

Jeremy glanced at me. 'You've still got that photo?'

'I sure have.'

We stood for a while looking on while Elgin Yaxley clapped Bart Underfield on the back and smiled like a crocodile and Bart Underfield looked happier than he had since soon after the trial.

'What will you do with it?'

'Just wait, I suppose,' I said, 'to see what happens.'

'I think I was wrong,' Jeremy said thoughtfully, 'to say you should burn all those things in the box.'

'Mm,' I smiled faintly. 'Tomorrow I'll have a go at the blue oblongs.'

'So you've worked out how?'

'Well, I hope so. Have to see.'

'How, then?'

He looked genuinely interested, his eyes switching from their customary scanning of the neighbourhood to a steady ten seconds in my direction.

'Um . . . do you want a lecture on the nature of light, or just the proposed order of events?'

'No lecture.'

'OK. Then I think if I enlarge the orange negatives through blue light onto high contrast black and white paper I might get a picture.'

He blinked. 'In black and white?'

'With luck.'

'How do you get blue light?'

'That's rather where the lecture comes in,' I said. 'Do you want to watch the last race?'

We had a slight return of angular elbow movements and of standing on one leg and of hesitated waffle, all on account, I guessed, of squaring the solicitorial conscience with the condoning of gambling.

I had done him an injustice, however. When we were watching on the stands for the race to start he said, 'I did . . . ah . . . in point of fact . . . er . . . watch you ride . . . this afternoon.'

'Did you?'

'I thought . . . it, ah, might be instructive.'

'And how did it grab you?'

'To be honest,' he said, 'rather you than me.'

He told me, as we drove towards St Albans, about his researches into the television company.

'I got them to show me the credits, as you suggested, and I asked if they could put me in touch with anyone who worked on the play at Pine Woods Lodge. It was only a single play, by the way. The unit was there for only about six weeks.'

'Not very promising,' I said.

'No. Anyway, they told me where to find the director. Still working in television. Very dour and depressing man, all grunts and heavy moustache. He was sitting on the side of a road in Streatham watching some electricians holding a union meeting before they went on strike and refused to light the scene he wanted to shoot in a church porch. His mood, in a word, was vile.'

'I can imagine.'

'I'm afraid,' Jeremy said regretfully, 'that he wasn't much help. Thirteen years ago? How the hell did I expect him to remember one crummy six weeks thirteen years ago? How the hell did I expect him to remember some crummy girl with a crummy brat? And much more to that effect. The only positive thing he said was that if he'd been directing there would have been no crummy hangers on anywhere near Pine Woods Lodge. He couldn't stand outsiders hanging about when he was working, and would I, too, please get the hell out.'

'Pity.'

'After that I tracked down one of the main actors in the play, who is temporarily working in an art gallery, and got much the same answer. Thirteen years? Girl with small child? Not a chance.'

I sighed. 'I had great hopes of the television lot.'

'I could carry on,' Jeremy said. 'They aren't difficult to find. I just rang up a few agents, to get the actor.'

'It's up to you, really.'

'I think I might.'

'How long were the musicians there?' I said.

Jeremy fished out a by now rather worn-looking piece of paper, and consulted.

'Three months, give or take a week.'

'And after them?'

'The religious fanatics.' He grimaced. 'I don't suppose your mother was religious?'

'Heathen.'

'It's all so long ago.'

'Mm.' I said, 'Why don't we try something else? Why not publish Amanda's photograph in the *Horse and Hound*, and ask specifically for an identification of the stable? Those buildings are probably still standing, and looking just the same.'

'Wouldn't a big enough picture cost a lot?'

'Not compared with private detectives,' I reflected. 'I think *Horse and Hound* charges for space, not for what you put in it. Photographs cost no more than words. So I could make a good sharp black and white print of Amanda . . . and we could at least see.'

He sighed. 'OK, then. But I can see the final expenses of this search costing more than the inheritance.'

I glanced at him. 'Just how rich is she . . . my grand-mother?'

'She may be broke, for all I know. She's incredibly secretive. I dare say her accountant has some idea, but he makes a clam look sloppy.'

We reached St Albans and detoured around to the nursing home; and while Jeremy read old copies of *The*

Lady in the waiting room I talked upstairs with the dying old woman.

Sitting up, supported by pillows, she watched me walk into her room. The strong harsh face was still full of stubborn life, the eyes as unrelentingly fierce. She said not something gentle like 'Hallo' or 'Good evening,' but merely 'Have you found her?'

'No.'

She compressed her mouth. 'Are you trying?'

'Yes and no.'

'What does that mean?'

'It means I've used some of my spare time looking for her but not my whole life.'

She stared at me with narrowed eyes, and presently I sat in the visitors' armchair and continued to stare back.

'I went to see your son,' I said.

Her face melted for a passing moment into an unguarded and revealing mixture of rage and disgust, and with a sense of surprise I saw the passion of her disappointment. I had already understood that a non-marrying non-child-producing son had essentially robbed her not of daughter-in-law and grand-children as such, to whom on known form she might anyway have behaved tyrannically, but of continuation itself: but I certainly hadn't realized that her search for Amanda sprang from obsession and not pique.

'Your genes to go on,' I said slowly. 'Is that what you want?'

'Death is pointless otherwise.'

I thought that life itself was pretty pointless, but I didn't say so. One woke up alive, and did what one could, and died. Perhaps she was in fact right . . . that the point of life was for genes to go on. Genes surviving, through generations of bodies.

'Whether you like it or not,' I said, 'your genes may go on through me.'

The idea still displeased her. The muscles tightened along her jaw, and it was in a hard unfriendly voice that at length she said, 'That young solicitor thinks I should tell you who your father was.'

I stood up at once, unable to stay calm. Although I had come to find out, I now didn't want to. I wanted to escape. To leave the room. Not to hear. I felt nervous in a way I hadn't done for years, and my mouth was sticky and dry.

'Don't you want to know?' she demanded.

'No.'

'Are you afraid?' She was scornful. Sneering.

I simply stood there, not answering, wanting to know and not wanting, afraid and not afraid: in an absolute muddle.

'I have hated your father since before you were born,' she said bitterly. 'I can hardly bear even now to look at you, because you're like him . . . like he was at your age. Thin . . . and physical . . . and with the same eyes.'

I swallowed, and waited, and felt numb.

229

'I loved him,' she said, spitting the words out as if they themselves offended her. 'I doted on him. He was thirty and I was forty-four. I'd been a widow for five years . . . I was lonely. Then he came. He lived with me . . . and we were going to marry. I adored him. I was stupid.'

She stopped. There really was no need to go on. I knew all the rest. All the hatred she had felt for me all those years was finally explained. So simply explained . . . and understood . . . and forgiven. Against all expectations what I suddenly felt for my grand-mother was pity.

I took a deep breath. I said, 'Is he still alive?'

'I don't know. I haven't spoken to him or heard of him since.'

'And what . . . was his name?'

She stared at me straightly, nothing in her own persistent hatred being changed a scrap. 'I'm not going to tell you. I don't want you seeking him out. He ruined my life. He bedded my seventeen-year-old daughter under my own roof and he was after my money. That's the sort of man your father was. The only favour I'll do you is not to tell you his name. So be satisfied.'

I nodded. I made a vague gesture with one hand and said awkwardly, 'I'm sorry.'

Her scowl if anything deepened.

'Now find Amanda for me,' she said. 'That solicitor said you would, if I told you. So go away and do it.' She closed her eyes and looked immediately more ill, more vulnerable. 'I don't like you,' she said. 'So go away.'

'Well?' Jeremy said, downstairs.

'She told me.'

'The milkman?'

'Near enough.' I relayed to him the gist of it, and his reaction was the same as mine.

'Poor old woman.'

'I could do with a drink,' I said.

CHAPTER THIRTEEN

In printing colour photographs one's aim was usually to produce a result that looked natural, and this was nowhere near as easy as it sounded. Apart from trifles like sharp focus and the best length and brightness of exposure, there was the matter of colour itself, which came out differently on each make of film, and on each type of photographic printing paper, and even on paper from two boxes of the same type from the same manufacturer: the reason for this being that the four ultra-thin layers of emulsion laid onto colour printing paper varied slightly from batch to batch. In the same way that it was almost impossible to dye two pieces of cloth in different dye baths and produce an identical result, so it was with light-sensitive emulsions.

To even this out and persuade all colours to look natural one used colour filters – pieces of coloured glass inserted between the bright light on the enlarger and the negative. Get the mixture of filters right, and in the finished print blue eyes came out blue and cherry lips, cherry.

In my enlarger, as on the majority worldwide, the three filters were the same colours as the colours of negatives: yellow, magenta, and cyan. Using all three filters together produced grey, so one only ever used two at once, and those two, as far as my sort of photographs were concerned, were always yellow and magenta. Used in delicate balance they could produce skin colours that were neither too yellow nor too pink for human faces, and it was to a natural-looking skin colour that one normally geared one's prints.

However, if one put a square of magenta-coloured glass on a square of yellow-coloured glass, and shone a light through both together, one saw the result as red.

Shine a light through yellow and cyan, and you got green. And through magenta and cyan . . . a pure royal blue.

I had been confused when Charlie had first shown me, because mixing coloured light produced dramatically different results from mixing coloured paints. Even the primary colours were different. Forget paint, Charlie had said. This is light. You can't make blue by mixing other coloured paints, but you can with light.

'Cyan?' I'd said. 'Like cyanide?'

'Cyanide turns you blue,' he said. 'Cyan is a Greek word for blue. Kyanos. Don't forget. Cyan is greeny blue, and not surprisingly you get it by mixing blue light with green.'

'You do?' I'd said doubtfully, and he had shown me

the six colours of light, and mixed them for me before my eyes until I got their relationship fixed in my head forever, until they were as basic in my brain as the shape of letters.

In the beginning were red, green, and blue . . .

I went into my darkroom on that fateful Sunday morning and adjusted the filters in the head of the enlarger so that the light which shone through the negatives would be that unheard-of combination for normal printing: full cyan and full magenta filtration, producing a deep clear blue.

I was going to print George's blank colour negatives onto black and white paper, which would certainly rid me of the blue of the oblongs: but all I might get instead were grey oblongs.

Black and white printing paper was sensitive only to blue light (which was why one could print in black and white in red safe-light). I thought that if I printed the black-looking negatives through heavy pure blue filtration I might get a greater contrast between the yellow dye image on the negative and the orange mask covering it. Make the image, in fact, emerge from its surroundings.

I had a feeling that whatever was hidden by the mask would not itself be sharply black and white anyway . . . because if it had been it would have been visible through and in spite of the blue. What I was looking for would in itself be some sort of grey.

I set out the trays of developer and stop bath and

fixer, and put all of the first thirty-six un-blotched negatives into a contact-printing frame. In this the negative was held directly against the printing paper when the light was passed through it, so that the print, when finished, was exactly the same size as the negative. The frame merely held all the negatives conveniently so that all thirty-six could be printed at once onto one eight-by-ten inch sheet of paper.

Getting the exposure time right was the biggest difficulty, chiefly because the heavy blue filtration meant that the light getting to the negatives was far dimmer than I was used to. I wasted about six shots in tests, getting useless results from grey to black, all the little oblongs still stubbornly looking as if there was nothing on them to see, whatever I did.

Finally in irritation I cut down the exposure time to far below what it was reasonable to think right, and came up with a print that was almost entirely white. I stood in the dim red light watching the white sheet lie in the developer with practically nothing happening except that the frame numbers of the negatives very palely appeared, followed by faint lines showing where the edges of the negatives had been.

Sighing with frustration I left it in the developer until nothing else emerged and then, feeling depressed, dipped it in the stop bath and then fixed it and washed it, and switched on the bright lights.

Five of the oblongs were not entirely white. Five of

the little oblongs, scattered at random through the thirty-six, bore very pale grey geometric shapes.

I had found them.

I could feel myself smiling with ridiculous joy. George had left a puzzle, and I had almost solved it. If I was going to take his place, it was right that I should.

If I . . . My God, I thought. Where did thoughts come from? I had no intention of taking his place. No conscious intention. That thought had come straight from the subconscious, unbidden, unwanted.

I shivered slightly and felt vaguely alarmed, and without any smile at all wrote down the frame numbers of the five grey-patterned prints. Then I wandered round the house for a while doing mindless jobs like tidying the bedroom and shaking out the bean bags and stacking a few things in the dishwasher. Made a cup of coffee and sat down in the kitchen to drink it. Considered walking down to the village to fetch a Sunday paper, and instead went compulsively back to the darkroom.

It made all the difference knowing which negatives to look at, and roughly what to look for.

I took the first one numerically, which happened to be number seven, and enlarged it to the full size of the ten-by-eight inch paper. A couple more bad guesses at exposure time left me with unclear dark grey prints, but in the end I came up with one which developed into mid-grey on white; and I took it out of the developer as soon as it had reached its peak of contrast, and stopped it and fixed it and washed it, and carried it out to the daylight in the kitchen.

Although the print was still wet one could see exactly what it was. One could read it without difficulty. A typewritten letter starting 'Dear Mr Morton' and ending 'Yours sincerely, George Millace.'

A letter typed onto white paper with an old greyish ribbon, so that the typing itself looked pale grey. Pale grey, but distinct.

The letter said:

Dear Mr Morton,

   I am sure you will be interested in the enclosed two photographs. As you will see, the first one is a picture of your horse Amber Globe running poorly in your colours in the two-thirty race at Southwell on Monday, May 12th.

   As you will also see, the second picture is of your horse Amber Globe winning the four o'clock race at Fontwell on Wednesday, August 27th.

   If you look closely at the photographs you will see that they are not of the same horse. Alike, but not identical.

   I am sure that the Jockey Club would be interested in this difference. I will ring you shortly, however, with an alternative suggestion.

Yours sincerely,
George Millace.

I read it through about six times, not because I didn't take it in the first time, but simply as an interval for assimilation and thought.

There were some practical observations to be made, which were that the letter bore no heading and no date and no handwritten signature. There was an assumption to be drawn that the other four pale grey geometric patterns would also turn out to be letters; and that what I had found was George's idiosyncratic filing system.

Beyond those flat thoughts lay a sort of chaos: a feeling of looking into a pit. If I enlarged and read the other letters I could find that I knew things which would make 'waiting to see what happens' impossible. I might feel, as in the case of the grey-smudge lovers I already did feel, that doing nothing was weak and wrong. If I learned all George's secrets I would have to accept the moral burden of deciding what to do about them . . . and of doing it.

To postpone the decision I went upstairs to the sitting room and looked through the form books to find out in which year Amber Globe had won at Fontwell on August 12th; and it had been four years previously.

I looked up Amber Globe's career from start to finish, and what it amounted to on average was three or four poorer showings followed by an easy win at high odds, this pattern being repeated twice a season for four years. Amber Globe's last win had been the one on August 12th, and from then on he had run in no more races at all.

A supplementary search showed that the trainer of Amber Globe did not appear in the list of trainers for any subsequent years, and had probably gone out of business. There was no way of checking from those particular books whether 'Dear Mr Morton' had subsequently owned or run any more horses, although such facts would be stored in central official racing records.

Dear Mr Morton and his trainer had been running two horses under the name of Amber Globe, switching in the good one for the big gambles, letting the poor one lengthen the odds. I wondered if George had noticed the pattern and gone deliberately to take his photographs; or whether he had taken the photographs merely in the course of work, and then had noticed the difference in the horses. There was no way of knowing or even guessing, as I hadn't found the two photographs in question.

I looked out of the window at the Downs for a while, and wandered round a bit fingering things and doing nothing much, waiting for the arrival of a comfortable certainty that knowledge did not involve responsibility.

I waited in vain. I knew that it did. The knowledge was downstairs, and I would have to acquire it. I had come too far to want to stop.

Unsettled, fearful, but with a feeling of inevitability, I went down to the darkroom and printed the other four negatives one by one, and read the resulting letters in the kitchen.

With all five in the drier I sat for ages staring into space, thinking disjointed thoughts.

George had been busy.

The sly malice of George's mind spoke out as clearly as if I could hear his voice.

George's ominous letters must have induced fear and despondency in colossal proportions.

The second of them said:

Dear Bonnington Ford,

I am sure you will be interested in the enclosed series of photographs, which, as you will see, are a record of your entertaining in your training stables on Sunday afternoons a person who has been 'warned off'. I don't suppose I need to remind you that the racing authorities would object strongly to this continuous association, even to the extent of reviewing your licence to train.

I could of course send copies of these photographs to the Jockey Club. I will ring you shortly, however, with an alternative suggestion.

Yours sincerely,
George Millace.

Bonnington Ford was a third-rate trainer who by general consensus was as honest and trustworthy as a pickpocket at Aintree, and he trained in a hollow in the Downs at a spot where any passing motorist could glance down into his yard. It would have been no trouble at all for George Millace, if he had wanted to, to sit in his car at that spot and take telephoto pictures at his leisure.

Again I hadn't found the photographs in question, so there was nothing I could do about that particular letter, even if I had wanted to. George hadn't even mentioned the name of the disqualified person. I was let off any worrying choice.

The last three letters were a different matter, one in which the dilemma sharply raised its head: where did duty lie, and from how much could one opt out.

Of these three letters the first said:

Dear Elgin Yaxley,

I am sure you will be interested in the enclosed photograph. As you will see, it clearly contradicts a statement you recently made on oath at a certain trial.

I am sure that the Jockey Club would be interested to see it, and also the police, the judge, and the insurance company. I could send all of them copies simultaneously.

I will ring you shortly, however, with an alternative suggestion.

Yours sincerely,
George Millace.

The one next to it on the film roll would have driven the nails right in. It said:

Dear Elgin Yaxley,

I am happily able to tell you that since I wrote to you yesterday there have been further developments.

Yesterday I also visited the farmer upon whose farm you boarded your unfortunate steeplechasers, and I showed him in confidence a copy of the photograph, which I sent to you. I suggested that there might be a full further enquiry, during which his own share in the tragedy might be investigated.

He felt able to respond to my promise of silence with the pleasing information that your five good horses were not after all dead. The five horses which died had been bought especially and cheaply by him (your farmer friend) from a local auction, and it was these which were shot by Terence O'Tree at the appointed time and place. Terence O'Tree was not told of the sub-stitution.

Your farmer friend also confirmed that when the veterinary surgeon had given your good horses their anti-tetanus jabs and had left after seeing them in good health, you yourself arrived at the farm in a horsebox to supervise their removal.

Your friend understood you would be shipping them out to the Far East, where you already had a buyer.

I enclose a photograph of his signed statement to this effect.

I will ring you shortly with a suggestion.

> Yours sincerely,
> George Millace.

The last of the five prints was different from the others in that its letter was handwritten, not typed: but as it had been apparently written in pencil, it was still of the same pale grey. It said:

Dear Elgin Yaxley,

I bought the five horses that T. O'Tree shot. You fetched your own horses away in a horsebox, to export them to the East. I am satisfied with what you paid me for this service.

> Yours faithfully,
> David Parker.

I thought of Elgin Yaxley as I had seen him the previous day at Ascot, smirking complacently and believing himself safe.

I thought of right and wrong, and justice. Thought of Elgin Yaxley as the victim of George Millace, and of the insurance company as the victim of Elgin Yaxley. Thought of Terence O'Tree who had gone to jail, and David Parker, who hadn't.

I couldn't decide what to do.

*

After a while I got up stiffly and went back to the darkroom. I put all of the magenta-splashed set of negatives into the contact-printing frame, and made a nearly white print: and this time there were not five little oblongs with grey blocks on, but fifteen.

With a hollow feeling of horror I switched off all the lights, locked the doors, and walked up the road to my briefing with Harold.

'Pay attention,' Harold said sharply.

'Er . . . yes.'

'What's the matter?'

'Nothing.'

'I'm talking about Coral Key at Kempton on Wednesday, and you're not listening.'

I dragged my attention back to the matter in hand.

'Coral Key,' I said. 'For Victor Briggs.'

'That's right.'

'Has he said anything . . . about yesterday?'

Harold shook his head. 'We had a drink after the race, but if Victor doesn't want to talk you can't get a word out of him, and all he uttered were grunts. But until he tells me you're off his horses you're still on them.'

He gave me a glass and a can of coke, and poured a large whisky for himself.

'I haven't much for you this week,' he said. 'Nothing Monday or Tuesday. Pebble was going to run at

Leicester but there's some heat in his leg... There's just Coral Key on Wednesday, Diamond Buyer and the mare Friday, and two on Saturday, as long as it doesn't rain. Have you any outside rides lined up?'

'A novice 'chaser at Kempton on Thursday.'

'I hope it can bloody jump.'

I went back to the quiet cottage and made prints from the fifteen magenta-splashed negatives, getting plain white and grey results as before, as the blotchy shapes were filtered out along with the blue.

To my relief they were not fifteen threatening letters: only the first two of them finished with the promise of alternative suggestions.

I had expected one on the subject of the lovers, and it was there. It was the second one which left me breathless and weakly laughing in the kitchen: and certainly it put me in a better frame of mind for any revelations to come.

The last thirteen prints, however, turned out to be George's own notes of where and when he had taken his incriminating pictures, and on what film, and at which exposures, and on what dates he had sent the frightening letters. I guessed he had kept his records in this form because it had turned out to be easy for him, and had seemed safer than leaving such damaging material lying legibly around on paper.

As a back-up to the photographs and letters they

were fascinating: but they all failed to say what the 'alternative suggestions' had been. There was no record of what monies George had extorted, nor of any bank, safe deposit, or hiding place where he could have stashed the proceeds. Even to himself, George on this subject had been reticent.

I went late to bed and couldn't sleep, and in the morning made some telephone calls.

One to the editor of *Horse and Hound*, whom I knew, begging him to include Amanda's picture in that week's issue, emphasizing that time was short. He said dubiously that he would print it if I got it to his office that morning, but after that it would be too late.

'I'll be there,' I said. 'Two columns wide, photograph seven centimetres deep, with some wording top and bottom. Say eleven centimetres altogether. On a nice right-hand page near the front where no one can miss it.'

'Philip!' he protested, but then sighed audibly, and I knew he would do it. 'That camera of yours . . . if you've got any racing pics I might use, bring them along. I'll have a look anyway. No promises, mind, but a look. It's people I want, not horses. Portraits. Got any?'

'Well . . . yes.'

'Good. Soon as possible, then. See you.'

I telephoned Marie Millace for Lord White's home number, and then I telephoned Old Driven Snow at his home in the Cotswolds.

'You want to see me?' he said. 'What about?'

'About George Millace, sir.'

'Photographer? Died recently?'

'Yes, sir. His wife is a friend of Lady White.'

'Yes, yes,' he said, impatiently. 'I could see you at Kempton, if you like.'

I asked if I could call on him at his home instead, and although he wasn't overpoweringly keen he agreed to my taking half an hour of his time at five o'clock the next day. With slightly sweating palms I replaced the receiver and said 'Phew' and thought that all I had to do to back out was to ring him again and cancel.

After that I telephoned to Samantha, which was a great deal easier, and asked if I could take her and Clare out to dinner. Her warm voice sounded pleased.

'Tonight?' she said.

'Yes.'

'I can't go. But I'm sure Clare can. She'd like it.'

'Would she?'

'Yes, you silly man. What time?'

I said I would pick her up at about eight, and Samantha said fine and how was the search for Amanda going, and I found myself talking to her as if I'd known her all my life. As indeed, in a way, I had.

I drove to London to the *Horse and Hound* offices and fixed with the editor to print Amanda's picture captioned '*Where is this stable? Ten pounds reward for the first person – and particularly for the first child – who can telephone Philip Nore to tell him.*'

'Child?' said the editor, raising his eyebrows and adding my telephone number. 'Do they read this paper?'

'Their mothers do.'

'Subtle stuff.'

He said, looking through the folder I'd brought of racing faces, that they were starting a series on racing personalities, and he wanted new pictures that hadn't already appeared all over the place, and he could use some of mine, if I liked.

'Er . . . yes.'

'Usual rates,' he said casually, and I said fine: and only after a pause did I ask him what the usual rates were. Even to ask, it seemed to me, was a step nearer to caring as much for the income as for the photographs themselves. Usual rates were a commitment. Usual rates meant joining the club. I found it disturbing. I accepted them, all the same.

Samantha was out when I went to fetch Clare.

'Come in for a drink first,' Clare said, opening the door wide. 'It's such a lousy evening.'

I stepped in out of the wind and cold rain of late November and we went not downstairs to the kitchen but into the long, gently lit ground-floor sitting room, which stretched from the front to the back of the house. I looked around, seeing its comfort, but feeling no familiarity.

'Do you remember this room?' Clare said.

I shook my head.

'Where's the bathroom?' she said.

I answered immediately, 'Up the stairs, turn right, blue ba . . .'

She laughed. 'Straight from the subconscious.'

'It's so odd.'

There was a television set in one corner with a programme of talking heads, and Clare walked over and switched it off.

'Don't, if you're in the middle of watching,' I said.

'It was just another anti-drug lecture. All these pontificating so-called experts. How about that drink? What would you like? There is some wine . . .' She held up a bottle of white Burgundy, opened, so we settled on that.

'Some smug little presenter was saying,' she said, pouring into the glasses, 'that one in five women take tranquillizers, but only one in ten men. Implying that poor little women are so much less able to deal with life, the feeble little dears.' She handed me a glass. 'Makes you laugh.'

'Does it?'

She grinned. 'I suppose it never occurs to the doctors who write out the prescriptions that the poor feeble little women sprinkle those tranquillizers all over their husbands' dinner when he comes home from work.'

I laughed.

'They do,' she said. 'The ones with great hulking

bastards who knock them about, and the ones who don't like too much sex . . . they mix the nice tasteless powder into the brute's meat and two veg, and lead a quiet life.'

'It's a great theory.'

'Fact,' she said.

We sat in a couple of pale velvet armchairs sipping the cool wine, she, in a scarlet silk shirt and black trousers, making a bright statement against the soft colouring of the room. A girl given to positive statements. A girl of decision and certainty and mental energy. Not at all like the gentle undemanding girls I occasionally took home.

'I saw you racing on Saturday,' she said. 'On television.'

'I didn't think you were interested.'

'Of course I am, since I saw your photos.' She drank a mouthful. 'You do take some frightful risks.'

'Not always like Saturday.' She asked why not, and rather to my surprise, I told her.

'But my goodness,' she said indignantly, 'that's not fair.'

'Life's not fair. Too bad.'

'What a gloomy philosophy.'

'Not really. Take what comes, but hope for the best.'

She shook her head. 'Go out looking for the best.' She drank and said, 'What happens if you're really smashed up by one of those falls?'

'You curse.'

'No, you fool. To your life, I mean.'

'Mend as fast as possible and get back in the saddle. While you're out of it, some other jockey is pinching your rides.'

'Charming,' she said. 'And what if it's too bad to mend?'

'You've got a problem. No rides, no income. You start looking at "sits vac".'

'And what happens if you're killed?'

'Nothing much,' I said.

'You don't take it seriously,' she complained.

'Of course not.'

She studied my face. 'I'm not used to people who casually risk their lives most days of the week.'

I smiled at her. 'The risk is less than you'd think. But if you're really unlucky, there's always the Injured Jockeys Fund.'

'What's that?'

'The racing industry's private charity. It looks after the widows and orphans of dead jockeys and gives succour to badly damaged live ones, and makes sure no one pops off in old age for want of a lump of coal.'

'Can't be bad.'

We went out a little later and ate in a small restaurant determinedly decorated as a French peasant kitchen with scrubbed board tables, rushes on the floor, and dripping candles stuck in wine bottles. The food turned out to be as bogus as the surroundings, never having seen the light of anyone's *pot au feu*. Clare however seemed not to mind and we ate microwaved veal in a blanket white sauce, trying not to remember the blanquettes in France, where she too had been frequently, though for holidays, not racing.

'You race in France?'

'After Christmas, if it freezes here, there's always the chance of some rides at Cagnes sur Mer . . . down on the south coast.'

'It sounds marvellous.'

'It's still winter. And still work. But yes, not bad.'

She returned to the subject of photographs, and said she would like to come down to Lambourn again to go through the Jockey's Life file.

'Don't worry if you want to change your mind,' I said.

'Of course I don't.' She looked at me in seeming alarm. 'You haven't sold any to anyone else, have you? You did say you wouldn't.'

'Not those.'

'What, then?'

I told her about *Horse and Hound*, and about Lance Kinship, and how odd I found it that all of a sudden people seemed to be wanting to buy my work.

'I would think,' she said judiciously, 'that the word has gone round.' She finished her veal and sat back, her face serious with thought. 'What you need is an agent.'

I explained about having to find one for Marie Millace anyway, but she brushed that aside.

252

'Not *any* agent,' she said. 'I mean me.'

She looked at my stunned expression and smiled. 'Well?' she said. 'What does any agent do? He knows the markets and sells the goods. Your goods will sell . . . obviously. So I'll learn pretty damn quick what the markets are, that I don't know already. The sports side of it, I mean. And what if I got you commissions for illustrations for other books . . . on any subject . . . would you do them?'

'Yes, but . . .'

'No buts,' she said. 'There's no point in taking super pics if no one sees them.'

'But there are thousands of photographers.'

'Why are you so defeatist?' she said. 'There's always room for one more.'

The candlelight shone on the intent expression and lay in apricot shadows under cheekbone and chin. Her grey eyes looked steadily at a future I still shied away from. I wondered what she'd say if I said I wanted to kiss her, when her thoughts were clearly more practical.

'I could try,' she said persuasively. 'I'd like to try. Will you let me? If I'm no good, I'll admit it.'

She'll bully you into things, Samantha had said.

Take what comes, and hope for the best.

I stuck to my old philosophy and said, 'All right', and she said 'Great' as if she meant it: and later, when I delivered her to her doorstep and kissed her, she didn't object to that either.

CHAPTER FOURTEEN

Four times on Tuesday morning I lifted the telephone to cancel my appointment with Lord White. Once I got as far as hearing the bell ring at the other end.

Four times I put the receiver down and decided I would have to go. I would have liked to have gone with more certainty that I was doing right; but anyway, I went.

Lord White's house in Gloucestershire turned out to be a weathered stone pile with more grandeur than gardeners. Noble windows raised their eyebrows above drifts of unswept leaves. A stubble of fawn stalks indicated lawn. A mat of dead weeds glued the gravel together. I rang the front doorbell and wondered about the economics of barony.

The third Baron White received me in a small sitting room which gave onto a view of straggly rose bushes and an unclipped hedge. Inside, everything was of venerable antiquity, dusted and gleaming. Holes in the chintz chair covers had been patched. Less money than was needed, I diagnosed briefly, but still enough to keep at bay a three-bedroomed semi.

Lord White shook hands and offered me a chair in a mixture of puzzlement and civility, waiting for me to say why I had come: and although I'd spent the whole journey inventing possible openings, I found it an agony to begin.

'Sir . . .' I said. 'I'm sorry . . . very sorry, sir . . . but I'm afraid what I've come about may be a great shock to you.'

He frowned slightly. 'About George Millace?' he said. 'You said it was something about George Millace.'

'Yes . . . about some photographs he took.'

I stopped. Too late, I wished fervently that I hadn't come. I should after all have adhered to the lifetime habit of non-involvement, of wait and see. I should never have set out to use George's wicked arsenal. But I had. I was there. I had made the decision and acted on it. What I was there for . . . had to be done.

My errand was to give pain. Purposely to hurt. To go against all the instincts of compassion I owed to Samantha and Charlie and Margaret and Bill. To serve as a wrecker, with a brutal celluloid axe.

'Get on with it, Nore,' Lord White said comfortably, unsuspecting.

With foreboding I opened the large envelope I carried. I pulled out the first of the three pictures of the lovers, and put it into his outstretched hand: and for all that I thought he was behaving foolishly over Dana den Relgan, I felt deeply sorry for him.

His first reaction was of extreme anger. How dared I, he said, standing up and quivering, how dared I bring him anything so filthy and *disgusting*.

With the greatest difficulty, I thought; but he wouldn't have appreciated it. I took the second and third photographs out of the envelope and rested them picture-side-down on the arm of my chair.

'As you will see,' I said, and my voice was hoarse, 'the others are if anything worse.'

I reckoned it took him a lot of courage to pick up the other two pictures. He looked at them in desperate silence, and slowly sank down again in his chair.

His face told of his anguish. Of his disbelief. Of his horror.

The man making love to Dana was Ivor den Relgan.

'They say,' Lord White said, 'that they can fake pictures of anything.' His voice shook. 'Cameras do lie.'

'Not this one,' I said regretfully.

'It can't be true.'

I took from the envelope a print of the letter George Millace had written, and gave it to him. He had difficulty in bringing himself to read it, so physically shaking was his distress.

The letter, which I knew by heart, read:

Dear Ivor den Relgan,

I am sure you will be interested in the enclosed photographs, which I was happily able to take a few days ago in St Tropez.

As you will see, they show you in a compromising position with the young lady who is known as your daughter. (It is surely unwise to do this sort of thing on hotel balconies without making sure that one cannot be seen by telephoto lenses?)

There seem to be two possibilities here.

One. Dana den Relgan IS your daughter, in which case this is incest.

Two. Dana den Relgan is NOT your daughter, in which case why are you pretending she is? Can it have anything to do with the ensnaring of a certain member of the Jockey Club? Are you hoping for entry to the Club, and other favours?

I could of course send these photographs to the Lord in question. I will ring you shortly, however, with an alternative suggestion.

> Yours sincerely,
> George Millace.

Lord White became much older before my eyes, the glow that loving had given him shrinking greyly back into deepening wrinkles. I looked away. Looked at my hands, my feet, the spindly rose bushes outside. Anywhere but at that devastated man.

After a very long time he said, 'Where did you get these?'

'George Millace's son gave me a box with some things of his father's in, after his father died. These photos were in it.'

He suffered through another silence, and said, 'Why did you bring them to me? For the sake of causing me ... mortification?'

I swallowed and said as flatly as possible, 'You won't really have noticed, sir, but people are worried about how much power has been given recently to Ivor den Relgan.'

He shuddered slightly at the name but raised the blue eyes to give me a long unfriendly inspection.

'And you have taken it upon yourself to try to stop it?'

'Sir ... yes.'

He looked grim, and as if seeking refuge in anger he said authoritatively, 'It's none of your business, Nore.'

I didn't answer at once. I'd had enough trouble in persuading myself that it *was* my business to last a lifetime. But in the end, diffidently, I said, 'Sir, if you are certain in your own mind that Ivor den Relgan's sudden rise to unheard-of power is nothing whatever to do with your affection for Dana den Relgan, then I do most abjectly beg your pardon.'

He merely stared.

I tried again. 'If you truly believe that racing would

benefit by Ivor den Relgan appointing paid Stewards, I apologize.'

'Please leave,' he said rigidly.

'Yes, sir.'

I stood up and walked over to the door, but when I reached it I heard his voice from behind me.

'Wait. Nore . . . I must think.'

I turned, hovering. 'Sir,' I said, 'you're so respected . . . and liked . . . by everyone. It's been no fun to watch what's been happening.'

'Will you please come back and sit down?' His voice was still stern, still full of accusation and judgement. Still full of defence.

I returned to the armchair, and he went and stood by the window with his back to me, looking out at the dead roses.

His thoughts took time. So would mine have done, in the same situation. The result of them was a deep change in his voice in both pitch and content, for when he finally spoke again he sounded not shattered nor furious, but normal. He spoke, however, without turning round.

'How many people,' he said, 'have seen these pictures?'

'I don't know how many George Millace showed them to,' I said. 'As for me, they've been seen only by one friend. He was with me when I found them. But he doesn't know the den Relgans. He doesn't often go racing.'

'So you didn't consult with anyone before you came here?'

'No, sir.'

Another long pause. I was good, anyway, at waiting. The house around us was very quiet: holding its breath, I thought fancifully, as I in a way, held mine.

'Do you intend,' he said quietly, 'to make jokes about this on the racecourse?'

'No.' I was horrified. 'I do not.'

'And would you . . .' he paused, but went on, 'would you expect any reward, in service . . . or cash . . . for this silence?'

I stood up as if he had actually hit me, not delivered his thrust from six paces with his back turned.

'I would not,' I said. 'I'm not George Millace. I think . . . I think I'll go now.' And go I did, out of the room, out of the house, out of his weedy domain, impelled by a severe hurt to the vanity.

On Wednesday nothing much happened; less, in fact, than expected, as I was met when I went to ride out first lot with the news that Coral Key wouldn't be running that day at Kempton after all.

'Bloody animal got cast in its box during the night,' Harold said. 'I woke and heard him banging. God knows how long he'd been down; he was halfway exhausted. It won't please Victor.'

With the riding fee down the drain it wasn't worthwhile spending money on petrol to go spectating at the races, so I stayed at home and did Lance Kinship's reprints.

Thursday I set off to Kempton with only one ride, thinking it was a very thin week on the earning front; but almost as soon as I'd stepped through the gate I was grabbed by a fierce little man who said his guv'nor was looking for me, and if I wanted his spare rides I should shift my arse.

I shifted, and got the rides just before the trainer in question thought I wouldn't get there in time and gave them to someone else.

'Very annoying,' he said, puffing as if breathless, though I gathered he had been standing still waiting for me for fifteen minutes. 'My fellow said yesterday he'd no ill effects from a fall he'd had. And then this morning, cool as you please, he rings to say he's got 'flu.'

'Well . . . er . . .' I swallowed a laugh. 'I don't suppose he can help it.'

'Damned inconsiderate.'

His horse turned out to have better lungs than their master, but were otherwise no great shakes. I got one of them round into third place in a field of six, and came down on the other two fences from home; a bit of a crash but nothing broken in either him or me.

The third horse, the one I'd gone originally to ride, wasn't much better: a clumsy underschooled baby of a horse with guts about equal to his skill. I took him round carefully in the novice 'chase to try to teach him his job, and got no thanks from the trainer who said I hadn't gone fast enough to keep warm.

'There were six or seven behind us,' I said mildly.

'And six or seven in front.'

I nodded. 'He needs time.' And patience, and weeks and months of jumping practice. He probably wouldn't get either, and I probably wouldn't be offered the mount again. The trainer would go for speed regardless, and the horse would crash at the open ditch, and it would serve the trainer right. Pity the poor horse.

The relief of the afternoon, as far as I was concerned, was the absence of Lord White.

The surprise of the afternoon was the presence of Clare.

She was waiting outside the weighing room when I'd changed back into street clothes and was leaving for home.

'Hullo,' she said.

'Clare!'

'Just thought I'd come and take a look at the real thing.' Her eyes smiled. 'Is today typical?'

I looked at the grey windy sky and the thin Thursday crowd, and thought of my three nondescript races.

'Pretty much,' I said. 'How did you get here?'

'By race-train. Very educational. And I've been walking around all afternoon all a-goggle. I never knew people actually *ate* jellied eels.'

I laughed. 'I've never looked one in the face. Er . . .

what would you like? A drink? A cup of tea? A trip to Lambourn?'

She thought it over briefly. 'Lambourn,' she said. 'I can get a train back from there, can't I?'

I drove her to Berkshire with an unaccustomed feeling of contentment. It felt right to have her sitting there in the car. Natural. Probably, I thought, rationalizing, because she was Samantha's daughter.

The cottage was dark and cold, but soon warmed. I went round switching on lights and heat and the kettle for tea; and the telephone rang. I answered it in the kitchen, which was where it happened to be plugged in, and had my ear-drum half-shattered by a piercing voice which shrieked, 'Am I first?'

'Um,' I said, wincing and holding the receiver away from my ear. 'Are you first what?'

'First!' A very young voice. A child. Female. 'I've been ringing every five minutes for *hours*. Honestly. So am I first? Do say I'm first.'

Realization dawned. 'Yes,' I said. 'You're the very first. Have you been reading *Horse and Hound*? It isn't published until tomorrow . . .'

'It gets to my auntie's bookshop on Thursdays.' She sounded as if anyone in their right mind would know things like that. 'I collect it for Mummy on my way home from school. And she saw the picture, and told me to ring you. So can I have the ten pounds? Can I really?'

'If you know where the stable is, yes, of course.'

'Mummy knows. She'll tell you. You'd better talk to her now, but you won't forget, will you?'

'I won't,' I said.

There were some background voices and clicks of the receiver at the far end, and then a woman's voice, pleasant and far less excited.

'Are you the Philip Nore who rides in National Hunt races?'

'Yes,' I said.

It seemed to be enough of a reference, because she said without reservation, 'I do know where that stable is, but I'm afraid you'll be disappointed, because it isn't used for horses any longer. Jane, my daughter, is afraid you won't send her the ten pounds when you know that, but I expect you will.'

'I expect so,' I agreed, smiling. 'Where is it?'

'Not far from here. That's Horley, in Surrey. Near Gatwick Airport. The stable's about half a mile from our house. It's still called Zephyr Farm Stables, but the riding school has been closed for years and years.'

I sighed. 'And the people who kept it?'

'No idea,' she said. 'I suppose they sold it. Anyway, it's been adapted into living quarters. Do you want the actual address?'

'I guess so,' I said, 'and yours, too, please.'

She read them out to me and I wrote them down, and then I said, 'Do you happen to know the name of the people living there now?'

'Huh,' she said scornfully. 'They're a real pest. You

won't get far with them, whatever it is you want, I'm afraid. They've got the place practically fortified to ward off furious parents.'

'To ... what?' I said, mystified.

'Parents trying to persuade their children to come home. It's one of those commune things. Religious brainwashing, something like that. They call themselves Colleagues of Supreme Grace. All nonsense. Pernicious nonsense.'

I felt breathless.

'I'll send Jane the money,' I said. 'And thanks very much.'

'What is it?' Clare said, as I slowly replaced the receiver.

'The first real lead to Amanda.'

I explained about the *Horse and Hound* advertisement, and about the tenants of Pine Woods Lodge.

Clare shook her head. 'If these Supreme Grace people know where Amanda is, they won't tell you. You must have heard of them, haven't you? Or others like them? They're all gentle and smiling on the surface, and like steel rat-traps underneath. They lure people my age with friendliness and sweet songs and hook them into Believing, and once they're in the poor slobs never get out. They're in love with their prison. Their parents hardly stand a chance.'

'I've heard of something like it. But I've never seen the point.'

'Money,' Clare said crisply. 'All the darling little

Colleagues go out with saintly faces and collecting boxes, and rake in the lolly.'

'To live on?'

'Sure, to live on. And further the cause, or in other words, to line the pockets of our great leader.'

I made the tea and we sat by the table to drink it.

Amanda in a stable-yard at Horley; Caroline twenty miles away at Pine Woods Lodge. Colleagues of Supreme Grace at Pine Woods Lodge, Colleagues ditto at Horley. Too close a connection to be a coincidence. Even if I never found out precisely what, there had been a rational sequence of events.

'She's probably not still there,' I said.

'But you'll go looking?'

I nodded. 'Tomorrow, I think, after racing.'

When we'd finished the tea Clare said she wanted to see the Jockey's Life folder again, so we took it upstairs, and I showed some of the pictures blown up on the wall to amuse her, and we talked of her life and mine and of nothing in particular; and later in the evening we went to the good pub at Ashbury for a steak.

'A great day,' Clare said, smiling over the coffee. 'Where's the train?'

'Swindon. I'll drive you there . . . or you could stay.'

She regarded me levelly. 'Is that the sort of invitation I think it is?'

'I wouldn't be surprised.'

She looked down and fiddled with her coffee spoon,

paying it a lot of attention. I watched the bent, dark, thinking head and knew that if it took her so long to answer, she would go.

'There's a fast train at ten thirty,' I said. You could catch it comfortably. Just over an hour to Paddington.'

'Philip . . .'

'It's all right,' I said easily. 'If one never asks, one never gets.' I paid the bill. 'Come on.'

She was distinctly quiet on the six-mile drive to the railway station, and she didn't share her thoughts. Not until I'd bought her a ticket (against her objections) and was waiting with her up on the platform did she give any indication of what was in her mind, and then only obliquely.

'There's a Board meeting in the office tomorrow,' she said. 'It will be the first I've been to. They made me a Director a month ago, at the last one.'

I was most impressed, and said so. It couldn't be often that publishing houses put girls of twenty-two on the Board. I understood, also, why she wouldn't stay. Why she might never stay. The regret I felt shocked me with its sudden intensity, because my invitation to her hadn't been a desperate plea but only a suggestion for a passing pleasure. I had meant it as a small thing, not a lifetime commitment. My sense of loss, on that railway platform, seemed out of all proportion.

The train came in and she climbed aboard, pausing with the door open to exchange kisses. Brief unpassionate kisses, no advance from Monday on the doorstep.

See you soon, she said, and I said yes. About contracts, she said. A lot to discuss.

'Come on Sunday,' I said.

'Let you know. Goodbye.'

'Goodbye.'

The impatient train ground away, accelerating last, and I drove home to the empty cottage with a most unaccustomed feeling of loneliness.

Newbury races, Friday, late November.

Lord White was there, standing under the expanse of glass roof outside the weighing room, talking earnestly to two fellow Stewards. He looked the same as always, grey-white hair mostly hidden by trilby, brown covert coat over dark grey suit, air of benign good sense. Hard to imagine him high as a kite on love. Impossible, if one hadn't seen it.

As always in those areas I had to pass near him to reach the weighing-room door. He steadfastly continued his conversation with the Stewards, and only through the barest flicker of his eyes in my direction did he show he knew I was there.

If he didn't want to talk to me, I didn't mind. Less embarrassing all round.

Inside the weighing room stood Harold, expansively telling a crony about a good place for cut-price new tyres. Hardly pausing for breath he told me he'd wait for my saddle if I'd do him a favour and change and weigh quickly, and when I went back to him in colours he was still on about cross-ply and radials. The crony took the opportunity to depart, and Harold, taking my saddle and weight cloth, said with mischievous amusement, 'Did you hear Ghengis Khan got the boot?'

I paid him sharp attention.

'Are you sure?' I said.

Harold nodded. 'Old Lanky . . .' he pointed to the disappearing crony, '. . . . was telling me just before you arrived. He says they held an emergency-type meeting of the Jockey Club this morning in London. He was at it. Lord White asked them to cancel plans for a committee chaired by Ivor den Relgan, and as it was old Driven Snow's idea in the first place, they all agreed.'

'It's something, anyway,' I said.

'Something?' Harold swung towards exasperation. 'Is that all you think? It's the best about-turn since the Armada.'

He stalked off with my saddle, muttering and shaking his head, and leaving me, had he but known, in a state of extreme relief. Whatever else my visit to Lord White had done, it had achieved its primary object. At least, I thought gratefully, I hadn't caused so much havoc in a man I liked for nothing at all.

I rode a novice hurdler which finished second, pleasing the owner mightily and Harold not much, and later a two-mile 'chase on a sensitive mare who had no real heart for the job and had to be nursed. Getting her round at all was the best to be hoped for, a successful conclusion greeted by Harold with a grunt. As we had also finished fourth I took it for a grunt of approval, but one could never be sure.

When I was changing back into street clothes a racecourse official stepped into the big bustling jockey's room and shouted down the length of it, 'Nore, you're wanted.'

I finished dressing and went out into the weighing room, and found that the person who was waiting was Lord White.

'I want to talk to you,' he said. 'Come over here into the Steward's room . . . and close the door, will you?'

I followed him into the room off the weighing room used by the Stewards for on-the-spot enquiries, and, as he asked, shut the door. He stood behind one of the chairs which surrounded the big table, grasping its back with both hands as if it gave him a shield, a barrier, the rampart of a citadel.

'I regret,' he said formally, 'what I imputed to you on Tuesday.'

'It's all right, sir.'

'I was upset . . . but it was indefensible.'

'I do understand, sir.'

'What do you understand?'

'Well . . . that when someone hurts you, you want to kick them.'

He half smiled. 'Poetically put, if I may say so.'

'Is that all, sir?'

'No, it isn't.' He paused, pondering. 'I suppose you've heard that the committee is cancelled?'

I nodded.

He drew a sober breath. 'I want to request den Relgan's resignation from the Jockey Club. The better to persuade him, I am of a mind to show him those photographs, which of course he has seen already. I think, however, that I need your permission to do so, and that is what I am asking.'

Talk about leverage, I thought; and I said, 'I've no objection. Please do what you like with them.'

'Are they . . . the only copies?'

'Yes,' I said, which in fact they were. I didn't tell him I also had the negatives. He would have wanted me to destroy them, and my instincts were against it.

He let go of the chair back as if no longer needing it, and walked round me to the door. His face, as he opened it, bore the firm familiar blameless expression of pre-Dana days. The cruel cure, I thought, had been complete.

'I can't exactly thank you,' he said civilly, 'but I'm in your debt.' He gave me a slight nod and went out of the room: transaction accomplished, apology given, dignity intact. He would soon be busy persuading himself, I thought, that he hadn't felt what he'd felt, that his infatuation hadn't existed.

Slowly I followed, satisfied on many counts, on many

levels, but not knowing if he knew it. The profoundest gifts weren't always those explicitly given.

From Marie Millace I learned more.

She had come to Newbury to see Steve ride now that his collarbone had mended, though she confessed, as I steered her off for a cup of coffee, that watching one's son race over fences was an agony.

'All jockeys' wives say it's worse when their sons start,' I said. 'Daughters too, I dare say.'

We sat at a small table in one of the bars, surrounded by people in bulky overcoats which smelled of cold damp air and seemed to steam slightly in the warmth. Marie automatically stacked to one side the debris of cups and sandwich wrappers left by the last customers, and thoughtfully stirred her coffee.

'You're looking better,' I said.

She nodded. 'I feel it.'

She had been to a hairdresser, I saw, and had bought some more clothes. Still pale, with smudged grieving eyes. Still fragile, thin-shelled, inclined to sound shaky, tears under control but not far. Four weeks away from George's death.

She sipped the hot coffee and said, 'You can forget what I told you last week about the Whites and Dana den Relgan.'

'Can I?'

She nodded. 'Wendy's here. We had coffee earlier on. She's very much happier.'

'Tell me about it,' I said.

'Are you interested? I'm not prattling on?'

'Very interested,' I assured her.

'She said that last Tuesday, sometime on Tuesday, her husband found out something he didn't like about Dana den Relgan. She doesn't know what. He didn't tell her. But she said he was like a zombie all evening, white and staring and not hearing a word that was said to him. She didn't know what was the matter, not then, and she was quite frightened. He locked himself away alone all Wednesday, but in the evening he told her his affair with Dana was over, and that he'd been a fool, and would she forgive him.'

I listened, amazed that women so easily relayed that sort of gossip, and pleased they did.

'And after that?' I said.

'Aren't men extraordinary?' Marie Millace said. 'After that he began to behave as if the whole thing had never happened. Wendy says that now he has confessed and apologized, he expects her to go on as before, as if he'd never gone off and slept with the wretched girl.'

'And will she?'

'Oh, I expect so. Wendy says his trouble was the common one among men of fifty or so, wanting to prove to themselves they're still young. She understands him, you see.'

'So do you,' I said.

She smiled with sweetness. 'Goodness, yes. You see it all the time.'

When we'd finished the coffee I gave her a short list of agents that she might try, and said I'd give any help I could. After that I told her I'd brought a present for her. I had been going to give it to Steve to give to her, but as she was there herself, she could have it: it was in my bag in the changing room.

I fetched out and handed to her a ten-by-eight inch cardboard envelope which said 'Photographs. Do not Bend' along its borders.

'Don't open it until you're alone,' I said.

'I *must*,' she said, and opened it there and then.

It contained a photograph I'd taken once of George. George holding his camera, looking towards me, smiling his familiar sardonic smile. George in colour. George in a typically George-like pose, one leg forward with his weight back on the other one, head back, considering the world a bad joke. George as he'd lived.

There and then in full public view Marie Millace flung her arms round me and hugged me as if she would never let go, and I could feel her tears trickling down my neck.

CHAPTER FIFTEEN

Zephyr Farm Stables was indeed fortified like a stockade, surrounded by a seven-foot-high stout wooden fence and guarded by a gate that would have done credit to Alcatraz. I sat lazily in my car across the street from it, waiting for it to open.

I waited while the cold gradually seeped through my anorak and numbed my hands and feet. Waited while a few intrepid pedestrians hurried along the narrow path beside the fence without giving the gate a glance. Waited in the semi-suburban street on the outskirts of Horley, where the street lamps faltered to a stop and darkness lay beyond.

No one went in or out of the gate. It stayed obstinately shut, secretive and unfriendly, and after two fruitless hours I abandoned the chilly vigil and booked into a local motel.

Enquiries brought a sour response. Yes, the receptionist said, they did sometimes have people staying there who were hoping to persuade their sons and daughters to come home from Zephyr Farm Stables.

Hardly any of them ever managed it, because they were never allowed to see their children alone, if at all. Proper scandal, said the receptionist: and the law can't do a blind thing about it. All over eighteen, they are, see? Old enough to know their own minds. Phooey.

'I just want to find out if someone's there,' I said.

She shook her head and said I didn't have a chance.

I spent the evening drifting around hotels and pubs talking about the Colleagues to a succession of locals propping up the bars. The general opinion was the same as the receptionist's: anything or anyone I wanted from Zephyr Farm Stables, I wouldn't get.

'Do they ever come out?' I asked. 'To go shopping, perhaps?'

Amid a reaction of rueful and sneering smiles I was told that yes indeed the Colleagues did emerge, always in groups, and always collecting money.

'They'd sell you things,' one man said. 'Try to sell you bits o' polished stone and such. Just beggin' really. For the cause, they say. For the love of God. Bunk, I say. I tell 'em to be off to church, and they don't like that, I'll tell ye.'

'Ever so strict, they are,' a barmaid said. 'No smokes, no drinks, no sex. Can't see what the nitwits see in it, myself.'

'They don't do no harm,' someone said. 'Always smiling and that.'

Would they be out collecting in the morning, I asked. And if so, where?

'In the summer they hang about the airport all the time, scrounging from people going on holiday and sometimes picking someone up for themselves ... recruits, like ... but your best bet would be in the centre of town. Right here. Saturday ... they're sure to be here. Sure to be.'

I thanked them all, and slept, and in the morning parked as near to the centre as possible and wandered about on foot.

By ten o'clock the town was bustling with its morning trade, and I'd worked out that I would have to leave by eleven-thirty at the latest to get back to Newbury, and even that was cutting it a bit fine. The first race was at twelve-thirty because of the short winter days, and although I wasn't riding in the first two, I had to be there an hour before the third, or Harold would be dancing mad.

I saw no groups of collecting Colleagues. No groups at all. No chanting people with shaven heads and bells, or anything like that. All that happened was that a smiling girl touched my arm and asked if I would like to buy a pretty paperweight.

The stone lay on the palm of her hand, wedge-shaped, greeny-brown, and polished.

'Yes,' I said. 'How much?'

'It's for charity,' she said. 'As much as you like.' She produced in her other hand a wooden box with a slit in the top but with no names of charities advertised on its sides.

277

'What charity?' I asked pleasantly, fishing for my wallet.

'Lots of good causes,' she said.

I sorted out a pound note, folded it, and pushed it through the slit.

'Are there many of you collecting?' I asked.

She turned her head involuntarily sideways, and I saw from the direction of her eyes that there was another girl offering a stone to someone waiting at a bus stop, and on the other side of the road, another. All pretty girls in ordinary clothes, smiling.

'What's your name?' I asked.

She broadened the smile as if that were answer enough, and gave me the stone. 'Thank you very much,' she said. 'Your gift will do so much good.'

I watched her move on down the street, pulling another stone from a pocket in her swirling skirt and accosting a kind-looking old lady. She was too old to be Amanda, I thought, though it wasn't always easy to tell. Especially not, I saw a minute later as I stood in the path of another stone-seller, in view of the other-worldly air of saintliness they wore like badges.

'Would you like to buy a paperweight?'

'Yes,' I said: and we went through the routine again.

'What's your name?' I asked.

'Susan,' she said. 'What's yours?'

I in my turn gave her the smile and the shake of the head, and moved on.

In half an hour I bought four paperweights. To the

fourth girl I said, 'Is Amanda out here this morning?'

'Amanda? We haven't got a . . .' She stopped, and her eyes, too, went on a giveaway trek.

'Never mind,' I said, pretending not to see. 'Thanks for the stone.'

She smiled the bright empty smile and moved on, and I waited a short while until I could decently drift in front of the girl she'd looked at.

She was young, short, smooth-faced, curiously blank about the eyes, and dressed in an anorak and swirling skirt. Her hair was medium brown, like mine, but straight, not slightly curling, and there was no resemblance that I could see between our faces. She might or she might not be my mother's child.

The stone she held out to me was dark blue with black flecks, the size of a plum.

'Very pretty,' I said. 'How much?'

I got the stock reply, and gave her a pound.

'Amanda,' I said.

She jumped. She looked at me doubtfully. 'My name's not Amanda.'

'What then?'

'Mandy.'

'Mandy what?'

'Mandy North.'

I breathed very slowly, so as not to alarm her, and smiled, and asked her how long she had lived at Zephyr Farm Stables.

'All my life,' she said limpidly.

'With your friends?'

She nodded. 'They're my guardians.'

'And you're happy?'

'Yes, of course. We do God's work.'

'How old are you?'

Her doubts returned. 'Eighteen . . . yesterday . . . but I'm not supposed to talk about myself . . . only about the stones.'

The childlike quality was very marked. She seemed not exactly to be mentally retarded, but in the old sense, simple. There was no life in her, no fun, no awakening of womanhood. Beside the average clued-up teenager she was like a sleep-walker who had never known day.

'Have you any more stones then?' I asked.

She nodded and produced another one from her skirt. I admired it and agreed to buy it, and said while picking out another note, 'What was your mother's name, Mandy?'

She looked scared. 'I don't know. You mustn't ask things like that.'

'When you were little did you have a pony?'

For an instant her blank eyes lit with an uncrushable memory, and then she glanced at someone over my left shoulder, and her simple pleasure turned to red-faced shame.

I half turned. A man stood there; not young, not smiling. A tough-looking man a few years older than myself, very clean, very neatly dressed, and very annoyed.

'No conversations, Mandy,' he said to her severely. 'Remember the rule. Your first day out collecting, and you break the rule. The girls will take you home now. You'll be back on housework, after this. Go along, they're waiting over there.' He nodded sharply to where a group of girls waited together, and watched as she walked leaden-footed to join them. Poor Mandy in disgrace. Poor Amanda. Poor little sister.

'What's your game?' the man said to me. 'The girls say you've bought stones from all of them. What are you after?'

'Nothing,' I said. 'They're pretty stones.'

He glared at me doubtfully, and he was joined by another similar man who walked across after talking to the now departing girls.

'This guy was asking the girls their names,' he said. 'Looking for Amanda.'

'There's no Amanda.'

'Mandy. He talked to her.'

They both looked at me with narrowed eyes, and I decided it was time to leave. They didn't try to stop me when I headed off in the general direction of the car park. They didn't try to stop me, but they followed along in my wake.

I didn't think much about it, and turned into the short side road which led to the park. Glancing back to see if they were still following I found not only that

they were, but there were now four of them. The two
new ones were young, like the girls.

It seemed too public a place for much to happen:
and I suppose by many standards nothing much did.
There was for instance no blood.

There were three more of them loitering around the
car park entrance, and all seven of them encircled me
outside, before I got there. I pushed one of them to
get him out of the way, and got shoved in return by a
forest of hands. Shoved sideways along the road a few
steps and against a brick wall. If any of the Great
British Public saw what was happening, they passed by
on the other side.

I stood looking at the seven Colleagues. 'What do
you want?' I said.

The second of the two older men said, 'Why were
you asking for Mandy?'

'She's my sister.'

It confounded the two elders. They looked at each
other. Then the first one decisively shook his head.
'She's got no family. Her mother died years ago. You're
lying. How could you possibly think she's your sister?'

'We don't want you nosing round, making trouble,'
the second one said. 'If you ask me, he's a reporter.'

The word stung them all into reconciling violence
with their strange religion. They banged me against the
wall a shade too often, and also pushed and kicked a
shade too hard, but apart from trying to shove all seven
away like a rugger scrum there wasn't a great deal I

could physically do to stop them. It was one of those stupid sorts of scuffles in which no one wanted to go too far. They could have half-killed me easily if they'd meant to, and I could have hurt them more than I did. Escalation seemed a crazy risk when all they were truly delivering was a warning off, so I pushed against their close bodies and hacked at a couple of shins, and that was that.

I didn't tell them the one thing which would have saved me the drubbing: that if they could prove that Mandy was indeed my sister she would inherit a fortune.

Harold watched my arrival outside the weighing room with a scowl of disfavour.

'You're bloody late,' he said. 'And why are you limping?'

'Twisted my ankle.'

'Are you fit to ride?'

'Yes.'

'Huh.'

'Is Victor Briggs here?' I said.

'No, he isn't. You can stop worrying. Sharpener's out to win, and you can ride him in your usual way. None of those crazy damn-fool heroics. Understood? You look after Sharpener or I'll belt the hide off you. Bring him back whole.'

283

I nodded, smothering a smile, and he gave me another extensive scowl and walked off.

'Honestly, Philip,' said Steve Millace, wandering past. 'He treats you like dirt.'

'No . . . just his way.'

'I wouldn't stand for it.'

I looked at the easy belligerence in the over-young face and realized that he didn't really know about affection coming sometimes in a rough package.

'Good luck, today,' I said neutrally, and he said 'Thanks,' and went on into the weighing room. He would never be like his father, I thought. Never as bright, as ingenious, as perceptive, as ruthless, or as wicked.

I followed Steve inside and changed into Victor Briggs's colours, feeling the effects of the Colleagues' attentions as an overall ache. Nothing much. A nuisance. Not enough, I hoped, to make any difference to my riding.

When I went outside the nearest conversation was going on loudly between Elgin Yaxley and Bart Underfield, who were slapping each other on the shoulder and looking the faintest bit drunk. Elgin Yaxley peeled off and rolled away, and Bart, turning with an extravagant lack of coordination, bumped into me.

'Hullo,' he said, giving a spirits-laden cough. 'You'll be the first to know. Elgin's getting some more horses. They're coming to me, of course. We'll make Lambourn sit up. Make the whole of racing sit up.' He gave me a patronizing leer. 'Elgin's a man of ideas.'

'He is indeed,' I said dryly.

Bart remembered he didn't much like me and took his good news off to other, more receptive ears. I stood watching him, thinking that Elgin Yaxley would never kill another horse for the insurance. No insurance company would stand for it twice. But Elgin Yaxley believed himself undetected . . . and people didn't change. If their minds ran to fraud once, they would do again. I didn't like the sound of Elgin Yaxley having ideas.

The old dilemma still remained. If I gave the proof of Elgin Yaxley's fraud to the police or the insurance company, I would have to say how I came by the photograph. From George Millace . . . who wrote threatening letters. George Millace, husband of Marie, who was climbing back with frail handholds from the wreck of her life. If justice depended on smashing her deeper into soul-racking misery, justice would still have to wait.

Sharpener's race came third on the card. Not the biggest event of the day, which was the fourth race, a brandy-sponsored Gold Cup, but a well-regarded two-mile 'chase. Sharpener had been made favourite because of his win at Kempton and with some of the same *joie de vivre* he sailed round most of Newbury's long oval in fourth place. We lay third at the third last fence, second at the second last, and jumped to the front over the last. I sat down and rode him out with hands and heels, and my God, I thought, I could do with the muscle-power I lost in Horley.

Sharpener won and I was exhausted, which was ridiculous. Harold, beaming, watched me fumble feebly with the girth buckles in the winners' enclosure. The horse, stamping around, almost knocked me over.

'You only went two miles,' Harold said. 'What the hell's the matter with you?'

I got the buckles undone and pulled off the saddle, and began in fact to feel a trickle of strength flow again through my arms. I grinned at Harold and said, 'Nothing . . . It was a damn good race. Nice shape.'

'Nice shape be buggered. You won. Any race you win is a nice bloody shape.'

I went in to be weighed, leaving him surrounded by congratulations and sportswriters: and while I was sitting on the bench by my peg waiting for vigour to amble back I decided what to do about Elgin Yaxley.

I had grown a habit, over the past two weeks, of taking with me in the car not only my favourite two cameras but also the photographs I seemed to keep on needing. Lance Kinship's reprints were there, although he himself hadn't turned up, and so were the four concerning Yaxley. Straight after the big race I went out and fetched them.

The second horse I was due to ride for Harold was a novice hurdler in the last race: and because there had been so many entries in the novice hurdle that they'd split it into two divisions, the last race on that day was the seventh, not the sixth. It gave me just enough extra time for what I wanted.

Finding Elgin Yaxley wasn't so difficult: it was detaching him from Bart Underfield that gave the trouble.

'Can I talk to you for a moment?' I said to Yaxley.

'You're not having the rides on our horses,' Bart said bossily. 'So don't waste time asking.'

'You can keep them,' I said.

'What do you want, then?'

'I want to give Mr Yaxley a message.' I turned to Yaxley 'It's a private message, for your ears only.'

'Oh very well.' He was impatient. 'Wait for me in the bar, Bart.'

Bart grumbled and fussed, but finally went.

'Better come over here,' I said to Elgin Yaxley, nodding towards a patch of grass by the entrance gate, away from the huge big-race crowd with their stretched ears and curious eyes. 'You won't want anyone hearing.'

'What the devil *is* all this?' he said crossly.

'A message from George Millace,' I said.

His sharp features grew rigid. The small moustache he wore bristled. The complacency vanished into a furious concentration of fear.

'I have some photographs,' I said, 'which you might like to see.'

I handed him the cardboard envelope. It seemed easier this second time, I thought, to deliver the chop. Maybe I was becoming hardened . . . or maybe I simply didn't like Elgin Yaxley. I watched him open the envelope with no pity at all.

He first went pale, and then red, and great drops of sweat stood out like blisters on his forehead. He checked through the four pictures and found the whole story was here, the café meeting and George's two letters, and the damning note from the farmer, David Parker. The eyes he raised to me were sick and incredulous, and he had difficulty finding his voice.

'Take your time,' I said. 'I expect it's a shock.'

His mouth moved as if practising, but no words came out.

'Any number of copies,' I said, 'could go off to the insurance company and the police and so on.'

He managed a strangled groan.

'There's another way,' I said.

He got his throat and tongue to shape a single hoarse unedifying word. '*Bastard.*'

'Mm,' I said. 'There's George Millace's way.'

I'd never seen anyone look at me with total hatred before, and I found it unnerving. But I wanted to find out just what George had extracted from at least one of his victims, and this was my best chance.

I said flatly, 'I want the same as George Millace.'

'No.' It was more a wail than a shout. Full of horror; empty of hope.

'Yes indeed,' I said.

'But I can't afford it. I haven't got it.'

The anxiety in his eyes was almost too much for me, but I spurred on my flagging resolution with the thought of five shot horses, and said again, 'The same as George.'

'Not ten,' he said wildly. 'I haven't got it.'

I stared at him.

He mistook my silence and gabbled on, finding his voice in a flood of begging, beseeching, cajoling words.

'I've had expenses, you know. It hasn't all been easy. Can't you let me alone? Let me off, won't you? George said once and for all ... and now *you* ... Five, then,' he said in the face of my continued silence. 'Will five do? That's enough. I haven't got any more. I haven't.'

I stared once more, and waited.

'All right, then. All *right*.' He was shaking with worry and fury. 'Seven and a half. Will that do? It's all I've got, you bloodsucking leech ... you're worse than George Millace ... bastard *blackmailers* ...'

While I watched he fumbled into his pockets and brought out a cheque book and a pen. Clumsily supporting the cheque book on the photograph envelope, he wrote the date, and a sum of money, and signed his name. Then with shaking fingers he tore the slip of paper out of the book and stood holding it.

'Not Hong Kong,' he said.

I didn't know at once what he meant, so I took refuge in more staring.

'Not Hong Kong. Not there again. I don't like it.' He was beseeching again, begging for crumbs.

'Oh . . .' I hid my understanding in a cough. 'Anywhere,' I said. 'Anywhere out of Britain.'

It was the right answer, but gave him no comfort. I stretched out my hand for the cheque.

He gave it to me, his hand trembling.

'Thank you,' I said.

'Rot in hell.'

He turned and stumbled away, half running, half staggering, utterly in pieces. Serve him right, I thought callously. Let him suffer. It wouldn't be for long.

I meant to tear up his cheque when I'd looked to see how much he thought my silence was worth: how much he'd paid George. I meant to, but I didn't.

When I looked at that cheque something like a huge burst of sunlight happened in my head, a bright expanding delight of awe and comprehension.

I had used George's own cruelty. I had demanded to be given what he himself had demanded. His alternative suggestion for Elgin Yaxley.

I had it. All of it.

Elgin Yaxley was going off into exile, and I held his cheque for seven thousand five hundred pounds.

It was made out not to me, or to Bearer, or even to the estate of George Millace, but to the Injured Jockeys Fund.

CHAPTER SIXTEEN

I walked around for a while trying to find the particular ex-jockey who had become one of the chief administrators of the Fund, and at length tracked him down in the private entertainment box of one of the television companies. There was a crowd in there, but I winkled him out.

'Want a drink?' he said, holding up his glass.

I shook my head. I was wearing colours, breeches, boots and an anorak. 'More than my life's worth, boozing with you lot before racing.'

He said cheerfully, 'What can I do for you?'

'Take a cheque,' I said, and gave it to him.

'Phew,' he said, looking at it. 'And likewise *wow*.'

'Is it the first time Elgin Yaxley's been so generous?'

'No, it isn't,' he said. 'He gave us ten thousand a few months ago, just before he went abroad. We took it of course, but some of the trustees wondered if it wasn't conscience money. I mean . . . he'd just been paid a hundred thousand by the insurance company for those horses of his that were shot. The whole business looked horribly fishy, didn't it?'

'Mm.' I nodded. 'Well ... Elgin Yaxley's going abroad again, so he says, and he gave me this cheque for you. So will you take it?'

He smiled. 'If his conscience is troubling him again, we might as well benefit.' He folded the cheque, tucked it away, and patted the pocket which contained it.

'Have you had any other huge cheques like that?' I enquired conversationally.

'People leave big amounts in their wills, sometimes, but no ... not many like Elgin Yaxley.'

'Would Ivor den Relgan be a generous supporter?' I asked.

'Well yes, he gave us a thousand at the beginning of the season. Some time in September. Very generous.'

I pondered. 'Do you keep lists of the people who donate?'

He laughed. 'Not all of them. Thousands of people contribute over the years. Old age pensioners. Children. Housewives. Anyone you can think of.' He sighed. 'We never seem to have enough for what we need to do, but we're always grateful for the smallest help ... and you know all that.'

'Yes. Thanks anyway.'

'Any time.'

He went back to the convivial crowd and I returned to the weighing room and got myself and my saddle weighed out for the last race.

I was as bad as George, I thought. Identically as bad. I had extorted money by threats. It didn't seem so wicked, now that I'd done it myself.

Harold in the parade ring said sharply, 'You're looking bloody pleased with yourself.'

'Just with life in general.'

I'd ridden a winner. I'd almost certainly found Amanda. I'd discovered a lot more about George. Sundry kicks and punches on the debit side, but who cared. Overall, not a bad day.

'This hurdler,' Harold said severely, 'is the one who ballsed-up the schooling session last Saturday. I know you weren't on him . . . it wasn't your fault . . . but you just mind he gets a good clear view of what he's got to jump. Understand? Go to the front and make the running, so he's got a clear view. He won't last the trip, but it's a big field and I don't want him being jostled and blinded in the pack early on. Got it?'

I nodded. There were twenty-three runners, almost the maximum allowed in this type of race. Harold's hurdler, walking edgily round the parade ring, was already sweating with nervous excitement, and he was an animal, I knew from experience, who needed a soothing phlegmatic approach.

'Jockeys, please mount,' came the announcement, and I and the hurdler in a decently quiet way got ourselves together and down to the start.

I was thinking only of bowling along in front out of trouble, and when the tapes went up, off we set. Over

293

the first, leading as ordered; good jump, no trouble. Over the second, just out in front; passable jump, no trouble. Over the third . . .

In front, as ordered, at the third. Rotten, disastrous jump, all four feet seeming to tangle in the hurdle instead of rising over it: exactly the mess he'd made over the schooling hurdle at home.

He and I crashed to the turf together, and twenty-two horses came over the hurdle after us.

Horses do their very best to avoid a man or a horse on the ground, but with so many, so close, going so fast, it would have been a miracle if I hadn't been touched. One couldn't ever tell at those times just how many galloping hooves connected: it always happened too fast. It felt like being rolled like a rag doll under a stampede.

It had happened before. It would happen again. I lay painfully on my side looking at a close bunch of grass, and thought it was a damn silly way to be earning one's living.

I almost laughed. I've thought that before, I thought. Every time I'm down here on the mud, I think it.

A lot of First Aid hands arrived to help me up. Nothing seemed to be broken. Thank God for strong bones. I wrapped my arms round my body, as if hugging would lessen the hurt.

The horse had got up and decamped, unscathed. I rode back to the stands in an ambulance, demonstrated to the doctor that I was basically in one piece, and winced my slow way into ordinary clothes.

When I left the weighing room most people had gone home, but Harold was standing there with Ben, his travelling head lad.

'Are you all right?' Harold demanded.

'Yeah.'

'I'll drive you home,' he said. 'Ben can take your car.'

I looked at the generous worry in both of their faces, and didn't argue. Dug into my pocket, and gave Ben my keys.

'That was a hell of a fall,' Harold said, driving out of the gates. 'A real brute.'

'Mm.'

'I was glad to see you stand up.'

'Is the horse all right?'

'Yes, clumsy bugger.'

We drove in companionable silence towards Lambourn. I felt beaten up and shivery, but it would pass. It always passed. Always would, until I got too old for it. I'd be too old in my mind, I thought, before my body gave out.

'If Victor Briggs comes down here again,' I said, 'would you tell me?'

He glanced at me sideways. 'You want to see him? Won't do any good, you know. Victor just does what he wants.'

'I want to know . . . what he wants.'

'Why not leave well alone?'

'Because it isn't well. I've left it alone . . . it doesn't work. I want to talk to him . . . and don't worry, I'll be diplomatic. I don't want to lose this job. I don't want you to lose Victor's horses. Don't worry. I know all that. I want to talk to him.'

'All right,' Harold said doubtfully. 'When he comes, I'll tell him.'

He stopped his car beside my front door.

'You're sure you're all right?' he said. 'You look pretty shaken . . . Nasty fall. Horrid.'

'I'll have a hot bath . . . get the stiffness out. Thanks for the lift home.'

'You'll be fit for next week? Tuesday at Plumpton?'

'Absolutely,' I said.

It was already getting dark. I went round in the cottage drawing the curtains, switching on lights, heating some coffee. Bath, food, television, aspirins, bed, I thought, and pray not to feel too sore in the morning.

Ben parked my car in the carport, gave me the keys through the back door, and said goodnight.

Mrs Jackson, the horse-box driver's wife from next door, came to tell me the rating officer had called.

'Oh?' I said.

'Yes. Yesterday. Hope I did right, letting him in, like. Mind you, Mr Nore, I didn't let him out of my sight. I went right round with him, like. He was only in here a matter of five minutes. He didn't touch a thing. Just counted the rooms. Hope it's all right. He had papers from the council, and such.'

'I'm sure it's fine, Mrs Jackson.'

'And your telephone,' she said. 'It's been ringing and ringing. Dozens of times. I can hear it through the wall, you know, when everything's quiet. I didn't know if you'd want me to answer it. I will, any time, you know, if you want.'

'Kind of you,' I said. 'I'll let you know if I do.'

She gave me a bright nod and departed. She would have mothered me if I'd let her, and I guessed she would have been glad to let the rating man in, as she liked looking round in my house. Nosy, friendly, sharp-eyed neighbour, taker-in of parcels and dispenser of gossip and advice. Her two boys had broken my kitchen window once with their football.

I telephoned Jeremy Folk. He was out: would I care to leave a message? Tell him I found what we were looking for, I said.

The instant I put the receiver down the bell rang. I picked it up again, and heard a child's breathless voice. 'I can tell you where that stable is. Am I the first?'

I regretfully said not. I also passed on the same bad news to ten more children within the next two hours. Several of them checked disappointedly to make sure I'd been told the right place – Zephyr Farm Stables? And several said did I know it had been owned for years and years by some Jesus freaks? I began asking them if they knew how the Colleagues had chanced to buy the stables, and eventually came across a father who did.

'We and the people who kept the riding school,' he said, 'we were pretty close friends. They wanted to move to Devon, and were looking for a buyer for their place, and these fanatics just turned up one day with suitcases full of cash, and bought it on the spot.'

'How did the fanatics hear of it? Was it advertised?'

'No . . .' He paused, thinking. 'Oh, I remember . . . it was because of one of the children who used to ride the ponies. Yes, that's right. Sweet little girl. Mandy something. Always there. She used to stay with our friends for weeks on end. I saw her often. There was something about her mother being on the point of death, and the religious people looking after her. It was through the mother that they heard the stables were for sale. They were in some ruin of a house at the time, I think, and wanted somewhere better.'

'You don't remember the mother's name, I suppose.'

'Sorry, no. Don't think I ever knew it, and after all these years . . .'

'You've been tremendously helpful,' I said. 'I'll send your Peter the tenner, even though he wasn't first.'

The father's voice chuckled. 'That'll please him.'

I took his address, and also the name of the people who had owned the stables, but Peter's father said he had lost touch with them over the years and no longer knew where they lived.

Jeremy could find them, I thought, if he needed to.

After I'd bathed and eaten I unplugged the telephone from the kitchen and carried it up to the sitting room, where for another hour it interrupted the television. God bless the little children, I thought, and wondered how many thousands were going to ring up. None of them themselves had ever been inside the high wooden walls: it was always their mummies and daddies who had ridden there when they were young.

By nine o'clock I was thoroughly tired of it. Despite the long hot soak my deeply bruised muscles were beginning to stiffen; and the best place to take them was bed. Get it over with, I thought. It was going to be lousy. It always was, for about twenty-four hours, after so many kicks. If I went to bed I could sleep through the worst.

I unplugged the telephone and went down to the bathroom in shirtsleeves for a scratch round the teeth; and the front doorbell rang.

Cursing, I went to see who had called.

Opened the door.

Ivor den Relgan stood there, holding a gun.

I stared at the pistol, not believing it.

'Back up,' he said. 'I'm coming in.'

It would be untrue to say I wasn't afraid. I was certain he was going to kill me. I felt bodiless. Floating. Blood racing.

For the second time that day I saw into the eyes of

hatred, and the power behind den Relgan's paled Elgin Yaxley's into petulance. He jerked the lethal black weapon towards me insisting I retreated, and I took two or three steps backwards, hardly feeling my feet.

He stepped through my door and kicked it shut behind him.

'You're going to pay,' he said, 'for what you've done to me.'

Be careful, Jeremy had said.

I hadn't been.

'George Millace was bad,' he said. 'You're worse.'

I wasn't sure I was actually going to be able to speak, but I did. My voice sounded strange: almost squeaky.

'Did you . . .' I said, ' . . . burn his house?'

His eyes flickered. His naturally arrogant expression, which had survived whatever Lord White had said to him, wasn't going to be broken up by any futile last-minute questions. In adversity his air of superiority had if anything intensified, as if belief in his own importance were the only thing left.

'Burgled, ransacked, burnt,' he said furiously. 'And you had the stuff all the time. You . . . you *rattlesnake*.'

I had destroyed his power base. Taken away his authority. Left him metaphorically as naked as on his St Tropez balcony.

George, I thought, must have used the threat of those photographs to stop den Relgan angling to be let into the Jockey Club. I'd used them to get him thrown out.

He'd had some sort of standing, of credibility, before, in racing men's eyes. Now he had none. Never to be in was one thing. To be in and then out, quite another.

George hadn't shown those photographs to anyone but den Relgan himself.

I had.

'Get back,' he said. 'Back there. Go on.'

He made a small waving movement with the pistol. An automatic. Stupid thought. What did it matter.

'My neighbours'll hear the shot,' I said hopelessly.

He sneered and didn't answer. 'Back past that door.'

It was the door to the darkroom, solidly shut. Even if I could jump in there alive . . . no sanctuary. No lock. I stepped past it.

'Stop,' he said.

I'd have to run, I thought wildly. Had at least to try. I was already turning on the ball of one foot when the kitchen door was smashed open.

I thought for a split second that somehow den Relgan had missed me and the bullet had splintered some glass, but then I realized he hadn't fired. There were people coming into the house from the back. Two people. Two bustling burly young men . . . with nylon stocking masks over their faces.

They were rushing, banging against each other, fast, eager, infinitely destructive.

I tried to fight them.

I tried.

God almighty, I thought. Not three times in one day.

301

How could I explain to them... Blood vessels were already severed and bleeding under my skin... Too many muscle fibres already crushed and torn... too much damage already done. How could I explain... and if I had it wouldn't have made any difference. Pleased them, if anything.

Thoughts scattered and flew away. I couldn't see, couldn't yell, could hardly breathe. They wore roughened leather gloves which tore my skin and the punches to my face knocked me silly. When I fell on the ground they used their boots. On limbs, back, stomach, head.

I drifted off altogether.

When I came back it was quiet. I was lying on the white tiled floor with my cheek in a pool of blood. In a dim way I wondered whose blood it was.

Drifted off again.

It's my blood, I thought.

Tried to open my eyes. Something wrong with the eyelids. Oh well, I thought, I'm alive. Drifted off again.

He didn't shoot me, I thought. Did he shoot me? I tried to move, to find out. Bad mistake.

When I tried to move, my whole body went into a sort of rigid spasm. Locked tight in a monstrous cramp from head to foot. I gasped with the crushing, unexpected agony of it. Worse than fractures, worse than dislocations, worse than anything...

Screaming nerves, I thought. Telling my brain to seize up. Saying too much was injured, too much was smashed, nothing must move. Too much was bleeding inside.

Christ, I thought. Leave go. Let me go. I won't move. I'll just lie here. Let me go.

After a long time the spasm did pass, and I lay in relief in a flaccid heap. Too weak to do anything but pray that the cramp wouldn't come back. Too shattered to think much at all.

The thoughts I did have, I could have done without. Thoughts like people died of ruptured internal organs . . . kidneys, liver, spleen. Thoughts like what exactly did I have wrong with me, to cause such a fierce reaction. Thoughts like den Relgan coming back to finish the job.

Den Relgan's mid-world voice, 'You'll pay for what you've done to me . . .'

Pay in cuts and internal haemorrhage and wretched pain. Pay in fear that I was lying there dying. Bleeding inside. Bleeding to death. The way people beaten to death died.

Ages passed.

If any of those things were ruptured, I thought . . . liver, kidneys, spleen . . . and pouring out blood, I would be showing the signs of it. Shallow breathing, fluttering pulse, thirst, restlessness, sweat. None of that seemed to be happening.

I took heart after a while, knowing that at least I wasn't getting worse. Maybe if I moved gently, cautiously, it would be all right.

Far from all right. Back into a rigid locked spasm, as bad as before.

It had taken only the intention to move. Only the outward message. The response had been not movement, but cramp. I dare say it was the body's best line of defence, but I could hardly bear it.

It lasted too long, and went away slowly, tentatively, as if threatening to come back. I won't move, I promised. I won't move .... just let go .... let me go.

The lights in the cottage were on, but the heating was off. I grew very cold; literally congealing. Cold stopped things bleeding, I thought. Cold wasn't all bad. Cold would contract all those leaking internal blood vessels and stop the red stuff trickling out into where it shouldn't be. Haemorrhage would be finished. Recovery could start.

I lay quiet for hours, waiting. Sore but alive. Increasingly certain of staying alive. Increasingly certain I'd been lucky.

If nothing fatal had ruptured, I could deal with the rest. Familiar country. Boring, but known.

I had no idea of the time. Couldn't see my watch. Suppose I move my arm, I thought. Just my arm. Might manage that, if I'm careful.

It sounded simple. The overall spasm stayed away, but the specific message to my arm produced only a twitch. Crazy. Nothing was working. All circuits jammed.

After another long while I tried again. Tried too

hard. The cramp came back, taking my breath away, holding me in a vice, worst now in my stomach, not so bad in my arms, but rigid, fearful, frightening, lasting too long.

I lay on the floor all night and well on into the morning. The patch of blood under my head got sticky and dried. My face felt like a pillow puffed up with gritty lumps. There were splits in my mouth, which were sore, and I could feel with my tongue the jagged edges of broken teeth.

Eventually I lifted my head off the floor.

No spasm.

I was lying in the back part of the hall, not far from the bottom of the stairs. Pity the bedroom was right up at the top. Also the telephone. I might get some help . . . if I could get up the stairs.

Gingerly I tried moving, dreading what would happen. Moved my arms, my legs, tried to sit up. Couldn't do it. My weakness was appalling. My muscles were trembling. I moved a few inches across the floor, still half lying down. Got as far as the stairs. Hip on the hall floor, shoulder on the stairs, head on the stairs, arms failing with weakness . . . the spasms came back.

Oh Christ, I thought, how much more?

In another hour I'd got my haunch up three steps and was again rigid with cramp. Far enough, I thought numbly. No farther. It was certainly more comfortable lying on the stairs than on the floor, as long as I stayed still.

I stayed still. Gratefully, wearily, lazily still. For ages.

Somebody rang the front door bell.

Whoever it was, I didn't want them. Whoever it was would make me move. I no longer wanted help, but just peace. Peace would mend me, given time.

The bell rang again. Go away, I thought. I'm better alone.

For a while I thought I'd got my wish, but then I heard someone at the back of the house, coming in through the back door. The broken back door, open to a touch.

Not den Relgan, I thought abjectly. Don't let it be den Relgan . . . not him.

It wasn't, of course. It was Jeremy Folk.

It was Jeremy, coming in tentatively, saying 'Er . . .' and 'Are you there . . .' and 'Philip? . . .' and standing still with shock when he reached the hall.

'Jesus Christ,' he said blankly.

I said 'Hello.'

'*Philip.*' He leaned over me. 'Your face . . .'

'Yeah.'

'What shall I do?'

'Nothing,' I said. 'Sit down . . . on the stairs.' My mouth and tongue felt stiff. Like Marie's, I thought. Just like Marie.

'But what happened? Did you have a fall at the races?'

He did sit down, on the bottom stair by my feet, folding his own legs into ungainly angles.

'But . . . the blood. You've got blood . . . all over your face. In your hair. Everywhere.'

'Leave it,' I said. 'It's dry.'

'Can you see?' he said. 'Your eyes are . . .' He stopped, reduced apparently to silence, not wanting to tell me.

'I can see out of one of them,' I said. 'It's enough.'

He wanted of course to move me, wash the blood off, make things more regular. I wanted to stay just where I was, without having to argue. Hopeless wish. I persuaded him to leave me alone only by confessing to the cramps.

His horror intensified. 'I'll get you a doctor.'

'Just shut up,' I said. 'I'm all right. Talk if you like, but don't *do* anything.'

'Well . . .' He gave in. 'Do you want anything? Tea, or anything?'

'Find some champagne. Kitchen cupboard.'

He looked as if he thought I was mad, but champagne was the best tonic I knew for practically all ills. I heard the cork pop and presently he returned with two tumblers. He put mine on the stair by my left hand, near my head.

Oh well, I thought. May as well find out. The cramps would have to stop sometime. I stiffly moved the arm and fastened the hand round the chunky glass, and tried to connect the whole thing to my mouth: and I got at least three reasonable gulps before everything seized up.

307

It was Jeremy, that time, who was frightened. He took the glass I was dropping and had a great attack of the dithers, and I said 'Just wait,' through my teeth. The spasm finally wore off, and I thought perhaps it hadn't been so long or so bad that time, and that things really were getting better.

Persuading people to leave one alone always took more energy than one wanted to spend for the purpose. Good friends tired one out. For all that I was grateful for his company, I wished Jeremy would stop fussing and be quiet.

The front door bell rang yet again, and before I could tell him not to, he'd gone off to answer it. My spirits sank even lower. Visitors were too much.

The visitor was Clare, come because I'd invited her.

She knelt on the stairs beside me and said, 'This isn't a fall, is it? Someone's done this to you, haven't they? Beaten you up?'

'Have some champagne,' I said.

'Yes. All right.'

She stood up and went to fetch a glass, and argued on my behalf with Jeremy.

'If he wants to lie on the stairs, let him. He's been injured countless times. He knows what's best.'

My God, I thought. A girl who understands. Incredible.

She and Jeremy sat in the kitchen introducing themselves and drinking my booze, and on the stairs things did improve. Small exploratory stretchings produced no cramps. I drank some champagne. Felt sore but less ill. Felt that some time soon I'd sit up.

The front doorbell rang.

An epidemic.

Clare walked through the hall to answer it. I was sure she intended to keep whoever it was at bay, but she found it impossible. The girl who had called wasn't going to be stopped on the doorstep. She pushed into the house physically past Clare's protestations, and I heard her heels clicking at speed towards me down the hall.

'I must see,' she said frantically. 'I must know if he's alive.'

I knew her voice. I didn't need to see the distraught beautiful face seeking me, seeing me, freezing with shock.

Dana den Relgan.

CHAPTER SEVENTEEN

'Oh my *God*,' she said.

'I am,' I said in my swollen way, 'alive.'

'He said it would be . . . a toss-up.'

'Came down heads,' I said.

'He didn't seem to care. Didn't seem to realize . . . If they'd killed you . . . what it would mean. He just said no one saw them, they'd never be arrested, so why worry?'

Clare demanded, 'Do you mean you know who did this?'

Dana gave her a distracted look. 'I have to talk to him. Alone. Do you mind?'

'But he's . . .' She stopped, and said, 'Philip?'

'It's all right.'

'We'll be in the kitchen,' Clare said. 'Just shout.'

Dana waited until she had gone, and then perched beside me on the stairs, half sitting, half lying, to bring her head near to mine. I regarded her through the slit of my vision, seeing her almost frantic and deadly anxiety and not knowing its cause. Not for my life,

since she could now see it was safe. Not for my
silence, since her very presence was an admission that
could make things worse. The gold-freckled hair fell
softly forward almost to touch me. The sweet scent she
was wearing reached my perception even through a
battered nose. The silk of her blouse brushed my hand.
The voice was soft in its cosmopolitan accent . . . and
beseeching.

'Please,' she said. '*Please* . . .'

'Please . . . what?'

'How can I ask you?' Even in trouble, I thought, she
had a powerful attraction. I'd only seen it before, not
felt it, as before she'd given me only passing and uninterested smiles; but now, with the full wattage switched
my way, I found myself thinking that I would help her,
if I could.

She said persuadingly, 'Please give me . . . what I
wrote for George Millace.'

I lay without answering, closing the persevering eye.
She misread my inaction, which was in truth born of
ignorance, and rushed into a flood of impassioned
begging.

'I know you'll be thinking . . . how can I ask you,
when Ivor's done this to you . . . how can I expect the
slightest favour. . . . or mercy . . . or kindness.' Her voice
was a jumble of shame and despair and anger and
cajoling, every emotion rising separately like a wave
and subsiding before the next. Asking a favour from
someone her father . . . husband? . . . lover . . . had had

mauled halfway to extinction wasn't the easiest of errands, but she was having a pretty good stab at it. 'Please, please, I beg of you, give it back.'

'Is he your father?' I said.

'No.' A breath; a whisper; a sigh.

'What then?'

'We have ... a relationship.'

You don't say, I thought dryly.

She said, 'Please give me the cigarettes.'

The what? I had no idea what she meant.

Trying not to mumble, trying to make my slow tongue lucid, I said, 'Tell me about your ... relationship ... with den Relgan ... and about ... your relationship with Lord White.'

'If I tell you, will you give it to me? Please, *please*, will you?'

She took my silence to mean that at least she could hope. She scurried into explanations, the words falling over themselves here and there, and here and there coming in faltering pauses: and all of it, overall, apologetic and self-excusing, a distinct flavour of 'poor little me, I've been used, none of it's my fault'.

I opened the slit eye, to watch.

'I've been with him two years ... not married, it's never been like that ... not domestic, just ...'

Just for sex, I thought.

'You talk like him,' I said.

'I'm an actress.' She waited a shade defiantly for me to dispute it, but indeed I couldn't. A pretty good

actress, I would have said. Equity card? I thought sardonically, and couldn't be bothered to ask.

'Last summer,' she said, 'Ivor came one day spilling
over with a brilliant idea. So pleased with himself . . .
if I'd co-operate, he'd see I didn't suffer . . . I mean, he
meant . . .' She stopped there, but it was plain what
he meant. Won't suffer financially . . . neat euphemism
for hefty bribe.

'He said there was a man at the races wanting to
flirt. He used not to take me to the races, not until
then. But he said, would I go with him and pretend to
be his daughter, and see if I could get the man to flirt
with *me*. It was a laugh, you see. Ivor said this man had
a reputation like snow, and he wanted to play a joke
on him . . . Well, that's what he said. He said the man
was showing all the signs of wanting a sexual
adventure . . . looking at pretty girls in that special way
that they do, patting their arms, you know what I mean.'

I thought, how odd it must be to be a pretty girl, to
find it normal for middle-aged men to be on the look-
out for sex, to expect them to pat one's arms.

'So you went,' I said.

She nodded. 'He was a sweetie . . . John White. It
was easy. I mean . . . I liked him. I just smiled . . . and
liked him . . . and he . . . well . . . I mean, it was true
what Ivor had said, he was on the look-out, and there
I was.'

There she was, I thought, beautiful and not too
dumb, and trying to catch him. Poor Lord White,

hooked because he wanted to be. Fooled by his foolish age, his nostalgia for youth.

'Ivor wanted to use John, of course. I saw it . . . it was plain, but I didn't see all that harm in it. I mean . . . why not? Everything was going fine until Ivor and I went to St Tropez for a week.' The pretty face clouded with remembered rage. 'And that beastly photographer wrote to Ivor . . . saying lay off Lord White, or else he'd show him those pictures of us . . . Ivor and me . . . Ivor was livid, I've never seen him so angry . . . not until this week.'

Each of us, I supposed, thought of the fury we'd witnessed that week in den Relgan.

'Does he know you're here?' I said.

'My God, no.' She looked horrified. 'He doesn't know . . . he hates drugs . . . it's all we have rows about . . . George Millace made me write that list . . . said he'd show the pictures to John if I didn't . . . I *hated* George Millace . . . but you . . . you'll give it back to me, won't you? Please . . . please . . . you must see . . . it would ruin me with anyone who matters . . . I'll pay you. I'll pay you . . . if you'll give it to me.'

Crunch time, I thought.

'What do you expect . . . me to give to you?' I said.

'The packet of cigarettes, of course. With the writing on.'

'Yes . . . why did you write on a cigarette packet?'

'I wrote on the wrapping with the red felt pen . . . George Millace said write the list and I said I wouldn't whatever he did and he said write it then with this pen on the cellophane wrapper round these cigarettes and you can pretend you haven't done it, because how could anyone take seriously a scrawl on wrapping paper ...' She stopped suddenly and said with awakening suspicion, 'You have got it, haven't you? George Millace gave it to you ... with the pictures ... didn't he?'

'What did you write ... on the list?'

'My God,' she said. 'You haven't got it: you haven't and I've come here ... I've told you ... it's all for nothing ... you haven't got it ...' She stood up abruptly, beauty vanishing in fury. 'You beastly *shit*. Ivor should have killed you. Should have made sure. I hope you *hurt*.'

She had her wish, I thought calmly. I felt surprisingly little resentment about den Relgan's tit for tat. I'd clobbered his life, he'd clobbered my body. I'd come off the better, I thought, on the whole. My troubles would pass.

'Be grateful,' I said.

She was too angry, however, at what she had given away. She whisked off through the hall in her silks and her scent, and slammed out of the front door. The air in her wake quivered with feminine impact. Just as well, I thought hazily, that the world wasn't full of Dana den Relgans.

Clare and Jeremy came out of the kitchen.

'What did she want?' Clare said.

'Something I . . . haven't got.'

They began asking what in general was happening, but I said 'Tell you . . . tomorrow,' and they stopped. Clare sat beside me on the stairs and rubbed one finger over my hand.

'You're in a poor way, aren't you?' she said.

I didn't want to say yes. I said, 'What's the time?'

'Half-past three . . . getting on for four.' She looked at her watch. 'Twenty to four.'

'Have some lunch,' I said. 'You and Jeremy.'

'Do you want any?'

'No.'

They heated some soup and some bread and kept life ticking over. It's the only day, I thought inanely, that I've ever spent lying on the stairs. I could smell the dust in the carpet. I ached all over, incessantly, with a grinding stiff soreness, but it was better than the cramps; and movement was becoming possible. Movement soon, I thought, would be imperative. A sign that things were returning to order . . . I needed increasingly to go to the bathroom.

I sat up on the stairs, my back propped against the wall.

Not so bad. Not so bad. No spasms.

A perceptible improvement in function in all muscles. The memory of strength no longer seemed remote. I could stand up, I thought, if I tried.

Clare and Jeremy appeared enquiringly, and without pride I used their offered hands to pull myself upright.

Tottery, but upright.

No cramps.

'Now what?' Clare said.

'A pee.'

They laughed. Clare went off to the kitchen and Jeremy said something, as he gave me an arm for support across the hall, about washing the pool of dried blood off the floor.

'Don't bother,' I said.

'No trouble.'

I hung onto the towel rail in the bathroom a bit and looked into the glass over the washbasin, and saw the state of my face. Swollen, misshapen landscape. Unrecognizable. Raw in patches. Dark red in patches. Caked with dried blood: hair spiky with it. One eye lost in puffy folds, one showing a slit. Cut, purple mouth. Two chipped front teeth.

Give it a week, I thought, sighing. Boxers did it all the time from choice, silly buggers.

Emptying the bladder brought an acute awareness of heavy damage in the abdomen but also reassurance. No blood in the urine. My intestines might have caught it, but not once had those feet, equine or human, landed squarely with exploding force over a kidney. I'd been lucky. Exceptionally lucky. Thanked God for it.

I ran some warm water into the washbasin and sponged off some of the dried blood. Wasn't sure, on the whole, that it was any improvement, either in comfort or visibility. Where the blood had been were

317

more raw patches and clotted cuts. Gingerly I patted the washed bits dry with a tissue. Leave the rest, I thought.

There was a heavy crash somewhere out in the hall.

I pulled open the bathroom door to find Clare coming through from the kitchen, looking anxious.

'Are you all right?' she said. 'You didn't fall?'

'No ... Must be Jeremy.'

Unhurriedly we went forward towards the front of the house to see what he'd dropped ... and found Jeremy himself face down on the floor. Half in and half out of the darkroom door. The bowl of water he'd been carrying spilled wetly all around him, and there was a smell ... a strong smell of bad eggs. A smell I knew. I ...

'Whatever ...' Clare began.

Dear Christ, I thought, and it was a prayer, not a blasphemy. I caught her fiercely round the waist and dragged her to the front door. Opened it. Pushed her outside.

'Stay there,' I said urgently. 'Stay outside. It's gas.'

I took a deep lungful of the dark wintry air and turned back. Felt so feeble ... so desperate. Bent over Jeremy, grabbed hold of his wrists, one in each hand, and pulled.

Pulled and dragged him over the white tiles, pulling him, sliding him, feeling the deadly tremors in my weak arms and legs. Out of the darkroom, through the hall, to the front door. Not far. Not more than ten feet. My

own lungs were bursting for air . . . but not that air . . .
not rotten eggs.

Clare took one of Jeremy's arms and pulled with
me, and between us we dragged his unconscious form
out into the street. I twitched the door shut behind me,
and knelt on the cold road, retching and gasping and
feeling utterly useless.

Clare was already banging on the house next door,
returning with the schoolmaster who lived there.

'Breathe . . . into him,' I said.

'Mouth to mouth?' I nodded. 'Right, then.' He knelt
down beside Jeremy, turned him over, and without
question began efficient resuscitation, knowing the
drill.

Clare herself disappeared but in a minute was back.

'I called the ambulance,' she said, 'but they want to
know what gas. There's no gas in Lambourn, they say.
They want to know . . . what to bring.'

'A respirator.' My own chest felt leaden. Breathing
was difficult. 'Tell them . . . it's sulphur. Some sort of
sulphide. Deadly. Tell them to hurry.'

She looked agonized, and ran back into the schoolmaster's house, and I leant weakly on my knees against
the front wall of my own house and coughed and felt
incredibly ill. From the new troubles, not the old. From
the gas.

Jeremy didn't stir. Dear God, I thought. Dear Christ,
let him live.

Gas in my darkroom had been meant for me, not

for him. Must have been. Must have been in there, somehow, waiting for me, all the hours I'd spent lying outside in the hall.

I thought incoherently: Jeremy, *don't die*. Jeremy, it's my fault. *Don't die*. I should have burned George Millace's rubbish . . . not used it . . . not brought us so near . . . so near to death.

People came out from all the cottages, bringing blankets and shocked eyes. The schoolmaster went on with his task, though I saw from his manner, from glimpses of his face, that he thought it was useless.

Don't die . . .

Clare felt Jeremy's pulse. Her own face looked ashen.

'Is he . . .?' I said.

'A flutter.'

Don't die.

The schoolmaster took heart and tirelessly continued. I felt as if there was a constricting band round my ribs, squeezing my lungs. I'd taken only a few breaths of gas and air. Jeremy had breathed pure gas. And Clare . . .

'How's your chest?' I asked her.

'Tight,' she said. 'Horrid.'

The crowd around us seemed to be swelling. The ambulance arrived, and a police car, and Harold, and a doctor, and what seemed like half of Lambourn.

Expert hands took over from the schoolmaster and pumped air in and out of Jeremy's lungs: and Jeremy himself lay like a log while the doctor examined him and while he was lifted onto a stretcher and loaded into the ambulance.

He had a pulse. Some sort of pulse. That was all they would say. They shut doors on him, and drove him to Swindon.

Don't die, I prayed. Don't let him die. It's my fault.

A fire engine arrived with men in breathing apparatus. They went round to the back of the cottage carrying equipment with dials, and eventually came out through my front door into the street. What I heard of their reports to the policemen suggested that there shouldn't be any close investigation until the toxic level inside the cottage was within limits.

'What gas is it?' one of the policemen asked.

'Hydrogen sulphide.'

'Lethal?'

'Extremely. Paralyzes the breathing. Don't go in until we give the all clear. There's some sort of source in there, still generating gas.'

The policeman turned to me. 'What is it?' he said.

I shook my head. 'I don't know. I've nothing that would.'

He had asked earlier what was wrong with my face. 'Fell in a race.'

Everyone had accepted it. Battered jockeys were commonplace in Lambourn. The whole circus moved up the road to Harold's house, and events became jumbled.

Clare telephoned twice to the hospital for news of Jeremy.

'He's in intensive care ... very ill. They want to know his next of kin.'

'Parents,' I said despairingly. 'Jeremy's home ... in St Albans.' The number was in my house, with the gas.

Harold did some work with directory enquiries and got through to Jeremy's father.

Don't die, I thought. Bloody well live ... *Please live.*

Policemen tramped in and out. An inspector came, asking questions. I told him, and Clare told him, what had happened. I didn't know how hydrogen sulphide had got into my darkroom. It had been a sheer accident that it had been Jeremy who breathed it. I didn't know why anyone should want to put gas in my darkroom. I didn't know who.

The inspector said he didn't believe me. No one had death traps like that set in their houses without knowing why. I shook my head. Talking was still a trial. I'd tell him why, I thought, if Jeremy died. Otherwise not.

How had I known so quickly that there was gas? My reaction had been instantaneous, Clare had said. Why was that?

'Sodium sulphide ... used to be used in photographic studios. Still sometimes used ... but not much ... because of the smell. I didn't have any. It wasn't ... mine.'

'Is it a gas?' he said, puzzled.

'No. Comes in crystals. Very poisonous. Comes in sepia toner kits. Kodak make one. Called T – 7 A . . . I think.'

'But you knew it *was* a gas.'

'Because of Jeremy . . . passing out. And I breathed it . . . it felt . . . wrong. You can make gas . . . using sodium sulphide . . . I just knew it was gas . . . I don't know how I knew . . . I just knew.'

'How do you make hydrogen sulphide gas from sodium sulphide crystals?'

'I don't know.'

He was insistent that I should answer, but I truthfully didn't know. And now, sir, he said, about your injuries. Your obvious discomfort and weakness. The state of your face. Are you sure, sir, that these were the result of a fall in a horse race? Because they looked to him, he had to say, more like the result of a severe human attack. He'd seen a few in his time, he said.

A fall, I said.

The inspector asked Harold, who looked troubled but answered forthrightly, 'A wicked fall, inspector. Umpteen horses kicked him. If you want witnesses . . . about six thousand people were watching.'

The inspector shrugged but looked disillusioned. Maybe he had an instinct, I thought, which told him I'd lied on some counts. When he'd gone Harold said, 'Hope you know what you're doing. Your face was OK when I left you, wasn't it?'

'Tell you one day,' I said, mumbling.

323

He said to Clare, 'What happened?' but she too shook her head in exhaustion and said she didn't know anything, didn't understand anything, and felt terrible herself. Harold's wife gave us comfort and food and eventually beds; and Jeremy at midnight was still alive.

Several rotten hours later Harold came into the little room where I sat in bed. Sat because I could breathe better that way, and because I couldn't sleep, and because I still ached abominably all over. My young lady, he said, had gone off to London to work, and would telephone that evening. The police wanted to see me. And Jeremy? Jeremy was still alive, still unconscious, still critically ill.

The whole day continued wretchedly.

The police went into my cottage, apparently opening doors and windows for the wind to blow through, and the inspector came to Harold's house to tell me the results.

We sat in Harold's office, where the inspector in daylight proved to be a youngish blond man with sensible eyes and a habit of cracking his knuckles. I hadn't taken him in much as a person the evening before, only his air of hostility; and that was plainly unchanged.

'There's a water filter on the tap in your darkroom,' he said. 'What do you use it for?'

'All water for photographs,' I said, 'has to be clean.'

Some of the worst swelling round my eyes and

mouth was beginning to subside. I could see better, talk better: at least some relief.

'Your water filter,' the inspector said, 'is a hydrogen sulphide generator.'

'It can't be.'

'Why not?'

'Well . . . I use it all the time. It's only a water softener. You regenerate it with salt . . . like all softeners. It couldn't possibly make gas.'

He gave me a long considering stare. Then he went away for an hour, and returned with a box and a young man in jeans and a sweater.

'Now, sir,' the inspector said to me with the studied procedural politeness of the suspicious copper, 'is this your water filter?'

He opened the box to show me the contents. One Durst filter with, screwed on to its top, the short rubber attachment which was normally pushed onto the tap.

'It looks like it,' I said. 'It looks just like it should. What's wrong with it? It couldn't possibly make gas.'

The inspector gestured to the young man, who produced a pair of plastic gloves from a pocket, putting them on. He then picked up the filter, which was a black plastic globe about the size of a grapefruit, with clear sections top and bottom, and unscrewed it round the middle.

'Inside here,' he said, 'there's usually just the filter cartridge. But as you'll see, in this particular object, things are quite different. Inside here there are two containers, one above the other. They're both empty now . . . but this lower one contained sodium sulphide crystals, and this one . . .' he paused with an inborn sense of the dramatic, ' . . . this upper one contained sulphuric acid. There must have been some form of membrane holding the contents of the two containers apart . . . but when the tap was turned on, the water pressure broke or dissolved the membrane, and the two chemicals mixed. Sulphuric acid and sodium sulphide, propelled by water . . . very highly effective sulphide generator. It would have gone on pouring out gas even if the water was turned off. Which it was . . . presumably by Mr Folk.'

There was a long, meaningful, depressing silence.

'So you can see, sir,' the inspector said, 'it couldn't in any way have been an accident.'

'No,' I said dully. 'But I don't know . . . I truthfully don't know . . . who could have put such a thing there . . . They would have to have known what sort of filter I had, wouldn't they?'

'And that you had a filter in the first place.'

'Everyone with a darkroom has a filter of some sort.'

Another silence. They seemed to be waiting for me to tell them, but I didn't know. It couldn't have been den Relgan . . . why should he bother with such a device when one or two more kicks would have finished me. It couldn't have been Elgin Yaxley: he hadn't had time. It couldn't have been any of the other people

George Millace had written his letters to. Two of them were old history, gone and forgotten. One of them was still current, but I'd done nothing about it, and hadn't told the man concerned that the letter existed. It wouldn't anyway be him. He would certainly not kill me.

All of which left one most uncomfortable explanation . . . that somebody thought I had something I didn't have. Someone who knew I'd inherited George Millace's blackmailing package . . . and who knew I'd used some of it . . . and who wanted to stop me using any more of it.

George Millace had definitely had more in the box than I'd inherited. I didn't have, for instance, the cigarette packet on which Dana den Relgan had written her drugs list. And I didn't have . . . what else?

'Well, sir,' the inspector said.

'No one's been into my cottage since I was using the darkroom on Wednesday. Only my neighbour, and the rating officer . . .' I stopped, and they pounced on it. 'What rating officer?'

Ask Mrs Jackson, I said: and they said yes they would.

'She said he didn't touch anything.'

'But he could have seen what type of filter . . .'

'Is it my own filter?' I asked. 'It does look like it.'

'Probably,' the younger man said. 'But our man would have had to see it . . . for the dimensions. Then he would come back . . . and it would take about thirty seconds, I'd reckon, to take the filter cartridge out and put the packets of chemicals in. Pretty neat job.'

'Will Jeremy live?' I said.

The younger man shrugged. 'I'm a chemist. Not a doctor.'

They went away after a while, taking the filter.

I rang the hospital. No change.

I went to the hospital myself in the afternoon, with Harold's wife driving because she insisted I wasn't fit.

I didn't see Jeremy. I saw his parents. They were abstracted with worry, too upset to be angry. Not my fault, they said, though I thought they would think so later. Jeremy was being kept alive by a respirator. His breathing was paralyzed. His heart was beating. His brain was alive.

His mother wept.

'Don't worry so,' Harold's wife said, driving home. 'He'll be all right.'

She had persuaded the casualty sister, whom she knew, to get me to have some stitches in my face. The result felt stiffer than ever.

'If he dies . . .'

'He won't die,' Harold's wife said.

*

The inspector telephoned to say I could go back to the cottage, but not into the darkroom: the police had sealed it.

I wandered slowly round my home feeling no sort of ease. Physically wretched, morally pulverized, neck-deep in guilt.

There were signs everywhere that the police had searched. Hardly surprising, I supposed. They hadn't come across the few prints I still had of George Millace's letters, which were locked in the car. They had left undisturbed on the kitchen dresser the box with the blank-looking negatives.

The box . . .

I opened it. It still contained, beside the puzzles I'd solved, the one that I hadn't.

The black light-proof envelope which contained what looked like a piece of clear plastic and two unused sheets of typing paper.

Perhaps . . . I thought . . . Perhaps it's because I have these that the gas trap was set.

But what . . . *what* did I have?

It was no good, I thought: I would have to find out . . . and pretty fast, before whoever it was had another go at killing me, and succeeded.

CHAPTER EIGHTEEN

I begged a bed again from Harold's wife, and in the morning telephoned Swindon hospital again.

Jeremy was alive. No change.

I sat in Harold's kitchen drinking coffee, suicidally depressed.

Harold answered his ringing telephone for about the tenth time that morning and handed the receiver to me.

'It's not an owner, this time,' he said. 'It's for you.'

It was Jeremy's father. I felt sick.

'We want you to know . . . he's awake.'

'Oh . . .'

'He's still on the respirator. But they say that by now if he'd been going to die, he'd have gone. He's still very ill . . . but they say he'll recover. We thought you'd like to know.'

'Thank you,' I said.

The reprieve was almost more unbearable than the anxiety. I gave the receiver to Harold and said Jeremy was better, and went out into the yard to look at the horses. In the fresh air I felt stifled. In relief, over-thrown. I stood in the wind waiting for the internal storm to abate, and gradually felt an incredible sense of release. I had literally been freed. Let off a life sentence. You bugger, Jeremy, I thought, dishing out such a fright.

Clare telephoned.

'He's all right. He's awake,' I said.

'Thank God.'

'Can I ask you a favour?' I said. 'Can I dump myself on Samantha for a night or two?'

'As in the old days?'

'Until Saturday.'

She swallowed a laugh and said why not, and when did I want to come.

'Tonight,' I said. 'If I may.'

'We'll expect you for supper.'

Harold wanted to know when I thought I'd be fit to race.

I would get some physiotherapy from the Clinic for Injuries in London, I said. By Saturday I'd be ready.

'Not by the look of you.'

'Four days. I'll be fit.'

'Mind you are, then.'

I felt distinctly unfit for driving, but less than inclined

to sleep alone in my cottage. I did some minimal packing, collected George's rubbish box from the kitchen, and set off to Chiswick, where despite wearing sunglasses I got a horrified reception. Black bruises, stitched cuts, three-day growth of beard. Hardly a riot.

'But it's *worse*,' Clare said, staring closely.

'Looks worse, feels better.' A good job, I thought, that they couldn't see the rest of me. My whole belly was black with the decaying remains of internal abdominal bleeding. The damage, I'd concluded, which had set off the spasms.

Samantha was troubled. 'Clare said someone had punched you . . . but I never thought . . .'

'Look,' I said, 'I could go somewhere else.'

'Don't be silly. Sit down. Supper's ready.'

They didn't talk much or seem to expect me to. I wasn't good company. Too drastically feeble. I asked with the coffee if I might telephone Swindon.

'Jeremy?' Clare said.

I nodded.

'I'll do it. What's the number?'

I told her, and she got through, and consulted.

'Still on the respirator,' she said, 'but progress maintained.'

'If you're tired,' Samantha said calmly, 'go to bed.'

'Well . . .'

They both came upstairs. I walked automatically, without thinking, into the small bedroom next door to the bathroom.

They both laughed. 'We wondered if you would,' Samantha said.

Clare went to work and I spent most of Wednesday dozing in the swinging basket chair in the kitchen. Samantha came in and out, went to her part-time job in the morning, shopped in the afternoon. I waited in a highly peaceful state for energy of any sort to return to brain or limbs and reckoned I was fortunate to have a day like that to mend in.

Thursday took me to the Clinic for Injuries for two long sessions of electric treatment, massage and general physio, with two more sessions promised for Friday.

On Thursday between the sessions I telephoned four photographers and one acquaintance who worked on a specialist magazine, and found no one who knew how to raise pictures from plastic or typing paper. Pull the other one, old boy, the specialist said wearily.

When I got back to Chiswick the sun was low on the winter horizon, and in the kitchen Samantha was cleaning the french windows.

'They always look so filthy when the sun shines on them,' she said, busily rubbing with a cloth. 'Sorry if it's cold in here, but I won't be long.'

I sat in the basket chair and watched her squirt liquid cleaner out of a white plastic bottle. She finished the outsides of the doors and came in, pulling them after her, fastening the bolts. The plastic bottle stood on a table beside her.

AJAX, it said, in big letters.

I frowned at it, trying to remember. Where had I heard the word Ajax?

I stood up out of the swinging chair and walked over for a closer look. Ajax Window Cleaner, it said in smaller red letters on the white plastic, With Ammonia. I picked the bottle up and shook it. Liquid. I put my nose to the top, and smelled the contents. Soapy. Sweet-scented. Not pungent.

'What is it?' Samantha said. 'What are you looking at?'

'This cleaner . . .'

'Yes?'

'Why would a man ask his wife to buy him some Ajax?'

'What a question,' Samantha said. 'I've no idea.'

'Nor did she have,' I said. 'She didn't know why.'

Samantha took the bottle out of my hands and continued with her task. 'You can clean any sort of glass with it,' she said. 'Bathroom tiles. Looking glass. Quite useful stuff.'

I went back to the basket chair and swung in it gently. Samantha cast me a sideways glance, smiling.

'You looked like death two days ago,' she said.

'And now?'

'Now one might pause before calling the undertaker.'

'I'll shave tomorrow,' I said.

'Who punched you?' Her voice sounded casual. Her eyes and attention were on the window. It was, all the same, a serious question. A seeking not for a simple one word answer, but for commitment to herself. A sort of request for payment for shelter unquestioningly given. If I didn't tell her, she wouldn't persist. But if I didn't tell her, we had already gone as far as we ever would in relationship.

What did I want, I thought, in that house that now increasingly felt like home. I had never wanted a family: people always close: permanence. I'd wanted no loving ties. No suffocating emotional dependents. So if I nested comfortably, deeply into the lives lived in that house, wouldn't I feel impelled in a short while to break out with wild flapping freedom-seeking wings. Did anyone ever fundamentally change?

Samantha read into my silence what I expected, and her manner did subtly alter, not to one of unfriendliness, but to a cut-off of intimacy. Before she'd finished the window I'd become her guest, not her . . . her what? Her son, brother, nephew . . . part of her.

She gave me a bright surface smile and put the kettle on for tea.

Clare returned from work with gaiety over tiredness, and she too, though not asking, was waiting.

I found myself, halfway through supper, just telling them about George Millace. In the end it was no great hard decision. No cut and dried calculation. I just naturally told them.

'You won't approve,' I said. 'I carried on where George left off.'

They listened with their forks in the air, taking mouthfuls at long intervals, eating peas and lasagne slowly.

'So you see,' I said at the end. 'It isn't finished yet. There's no going back or wishing I hadn't started . . . I don't know that I do wish that . . . but I asked to come here for a few days because I didn't feel safe in the cottage, and I'm not going back there to live permanently until I know who tried to kill me.'

Clare said, 'You might never know.'

'Don't say that,' Samantha said sharply. 'If he doesn't find out . . .' She stopped.

I finished it for her, 'I'll have no defence.'

'Perhaps the police . . .' Clare said.

'Perhaps.'

We passed the rest of the evening more in thoughtfulness than depression, and the news from Swindon was good. Jeremy's lungs were coming out of paralysis. Still on the respirator, but a significant improvement during the past twenty-four hours. The prim voice reading the written bulletin sounded bored. Could I speak to Jeremy himself yet, I asked. They'd check. The prim voice came back; not in intensive care: try on Sunday.

*

I spent a long time in the bathroom on Friday morning scraping off beard and snipping out unabsorbed ends of the fine transparent thread the casualty sister had used in her stitching. She'd done a neat job, I had to confess. The cuts had all healed, and would disappear probably without scars. All the swelling, also, had gone. There were still remains of black bruises turning yellow, and still the chipped teeth, but what finally looked out of the mirror was definitely a face, not a nightmare.

Samantha looked relieved over the re-emergence of civilization and insisted on telephoning to her dentist. 'You need caps,' she said, 'and caps you'll have.' And caps I had, late that afternoon. Temporaries, until porcelain jobs could be made.

Between the two sessions in the clinic I drove north out of London to Basildon in Essex, to where a British firm manufactured photographic printing paper. I went instead of telephoning because I thought they would find it less easy to say they had no information if I was actually there; and so it proved.

They did not, they said in the front office politely, know of any photographic materials which looked like plastic or typing paper. Had I brought the specimens with me?

No, I had not. I didn't want them examined in case they were sensitive to light. Could I see someone else?

Difficult, they said.

I showed no signs of leaving. Perhaps Mr

Christopher could help me, they suggested at length, if he wasn't too busy.

Mr Christopher turned out to be about nineteen with an antisocial hair-cut and chronic catarrh. He listened, however, attentively.

'This paper and this plastic've got no emulsion on them?'

'No, I don't think so.'

He shrugged. 'There you are, then.'

'There I am where?'

'You got no pictures.'

I sucked at the still broken teeth and asked him what seemed to be a nonsensical question.

'Why would a photographer want ammonia?'

'Well, he wouldn't. Not for photographs. No straight ammonia in any developer or bleach or fix, that I know of.'

'Would anyone here know?' I asked.

He gave me a pitying stare, implying that if he didn't know, no one else would.

'You could ask,' I said persuasively. 'Because if there's a process which does use ammonia, you'd like to know, wouldn't you?'

'Yeah. I reckon I would.'

He gave me a brisk nod and vanished, and I waited a quarter of an hour, wondering if he'd gone off to lunch. He returned, however, with a grey elderly man in glasses who was none too willing but delivered the goods.

'Ammonia,' he said, 'is used in the photographic sections of engineering industries. It develops what the public call blueprints. More accurately, of course, it's the diazo process.'

'Please,' I said humbly and with gratitude, 'could you describe it to me.'

'What's the matter with your face?' he said.

'Lost an argument.'

'Huh.'

'Diazo process,' I said. 'What is it?'

'You get a drawing . . . a line drawing, I'm talking about . . . from the designer. Say of a component in a machine. A drawing with exact specifications for manufacture. Are you with me?'

'Yes.'

'The industry will need several copies of the master drawing. So they make blueprints of it. Or rather, they don't.'

'Er . . .' I said.

'In blueprints,' he said severely, 'the paper turns blue, leaving the design in white. Nowadays the paper turns white and the lines develop in black. Or dark red.'

'Please . . . go on.'

'From the beginning?' he said. 'The master drawing, which is of course on translucent paper, is pinned and pressed tightly by glass over a sheet of diazo paper. Diazo paper is white on the back, and yellow or greenish on the side covered with ammonia-sensitive dye. Bright carbon arc light is shone onto the master drawing for a measured length of time. This light bleaches out all the dye on the diazo paper underneath except for the parts under the lines on the master drawing. The diazo paper is then developed in hot ammonia fumes, and the lines of dye emerge, turning dark. Is that what you want?'

'Indeed it is,' I said with awe. 'Does diazo paper look like typing paper?'

'Certainly it can, if it's cut down to that size.'

'And how about a piece of clear-looking plastic?'

'Sounds like diazo film,' he said calmly. 'You don't need hot ammonia fumes for developing that. Any form of cold liquid will do. But be careful. I said carbon arc lights, because that's the method that's used in engineering, but of course a longer exposure to sunlight or any other form of light would also have the same effect. If the piece of film you have looks clear, it means that most of the yellow-looking dye has been already bleached out. If there is a drawing there, you must be careful not to expose it to too much more light.'

'How much more light is too much?' I said anxiously.

He pursed his lips. 'In sunlight, you'd have lost any trace of dye for ever in thirty seconds. In normal room light . . . five to ten minutes.'

'It's in a light-proof envelope.'

'Then you might be lucky.'

'And the sheets of paper . . . they look white on both sides.'

'The same applies,' he said. 'They've been exposed

to light. You might have a drawing there, or you might not.'

'How do I make hot ammonia fumes, to find out?'

'Simple,' he said, as if everyone would know items like that. 'Put some ammonia in a saucepan and heat it. Hold the paper over the top. Don't get it wet. Just steam it.'

'Would you,' I said carefully, 'like some champagne for lunch?'

I returned to Samantha's house at about six o'clock with a cheap saucepan, two bottles of Ajax, an anaesthetized top lip, and a set of muscles that had been jerked, pressed and exercised into some sort of resurrection. I also felt dead tired which wasn't a good omen for fitness on the morrow, when, Harold had informed me on the telephone, two 'chasers would be awaiting my services at Sandown Park.

Samantha had gone out. Clare, with work scattered all over the kitchen table, gave me a fast, assessing scrutiny and suggested a large brandy.

'It's in that cupboard with the salt and flour and herbs. Cooking brandy. Pour me some too, would you?'

I sat at the table with her for a while, sipping the repulsive stuff neat and feeling a lot better for it. Her dark head was bent over the book she was working on, the capable hand stretching out now and again for the glass, the mind engrossed in her task.

341

'Would you live with me?' I said.

She looked up; abstracted, faintly frowning, questioning.

'Did you say . . .?'

'Yes, I did,' I said. 'Would you live with me?'

Her work at last lost her attention. With a smile in her eyes she said, 'Is that an academic question or a positive invitation?'

'Invitation.'

'I couldn't live in Lambourn,' she said. 'Too far to commute. You couldn't live here . . . too far from the horses.'

'Somewhere in between.'

She looked at me wonderingly. 'Are you serious?'

'Yes.'

'But we haven't . . .' She stopped, leaving a clear meaning.

'Been to bed.'

'Well . . .'

'In general,' I said. 'What do you think?'

She took refuge and time with sips from her glass. I waited for what seemed a small age.

'I think,' she said finally, 'why not give it a try.'

I smiled from intense satisfaction.

'Don't look so smug,' she said. 'Drink your brandy while I finish this book.'

She bent her head down again but didn't read far.

'It's no good,' she said. 'How can I work . . .? Let's get the supper.'

Cooking frozen fish fillets took ages because of her trying to do it with my arms round her waist and my chin on her hair. I didn't taste the stuff when we ate it. I felt extraordinarily light-headed. I hadn't deeply hoped she would say yes, and still less had I expected the incredible sense of adventure since she had. To have someone to care about seemed no longer a burden to be avoided, but a positive privilege.

Amazing, I thought dimly; the whole thing's amazing. Was this what Lord White had felt for Dana den Relgan?

'What time does Samantha get back?' I said.

Clare shook her head. 'Too soon.'

'Will you come with me tomorrow?' I said. 'To the races . . . and then stay somewhere together afterwards.'

'Yes, I will.'

'Samantha won't mind?'

She gave me an amused look. 'No, I don't think so.'

'Why do you laugh?'

'She's gone to the pictures. I asked her why she had to go on your last night here. She said she wanted to see the film. I thought it odd . . . but I believed her. She saw . . . more than I did.'

'My God,' I said. '*Women.*'

While she did try again to finish her work, I fetched the rubbish box and took out the black light-proof envelope.

I borrowed a flat glass dish from a cupboard. Took the piece of plastic film from the envelope. Put it in the dish. At once poured liquid Ajax over it. Held my breath.

Almost instantly dark brownish-red lines became visible. I rocked the dish, sloshing the liquid across the plastic surface, conscious that all of the remaining dye had to be covered with ammonia before the light bleached it away.

It was no engineering drawing, but handwriting.

It looked odd.

As more and more developed, I realized that from the reading point of view the plastic was wrong side up.

Turned it over. Sloshed more Ajax over it, tilting it back and forth. Read the revealed words, as clear as when they'd been written.

They were . . . they had to be . . . what Dana den Relgan had written on the cigarette packet.

Heroin, cocaine, cannabis. Quantities, dates, prices paid, suppliers. No wonder she had wanted it back.

Clare looked up from her work.

'What have you found?'

'What that Dana girl who came last Sunday was wanting.'

'Let's see.' She came across and looked into the dish, reading. 'That's pretty damning, isn't it?'

'Mm.'

'But how did it turn up . . . like this?'

I said appreciatively, 'Crafty George Millace. He got her to write on cellophane wrapping with a red felt-tip pen . . . she felt safer that way, because cigarette packet wrapping is so fragile, so destructible . . . and I expect the words themselves looked indistinct, over the printed packet. But from George's point of view all he wanted was solid lines on transparent material, to make a diazo print.'

I explained to her all that I'd learned in Basildon. 'He must have cut the wrapping off carefully, pressed it flat under glass on top of this piece of diazo film, and exposed it to light. Then with the drugs list safely recorded, it wouldn't matter if the wrapping came to pieces . . . and the list was hidden, like everything else.'

'He was an extraordinary man.'

I nodded. 'Extraordinary. Though, mind you, he didn't mean anyone else to have to solve his puzzles. He made them only to please himself . . . and to save the records from angry burglars.'

'In which he succeeded.'

'He sure did.'

'What about all your photographs?' she said in sudden alarm. 'All the ones in the filing cabinet. Suppose . . .'

'Calm down,' I said. 'Even if anyone stole them or burned them they'd miss all the negatives. The butcher has those down the road in his freezer room.'

'Maybe all photographers,' she said, 'are obsessed.'

It wasn't until much later that I realized I hadn't disputed her classification. I hadn't even *thought* 'I'm a jockey.'

I asked her if she'd mind if I filled the kitchen with the smell of boiling ammonia.

'I'll go and wash my hair,' she said.

When she'd gone I drained the Ajax out of the dish into the saucepan and added to it what was left in the first bottle, and while it heated opened the french windows so as not to asphyxiate. Then I held the first of the sheets of what looked like typing paper over the simmering cleaner, and watched George's words come alive as if they'd been written in secret ink. Ammonia clearly evaporated quickly, because it took the whole second bottle to get results with the second sheet, but it too, grew words like the first.

Together they constituted one handwritten letter in what I had no doubt was George's own writing. He must himself have written on some sort of transparent material ... and it could have been anything: a polythene bag, tracing paper, a piece of glass, film with all the emulsion bleached off ... anything. When he'd written, he had put his letter over diazo paper and exposed it to light, and immediately stored the exposed paper in the light-proof envelope.

And then what? Had he sent his transparent original? Had he written it again on ordinary paper? Had he typed it? No way of knowing. But one thing was certain: in some form or other he had despatched his letter.

I had heard of the results of its arrival.

I could guess, I thought, who wanted me dead.

CHAPTER NINETEEN

Harold met me with some relief on the verandah outside the weighing room at Sandown.

'You at least look better ... have you passed the doctor?'

I nodded. 'He signed my card.' He'd no reason not to. By his standards a jockey who took a week off because he'd been kicked was acting more self-indulgently than usual. He'd asked me to do a bend-stretch, and nodded me through.

'Victor's here,' Harold said.

'Did you tell him . . .?'

'Yes, I did. He says he doesn't want to talk to you on a racecourse. He says he wants to see his horses work on the Downs. He's coming on Monday. He'll talk to you then. And, Philip, you bloody well be careful what you say.'

'Mm,' I said non-committally. 'How about Coral Key?'

'What about him? He's fit.'

'No funny business?'

'Victor knows how you feel,' Harold said.

'Victor doesn't care a losing tote ticket how I feel. Is the horse running straight?'

'He hasn't said anything.'

'Because I am,' I said. 'If I'm riding it, I'm riding it straight. Whatever he says in the parade ring.'

'You've got bloody aggressive all of a sudden.'

'No . . . just saving you money. You personally. Don't back me to lose, like you did on Daylight. That's all.'

He said he wouldn't. He also said there was no point in holding the Sunday briefing if I was talking to Victor on Monday, and that we would discuss next week's plans after that. Neither of us said what was in both of our minds . . . after Monday, would there be any plans?

Steve Millace in the changing room was complaining about a starter letting a race off when he, Steve, hadn't been ready, with the consequence that he was left so flat-footed that the other runners had gone half a furlong before he'd got started . . . the owner was angry and said he wanted another jockey next time, and, as Steve asked everyone *ad infinitum*, was it fair?

'No,' I said. 'Life isn't.'

'It should be.'

'Better face it,' I said smiling. 'The best you can expect is a kick in the teeth.'

'Your teeth are all right,' someone said.

'They've got caps on.'

'Pick up the pieces, huh? Is that what you're saying?'

I nodded.

Steve said, not following this exchange, 'Starters should be fined for letting a race off when the horses aren't pointing the right way.'

'Give it a rest,' someone said: but Steve as usual was still going on about it a couple of hours later.

His mother, he said when I enquired, had gone to friends in Devon for a rest.

Outside the weighing room Bart Underfield was lecturing one of the more gullible of the pressmen on the subject of unusual nutrients.

'It's rubbish giving horses beer and eggs and ridiculous things like that. I never do it.'

The pressman refrained from saying – or perhaps he didn't know – that the trainers addicted to eggs and beer were on the whole more successful than Bart.

Bart's face when he saw me changed from bossy know-all to tight-lipped spite. He jettisoned the pressman and took two decisive steps to stand in my path, but when he'd stopped me he didn't speak.

'Do you want something, Bart?' I said.

He still didn't say anything. I thought that quite likely he couldn't find words intense enough to convey what he felt. I was growing accustomed, I thought, to being hated.

He found his voice. 'You wait,' he said with bitter quiet. 'I'll get you.'

If he'd had a dagger and privacy, I wouldn't have turned my back on him, as I did, to walk away.

Lord White was there, deep in earnest conversation

with fellow Stewards, his gaze flicking over me quickly as if wincing. He would never, I supposed, feel comfortable when I was around. Never be absolutely sure that I wouldn't tell. Never like me knowing what I knew.

He would have to put up with it for a long time, I thought. One way or another the racing world would always be my world, as it was his. He would see me, and I him, week by week, until one of us died.

Victor Briggs was waiting in the parade ring when I went out to ride Coral Key. A heavy brooding figure in his broad-brimmed hat and long navy overcoat: unsmiling, untalkative, gloomy. When I touched my cap to him politely there was no response of any sort, only the maintenance of an expressionless stare.

Coral Key was an oddity among Victor Briggs's horses, a six-year-old novice 'chaser bought out of the hunting field when he had begun to show promise in point-to-points. Great horses in the past had started that way, like Oxo and Ben Nevis which had both won the Grand National, and although Coral Key was unlikely to be of that class, it seemed to me that he, too, had the feel of good things to come. There was no way that I was going to mess up his early career, whatever my instructions. In my mind and very likely in my attitude I dared his owner to say he didn't want him to try to win.

He didn't say it. He said nothing at all about anything. He simply watched me unblinkingly, and kept his mouth shut.

Harold bustled about as if movement itself could dispel the atmosphere existing between his owner and his jockey; and I mounted and rode out to the course feeling as if I'd been in a strong field of undischarged electricity.

A spark ... an explosion ... might lie ahead. Harold sensed it. Harold was worried to the depths of his own explosive soul.

It might be going to be the last race I ever rode for Victor Briggs. I lined up at the start thinking that it was no good speculating about that; that all I should be concentrating on was the matter in hand.

A cold windy cloudy day. Good ground underfoot. Seven other runners, none of them brilliant. If Coral Key jumped as he had when I'd schooled him at home, he should have a good chance.

I settled my goggles over my eyes and gathered the reins.

'Come in, now, jockeys,' the starter said. The horses advanced towards the tapes in a slow line and as the gate flew up accelerated away from bunched haunches. Thirteen fences; two miles. I would find out pretty soon, I thought ruefully, if I wasn't yet fit.

Important, I thought, to get him to jump well. It was what I was best at. What I most enjoyed doing. There were seven fences close together down the far side of the course ... If one met the first of them just right they all fitted, but a brakes-on approach to the first often meant seven blunders by the end, and countless lengths lost.

From the start there were two fences, then the uphill stretch past the stands, then the top bend, then the downhill fence where I'd stepped off Daylight. No problems on Coral Key: he cleared the lot. Then the sweep round to the seven trappy fences, and if I lost one length getting Coral Key set right for the first, by the end of the seventh I'd stolen ten.

Too soon for satisfaction. Round the long bottom curve Coral Key lay second, taking a breather. Three fences to go . . . and the long uphill to home.

Between the last two fences I caught up with the leader. We jumped the last fence alongsides, nothing between us. Raced up the hill, stretching, flying . . . doing everything I could.

The other horse won by two lengths.

Harold said, 'He ran well,' a shade apprehensively, patting Coral Key in the unsaddling enclosure; and Victor Briggs said nothing.

I pulled the saddle off and went in to weigh. There wasn't any way that I could think of that I could have won the race. The other horse had had enough in hand to beat off my challenge. He'd been stronger than Coral Key, and faster. I hadn't felt weak. I hadn't thrown anything away in jumping mistakes. I just hadn't won.

I had needed a strong hand for talking to Victor Briggs; and I hadn't got it.

When life kicks you in the teeth, get caps.

I won the other 'chase, the one that didn't matter so much except to the owners, a junketing quartet of businessmen.

'Bloody good show,' they said, beaming. 'Bloody well ridden.'

I saw Victor Briggs watching from ten paces away, balefully staring. I wondered if he knew how much I'd have given to have those two results reversed.

Clare said, 'I suppose the wrong one won?'

'Yeah.'

'How much does it matter?'

'I'll find out on Monday.'

'Well . . . let's forget it.'

'Shouldn't be difficult,' I said. I looked at the trim dark coat, the white puff-ball hat, the long polished boots. Looked at the large grey eyes and the friendly mouth. Incredible, I thought, to have someone like that waiting for me outside the weighing room. Quite extraordinarily different from going home alone. Like a fire in a cold house. Like sugar on strawberries.

'Would you mind very much,' I said, 'if we made a detour for me to call on my grandmother?'

The old woman was markedly worse.

No longer propped more or less upright, she sagged back without strength on the pillows; and even the eyes seemed to be losing the struggle, with none of the beady aggression glittering out.

'Did you bring her?' she said.

Still no salutation, no preliminaries. Perhaps it was a mistake to expect changes in the mind to accompany changes in the body. Perhaps my feelings for her were different . . . and all that remained immutable was her hatred for me.

'No,' I said. 'I didn't bring her. She's lost.'

'You said you would find her.'

'She's lost.'

She gave a feeble cough, the thin chest jerking. Her eyelids closed for a few seconds and opened again. A weak hand twitched at the sheet.

'Leave your money to James,' I said.

With a faint outer echo of persistent inner stubbornness, she shook her head.

'Leave some to charity, then,' I said. 'Leave it to a dog's home.'

'I hate dogs.' Her voice was weak. Not her opinions.

'How about lifeboats?'

'Hate the sea. Makes me sick.'

'Medical research?'

'Hasn't done me much good, has it?'

'Well,' I said slowly, 'how about leaving it to a religious order of some sort.'

'You must be mad. I hate religion. Cause of trouble. Cause of wars. Wouldn't give them a penny.'

I sat down unbidden in the armchair.

'Can I do anything for you?' I asked. 'Besides, of course, finding Amanda. Can I fetch anything? Is there anything you want?'

She raised a faint sneer. 'Don't think you can soft soap me into leaving any money to you, because I'm not going to.'

'I'd give water to a dying cat,' I said. 'Even if it spat in my face.'

Her mouth opened and stiffened with affront.

'How . . . dare . . . you?'

'How dare you still think I'd shift a speck of dust for your money?'

The mouth closed into a thin line.

'Can I fetch you anything? I said again, levelly. 'Is there anything you want?'

She didn't answer for several seconds. Then she said, 'Go away.'

'Well, I will, in a minute,' I said. 'But I want just to suggest something else.' I waited a fraction, but as she didn't immediately argue I continued. 'In case Amanda is ever found . . . why don't you set up a trust for her? Tie up the capital tight with masses of excellent trustees. Make it so that she couldn't ever get her hands on the money herself . . . and nor could anyone who was . . . perhaps . . . after her fortune. Make it impossible for anyone but Amanda herself to benefit . . . with an income paid out only at the direction of the trustees.'

She watched me with half-lowered eyelids.

'Wherever she is,' I said, 'Amanda is still only

seventeen or eighteen. Too young to inherit a lot of money without strings. Leave it to her ... with strings like steel hawsers.'

'Is that all?'

'Mm.'

She lay quiet, immobile.

I waited. I had waited all my life for something other than malevolence from my grandmother. I could wait forever.

'Go away,' she said.

I stood up and said, 'Very well.'

Walked to the door. Put my hand on the knob.

'Send me some roses,' my grandmother said.

We found a flower shop still open in the town, though they were sweeping out ready to close.

'Doesn't she realize it's December?' Clare said. 'Roses will cost a fortune.'

'If you were dying, and you wanted roses, do you think you'd care?'

'Maybe not.'

All they had in the flower shop were fifteen very small pink buds on very long thin stems. Not much call for roses. These were left over spare from a wedding.

We drove back to the nursing home and gave them to a nurse to deliver at once, with a card enclosed saying I'd get some better ones next week.

'She doesn't deserve it,' Clare said.

'Poor old woman.'

We stayed in a pub by the Thames which had old beams and good food and bedroom windows looking out to bare willows and sluggish brown water.

No one knew us. We signed in as Mr and Mrs and ate a slow dinner, and went unobtrusively to bed. Not the first time she'd done it, she said: did I mind? Preferred it, I said. No fetishes about virgins? No kinks at all, that I knew of. Good, she said.

It began in friendship and progressed to passion. Ended in breathlessness and laughter, sank to murmurs and sleep. The best it had ever been for me. Couldn't tell about her. She showed no hesitation, however, about a repeat programme in the morning.

In the afternoon, in peaceful accord, we went to see Jeremy.

He was lying in a high bed in a room on his own, with a mass of breathing equipment to one side. He was, though, breathing for himself with his own lungs. Precariously, I guessed, since a nurse came in to check on him every ten minutes while we were there, making sure that a bell-push remained under his fingers the whole time.

He looked thinner than ever, and greyly pale, but there had been no near-execution in his brain. The eyes were as intelligent as ever, and the silly-ass manner appeared strongly as a defence against the indignities of his position. The nurse, on every visit, got a load of weary waffle.

I tried to apologize for what he'd suffered. He wouldn't have it.

'Don't forget,' he said, 'I was there because I wanted to be. No one exactly twisted my arm.' He gave me a travelling inspection. 'Your face looks OK. How do you heal so fast?'

'Always do.'

'Always . . .' he gave a weak laugh. 'Funny life you lead. Always healing.'

'How long will you be in here?'

'Three or four days.'

'Is that all?' Clare said, surprised. 'You look . . . er . . .'

He looked whiter than the pillow his head lay on. He nodded, however, and said, 'I'm breathing much better. Once there's no danger the nerves will pack up again, I can go. There's nothing else wrong.'

'I'll take you home if you need transport,' I said.

'Might hold you to that.'

We didn't stay very long because talking clearly tired him, but just before we went he said, 'You know, that gas was so quick. Not slow, like gas at the dentist. I'd no time to do anything . . . it was like breathing a brick wall.'

Into a short reflective silence Clare said, 'No one would have lived if they'd been there alone.'

'Makes you think . . . what?' said Jeremy cheerfully.

As we drove back towards the pub Clare said, 'You didn't tell him about Amanda.'

'Plenty of time.'

'He came down last Sunday because he'd got your message that you'd found her. He told me while we were in the kitchen. He said your phone was out of order, so he came.'

'I'd unplugged it.'

'Odd how things happen.'

'Mm.'

Our second night was a confirmation of the first. Much the same, but new and different. A tingling, fierce, gentle, intense, turbulent time. A matter, it seemed, as much to her liking as mine.

'Where's this depression one's supposed to get?' she said, very late. 'Post what's-it.'

'Comes in the morning, when you go.'

'That's hours off yet.'

'So it is.'

The morning came, as they do. I drove her to a station to catch a train, and went on myself to Lambourn.

When I got there, before going to Harold's, I called at my cottage. All seemed quiet. All cold. All strangely unfamiliar, as if home was no longer the natural embracing refuge it should be. I saw for the first time the bareness, the emotional chill which had been so apparent to Jeremy on his first visit. It no longer seemed to fit with myself. The person who had made that home was going away, receding in time. I felt oddly nostalgic . . . but there was no calling him back. The maturing change had gone too far.

Shivering a little I spread out on the kitchen table a variety of photographs of different people, and then I asked my neighbour Mrs Jackson to come in and look at them.

'What am I looking for, Mr Nore?'

'Anyone you've seen before.'

Obligingly she studied them carefully one by one, and stopped without hesitation at a certain face.

'How extraordinary!' she exclaimed. 'That's the council man who came about the rates. The one I let in here. Ever so sarcastic, the police were about that, but as I told them, you don't *expect* people to say they're rating officers if they aren't.'

'You're sure he's the one?'

'Positive,' she said, nodding. 'He had that same hat on, and all.'

'Then would you write on the back of the photo for me, Mrs Jackson?' I gave her a Lumocolor pen that would write boldly and blackly on the photographic paper, and dictated the words for her, saying that this man had called at the house of Philip Nore posing as a rating officer on Friday, 27 November.

'Is that all?' she asked.

'Sign your name, Mrs Jackson. And would you mind

repeating the whole message on the back of this other photograph?'

With concentration she did so. 'Are you giving these to the police?' she said. 'I don't want them bothering me again really. Will they come back again with their questions?'

'I shouldn't think so,' I said.

CHAPTER TWENTY

Victor Briggs had come in his Mercedes, but he went up to the Downs with Harold in the Land Rover. I rode up on a horse. The morning's work got done to everyone's reasonable satisfaction, and we all returned variously to the stable.

When I rode into the yard Victor Briggs was standing by his car, waiting. I slid off the horse and gave it to one of the lads to see to.

'Get in the car,' Victor said.

No waster of words, ever. He stood there in his usual clothes, gloved as always against the chilly wind, darkening the day. If I could see auras, I thought, his would be black.

I sat in the front passenger seat, where he pointed, and he slid himself in beside me, behind the steering wheel. He started the engine, released the brake, put the automatic gear into drive. The quiet hunk of metal eased out of Lambourn, going back to the Downs.

He stopped on a wide piece of grass verge from

where one could see half of Berkshire. He switched off the engine, leaned back in his seat, and said, 'Well?'

'Do you know what I'm going to say?' I asked.

'I hear things,' he said. 'I hear a lot of things.'

'I know that.'

'I heard that den Relgan set his goons on you.'

'Did you?' I looked at him with interest. 'Where did you hear that?'

He made a small tight movement of his mouth, but he did answer. 'Gambling club.'

'What did you hear?'

'True, isn't it?' he said. 'You still had the marks on Saturday.'

'Did you hear any reasons?'

He produced the twitch that went for a smothered smile.

'I heard,' he said, 'that you got den Relgan chucked out of the Jockey Club a great deal faster than he got in.'

He watched my alarmed surprise with another twitch, a less successful effort this time at hiding amusement.

'Did you hear how?' I said.

He said with faint regret. 'No. Just that you'd done it. The goons were talking. Stupid bone-headed bull-muscle. Den Relgan's heading for trouble, using them. They never keep their mouths shut.'

'Are they ... um ... out for general hire?'

'Chuckers out at a gaming club. Muscle for hire. As you say.'

'They beat up George Millace's wife . . . did you hear that too?'

After a pause he nodded, but offered no comment.

I looked at the closed expression, the dense whitish skin, the black shadow of beard. A secretive, solid, slow-moving man with a tap into a world I knew little of. Gaming clubs, hired bully-boys, underworld gossip.

'The goons said they left you for dead,' he said. 'A week later, you're winning a race.'

'They exaggerated,' I said dryly.

I got a twitch but also a shake of the head. 'One of them was scared. Rattled. Said they'd gone too far . . . with the boots.'

'You know them well?' I said.

'They talk.'

There was another pause, then I said without emphasis, 'George Millace sent you a letter.'

He moved in his seat, seeming almost to relax, breathing out in a long sigh. He'd been waiting to know, I thought. Patiently waiting. Answering questions. Being obliging.

'How long have you had it?' he said.

'Three weeks.'

'You can't use it.' There was a faint tremor of triumph in the statement. 'You'd be in trouble yourself.'

'How did you know I'd got it?' I said.

He blinked. The mouth tightened. He said slowly, 'I heard you had George Millace's . . .'

'George Millace's what?'

'Files.'

'Ah,' I said. 'Nice anonymous word, files. How did you hear I had them? Who from?'

'Ivor,' he said. 'And Dana. Separately.'

'Will you tell me?'

He thought it over, giving me a blank inspection, and then said grudgingly, 'Ivor was too angry to be discreet. He said too much about you . . . such as poisonous creep . . . he said you were fifty times worse than George Millace. And Dana . . . another night . . . she said did I know you had copies of some black-mailing letters George Millace had sent, and were using them. She asked if I could help her get hers back.'

I smiled in my turn. 'What did you say?'

'I said I couldn't help her.'

'When you talked to them,' I said, 'was it in gaming clubs?'

'It was.'

'Are they . . . your gaming clubs?'

'None of your business,' he said.

'Well,' I said, 'why not tell me?'

He said after a pause, 'I have two partners. Four gaming clubs. The clientele in general don't know I'm a proprietor. I move around. I play. I listen. Does that answer your question?'

I nodded. 'Yes, thank you. Are those goons your goons?'

'I employ them,' he said austerely, 'as chuckers out. Not to smash up women and jockeys.'

'A little moonlighting, was it? On the side.'

He didn't answer directly. 'I have been expecting,' he said, 'that you would demand something from me if you had that letter. Something more than . . . answers.'

I thought of the letter, which I knew word for word:

Dear Victor Briggs,

I am sure you will be interested to know that I have the following information. You did on five separate occasions during the past six months conspire with a bookmaker to defraud the betting public by arranging that your odds-on favourites should not win their races.

There followed a list of five races, complete with the sums Victor had received from his bookmaker friend. The letter continued:

I hold a signed affidavit from the bookmaker in question.

As you see, all five of these horses were ridden by Philip Nore, who certainly knew what he was doing.

I could send this affidavit to the Jockey Club, in which case you would both be warned off. I will

telephone you soon, however, with an alternative
suggestion.

The letter had been sent more than three years earlier.
For three years Victor Briggs had run his horses
straight. When George Millace died, a week to the day,
Victor Briggs had gone back to the old game. Had gone
back . . . to find that his vulnerable jockey was no longer
reliable.

'I didn't want to do anything about the letter,' I
said. 'I didn't mean to tell you I had it. Not until now.'

'Why not? You wanted to ride to win. You could
have used it to make me agree. You'd been told you'd
lose your job anyway if you wouldn't ride as I wanted.
You knew I couldn't face being warned off. Yet you
didn't use the letter for that. Why not?'

'I wanted . . . to make you run the horses straight
for their own sakes.'

He gave me another of the long uninformative
stares.

'I'll tell you,' he said at last. 'Yesterday I added up
all the prize money I'd won since Daylight's race at
Sandown. All those seconds and thirds, as well as
Sharpener's wins. I added up my winnings from betting,
win and place. I made more money in the past month
with you riding straight than I did with you stepping
off Daylight.' He paused, waiting for a reaction, but,
catching it from him, I simply stared back. 'I've seen,'
he went on, 'that you weren't going to ride any more

crooked races. I've understood that. I know you've changed. You're a different person. Older. Stronger. If you go on riding for me, I won't ask you again to lose a race.' He paused once more. 'Is that enough? Is that what you want to hear?'

I looked away from him, out across the windy landscape.

'Yes.'

After a bit he said, 'George Millace didn't demand money, you know. At least . . .'

'A donation to the Injured Jockeys?'

'You know the lot, don't you?'

'I've learned,' I said. 'George wasn't interested in extorting money for himself. He extorted . . .' I searched for the word ' . . . frustration.'

'From how many?'

'Seven, that I know of. Probably eight, if you ask your bookmaker.'

He was astonished.

'George Millace,' I said, 'enjoyed making people cringe. He did it to everybody in a mild way. To people he could catch out doing wrong, he did it with gusto. He had alternative suggestions for everyone . . . disclosure, or do what George wanted. And what George wanted, in general, was to frustrate. To stop Ivor den Relgan's power play. To stop Dana taking drugs. To stop other people . . . doing other things.'

'To stop me,' Victor said with a hint of dry humour, 'from being warned off.' He nodded. 'You're right, of course. When George Millace telephoned I was expecting straight blackmail. Then he said all I had to do was behave myself. Those were his words. As long as you behave, Victor, he said, nothing will happen. Victor. He called me Victor. I'd never met him. Knew who he was, of course, but that was all. Victor, he said, as if I were a little pet dog, as long as we're a good boy, nothing will happen. But if I suspect anything, Victor, he said, I'll follow Philip Nore around with my motorized telephotos until I have him bang to rights, and then Victor, you'll both be for the chop.'

'Do you remember word for word what he said, after all this time?' I asked, surprised.

'I recorded him. I was expecting his call ... I wanted evidence of blackmail. All I got was a moral lecture and a suggestion that I give a thousand pounds to the Injured Jockeys Fund.'

'And was that all? For ever?'

'He used to wink at me at the races,' Victor said.

I laughed.

'Yes, very funny,' he said. 'Is that the lot?'

'Not really. There's something you could do for me, if you would. Something you know, and could tell me. Something you could tell me in future.'

'What is it?'

'About Dana's drugs.'

'Stupid girl. She won't listen.'

'She will soon. She's still ... saveable. And besides her ...'

370

I told him what I wanted. He listened acutely. When I'd finished I got the twitch of a throttled smile.

'Beside you,' he said, 'George Millace was a beginner.'

Victor drove off in his car and I walked back to Lambourn over the Downs.

An odd man, I thought. I'd learned more about him in half an hour than I had in seven years, and still knew next to nothing. He had given me what I'd wanted, though. Given it freely. Given me my job without strings for as long as I liked . . . and help in another matter just as important. It hadn't all been, I thought, because of my having that letter.

Going home in the wind, out on the bare hills, I thought of the way things had happened during the past few weeks. Not about George and his bombshells, but of Jeremy and Amanda.

Because of Jeremy's persistence, I'd looked for Amanda, and because of looking for Amanda I had now met a grandmother, an uncle, a sister. I knew something at least of my father. I had a feeling of origin that I hadn't had before.

I had people. I had people like everyone else had. Not necessarily loving or praiseworthy or successful, but *there*. I hadn't wanted them, but now that I had them they sat quietly in the mind like foundation stones.

371

Because of looking for Amanda I had found Samantha, and with her a feeling of continuity, of belonging. I saw the pattern of my childhood in a different perspective, not as a chopped up kaleidoscope, but as a curve. I knew a place where I'd been, and a woman who'd known me, and they seemed to lead smoothly now towards Charlie.

I no longer floated on the tide.

I had roots.

I reached the point on the hill where I could see down to the cottage, the brow that I looked up to from the sitting room windows. I stopped there. I could see most of Lambourn, stretched out. Could see Harold's house and the yard. Could see the whole row of cottages, with mine in the centre.

I'd belonged in that village, been part of it, breathed its intrigues for seven years. Been happy, miserable, normal. It was what I'd called home. But now in mind and spirit I was leaving that place ... and soon would in body as well. I would live somewhere else, with Clare. I would be a photographer.

The future lay inside me; waiting, accepted. One day fairly soon I'd walk into it.

I would race, I thought, until the end of the season. Five or six more months. Then in May or June, when summer came, I'd hang up the boots: retire, as every jockey had to, some time or other. I would tell Harold soon, to give him time to find someone else for the autumn. I'd enjoy what was left, and maybe have a last chance at the Grand National. Anything might happen. One never knew.

I still had the appetite, still the physique. Better to go, I supposed, before both of them crumbled.

I went on down the hill without any regrets.

CHAPTER TWENTY-ONE

Clare came down on the train two days later to sort out what photographs she wanted from the filing cabinet: to make a portfolio, she said. Now that she was my agent, she'd be rustling up business. I laughed. It was serious, she said.

I had no races that day. I'd arranged to fetch Jeremy from hospital and take him home, and to have Clare come with me all the way. I'd also telephoned to Lance Kinship to say I'd had his reprints ready for ages, and hadn't seen him, and would he like me to drop them in as I was practically going past his house.

That would be fine, he said. Afternoon, earlyish, I suggested, and he said 'Right' and left the 't' off. And I'd like to ask you something, I said. 'Oh? All right. Anything you like.'

Jeremy looked a great deal better, without the grey clammy skin of Sunday. We helped him into the back of my car and tucked a rug round him, which he plucked off indignantly saying he was no aged invalid but a perfectly viable solicitor.

'And incidentally,' he said, 'my uncle came down here yesterday. Bad news for you, I'm afraid. Old Mrs Nore died during Monday night.'

'Oh no,' I said.

'Well, you knew,' Jeremy said. 'Only a matter of time.'

'Yes, but . . .'

'My uncle brought two letters for me to give to you. They're in my suitcase somewhere. Fish them out, before we start.'

I fished them out, and we sat in the hospital car park while I read them.

One was a letter. The other was a copy of her will.

Jeremy said, 'My uncle said he was called out urgently to the nursing home to make her will, and the doctor there told my uncle there wasn't much time.'

'Do you know what's in it?' I asked.

He shook his head. 'My uncle just said she was a stubborn old woman to the last.'

I unfolded the typewritten sheets.

I, Lavinia Nore, being of sound mind, do hereby revoke all previous wills . . .

There was a good deal of legal guff and some complicated pension arrangements for an old cook and gardener, and then the two final fairly simple paragraphs.

' . . . *Half the residue of my estate to my son James Nore . . .*'

' . . . *Half the residue of my estate to my grandson*

375

Philip Nore, to be his absolutely, with no strings or steel hawsers attached.'

'What's the matter?' Clare said. 'You look so grim.'

'The old witch . . . has defeated me.'

I opened the other envelope. Inside there was a letter in shaky handwriting, with no beginning, and no end.

It said:

I think you did find Amanda, and didn't tell me because it would have given me no pleasure.

Is she a nun?

You can do what you like with my money. If it makes you vomit, as you once said . . . then VOMIT.

Or give it to my genes.

Rotten roses.

I handed the will and the letter to Clare and Jeremy, who read them in silence. We sat there for a while, thinking, and then Clare folded up the letter, put it in its envelope, and handed it back to me.

'What will you do?' she said.

'I don't know. See that Amanda never starves, I suppose. Apart from that . . .'

'Enjoy it,' Jeremy said. 'The old woman loved you.'

I listened to the irony in his voice and wondered if it was true. Love or hate. Love and hate. Perhaps she'd felt both at once when she'd made that will.

We drove from Swindon towards St Albans, making a short detour to deliver Lance Kinship's reprints.

'Sorry about this,' I said. 'But it won't take long.'

They didn't seem to mind. We found the house without much trouble ... typical Kinship country, fake Georgian, large grandiose front, pillared gateway, meagre drive.

I picked the packet of photographs out of the boot of the car, and rang the front doorbell.

Lance opened the door himself, dressed today not in country gent togs but in white jeans, espadrilles, and a red and white horizontally striped T-shirt. International film-director gear, I diagnosed. All he needed was the megaphone.

'Come inside,' he said. 'I'll pay you for these.'

'OK. Can't be long though, with my friends waiting.'

He looked briefly towards my car, where Clare and Jeremy's interested faces showed in the windows, and went indoors with me following. He led the way into a large sitting room with expanses of parquet and too much black lacquered furniture. Chrome and glass tables. Art deco lamps.

I gave him the packet of pictures.

'You'd better look at them,' I said, 'to make sure they're all right.'

He shrugged. 'Why shouldn't they be?' All the same, he opened the envelope and pulled out the contents.

The top picture showed him looking straight at the

camera in his country gent clothes. Glasses. Trilby hat. Air of bossy authority.

'Turn it over,' I said.

With raised eyebrows he did so: and read what Mrs Jackson had written. *This is the rating officer . . .*

The change in him from one instant to the next was like one person leaving and another entering the same skin. He shed the bumptiously sure-of-himself phoney; slid into a mess of unstable ill-will. The gaudy clothes which had fitted one character seemed grotesque on the other, like gift-wrap round a hand-grenade. I saw the Lance Kinship I'd only suspected existed. Not the faintly ridiculous poseur pretending to be what he wasn't, but the tangled psychotic who would do anything at all to preserve the outward show.

It was in his very inadequacy, I supposed, that the true danger lay. In his estrangement from reality. In his theatrical turn of mind, which had allowed him to see murder as a solution to problems.

'Before you say anything,' I said, 'you'd better look at the other things in that envelope.'

With angry fingers he sorted them out. The regular reprints . . . and also the black and white glossy reproductions of Dana den Relgan's drugs list and the letter I'd found on the diazo paper.

They were for him a fundamental disaster.

He let the pictures of the great film producer fall to the ground around him like ten-by-eight coloured leaves, and stood holding the three black and white sheets in visible horror.

'She said . . .' he said hoarsely, 'she swore you didn't have it. She swore you didn't know what she was talking about . . .'

'She was talking about the drugs you supplied her with. Complete with dates and prices. That list which you hold, which is recognizably in her handwriting, for all that it was originally written on cellophane. And of course, as you see, your name appears on it liberally.'

'I'll kill you,' he said.

'No, you won't. You've missed your chance. It's too late now. If the gas had killed me you would have been all right, but it didn't.'

He didn't say 'What gas?' He said, 'It all went wrong. But it didn't matter. I thought . . . it didn't matter.' He looked down helplessly at the black and white prints.

'You thought it didn't matter because you heard from Dana den Relgan that I didn't have the list. And if I didn't have the list, then I didn't have the letter. Whatever else I'd had from George Millace, I didn't after all have the list and the letter . . . Is that what you thought? . . . so if I didn't have them there was no more need to kill me. Was that it?'

He didn't answer.

'It's far too late to do it now,' I said, 'because there are extra prints of those pages all over the place. Another copy of that picture of you, identified by Mrs Jackson. Bank, solicitors, several friends, all have instructions about taking everything to the police if any accidental death should befall me. You've a positive interest in keeping me alive from now on.'

The implication of what I was saying only slowly sank in. He looked from my face to the photographs and back again several times, doubtfully.

'George Millace's letter . . .' he said.

I nodded. George's letter, handwritten, read:

Dear Lance Kinship,

I have received from Dana den Relgan a most interesting list of drugs supplied to her by you over the past few months. I am sure I understand correctly that you are a regular dealer in such illegal substances.

It appears to be all too well known in certain circles that in return for being invited to places which please your ego, you will, so to speak, pay for your pleasure with gifts of cannabis, heroin and cocaine.

I could of course place Dana den Relgan's candid list before the proper authorities. I will telephone you shortly, however, with an alternative suggestion.

Yours sincerely,
George Millace.

'It was typed when I got it,' Lance Kinship said dully. 'I burnt it.'

'When George telephoned,' I said, 'did he tell you his alternative suggestion?'

The shock in Lance Kinship began to abate, with enmity growing in its place.

'I'm telling you nothing.'

I said, disregarding him, 'Did George Millace say to stop supplying drugs . . . and donate to the Injured Jockeys Fund?'

His mouth opened and snapped shut viciously.

'Did he telephone . . .' I asked, 'or did he tell you his terms when he called here?'

A tight silence.

'Did you put . . . something . . . from your store cupboard into his whisky?'

'Prove it!' he said with sick triumph.

One couldn't, of course. George had been cremated, with his blood tested only for alcohol. There had been no checks for other drugs. Not for perhaps tranquillizers, which were flavourless, and which in sufficient quantity would certainly have sent a driver to sleep.

George, I thought regretfully, had stepped on one victim too many. Had stepped on what he'd considered a worm and never recognized the cobra.

George had made a shattering mistake if he'd wanted for once to see the victim squirm when he came up with his terms. George hadn't dreamt that the inadequate weakling would lethally lash out to preserve his sordid life style: hadn't really understood how fanatically Lance Kinship prized his shoulder-rubbing with a jet-set that at best tolerated him. George must have enjoyed seeing Lance Kinship's fury. Must have driven off laughing. Poor George.

'Didn't you think,' I said, 'that George had left a copy of his letter behind him?'

From his expression, he hadn't. I supposed he'd acted on impulse. He'd very nearly been right.

'When you heard that George had blackmailed other people . . . including Dana . . . is that when you began thinking I might have your letter?'

'I heard,' he said furiously, 'I heard . . . in the clubs . . . Philip Nore has the letters . . . he's ruined den Relgan . . . got him sacked from the Jockey Club . . . Did you think . . . once I knew . . . did you really think I'd wait for you to come around to *me*?'

'Unfortunately,' I said slowly, 'whether you like it or not, I now have come around to you.'

'No.'

'Yes,' I said. 'I'll tell you straight away that like George Millace I'm not asking for money.'

He didn't look much reassured.

'I'll also tell you it's your bad luck that my mother died from addiction to heroin.'

He said wildly, 'But I didn't know your mother.'

'No, of course not. And there's no question of your ever having supplied her yourself . . . It's just that I have a certain long-standing prejudice against drug-pushers. You may as well know it. You may as well understand why I want . . . what I want.'

He took a compulsive step towards me. I thought of the brisk karate kick he had delivered to den Relgan at Kempton and wondered if in his rope-soled sandals on parquet he could be as effective. Wondered if he had any real skill . . . or whether it was more window-dressing to cover the vacuum.

He looked incongruous, not dangerous. A man not young, not old, thinning on top, wearing glasses . . . and beach clothes indoors in December.

A man pushed . . . who could kill if pushed too far. Kill not by physical contact, when one came to think of it, but in his absence, by drugs and gas.

He never reached me to deliver whatever blind vengeful blow he had in mind. He stepped on one of the fallen photographs, and slid, and went down hard on one knee. The inefficient indignity of it seemed to break up conclusively whatever remained of his confidence, for when he looked up at me I saw not hatred or defiance, but fear.

I said, 'I don't want what George did. I don't ask you to stop peddling drugs. I want you to tell me who supplies you with heroin.'

He staggered to his feet, his face aghast. 'I can't. I . . . *can't.*'

'It shouldn't be difficult,' I said mildly. 'You must know where you get it from. You get it in sizeable quantities, to sell, to give away. You always have plenty, I'm told. So you must have a regular supplier . . . mustn't you? He's the one I want.'

The source, I thought. One source supplying several pushers. The drug business was like some monstrous tentacled creature: cut off one tentacle and another grew in its place. The war against drugs would never be won . . . but it had to be fought, if only for the sake of silly girls who were sniffing their way to perdition. For the sake of the pretty ones. For Dana. For Caroline . . . my lost butterfly mother, who had saved me from an addiction of my own.

'You don't know . . .' Lance Kinship seemed to be breathless. 'It's impossible. I can't tell you. I'd be . . . dead.'

I shook my head. 'It will be between the two of us. No one will ever know you told me . . . unless you yourself talk, like den Relgan did in the gaming clubs.'

'I can't,' he said despairingly.

'If you don't,' I said conversationally, 'I will first tell the policemen investigating an attempted murder in my house that my neighbour positively identifies you as having posed as a rating officer. This isn't enough on its own to get you charged, but it could certainly get you *investigated* . . . for access to chemicals, and so on.'

He looked sick.

'Secondly,' I said, 'I'll see that it gets known all over the place that people would be unwise to ask you to their parties, despite your little goodies, because they might at any time be raided. Unlawful possession of certain drugs is still an offence, I believe.'

'You . . . you . . .'

I nodded. He couldn't find a word bad enough.

'I know where you go . . . to whose houses. Everyone talks. I've been told. A word in the ear of the drugs squad . . . and you'd be the least welcome guest in Britain.'

'I . . . I . . .'

'Yes, I know,' I said. 'Going to these places is what makes your life worth living. I don't ask you not to go. I don't ask you to stop your gifts. Just to tell me where the heroin comes from. Not the cocaine, not the cannabis, just the heroin. Just the deadly one.'

The faintest of crafty looks crept in round his anguished eyes.

'And don't,' I said, watching for it, 'think you can get away with any old lie. You may as well know that what you tell me will go to the drugs squad. Don't worry . . . by such a roundabout route that no one will ever connect it with you. But your present supplier may very likely be put out of business. If that happens, you'll be safe from me.'

He trembled as if his legs would give way.

'Mind you,' I said judiciously, 'with one supplier out of business, you might have to look around for another. In a year or so, I might ask you his name.'

His face was sweating and full of disbelief. 'You mean . . . it will go on . . . and on . . .'

'That's right.'

'But you *can't*.'

'I think you killed George Millace. You certainly

tried to kill me. You very nearly killed my friend. Why should you think I shouldn't want retribution?'

He stared.

'I ask very little,' I said. 'A few words written down . . . now and then.'

'Not in my writing,' he said, appalled.

'Certainly, in your writing,' I said matter-of-factly, 'to get the spelling right, and so on. But don't worry, you'll be safe. I promise you no one will ever find out where the tip-offs come from. No one will ever know they come via me. Neither my name nor yours will ever be mentioned.'

'You . . . you're *sure*?'

'Sure.'

I produced a small notebook and a fibre-tipped pen, 'Write now,' I said. 'Your supplier.'

'Not *now*,' he said, wavering.

'Why not?' I said calmly. 'May as well get it over. Sit down.'

He sat by one of his glass and chrome coffee tables, looking totally dazed. He wrote a name and address on the notepad.

'And sign it,' I said casually.

'*Sign* . . .'

'Of course. Just your name.'

He wrote: *Lance Kinship*. And then, underneath, with a flourish, added '*Film Director*.'

'That's great,' I said, without emphasis. I picked up

the pad, reading what he'd written. A foreign name. An address in London. One tentacle under the axe.

I stored away in a pocket the small document that would make him sweat next year . . . and the next, and the next. The document that I would photograph, and keep safe.

'That's . . . all?' he said numbly.

I nodded. 'All for now.'

He didn't stand up when I left him. Just sat on his black lacquer chair in his T-shirt and white trousers, stunned into silence, staring at space.

He'd recover his bumptiousness, I thought. Pseuds always did.

I went out to where Clare and Jeremy were still waiting, and paused briefly in the winter air before getting into the car.

Most people's lives, I thought, weren't a matter of world affairs, but of the problems right beside them. Not concerned portentously with saving mankind, but with creating local order: in small checks and balances.

Neither my life nor George Millace's would ever sway the fate of nations, but our actions could change the lives of individuals; and they had done that.

The dislike I'd felt for him alive was irrelevant to the intimacy I felt with him dead. I knew his mind, his intentions, his beliefs. I'd solved his puzzles. I'd fired his guns.

I got into the car.

'Everything all right?' Clare asked.

'Yes,' I said.